In Memory of Memory

Maria Stepanova

IN
MEMORY
OF MEMORY

A ROMANCE

translated by Sasha Dugdale

A NEW DIRECTIONS
PAPERBOOK ORIGINAL

Originally published in Russian by Novoe Izdatelstvo as Памяти памяти.
Published in arrangement with Suhrkamp Verlag.

Manufactured in the United States of America
First published as a New Directions Paperbook (NDP1489) in 2021
Design by Erik Rieselbach

Library of Congress Cataloging-in-Publication Data
Names: Stepanova, Maria, author. | Dugdale, Sasha, translator.
Title: In memory of memory : a romance / by Maria Stepanova ;
translated by Sasha Dugdale.
Other titles: Pamiati pamiati. English
Description: First edition. | New York: New Directions Publishing, [2021]
Identifiers: LCCN 2020042654 | ISBN 9780811228831 (paperback) |
ISBN 9780811228848 (ebook)
Classification: LCC PG3488.T4755 P3613 2021 | DDC 891.73/5—dc23
LC record available at https://lccn.loc.gov/2020042654

2 4 6 8 10 9 7 5 3 1

New Directions Books are published for James Laughlin
by New Directions Publishing Corporation
80 Eighth Avenue, New York 10011

"And what is the use of a book," thought Alice, "without pictures or conversations?"

—Lewis Carroll

Grandmother said, "He's old enough to be told. Drink in the company of the living, drink as much as you like. But never drink with the dead." I was bewildered, "How can you drink with the dead? I don't understand."

"Very easily," grandmother replied. "Most of the time that's what people do, they drink with the dead. Don't do it. Drink a glass and a hundred years will pass. Drink another and another hundred will pass. Drink a third and it's another hundred. By the time you leave, three hundred years will have passed and no one will recognize you, you'll be out of joint with time."

I thought she was trying to frighten me.

—Viktor Sosnora

"How awful!" said the ladies, "whatever do you find interesting in that?"

— Aleksandr Pushkin

Contents

PART THREE

PART ONE

1. Someone Else's Diary

Aunt Galya, my father's sister, died. She was just over eighty. We hadn't been close—there was an uneasiness between the families and a history of perceived snubs. My parents had what you might call troubled dealings with Aunt Galya, and we almost never saw her. As a result I had little chance to form my own relationship with her. We met infrequently, we had the odd phone call, but toward the end she unplugged her phone, saying "I don't want to talk to anyone." Then she disappeared entirely into the world she had built for herself: layered strata of possessions, objects, and trinkets in the cave of her tiny apartment.

Galya lived her life in the pursuit of beauty: the dream of rearranging her possessions into a definitive order, of painting the walls and hanging the curtains. At some point, years ago, she began the process of decluttering her apartment, and this gradually consumed her. She was permanently shaking things out, checking anew what objects were essential. The contents of the apartment constantly needed sorting and systematizing, each and every cup required careful consideration, books and papers stopped existing for themselves and became mere usurpers of space, forming barricades that crossed the apartment in little heaps. The apartment consisted of two rooms, and as one room was overcome by more objects, Galya would move to the other, taking only the absolute essentials with her—but then the tidying and reevaluating would begin again. The home wore its own viscera on the outside, unable to draw it all back into itself again. There was no longer any deciding whether a particular thing was important or not, because everything had significance in some way, especially the yellowing newspapers collected over decades, tottering piles of clippings that propped up the walls and the bed. At a later point the only spare living space was a divan, worn concave, and I remember we were sitting there on one occasion, the two of us, in the middle of a raging sea of postcards and TV guides. She was attempting to feed me the chocolates she kept reserved for special occasions, and I was attempting to turn down these precious offerings with anxious politeness. A newspaper clipping at the top of a pile bore the headline: "Which saint rules your sign of the Zodiac?" and the name of the paper and the publication date were written carefully at the top in her beautifully neat handwriting, blue ink across the dead paper.

*

We got there about an hour after her caretaker rang. The stairwell was in half darkness and there was a hum in the air. People we didn't know stood around on the landing and sat on the stairs, they had heard about her death somehow and had rushed round to offer their undertaker services, to help with registering the death, dealing with the paperwork. How on earth did they know? Had the doctor told them? The police? One of them came into the apartment with us, and stood there without taking off his coat.

Aunt Galya died in the early evening on March 8, Women's Day, that Soviet festival of mimosa and greeting cards festooned with chicks. Women's Day had been one of those celebration days in our family, when everyone gathered around a single enormous table and the minerals splashed liberally into ruby-colored wine glasses. On Women's Day there were always at least four different types of salad on the table: carrot and walnut; cheese; beetroot and garlic; and, of course, the common denominator of all Russian salads, *olivye*. But all that had ceased thirty years ago, long before my parents had emigrated to Germany. Galya was left behind, fuming, and in the new post-Soviet world her newspapers began publishing unprecedented and titillating things: horoscopes, recipes, homemade herbal remedies.

She desperately didn't want to end her life in a hospital, and she had her reasons. She'd seen her own parents, my grandparents, die in one, and she'd already had some sobering experiences of state medical care. But still the moment came for summoning an ambulance, and we might well have done so if it hadn't been a holiday weekend. It was decided to wait for Monday and the working week, and in this way Galya was given her chance to turn onto her side and die in her sleep.

In the other room, where her caretaker slept, photographs and sketches by my father Misha hung like squares on a chessboard, covering the whole wall. By the door was a black-and-white photograph taken in the 1960s, one from my favorite series of "pictures taken at the vets," a beautiful picture: a boy and his dog waiting their turn, sitting against a wall, the boy a sullen fourteen-year-old, and the dog, a boxer, leaning into him with its shoulder.

*

Her apartment now stood silent, stunned and cowering, filled with suddenly devalued objects. In the bigger room television stands squatted grimly in each corner. A huge new fridge was stuffed to the gills with icy cauliflower and frozen loaves of bread ("Misha loves his bread, get me a couple of loaves in case he comes over"). The same books stood in lines, the ones I used to greet like family members whenever I went around. *To Kill a Mockingbird*, the black Salinger with the boy on the cover, the blue binding of the Library of Poets series, a gray-bound Chekhov set, the green *Complete Works of Dickens*. My old acquaintances on the shelves: a wooden dog, a yellow plastic dog, and a carved bear with a flag on a thread. All of them crouched, as if preparing themselves for a journey, their own stolid usefulness in sudden doubt.

A few days later when I sat down to sort through papers, I noticed that in the piles of photographs and postcards there was hardly anything *written*. There were hoards of thermal vests and leggings; new and beautiful jackets and skirts, set aside for some great sallying forth and so never worn and still smelling of Soviet emporia; an embroidered men's shirt from before the war; and tiny ivory brooches, delicate and girlish: a rose, another rose, a crane with wings outstretched. These had belonged to Galya's mother, my grandmother, and no one had worn them for at least forty years. All these objects were inextricably bound together, everything had its meaning only in the whole, in the accumulation, within the frame of a continuing life, and now it was all turning to dust before me.

In a book about the working of the mind, I once read that the important factor in discerning the human face was not the combination of features, but the oval shape. Life itself, while it continues, can be that same oval, or after death, the thread of life running through the tale of what has been. The meek contents of her apartment, feeling themselves to be redundant, immediately began to lose their human qualities and, in doing so, ceased to remember or to mean anything.

I stood before the remnants of her home, doing the necessary tasks. Bemused at how little had been written down in this house of readers, I began to tease out a melody from the few words and scrappy phrases I could remember her saying: a story she had told me; endless questions about how the boy, my growing son, was doing; and anecdotes from the far-off past—country rambles in the 1930s. The woven fabric of language decomposes instantly, never again to be felt between the fingers: "I would never say 'lovely,' it sounds so terribly *common*," Galya admonished me once. And there were other prohibited words I can't recall, her talk of one's *people*, gossip about old friends, the neighbors, little reports from a lonely and self-consuming life.

I soon found that there was in fact much evidence of the written word in the apartment. Among the possessions she kept till her dying day, the possessions she often asked for, sometimes just to touch with her hand, were countless used notebooks and diaries. She'd kept a diary for years, not a day passed without her scribbling a note, as much a part of her routine as getting out of bed or washing. These diaries were stored in a wooden box by her headboard and there were a lot of them, two full bag loads, which I carried home to Banny Pereulok. There I sat down at once to read them, in search of stories, explanations: the oval shape of her life.

*

For the interested reader, diaries and notebooks can be placed in two categories: in the first the text is intended to be official, manifest, aimed at a readership. The notebook becomes a training ground for the outward self, and, as in the case of the nineteenth-century artist and diarist Marie Bashkirtseff, an open declaration, an unending monologue, addressed to an invisible but sympathetic ear.

Still I'm fascinated by the other sort of diary, the working tool, the sort the writer-as-craftsperson keeps close at hand, of little apparent use to the outsider. Susan Sontag, who practiced this art form for decades, said of her diary that it was "an instrument, a tool"—I'm not sure this is entirely apt. Sontag's notebooks (and the notebooks of other writers) are not just for the storage of ideas, like nuts in squirrels' cheeks, to be consumed later. Nor are they filled with quick outlines of events, to be recollected when needed. Notebooks are an essential daily activity for a certain type of person, loose-woven mesh on which they hang their clinging faith in reality and its continuing nature. Such texts have only one reader in mind, but this reader is utterly implicated. Break open a notebook at any point and be reminded of your own reality, because a notebook is a series of proofs that life has continuity and history, and (this is most important) that any point in your own past is still within your reach.

Sontag's notebooks are filled with such proofs: lists of films she has seen, books she has read, words that have charmed her, the dried husks of completed endeavors—and these are largely limited to the notebooks; they almost never feed into her books or films or articles, they are neither the starting point, nor the underpinning for her public work. They are not intended as explanations for another reader (perhaps for the self, although they are scribbled down at such a pace that sometimes it's hard to make out what is meant). Like a fridge, or as it was once called, an icehouse, a place where the fast-corrupting memory-product can be stored, a space for witness accounts and affirmations, or the material and outward signs of immaterial and elusive relations, to paraphrase Goncharov.

There is something faintly displeasing, if only in the excess of material, and I say this precisely because I am of the same disposition, and far too often my working notes seem to me to be heaped deadweight: ballast I would dearly love to be rid of, but what would be left of me then? In *The Silent Woman*, Janet Malcolm describes an interior that is, in some ways, the image of my own notebook (and this was a horrible realization). It is littered with newspapers, books, overflowing ashtrays, dusty Peruvian tat, unwashed dishes, empty pizza boxes, cans, flyers, books along the lines of *Who's Who*, attempting to pass as real knowledge, and other objects passing as nothing at all, because they lost all resemblance to anything years ago. For Malcolm this living space is Borges's Aleph, a "monstrous allegory of truth," a gristly mass of crude fact and versions that never attained the clean order of history.

*

My Aunt Galya's diaries were completely peculiar, and their strangely woven texture, which reminded me above all of chain-link fencing, intrigued me more and more as I read them.

At any of the big art exhibitions I visited as a child, there were always a few viewers who stood out to me, and they were usually, and inexplicably, women. These women went from one picture to another, bending over the captions and making notes on pieces of paper or in exercise books. It dawned on me at some point that they were simply copying down the names of all the pictures, making for themselves a sort of homemade catalog—a shadow copy of what they'd seen. And I wondered why they were doing it, and hadn't yet realized that a list creates the illusion of possession: the exhibition would pass and dissolve in the air, but the piece of paper held the order of sculptures and pictures, as freshly as when they first saw them, long after the actual images had faded.

Galya's diaries were just such lists, but of daily occurrences, recorded with astonishing exactness, and with astonishing opacity. The diaries documented the time she got up and when she went to sleep, the television programs she'd watched, the number of phone conversations she'd had, who they'd been with, what she'd eaten, whatever else she'd done. There was a minute and virtuosic avoidance of *content*—how she'd actually filled her hours. It might say "read," for example, but with no mention of what the reading material had been or what it had meant to her—in fact everything in her long and exhaustively documented life was the same. Nothing indicated what this life had been for, there was nothing about herself, nothing about other people, only the fastidious details, the fixing of the passing of time with the exactitude of a medieval chronicler.

I kept thinking that surely life would rear its head, if only once, and reveal itself in all its color. Hadn't she spent her life reading—wouldn't that alone have provoked intense reflection? There were also the constant slights and grievances that my aunt clung to, and only reluctantly relinquished. Surely something of this would be preserved and laid out in a final furious paragraph, in which Galya would tell the world, and us, its representatives, what she thought of us—the unexpurgated truth.

But there was nothing of the sort in the diaries. There were hints and semitones of meaning, folds in the weave that denoted emotion, "hurray" written in the margin against the note of a phone call with my father or with me, a few opaquely bitter comments on her parents' anniversaries. And that was it. It was as if the main task of each and every note, each completed year's diary, was a faithful witnessing of the exterior, and a concealment of the authentic and interior. Show everything. Hide everything. Preserve it forever.

What was it she held to be of such value in these diaries? Why did she keep them by her bedside until her dying day, frightened they would be lost, often asking for them to be moved closer to her? Perhaps the written text as it stood—and it was the tale of a life of loneliness and the imperceptible slide toward nonexistence—still had the force of an indictment. The world needed to read all this, to realize just how shoddily we had dealt with her.

Or, strange as it seems, for her these pinched records might have contained the substance of joy, which she needed to immortalize, to add to the pile of manuscripts that, as Bulgakov wrote, don't burn, and which speak without any intention toward the future. If that's the case then she succeeded.

October 11, 2002

Working backward again. It's 1:45 p.m. Just put the towels, night-gown etc. except dark colors in to soak. Will do the bedlinen later. Before that I brought everything in from balcony. 3 degrees, the vegetables might have frozen. Peeled and chopped pumpkin and put in a box ready for freezer. Very slow work! Watched television and did it in two hours and a little more. Before that I had tea with milk.

Slept from 4:00–6:00 p.m., couldn't resist a little nap. Before that T. V. rang about the telephone. And he rang before 12 as well to check whether the television was working. This morning not a single channel worked. Got up at 8 when Seryozha was washing in the bathroom. Left after nine, took my time to get ready. Bus No. 3 didn't come till 9:45. We waited an age. Should have taken the 171. There were crowds everywhere and it took far longer than usual.

Bus station. Newspapers. But I did manage to buy the pumpkin, first I've seen this year. And carrots. Got home around 12. Wanted to watch Columbo. Took my hypertension pills last night just after 1:45 after measuring B. P. Waited for it to come down so I could take more pills. Spent 20 mins trying. Couldn't measure B. P. Got to bed at 3 a.m.

July 8, 2004
Lovely sunny morning, not the rain promised. Had coffee with condensed milk and went out around 11. Crowds everywhere. Sat for a long time, until 1:00 p.m., by the pond, looked at the grass, the trees and the sky, sang, felt very well in myself.

People were out walking their dogs along the paths, and pushing babies in strollers, and lots of parties of youngsters in their swimsuits, relaxing and having fun.

Managed to pay without standing in line, bought cream cheese. Strolled home. New school has a beautiful border. Tall plumes of bedstraw and wild rose. Just perfect! On the way home saw some boys playing in an abandoned old car. They had a plastic bottle stuffed full of seed pods. Apparently they're edible.

October 11, 2005
Couldn't sleep. Didn't much want to get up or get going or do anything. 10:40 mail was delivered and I went back to bed after that. Sveta came just after that. She's such a good girl, she gets the best of everything for me. Had tea and spent the day in bed. Thanked V. V. for bringing up mail.

Bobrova rang after 12. She came on Thursday.

I rang the clinic. Ira from Social Services, and Yura in the evening. Watched television and tidied all the washing on the chair. Went to bed at 11:30 p.m.

Hot day. I wore the skirt Tonya got me. "Dreary sort of life, of no use to anyone," as you might say. Tea in the afternoon, coffee in the evening. No appetite whatsoever.

But there was one note, quite different from the rest. On July 17, 2005 she wrote:

Sima rang this morning. I got down the photo album afterward. Shook all the photos out and spent a long while looking at them. I didn't want to eat, and looking at the photos gave me such a feeling of melancholy, tears, real sadness for the times passed, and for those who aren't with us anymore. This pointless life of mine, a life lived for nothing, the emptiness in my soul ... I wanted to lose myself, forget it all.

I went back to bed and slept for the rest of the day, strange, can't think how I could have slept so long, didn't get up till the evening, till 8:oo p.m. Drank some milk, closed the curtains and lay down, and again this sleep to transport me away from reality. Sleep is my salvation.

*

Months passed, maybe years. Galya's diaries lay around the place, caught up in piles of other papers, the sort of papers you leave out, thinking they will come in handy, and instead they discolor and age like old kitchenware. I suddenly and involuntarily remembered them when I arrived in the town of Pochinky.

Pochinky had a dubious claim to fame in our household. This one-horse, dead-end little town, over two hundred kilometers from Nizhny Novgorod, was the place we'd all come from and no one had ever returned to. No one had even made an attempt to return there in the last seventy-odd years. Nabokov writes about existence as "but a brief crack of light between two eternities of darkness"—well, this quiet little provincial town, of little interest to anyone, became over the years that first dark eternity in the collective memory of our family.

Ours was a large family back then. I dimly remember accounts of dozens of brothers and sisters, photographs of carts and horses and wooden buildings. But these accounts were eclipsed by the tales of the wild adventures of my great-grandmother, Sarra Ginzburg, a native of Pochinky. She had been in prison in Tsarist times and had even lived in Paris, and trained as a doctor and then treated Soviet children, including my mother and me, and everything I was told about her had the laurel-leaf taste of legend. There was no one left to verify all these fantastic tales and no one would have wanted to.

We had a relative, Leonid, who was constantly on the brink of visiting the shrunken husk of this nineteenth-century town. He talked about it as one might an imaginary polar expedition. He spent his days attempting to instill this enthusiasm in others, his near and distant relatives (I was one of his last converts). He had striking pale eyes, almost transparent, and his enthusiasm was a constantly running motor. On the rare occasions when he found himself in Moscow he would visit to discuss his plans with my parents. Then one day he arrived unexpectedly and found my parents gone, they'd emigrated to Germany. I was the family's sole remaining representative in Moscow. I'd never considered a sentimental journey like this, and I was intoxicated: for the first time it seemed as if our family's native home was within reach, and therefore a real place. The more Leonid insisted on the hardships we would face, the distances we would travel, and the elaborate preparations that would need to be made, the more the journey seemed quite against the odds—and the more promise it held for me. In the end this Leonid, who spent so many years planning a trip with the whole extended family, a sort of return of the Tribes of Israel, died without ever realizing his dream. Pochinky remained as fantastical and unknown to us all as the fairy-tale city of Kitezh.

And here I was, just that little bit closer to Pochinky. Why I went I can't say, and I can't remember what I hoped to discover there, but before I left I spent a long time online, turning up facts. Pochinky was at the outer limits of the known world, I found it on an ancient map: beyond Arzamas, tucked in the wilds beyond

Pushkin's estate at Boldino, surrounded by villages with dooms-day names. There were no railway lines in these parts, the nearest station was three hours' drive. I decided to cut my losses and hired a driver in Nizhny Novgorod.

We left Nizhny Novgorod early in the morning along wide, pink, still-wintery streets. The town slipped into valleys and then reappeared in the car windows with its peculiar, not-quite-heed-less clutter of industrial sites and picket-fenced wooden houses, conceding nothing to the modern world. When we reached the road out of town the car seemed to move by itself, racing along with unnecessary speed: the driver, father of a three-month-old baby, kept his hands on the wheel and was disdainfully silent. The road flexed up and down in tight little waves, frail remains of snow clung to the ground under the fir trees. The world grew poorer with every kilometer. In the blackened villages new churches gleamed like china, white as new crowns on old teeth. I had a guidebook extolling the beauty of Arzamas, now long behind us, and a little book on Pochinky, published twenty years before: it mentioned a shop owned by *the Jew Ginzburg*, who traded in sewing machines, and that was all. There was no men-tion of the legendary Sarra.

We traveled for long hours. At last the hills began, a dusky ridge of them, Umbrian hills, the color of dark copper, rising and falling as evenly as breath. Sometimes a brief flash of water. After we passed the exit for Pushkin's Boldino estate there was a series of Pushkin memorials along the road. According to legend his local mistress had lived in the village of Lukoyanov. Little groups of trees like herds of animals.

Pochinky was built along a long main street: little side streets departed from the high street at tidy right angles. An attractive church in a classical style stood on the far side of the road. I learned from the guidebook that this was the Cathedral of the Nativity, where a certain Orfanov had once been priest. I knew the name, Valya Orfanova often sent us greetings when I was a child, and once she had asked my mother to buy me a book from her, so *Masha will have something to remember me by.* Mother picked out a poetry collection by the Symbolist poet Fyodor Sologub at the secondhand bookshop, but unfortunately it turned out to be a late work, *The Great Good News Herald,* a book of Communist poems published in 1923, filled with proletarians with flaming ideals. Useless to me, as I judged it then, not yet able to appreciate the exquisite soundplay underlying the hackneyed sentiments:

The officer's horse
The enemy force
Treads in its dance
Treads on my heart

I had a strong desire to abandon the deserted main square in search of a place where there was something I could see and touch, but Maria Fufayeva, a local historian, was waiting for us there. It was a Sunday but they'd opened up the town library just for us. An exhibition of watercolors of Pochinky's streets hung in the library; painted a hundred years before, they'd been sent from Germany for the exhibition. A German family had lived in Pochinky toward the end of the nineteenth century, and I had a sudden memory of the painter's name, Gethling, being mentioned when I was a child.

The pictures were gemütlich, cheery: a pretty house with a chemist's sign and some flowering mallow, the house of Augusta Gethling, the painter's sister, who had tutored my great-grandmother for her school entrance exam. The house was still standing, but its little porch was gone, the facade had been concreted over and the mallow and the carved window frames had disappeared. No one could tell me anything about the house with the large yard and the horse and cart, the home of Sarra and her family at the beginning of the twentieth century.

And that was all. Much like the diaries of Aunt Galya, the reader had to content herself with shopping lists, notes of television programs, descriptions of the weather. Whatever stood behind this, swaying and rustling, was in no hurry to show itself, and perhaps didn't intend to show itself at all. We were offered tea; we were taken for a guided tour of the town. I searched the ground beneath my feet constantly as if hoping to find a dropped kopeck.

The village had the shrunken feel of a vanished town, a once bustling center which had sprung up around the largest horse fair in the whole region. We crossed a vast market square, a vacant space now overgrown with trees, somewhere in its center a lead-gray statue of Lenin, but otherwise a place abandoned by people, too large to be useful in any new reincarnation. It was fringed by pretty little wooden houses, like the ones in the watercolors, some showing the signs of hasty, ugly renovation. And we were shown another square, a little asphalted space where Solomon Ginzburg, Sarra's brother, had owned a shop in the 1920s. Here we stood a while and took photos, a group of us, surly women in coats and hats. The wind was too icy for smiles. On a curb by the main road another monument glittered in the grass, dedicated to Kapral, a mighty stallion and a stud horse for a full twenty years.

A little drive beyond the bridge over the river Rudnya was a derelict complex of buildings, the size of a small town, used for horse breeding. They had been built at the beginning of the nineteenth century and had once belonged to the cavalry regiment of the Imperial Guard. But even before this, horses had been bred here: *kabarda and Nogay, stallions, horses, geldings and Nogay mares, and Russian colts and herding horses.*

Catherine the Great built up the business to an industrial scale. The resulting huge square building with its classical lines and peeling whitewashed walls, its subsiding central tower and the arched entrance, symmetrically matched on the far side of the square, was intended to be an outpost of civilization, a little island of Petersburgian refinement. It had fallen into total disrepair relatively recently, in the 1990s, and it now stood surrounded by bare earth, blasted by the long winter. The last horses moved about the open paddocks: heavyset chestnut horses with pale and tufty manes. They lifted their heads and pushed their muzzles into our palms. By now the sky was dazzling, the clouds formed a mountain ridge across the horizon, and a skin-pink light glowed under the crazed white facade of the buildings.

We'd already traveled halfway back when I realized I'd forgotten the most important thing: there must have been a cemetery of some sort, Jewish or otherwise, where my ancestors were buried. The driver had his foot on the accelerator, the names of villages were flashing past: surreal, earthy names. I called Maria Fufayeva on my mobile. There was no cemetery, just as there were no longer any Jews left in Pochinky. Actually, no, in fact there was one Jew left in Pochinky, she even knew his name: Gurevich. Strangely enough it was my mother's maiden name.

2. On Beginnings

I stopped writing this text for the very first time thirty-something years ago, after filling two or three pages of a lined school exercise book. The size and ambition of the task were simply too much for me. I put it aside, left it to grow into. I comforted myself with the thought that I could leave it be for now.

The history of this book consists of a number of such denials: moments when I managed to escape it in various ways: I put it off for my older, better self to complete, or I made tiny, painless, and deliberately inadequate sacrifices: jotting notes on scraps of paper or on my mobile while on the train or on the phone, a little like notching a stick (*to remind me*, so that from these two- and three-word distillations the memory would be able to put together a whole viable and elegant construction, a silken tent for the narrative to reside in). In place of a memory I did not have, of an event I did not witness, my memory worked over someone else's story; it rehydrated the driest little note and made of it a pop-up cherry orchard.

Early twentieth-century Russian memoirs sometimes mention an amusement for children that consisted of placing yellow discs in the bottom of a teacup and then filling the cup with water. Under water the discs began to glow with the extraordinary, exotic, and otherworldly intensity of Japanese and Chinese paints. I've never seen these discs—where did all that go? But in the family treasure trove of Christmas decorations handed down from my grandmother, there was a little incense burner, the height of a match, in the shape of a swarthy-faced boy smoking microscopic white cigarettes, and the smoke kept rising and the pinpoint of light endlessly disintegrated to ash, until our tiny cigarette supplies ended for good. Now all I can do is describe its workings, and perhaps this is a happy end of sorts? Paradise for the disappearing objects and everyday diversions of the past might simply exist in being remembered and mentioned.

I began writing this book when I was ten, in the apartment on Banny Pereulok in Moscow, where I am typing the first lines of this chapter now. In the 1980s there was a battered desk by the window with an orange desk lamp, I would stick my favorite transfers to its white plastic base: a plush mama bear, pulling a sleigh with a Christmas tree, a sack of gifts, and her baby bear sitting sideways on it under a snowy sky. On each sheet of trans-fers there were usually five or six drab pictures, gleaming with a sticky finish. Each one was cut out separately and wetted in a bowl of warm water. Then the transparent colored image had to be peeled free of the backing with a practiced movement, placed on a flat surface, and smoothed out, all the creases removed. I re-member the little cat boy wearing a raincoat and a carnival mask on the door of the kitchen cupboard, and the penguin couple on a background of pink-green wheeling Northern Lights. Still the bears were my very favorite.

It is as if it brings some relief to share all these scraps from the past as I remember them, half-wryly, the transfers dirty and rubbed away a good twenty years even before the kitchen was redecorated, and only now reanimated, illuminated again—fat little boy in a sombrero and yellow-green domino mask but with no face behind the mask, a mass of gold curlicues around his head ... As if, like a vanquished wizard, I could disappear, be-coming a thousand ancient, neglected, blackening objects. As if my life's work was to catalog them all. As if that is what I grew up to do.

The second time I started to write this book without even real-izing it, I was sixteen, wild, errant, in the afterglow of a love affair that felt as if it had defined everything in my life. With the passing of years this love has dissipated and paled to such an extent that I can no longer conjure up the sensation of "everything beginning" that I felt while I was in its grip. But I remember one thing with absolute clarity—when it became clear that the relationship was over, to all intents and purposes even if not in my head, I decided it was of vital importance to record a sort of "selected impressions": details, assemblage points, the turns our conversations took, the phrases we used. I wanted to fix them in my mind, to prepare for future writing-up. A linear narrative made no sense for this: the line itself was so shakily drawn. I simply noted down everything that seemed important not to forget; on each square of paper a single word or a few words, which straightaway reconstructed a location and happening in my memory; a conversation, street corner, a joke, or a promise. Every incident struggled desperately against my attempt to contain it, to give it order and sequence—alphabetical or chronological—and so I set on the idea of one day putting all these little twists of paper into a hat (my father's hat, he had a wonderful gray hat that he never wore) and of pulling them out one by one, and then, one by one, noting them down, point by point, until I was able to leave alone this chartered land of tenderness: a memorial to my own self. After a while these forty or so bits of paper ended up in various drawers of a table we had, and then dissolved somehow, lost in a procession of moves and spring cleans.

Do I need to mention that I don't remember a single one of the forty words I was so frightened I would forget all those years ago?

*

And yet I am still smitten with the idea of blindly retrieving and reliving scraps from my life, or from a collective life, rescued from the shadows of the known and accepted histories. The first step of this salvaging is my habitual working process: notes on the back of an envelope, scrawls during a phone call, three words in a notebook, invisible library cards piling up in a hasty and unsystematic manner, never to be reread. All this is the continuing mounting up of my life to date. Only there are ever fewer people with whom I can still discuss *how things were.*

I always knew I would someday write a book about my family, and there were even periods when this seemed to be my life's purpose (summarizing lives, collecting them into one narrative) because it was simply the case that I was the first and only person in the family who had a reason to speak facing outward, peering out from intimate family conversations as if from under a fur cap, and addressing the railway station concourse of collective experience. None of these people, not those still alive, nor those already dead, were ever *seen.* Life gave them no opportunity to be remembered or to remain in view, to stand briefly in the spotlight; their ordinariness put them beyond the usual human interest and this seemed unfair. There was, it felt to me, an urgency in speaking about them and on their behalf, and the endeavor frightened me. To start writing was to cease to be a curious listener, an addressee, and to become instead the horizon point of the family line, the destination for the many-eyed, many-decked ship of family history. I would become a stranger, a teller of tales, a selector and a sifter, the one who decides what part of the huge volume of the unsaid must fit in the spotlight's circle, and what part will remain outside it in the darkness.

It struck me that my grandparents' efforts in life were largely dedicated to remaining invisible, to achieving a desired incon- spicuousness, to hiding in the dim household light and keep- ing themselves apart from the wide current of history, with its extragrand narratives and its margins of error: the deaths of millions. Perhaps this was a conscious choice, perhaps not— who knows. In Autumn 1914, when my great-grandmother was a young woman, she returned to Russia from war-torn France, taking a detour to stay clear of the war. She might have gone back to her old ways, her revolutionary activity; she might have had her name in school history books or, just as likely, in the lists of the executed. But she remained well beyond the reach of the textbooks and their footnotes, in a place where all we can see is swirly-patterned wallpaper and an ugly old yellow butter dish, which survived its owner and the old world, and even the twentieth century.

Earlier in my life this gave me cause for some embarrassment, although the reason for this is hard to put into words and shameful to admit. I suppose the embarrassment had something to do with the "narrative drive." I felt bound to notice that my ancestors had hardly made any attempt to make our family history interesting. This was particularly clear to me when we commemorated the war each year at school. The war had happened forty odd years before. Other peoples' grandfathers came into school with their medals and bouquets of flowers, they never said much (because what had happened to them hardly bore being salami-sliced into episodes of derring-do), but they stood very upright by the blackboard, and even if they gave no witness accounts, they were in themselves pieces of evidence. My grandfather Lyonya did not fight: he was an engineer in the rear guard. I pinned more hope on Kolya, my other grandfather, with his officer ranking and his Order of the Red Star. But it turned out he had served in the Far East during the war, and I could never quite establish whether or not he did any fighting.

When I conducted further research, it began to look like he hadn't fought after all. He had been under suspicion, *something had happened*—and the shadowy tale hung untold, like a dark cloud, over that side of the family. This story had a title— "When father was an enemy of the people"—and it took place in 1938–39, during an "unspoken" Beria amnesty, when some were suddenly set free and others, like my grandfather, escaped imprisonment. It was only when I compared dates that I realized that my grandmother was pregnant with her second child during those dark days: my father was born on August 1, 1939, exactly a month before the outbreak of the Second World War, and the composition of Auden's poem:

Waves of anger and fear
Circulate over the bright
And darkened lands of the earth,
Obsessing our private lives;
The unmentionable odor of death
Offends the September night.

Lord knows by what miracle he survived and even grew up in an intact family with a mother and a father and a sister. I know two versions of the story. The one they told me in my childhood now seems a confection and apocryphal—I'll write of it later. But the image of my grandfather the warrior didn't really stick: in the story told at home he was a mere splinter in a whirlpool—hardly the hero of a stirring tale of war and victory.

Everyone else's ancestors had taken part in history, but mine seemed to have been mere lodgers in history's house. None of them had fought or been repressed or executed (there were dark rumors of arrest and interrogation surrounding the other grandfather, but it seems the affair died down and he escaped persecution), none had lived under German occupation or fought in the battles of the century. One story stood like an obelisk in all this: the life of my great-great-aunt's twenty-year-old son, who died defending Leningrad. This was a tale of the unfairness of life, and no amount of icy anesthetic running through the veins could dull its horror. Wasn't it impossible for the little boy in the photos in his round-toed felt boots to die? The news of his death is so inconceivable that sometimes just the mention of the boy's name is enough to make me *go dark before the eyes,* as my mother used to say—both the story and my response to it, learned from her.

It's hardly worth saying, but there were no famous people among my relatives; they seemed almost to insist on their inconspicuousness. They were doctors, engineers, architects (but not of dreaming spires and facades, only of workaday constructions like roads and bridges). They were accountants and librarians.

They led very quiet lives, appearing to live utterly apart from the grinding mills of the era. Almost no one belonged to the Communist Party, but at the same time there was nothing demonstrative in this—it was simply that their lives ran deep under the skin, that nothing was acted out on the surface, where every little movement is scaled up, noticed, and has consequences. Now that they have departed into permanent darkness and their personal histories are concluded, I can examine these lives, talk about them, and hold them up to the light for inspection. And, at the end of the day, there is a sort of inevitability to being seen— would this one last time really harm them?

*

From time to time, always in the evening, and usually on a school holiday, or a day when I was recuperating from sickness, my mother would call me to look at the photo albums. We'd prize open the cupboard door—the cupboard was jammed up against the divan so it took some skill to open it—and before we got out the albums we'd pull out a drawer filled with boxes (this extra diversion was the icing on the cake). The boxes contained all sorts of objects that were very dear to me, passport photos and pictures from different generations, prewar pebbles collected from Crimean beaches, an antediluvian baby's rattle, grandfather's drawing instruments (you can have these when you're old enough), other odds and ends. The photo albums themselves were kept in the main cupboard, and there were a lot of them. Some of them were stuffed so tight with photographs that the leather binding was stretched thin. Others were nearly empty, but we still took them out. The most impressive album was bound in orange leather and had silver buckles and straps; another was black patent leather with the emblem of a yellow castle on a hill on the front, and "Lausanne" printed slantwise. There was an art nouveau album, decorated in metallic curls and the image of a Japanese geisha, which would have looked dated even a hundred years ago. There were thinner albums and thicker ones, larger and smaller ones. The pages had a certain old-fashioned weight to them, with wide silver edges and slits for the corners of photographs. There was a touch of melancholy in the fact that our modern glossy, slippery photos didn't fit in the albums. They were either too narrow for the slots, or they bulged between the slits, and they were always too lightweight. The old photographs had an abiding quality, they were intended for a different life span, they cast into doubt all my efforts to fit my own image into a neighboring slot in the album.

And then the photographs themselves, each with a story attached. Men with thick beards and men in glasses with thin gold frames, who were directly related to us, our great-grandfathers, or great-great-grandfathers (and sometimes I added another "great" in my head quietly just because it gave them an air of grandeur), their friends and acquaintances. Young girls, who turned out to be grandmothers or aunties, with interchangeably dull names. Auntie Sanya, Auntie Sonya, Auntie Soka, a long line of them, swapping ages with ease, their expressions unchanging; standing, sitting, against a backdrop of dim interiors or staged landscapes. We began looking from the beginning, from the very first beards and collars, and somewhere toward the middle of the evening everything began to swim out of focus, except my sense of the enormity of it all. The geographical reach alone was huge: these people and their sepia-faded children lived in Khabarovsk, Gorky, Saratov, Leningrad. But no sense of family history attached itself to the city names, family history was merely made more distant and foreign by their roll call. At last, and with a sense of contentment, we reached a small album that contained photos of my mother as a child: looking gloomy in wartime evacuation in Yalutorovsk; standing holding a doll in a pioneer camp; wearing a sailor suit and holding flags in her nursery school. I could understand this scale, it was proportional to me. In some ways the whole evening's activity culminated in this: to see the child who was my mother, sullen, frightened, running as fast as she could along some long-forgotten dirt track, was to enter into a new territory of anticipated closeness, a place in which I was older than her and could look after her and feel sorry for her. When I look back at this now, I realize that the sting of pity and equality I felt back then came too early in my life. But at least it came. I had no other chance to feel older than her, or to pity her.

Only much later I noticed that all the bound albums, the stories and the golden-edged photographs (for they all had milled and gilded edges and monograms and the name of the photographer and the place the photograph was taken on the back) were of my mother's family. There were in the whole house only two or three photos of my father's family standing out on a bookshelf. In these pictures my grandmother Dora as a young woman looked surprisingly like my own young mother, and stern-faced grandfather Kolya looked for all the world like Pasternak in his old age. They were silently present, like icons in the corner of a room, almost as if they stood outside the wide current of family history, its river source, its jetties and shallows.

There were also albums of postcards (these later turned out to be the remains of great-grandmother Sarra's correspondence, dashed-off lines from Paris, Nizhny Novgorod, Venice, Montpellier), a whole miniature library of a disappeared visual aesthetic: beautiful full-cheeked women, mustachioed men, children in little Russian high-necked jackets, Symbolist death-and-the-maidens, gargoyles, and beggar girls. And other cards without scribbles on the back: *vedute* of the even brown walls of Italian, French, and German cities.

I loved best of all a series of postcards with night views of cities, parks at dusk, a bright streetcar turning a tight corner, an empty carousel, a lost child standing by a flower bed and clutching a useless hoop, tall houses, windows so impossibly red they could have been lipsticked in, and behind them the old world lived on. This dark-blue world with its lit lamps radiated the purest sense of yearning and was doubly and triply unattainable. Unattainable because the impossibility of foreign travel was a constant ungainsayable presence in our everyday lives—people in our world didn't travel. (Our two or three acquaintances who had been given permission to travel abroad seemed to glow in the golden light of a rare fortune—it happened so infrequently and to so few people.) And modern Paris, as described in André Maurois's *Paris*, had nothing in common with that dark-blue-and-black Paris, which seemed to prove conclusively that it had disappeared long ago, with no hope of ever returning. The postcards, like the visiting cards and the pale envelopes with their raspberry-colored paper lining, were all just waiting to be used in some way, but we couldn't imagine how to make use of them in this very different era. So we closed up the albums again and put them back on their shelf and placed the postcards back in their boxes and the evening came to a close as all evenings do.

Some of the objects from this old world (and our home was full of them, even seeming to rest on them, like hen's legs) had made a place for themselves in the new world. Yellowing lace was sewn onto the cuffs of a musketeer's greatcoat for a school carnival, a black hat from Paris with an ostrich feather of insane length and curliness came in handy over and over again. I couldn't pull the kid gloves over my hands (they had shrunk with time, but it looked as if they were simply too small for me, and I felt shamed by the breadth of my hands, like a wicked stepsister trying on a glass slipper). We drank tea from hundred-year-old cups once or twice a year when guests came over. Everything came out for high days and holidays, those days that were mismatched to the everyday, like two odd boots; those days when all the rules slipped sideways and you were permitted the impermissible. On other days the albums lay on the shelf and time merely passed.

I need to make it very clear at this point that our family was quite ordinary. After the Soviet Union disappeared, everything began rising up to the surface, objects regained little by little their primary function, and our accumulated and preserved past became once again what it was to begin with: a museum of cultured life at the beginning of the twentieth century, complete with battered bentwood furniture, a pair of oak armchairs, and a black leather-bound *Complete Works of Tolstoy*. It genuinely was buried treasure, but in a different sense from the usual. The clock struck the hour, the barometer indicated stormy weather, and the owl paperweight did nothing in particular. Remaining together was the sole purpose of these mild-mannered, uncomplicated objects, and they achieved it.

*

Strange really to think that this task—of committing everything to memory—has hung over me all my life. I didn't feel ready for it, not then, not now.

I couldn't get it all off by heart, however often I went over the same ground—and every dive down to the underwater caves of the past meant doing just that: the recounting of the same old names and circumstances, nothing gained, no new slant on things. Some things leaped into my memory ticketless, like a kid on a streetcar, usually a legend or a curiosity, the narrative equivalent of Barthes's *punctum*. Among these were the stories that could more easily be retold. And how much did it matter anyway if one starch-collared ancestor became a lawyer in the retelling, rather than a doctor? But guilt at the missing details hampered my ability to remember, forced me to put off asking more detailed questions. It was already clear that I would one day (when I became that better version of myself) open a special notebook and sit down with my mother, and she would start at the very beginning, and then there would be some meaning to it all—and a system, a family tree, and every cousin and nephew would be in their rightful place, and at the end of it there would be a book. I never once doubted that this moment of setting things straight would be essential to the process.

But I never did ask those questions or set things straight in that way, despite my ability to retain inessential facts and my chimp's memory for anything to do with words. The puzzle was never completed; I was left with the tongue twister of my aunt's names, Sanya, Sonya, Soka, a lot of photographs of the nameless and the noteless, some ethereal and unattached anecdotes, and the familiar faces of unfamiliar people.

To some extent this resembled a mah-jongg set that was kept at the dacha. The dacha (a little one-room place with a tiny kitchen, a terrace, and a scrap of boggy ground where some stubborn apple trees clung to life) was just outside Moscow, and for decades my family had been taking anything worn or shabby out there to assume its rightful place and live out its second life. Nothing was ever thrown away, and these elderly objects made the world more densely present, less ethereal. The *former* furniture aged with its summer's hard labor: harvesting, storing, the seasonal tasks. Ink stands kept pointlessly in the shed, drawers full of hundred-year-old nightshirts, and, on a shelf behind the mirror, a mah-jongg set in a little canvas bag. For years I was intrigued by this mah-jongg set, and every summer holiday I nursed the forlorn hope that I would set it all out, work out what to do with it, and return it to useful service. It never happened.

We knew that my great-grandmother had brought the set back from her travels abroad (and as we possessed two kimonos in the house, a large one and my smaller one, both gossamer-light with age, I had no doubt that abroad in this case meant Japan). The little bag contained lots of ivory pieces, brown with age, each with a white front covered in hieroglyphics, which I was never able to decipher or match to another piece, domino-fashion: a sailing boat to a sailing boat, a flourish of leaves to a flourish of leaves. There were simply too many different images, and alarmingly few common elements. And then I had the sudden thought that probably over the years some of the pieces had gone astray, and that made me feel completely lost. I could see there was a clear system, but just as clearly I knew I couldn't work out what it was, or even design a simpler version for myself. I couldn't even keep a piece in my pocket, because I didn't want to take a part from the whole.

When I began to think seriously about my memories I had the startling realization that I had nothing left. Almost nothing from those evenings looking at old photographs in the lamplight: no dates, no details, not even the skeleton of a family tree. Who was whose brother or nephew? The little boy with the sticking-out ears, in a short jacket with gold buttons, and the man with his sticking-out ears, wearing an officer's woolen coat were clearly the same person—but who was he? I had the faint stirring of a recollection that his name was Grigory, but it didn't help me much. The people who had once populated that other world with all its valencies, family connections, and warm embraces across the miles had all gone: they were dead, or displaced, lost. The history of a family that I had at the outset learned at the speed of a straight line was now fragmenting in my head into tesserae, into notes indicating textual omissions, into hypotheses there was no one left to prove.

Perhaps, for this reason, a number of unverifiable stories hovered around the edges of my mother's recollections. The sort of tales that add piquancy to the usual movement between generations but exist as apocrypha, the friable appendices to firm facts. Such fables are mostly like sprouting twigs, still to unfurl and grow to their life's proportions, and they take the form of half-spoken phrases in the margins of the story: "I've heard he lived in …"; "She must have been this or that …"; "There's a story about him …" It's the sweetest part of the tale-telling, the fairy-tale element. These are the embryos of a novel, what we remember forever, over and above the boring circumstances of time and place. I want to take them and blow life into them, tell them anew, stuff them with details I have prepared myself. I remember these stories so much more easily. The pity is that even they become meaningless without a subject to hang them on; they cannot be verified, and over the years they lose their individual quality and are incorporated into the memory as part of the wide current of the everyday, the typical. It is hard to say now what actually exists of the stories I have retained. By that I don't even mean what actually happened, but rather: was it passed down from mother to daughter, or simply a product of my imagination, invented without me even realizing?

Although sometimes I did realize. I remember once, a terrible teenager with a desire to fascinate, I told someone the family story of a curse. "And so, passionately in love" (I intoned) "with an impoverished Polish aristocrat, he converted to Christianity and married her, and his father cursed him and never spoke to him again, and so they lived in poverty and soon they died of consumption."

This wasn't *exactly* true—no one died of consumption. In the photo albums there are pictures of the cast-out son, looking happy in his prodigal state, wearing glasses, with grandchildren, all against an ordinary Soviet backdrop. But what about the Polish aristocrat? Did she exist or did I add her merely to embroider the story? Polish, to add the "exotic," an aristocrat to add spice to the line of merchants, doctors, and lawyers? I don't know. I can't remember. There was something in my mother's story, the faintest lighting of the way forward for my imagination. But there's no way back: fantasy can't be placed under the microscope to discover its kernel of truth. So my story continues to feature an unreliable Polish aristocrat—the doubtful cause of real and doubtless hardship. There was a curse, and there was genuine poverty, and my great-great-grandfather never did set eyes on his firstborn son again, and then they did all die, so in one way or another it is true.

I inherited one other thing that bears on the construction of this story, on how it was told and by whom. It's the sense of our family as a matriarchy, a tribe of strong, individual women standing like milestones spanning the century. Their fates loomed large in my life, here they are in the front row—holding on to each other, merging into each other—of the many-headed family photograph. Strange when you consider that they all had husbands. The men in this family are barely illuminated, as if history consisted only of heroines, and couldn't quite stretch to heroic men. There is truth to this, though it's hardly the men's fault. Women kept the family line going—one husband died young, another died even younger, a third was busy with other out-of-frame matters. In my head, and perhaps in my mother's too, the line of transmission (that part of the story left, once the cheerful bustle of life has been tidied neatly into prehistory) was a staircase leading steadily toward me, consisting entirely of women. Sarra begat Lyolya, Lyolya begat Natasha, and Natasha begat me. The matryoshka (nesting) doll insisted on the preeminence of single daughters, each emerging from the one before and inheriting, with everything else, the gift and the opportunity to be the single teller of the tale.

*

What did I think I was up to all those years? I clearly wanted to build a monument to those people, making sure they didn't simply dissipate into the air, unremembered and unremarked upon. But in fact it seemed I didn't even remember them myself. My family history was a confection of anecdotes, barely attached to names or faces, unrecognizable figures in photographs, questions I couldn't quite formulate because they had no starting point and, in any case, there was no one to ask. Despite all this, I had to write the book and here is why.

Jacques Rancière's essay *Figures of History* makes many arguments that seem urgent for our times. He says, for example, that the artist's duty is to show "what can't be seen, what lies beneath the visible." This pleases me, because the late Russian poet Grigory Dashevsky always saw this as the role of poetry, to bring the invisible to the point of visibility. Rancière's most important point is this: in his writing about history, he contrasts "document" and "monument." A "document," for him, is any record of an event that aims to be exhaustive, to tell history, to make "a memory official." A "monument" is the opposite of "document," in "the primary sense of the term":

that which preserves memory through its very being, that which speaks directly, through the fact that it was not intended to speak—the layout of a territory that testifies to the past activity of human beings better than any chronicle of their endeavors; a household object, a piece of fabric, a piece of pottery, a stele, a pattern painted on a chest or a contract between two people we know nothing about ...

With this in mind, I began to see that the monument-memorial I'd hoped to raise was in fact built long ago. It seemed I even lived in its pyramid chambers, between the piano and the armchair, in a space marked out by photographs and objects, which were mine and not mine, which belonged simply to the continuing and disappearing thread of life. Those boxes of our domestic archive hardly spoke directly, but they were the silent witnesses, those piles of greetings cards and trade union cards were the epidermal cells of the lived and unspoken past, and, as storytellers, they were hardly worse than the documents that could speak for themselves. A list was all that was needed, a simple list of objects.

Perhaps I hoped to reassemble and reanimate from all these objects the corpse of Osiris, the collective family body, which had disappeared from the home. All these fragments of memory and pieces of the old world did create a whole, a unity of a particular sort. A whole vessel, but flawed and empty, consisting mostly of cracks and gaps, no better and no worse than any single person who has lived her term and survived—or, more accurately, that person's final and unmoving *corpus*.

And of this twisted body, no longer capable of connecting its memories into a sequence—would it want to be seen? Even supposing it wants nothing, am I right to make it the subject of my story, a museum exhibit, like the pink stocking of Empress Sisi, or the rusty file with traces of blood that brought her story to its end? Putting my family on general view, even if I do it with as much love as I can muster and with the best words in the best order, is, after all, something of a Ham's deed, exposing the vulnerable and naked body of the family, its dark armpits, its pale belly.

And most likely I would learn nothing new in writing it, and just knowing this made the act of writing even more fraught. Yes, free of scandalous revelation, far from the hell of Péter Esterházy, who found out that his beloved father had worked for the secret police, but also far from the bliss of having always known everything about your people, and bearing this knowledge with pride. Neither of these outcomes were mine. This book about my family is not about my family at all, but something quite different: the way memory works, and what memory wants from me.

*

In late spring 2011 a colleague visited me in Moscow to invite me to Saratov to give a talk about the internet journal where I was working. Our conversation very quickly turned to Saratov itself, a city I had never visited, and the birthplace of my great-grandfather. My colleague pulled out a tablet. He had a wondrous digital haul of scanned prerevolutionary postcards with views of Saratov: predominantly green-white vistas with trees and churches. As I flicked through, the lines faded into each other, and now I can only remember the wide expanse of river, dotted with ships. The tablet contained other wonders, a downloaded directory for 1908: gray lists of names and streets. "I've tried looking for my family," said the colleague. "Hopeless task, really. There are ten pages of my surname."

My great-grandfather was called Mikhail Davidovich Fridman, and this gave us a head start. We found him easily—he was the only one of that name in Saratov, and a hundred years before he had lived on Moscow Street, clearly an important street in the town back then. I asked if the street was still there, and it was.

So I set off for Saratov. The Volga river basin was as bare as an empty soup dish, and the narrow streets descended toward it like tourniquets. Where there were once just spaces of green and white, now shopping centers and Japanese restaurants vied for space. The steppe pressed in: mannequins stood outside the open doors of dress shops, wearing lavish wedding dresses with fluttering ruched skirts, soiled yellow by the dusty steppe wind. I went to Moscow Street the next morning, after checking the address again.

The house was unrecognizable, but then I'd never seen it before to recognize it. The wide gray facade had been smeared with a layer of cement and shop windows cut into its front. A shoe shop. But it was still possible to pass through an archway into the yard.

I spent a good while in the yard just running my hands over the rough Saratov brickwork. Everything was as I'd hoped, perhaps even more so than I'd hoped. I recognized my great-grand-father's yard unhesitatingly. There was no doubt in my mind, even though I'd never seen it or had it described to me. The wooden slatted palisade with the Rudbeckia growing up against it, the crooked walls with their bricks and wood, and a useless old chair with a broken frame standing by a fence—all of it was mine, all of it instantly part of my family. It seemed to speak to me, saying: here, you needed to come here. There was a strong smell of cat, but a stronger smell of plants and greenery, and there was absolutely nothing I could pick up to take with me. But I didn't need souvenirs, I remembered everything beneath the high windows with such a sense of heightened native precision that I seemed to know how it had all been, in this, *our*, place, how we had lived and why we had left. The yard put its arms around me in an embrace—that's what it was. I hung around another ten minutes or so, making huge efforts to commit it all to memory, to extract the picture, as you might a mirror from its frame, and fix it for once and for all in the memory's grooves. Then I left. And it worked. From the train window I saw long, bright drainage ditches running alongside the tracks, and once a little tornado of dust, twisting over a deserted crossroads.

About a week later my colleague from Saratov rang me sheepishly. He'd mixed up the address. That street all right, but a different house. God, I'm so sorry, Masha.

And that is just about everything I know about memory.

3. A Handful of Photographs

1.

A large hospital ward with a black-and-white checkered floor. The sun beats down through the tall arched windows and the right-hand side of the picture is bleached white by the light. There is altogether plenty of white in the picture; the beds stand feet-forward, their metal frames covered in canvas and on them high-stacked pillows, the heads of the patients. Men with whiskers stare toward the camera, one has propped himself up on his elbow and a nurse is making a quick adjustment to something at his shoulder. Only one woman in the whole huge room. In the left-hand corner of the picture a swarthy man in a hospital gown sits by a table, leaning on crutches, his face creased into a toothy beaming smile. This table is covered with paper, doctor's notes, discharge papers. Two men are sitting at the table, radiating the untroubled contentment of the hospital visitor—they are the focus of the composition, the event, the reason for the photographer's visit. One sits back in his bentwood chair; he wears a black suit, his shoes shine, his collar is brilliant white. The other wears gray and a flash of starched collar beneath his transparent mustache. A row of auxiliaries stand farther back, their arms crossed over their chests and stomachs, as if waiting for orders. The iron bed legs and the ribs of columns run in parallel; someone peeps out from behind a column as if everyone is obliged to be present in this picture. The fronds of an institutional potted palm wave from a corner. The window is a pool of light, and the picture is most interesting where the light washes out the detail of the window frame and even eats away at the nurse and her patient.

2.

If you didn't know you might never guess that this is a body. It looks like a pile of rags on a low marble table, and some attentive students sit behind it. Anatomy class. Closer to the camera there's another little table with something indistinct on it, a sack or a bundle or some such, I can't quite make it out. Six women crowd around the table, white lab coats over their dark everyday dresses. The only man stands a little apart, he has turned away and is deciding whether to smile or frown while the others are occupied. He wears a comic pince-nez, behind him a school blackboard covered in chalk scrawlings, and if you look closely you can see a mass of information: a diagram of the vegetative nervous system left on the board after a lecture; the profile of a soldier in a high peaked cap; another profile of a beautiful woman with a cigarette in her mouth and a determined jaw; a smiling round face, presented straight on with a huge pair of ears added on each side. The blackboard is to the side of the picture, and at the table we see a restaging of Rembrandt's *The Anatomy Lesson of Dr. Nicolaes Tulp* but with an all-female cast: a black-haired girl with a stethoscope around her neck is reading from a book and her listeners are sitting absolutely still. Their faces are as impassive as the faces of watchmen on duty, only one has allowed a smile to soften her features. But if you thought at first that they were all listening attentively then you would have been wrong: one is stretched out on her chair and her gaze is remote, another is sitting up with a sudden start as if her name had been called. One student in glasses hasn't managed to put on her doctor's coat, and is attempting to pass off her heavy embroidered bodice as a medical robe. The woman sitting with a book, her hair gathered into a bun at the nape of her neck, is my great-grandmother, Sarra. The women direct their gazes in different directions, like a bundle of badly behaved twigs, anywhere except at the articulated pile of rags that is the corpse in front of them.

3.

All the French doctors are whiskered and their whiskers point skyward like wings; all the women are in white with their sleeves pushed up; an electric light hangs down from the ceiling. You can tell the nurses from the students by the huge cornettes they wear. Constant collective activity like a spindle turning, faces peeking out from behind backs, glances over the shoulder at a point in the picture where there is a mound under sheets, and the gray-bearded head doctor is holding a clamp or a lancet: this is the dead zone, the static center of the composition and the operation, so silent you can hear the ticking in your own head, and the women, who are standing so close to the hands and what is under them, are turned away to look at the camera, and seem to be frowning.

4.

The picture is the color of wood, and even seems to be wood-paneled, everything in it is planked, the walls, the fence, the shed, a little lean-to at the side of the house. There's a cat nearby, but the chickens are maintaining their dignity. A girl, wearing a new school dress, you can tell that the wide sleeves are newly stitched. Her whole being says that she is resigned to being photographed but doesn't quite see the need. A bentwood chair has been brought outside for the occasion and she is seated in it and the camera readied, and there she is, her smile both proud and ironic.

5.

There's no note on this one, but it's Switzerland, around 1910. Wedges of pine forest to the left and right and cone-shaped white mountains in the gap between. A few pine trees are visible, higher up in the whiteness, a couple of different-sized trees on the edges of the plantations, and beyond them the regular spikes of saplings growing under the trees. Above, the indistinct

Alpine cloudscape, and just below the top edge of the picture a fringe of greenery, from which *we*, Russian travelers, have only just emerged.

6.
A little photograph, old, and it looks even older than it is, because it's so faded. On the lower edge, printed in pink: CHERSON and B. WINEERT. It looks like the mid-1870s, a bride stands, immovable as an upturned cup on a tablecloth, her wedding dress falls in a triangle of thick material around her, a cliff of fabric descending from her stomach to the ground, buttons all aligned. Her wide face is fringed by lace. She stands, calm and steadfast, and beside her the groom seems barely to exist, leaning against her, as he might against a gate. Not unequal in the crude and obvious sense of an unequal marriage, but almost as if they presented to us the union of a triangle and an exclamation mark. He is thin-faced, long-boned, like a taper, or the last splinter of soap, and stretched to attenuation, even appears to be growing still in his frock coat with its lapels drawn on, his wife holding on to his elbow. The frock coat is almost too straight, the top hat unexpected, like a rabbit in a conjurer's hand. My great-great-grandfather's particular beauty seems so ephemeral that it's hard to imagine him twenty or thirty years later, an established man, a *paterfamilias*. As a child I used to think that the other great-great-grandfather with his bushy beard was the same man, except much older, and the difference between them horrified me. But there are only two photos of Leonty Liberman, and in both he looks the same: as if he might disappear into the background before he even reached adulthood.

7.
Children are playing croquet on a lawn in a Moscow suburb. The adults are sitting on a bench, or standing, leaning against a tall

pine. An old timbered dacha with a mansard roof and little onion domes continues out of the frame. The windows are wide open. The game has been broken off and everyone there has turned to face the photographer: little girls in knee-high socks and white dresses that are short like little smocks; barefooted little boys from next door's dacha; the croquet mallets are still, the balls lie motionless. Only the girl on the right is still intent on the game, she is bent over and her bare shoulders are crookedly but determinedly curled over the mallet, her right foot is extended, her face in profile. Her pageboy haircut exposes her long, soft neck. She looks like an ancient Greek boy, she radiates a dark concentration and is entirely focused inwardly, in the emblematic manner of a bas-relief. All the others stand and sit in little groups and pairs, but she is alone in the foreground. She is not far from the others, but all the same she seems to be at the edge of the photograph, like the far wing of a large house.

8.

A floor-length black skirt and a light blouse: an unknown woman standing in front of a fence. An ivy-clad brick house, the painted shutters open. Two children, of about two and five, flicker at her shoulders like wings. She is holding their hands, and her hands are crossed over her chest. Two men stand to each side, slightly closer to us. One is taller and he stands with his legs crossed, his hands thrust in his pockets—his shirt is belted, not tucked in, his curls are ruffled. This is Sashka, or *Sancho Pancho*, a friend and an admirer of my great-grandmother Sarra. The other man is older. He is wearing a pince-nez and a blouse made of coarse material. He has a gloomy expression and I suddenly realize that I recognize his face. Yakov Sverdlov. Ten years later in 1917 he becomes the Chairman of the All-Russia Central Executive Committee and signs a decree beginning the Red Terror and "the turning of the Soviet Republic into a single military camp."

41

9.

A dim yellow rectangle, a little brighter in the left-hand corner, but you can just about make out a table, a shoulder, a woman in profile. On the back, a note: "Don't let it put you off that the picture is so dark, it's not too bad if you take a good look." A little lower in the corner, same handwriting: "Paris."

10.

The first thing you notice are the words on a banner against a backdrop of endless birch trees:

FOR BEAUTY AND HEALTH IN WORKING LIVES
THE WAY AHEAD IS EXERCISE!

The lower part of the picture is such a tangle of women's bodies that the eye directs itself involuntarily to a point above their heads, to the regular white letters and tree trunks. The composition of women's bodies looks like a complex chemical equation. The upper row is standing tall and each subsequent row is squatting a little lower than the last, the final row lying spread out like mermaids in a sea of arms, PE knickers and identical PE shirts. About ninety women in all, but all their faces look surprisingly similar, or perhaps they all wear the same blankness, the same refusal to allow any expression to cross their faces. For this very reason I look at each individual face, and as I move between one woman and the next, I appear to see the different phases of a single mimetic movement. This is the Raiki Holiday Camp where Great-Grandmother Sarra worked as a doctor in around 1926. Her ten-year-old daughter Lyolya is lying in the front row, a long plait extending from her head and an absurd-looking fringed shawl on her shoulders. To make her easy to find, *our* Lyolya, someone's added a blue-inked cross over her head. But you could just as easily tell her apart by her estrangement from the scene, how she looks away and to one side.

11.

Heavy card, a golden surround, a backdrop with a misty landscape—against it, the fat-pawed iron bench with its fancy wrought armrests looks particularly squat and solid. David Fridman, a doctor and the father of my great-grandfather, sits on the bench, his hand rests on the collar of an Irish red setter (the breed standard for this type of setter had been set only twenty years before the picture was taken, in Dublin, in 1886). The clothes he wears are almost unnoticeable, begging not to be scrutinized: a good overcoat with an astrakhan collar, a matching black astrakhan hat, unremarkable trousers, even more unremarkable shoes, a pince-nez on a long chain, which only serves to focus attention on his troubled eyes. But perhaps it is not the eyes that give the impression of a troubled man, but rather the legs, held close together, as if he was just about to get up and leave. In our family we keep the common custom of sitting down briefly before the road, half a minute's respite to allow the journey to assume its proper proportions. The dog is nervy, it stirs. Both dog and man die in 1907, on the same day, or so my mother told me.

12.

A portrait photograph, just a face and nothing else—but my goodness, what a face: a long beard spreads into two points on the chest; the nostrils are flared wide; brows drawn together, and above them a head that appears bald despite its gray fuzz. There's no backdrop, just absence. This is Abram Osipovich Ginzburg, my other great-great-grandfather, the father of fourteen children, a merchant of the 1st Guild, the highest rank a merchant could achieve. He started his business in Pochinky, although he is not mentioned in the local archives, and in this picture he resembles "a God-Sent Tempest." The eyes are the first thing you notice in an old picture: they seem lost because their gaze is searching for a person who is no longer there, a person who once recognized them. But his gaze in this photograph is directed to the side—it's not a searching gaze, he has already fixed someone or something in his sights. You are drawn almost against your will to put yourself in their place, out of frame, in a space where nothing has been visible for a long time. The actual composition of the photograph, where your attention had been hitherto wandering, seems suddenly a cramped little triangle, and everything in it is regulated by that fiercely unbending gaze.

13.

A beautiful woman, wearing white, and a little boy in a sailor suit who looks like her. She is sitting and he is standing by her armchair. The white is a class signifier, a sign of affluence, of the creak of starched cloth and unlimited leisure. The boy is about six, his father will die two years later, in another three years he and his mother will find themselves in Moscow, who knows how, perhaps washed up in a basket of reeds, like Moses. I have on my shelf an old typewriter, a heavy Mercedes with the prosthetic jaw of a second keyboard. Betya took on any job she could find when she first came to Moscow, mostly typing work.

14.

A large copy (approx. 20cm by 30cm) of an old photograph, on the back: "1905. Left to right: Ginzburg, Baranov, Galper, Sverd-lova. The original is in the Gorky Memorial Museum No. 11 281. Research Associate Gladinina (?) A round blue stamp above the number."

It's winter and the snow under their feet is trampled. Dark, shaggy fur coats and hats with a spotting of white—the usual smudging you get on an old photograph, the dots and lines that obscure the picture. Great-Grandmother Sarra, first on the left, looks older than her seventeen years. Her hat, the sort that's fastened with pins, has slipped to the back of her head, a strand of hair has escaped and her round-cheeked face is red raw, you can see how cold she is. One of her hands is tucked into her coat's cuffs, another is balled into a fist. Her right eye, injured on the barricades, is covered with a black bandage, like a pirate's patch. This was in Nizhny Novgorod, the barricades were built during the uprising that began on December 12, 1905, and was put down by artillery after three days of street fighting.

In our family folklore this photograph is actually called "Babushka on the Barricades," although of course you can't see the barricades, just a white brick wall and to the side a little fence engulfed by a pile of snow. When you look carefully you can see how young they all are: the handsome young mustache in his gray fur cap, and Galper, with the prominent ears, whom I do not know, and her friend, with the childish face and high cheekbones. Sixty years later only the women have survived in the archival memory: Sarra Ginzburg and Sarra Sverdlova ("little Sarra"), the sister of Yakov Sverdlov, sitting on the bench outside the "Home for Old Bolsheviks," two gray-haired old ladies in thick coats, warming themselves in the winter sun, pressing old-fashioned muffs to their stomachs.

15.

Morning on the open terrace of a dacha: someone is sitting in a wicker chair but all you can see are legs and the corner of a striped dress. An oilcloth over the table, and on it a cornucopia of china dishes, cups, sugar bowls, the old yellow butter dish, a tall vase filled with flowers and foliage, and beyond that a saucepan, but the contents aren't visible. A girl in a summer dress is eating breakfast fastidiously. Her elbows are resting on the corner of the tablecloth, her right hand holds the knife, and in her left hand, the fork. Her feet, in fashionable shoes (rounded toes and little ankle straps), rest on the bar of the chair. The second girl, sitting opposite her, is bent over her teacup, stirring in sugar. Her suntanned knees stick out from under her skirt, her bare arms reflect the light, her hair is drawn up under a hairnet. An older woman in an apron, encased in a blinding white scarf, is watching Lyolya from afar to make sure she gets a good breakfast. This is Nanny Mikhailovna, who attached herself to the family and never left. It must be about 1930. There's a pile of papers and on the top a copy of the weekly *Ogoniok*, with a faint outline of a woman on the cover. You can't quite tell what the woman is doing.

16.

A gravel-tinted picture, you almost expect to feel granular dust when you touch its surface. Everything is gray: the face, the dress, the coarse woolen stockings, the brick wall, the wooden door, the twisting branch of a shrub. An older woman is sitting on a bentwood chair, her hands half-resting in front of her, she looks like she had started to move and then forgot what she was doing, and simply froze in that position, one hand half-covering her stomach. Her smile hasn't quite reached her whole face yet and her expression is serene, as if the clock had stopped at midday, that quiet hour of moderate approval. Everything in the picture is underpinned by a sense of abject poverty, it is the unspoken language of the image: the heavy hands, unadorned by rings, the only dress of canvas, it is all kith and kin with the sparse weeds under her feet, they share the same root. She has made no attempt to clothe herself for eternity, to allow her workaday appearance a moment's Sunday best. But this is as it is, because she has nothing else to choose from. This is my great-grandmother Sofia Akselrod, who used to read Sholem Aleichem in her village not far from Rzhev. This could be any year: 1916, 1926, 1936, it isn't as if anything changed with the passing of time.

17.

A five-year-old girl holding a huge doll that isn't hers. It's a sumptuous doll, dressed in folk costume, an embroidered skirt and ornate headpiece, with a thick braid of hair and rosy cheeks. The mysterious thrill of the object! The little girl can't even bring herself to look at the doll, and instead she directs her delighted gaze at the camera: Look at her! Look at us! So many contrasts: the little girl is frail and thin, and the doll is disproportionately large and plump; the little girl is dark-haired, her curls stick out in all directions, and the doll has a smooth flaxen plait. The lover and the beloved. The childish little hands hold the doll with a fervent tenderness: one palm cups the waist with care, the other hand encircles the doll's porcelain fingers with the lightest of touches. The image is black-and-white, and so I can't tell the color of the dress, with its embroidered cherries, or the color of the extravagant bow on the top of my mother's head.

18.

A tiny picture, the epaulets are faded and impossible to read, but I know my grandfather reached the rank of major and was only demobilized in 1944. This is clearly a picture taken before all that. The face is as closed as a fist, it expresses nothing but strength: the arched brows, the ears close to the head, the whites of his eyes, the mouth. All of it molded to form a single billiard ball: a single typical portrait of the military officer at the end of the 1930s. A collective image of a face, one portrait standing for everyone, like the faces of the heroes in Aleksei German's film *My Friend Ivan Lapshin*. I watched it when I was fifteen and I'd hardly seen any proper films, and I couldn't be sure of what was happening, or who the main character was, who was in love with whom—all the characters seemed interchangeable to me, all cut from the same piece of boiled army wool. There was something familiar about them, their speech and posture all seemed vaguely familiar, as if I'd known it for a long time, and only years later I realized that every one of them was in some sense my grandfather, his antique courtesy and eau de cologne, his sternness, his shaved cheeks and bald head.

19.

Somewhere by a stream in the mid- to late 1930s two young women are posing for a photograph and they can't stop laughing. One has let her hair loose, she leans down and is about to lay her white knitted shawl in the grass. The other is holding her hat to her head in the invisible breeze. They wear short, lightweight dresses. Their bags are already lying on the ground and their underclothes are crumpled at their feet.

20.

It's raining and people are wandering through the wet meadow like lost souls. A whole crowd of people, about twenty in all, the men in straw boaters, the women in long skirts, the hems brushing the damp grass, above their heads the hopeless domes of parasols. A long way off, on the horizon, there is a wall, but who knows what was behind it. To the right is the glimmer of gray water. They stand in groups of twos and threes, some apart, some closer, some farther away, and the longer you stare at them, the clearer it becomes that this might resemble the landscape of the afterlife, its shoreline, where each of us is quite alone.

On the back of the photograph is a note written in French. Handsomely written, all curlicues and flourishes. I translate it as I read: "*Montpellier, 22 of the VI month, 1909. To remind us of our zoological excursion to Palavas. How sad it was … The weather let us down. D. K. Genchev. For Mademoiselle S. Ginzburg, Pochinky.*" Palavas-Les-Flots is a small resort south of Montpellier where a long spit of dunes divides the Mediterranean from inland freshwater lakes. The flat beaches are covered with gray sand, and there are colonies of pink flamingos not so far away, which perhaps in part explains the zoological nature of the trip. Nowadays, Palavas is a busy and inexpensive holiday destination, but one hundred years ago there was nothing there, the hotels had not yet appeared, only the newly built church of St. Peter.

Among the wanderers in the meadow there is one woman who holds herself very erect. She stands on her own, turned away from the camera, her slender back in a light summer jacket is the axis of the image, she is the central pole of the stopped carousel wheel. She wears a stiff-brimmed hat and her head is thrown back, she is carrying a ragged bunch of flowers. I like to think it is my great-grandmother Sarra.

4. Sex and the Dead

I must have been about twelve. I was hunting around for something interesting to look at. There was plenty of interesting stuff: with every death a pile of new objects appeared in our apartment, deposited *just as they were*, trapped in a sudden end state, because their previous owner, the only person who could have freed them, was no longer among the living. The contents of Grandmother's last handbag, her bookshelves, buttons in a box, everything had simply stopped, like a clock, on a particular hour of a particular day. So many objects like this in our house. And then one day I found an old leather wallet in a far drawer. It contained a single photograph.

I could see right away what sort of a picture it was. Not a picture, or a postcard or, say, a picture calendar. A naked woman lay on a divan, looking at the camera. It was an amateur shot, taken long ago, already yellowing with age, but the feelings it aroused in me were utterly unlike the way great-grandmother's Paris letters or grandfather's jokey poems had made me feel. This picture added nothing to the throat-tightening feeling of family collectivity, to the black-and-white many-headed chorus of unknown relatives, always happening just behind my back, or to the hunger I felt when I saw something unknown and foreign: The promenade at Nice by night, on a prerevolutionary postcard. There was something clearly illicit about the photograph, although that could hardly have bothered me, quietly avoiding my parents, and on my own private search for the forbidden. There was a faint licentiousness in it, too, although the woman's nakedness was open, straightforward, and full to the camera. Strangest of all, the photograph had no relationship to me at all. It belonged to someone else. The fact that the wallet had lost its owner long before did not change this feeling of strangeness.

The woman lying on the leather sofa was not beautiful. My sense of aesthetics had been formed by the cast gallery in the Pushkin Museum and a book on ancient Greek myth, I was affronted by her many bodily defects. Her legs were shorter than they were supposed to be and her breasts smaller, but her bottom was much larger and her tummy pudgy in a way that was very unlike marble. All these defects made her look lively, as anything living in ignorance of perfection looks lively. She was grown-up, in her thirties, as I now realize, and not a "nude," simply a completely naked woman, although that wasn't the most striking thing. The woman was looking straight at the viewer—that is, at the camera, that is, at me. Her stare had such intensity: it was utterly unlike the radiantly unfocused gaze of a goddess, or a model in an artist's studio.

Her gaze had a very direct purpose to it: between the woman and her witness something was happening, or was going to happen. Strictly speaking, her stare was already that happening: it was the conduit or the corridor; the black hole. Her face was wide, flat, with slits for eyes, and there was nothing else in it apart from the intensity of the stare. Her communication was intended for the bearer of the photo, but I had somehow taken his place, and this made the situation both tragic and absurd. It was so very obvious that The Lady On The Leather Sofa (unlike the whole of art and the whole of history, which was definitely intended for me and took me into account) didn't have me in mind as a viewer, didn't want me, and I knew with certainty that someone else should have been in my place, someone with a name and a surname, and possibly even a mustache.

The absence of this other viewer made the whole thing feel indecent, coitus interruptus in its most basic sense, and I was the one interrupting. I'd turned up at the wrong time, and in the wrong place, and I'd witnessed what I shouldn't have witnessed:

sex. The sex was not in the body or the pose, or even the surroundings (although I remember them well)—it was in the directness of the gaze, its lack of ambiguity, the way it paid no attention to anything beyond the scene. Strange when you think that even thirty years ago both participants were probably dead and most certainly are now. They have died and left the sex act orphaned in an empty room.

*

What do I have against images? Perhaps it is that they all have the same flaw: euphoric amnesia. They no longer remember what they signify, where they came from, who they are related to, and yet none of this bothers them. For the beholder (I no longer know whether to call her a reader or a viewer) the picture seems to do more, to serve better. It delivers its message quicker, without wasting words, never tiring of actively engaging with the message: to stun us, to grasp hold of us, to occupy our thoughts. The picture seduces with its illusion of economy: as text begins to unwind its first phrases, a photograph has already come, confounded, conquered—and then it graciously condescends to allow the text to speak, to add the inessentials of what happened, and where.

For a whole century now the overproduction of visual material has been called the problem of the age, and its defining sign: heavy carts of descriptive text, loaded with meaning, have been overtaken by the image's swift sleighs. It's doubtless true, even if the sleighs only appear swifter to begin with. It's not just the dead who disappear in the mirrored corridor of reproduction—the living do, too. Siegfried Kracauer describes the process with photographic precision in his essay on photography: we can break down what our attention does to a photo of our grandmother into its various phases, how she literally disappears before us, vanishes into the folds of her crinoline, leaving only a collar, a chignon, and a skirt bustle on the surface of the image.

The same thing happens to us. With every new selfie we take, every group shot or passport photo, our lives become arranged into a chain of images, a history that is quite different from the one we tell ourselves and want others to believe. The line of was-and-will-be, a compendium of single moments, poses, mouths open to speak, blurry chins, none of which we chose ourselves. Balzac foresaw some of this and refused to have his photograph taken, reflecting that each new picture removed a layer of *balzac*, pared it away, and if you let it happen, soon nothing would be left of you (or what would be left was only a puff of smoke, the vegetable heart, and the very last layer, the thickness of a death mask).

The mechanics of photography never intended to preserve the essence. The project of photography better resembles those time capsules intended for our descendants, or for aliens from outer space, filled with evidence of humanity: an anthology of our greatest moments an attempt to define ourselves through our civilization's crowning achievements—Shakespeare/Mona Lisa/cigar, or penicillin/iPhone/Kalashnikov. They remind me of Egyptian burial sites, expanding suitcases stuffed with life's essentials. If we imagine our descendants or the aliens to be curious, and this curiosity to be unlimited by time, then it will only be satisfied by a bank of infinite images, a cupboard where *everything* is packed away, every last person's every last moment. And if this terrifying documentary mass could be gathered and kept ready for use, it would hardly be different from the incomplete but ever-increasing mass of data kept somewhere in the shapeless pockets of the atmosphere and called into being by the twitch of a computer mouse.

Photography observes change first and foremost—and always the same change: growth becoming dissolution and disappearance. I've seen a few photography projects that have documented change over decades, they flash up on social media now and again, giving rise to a bittersweet tenderness, and the almost improper curiosity with which young, healthy people regard a future that hasn't even dawned for them yet. A young Japanese man takes a photograph of himself with his young son. Time passes, the boy is one, four, then twelve years old, then twenty: it's like speeded-up film—we watch one being fill with life, as a balloon fills with air, while the other being diminishes and creases; its light gutters. Or another: Australian sisters who take a picture of themselves every year over a period of forty years in the same room, same spot, and in every picture they age a little more, slowly resigning themselves to aging and to those tiny visible signals of their eventual demise. In this sense at least, art's endeavor is diametrically opposed to photography: any successful body of text is a chronicle of growth, a thing that is not completely in line with the parallel chronology of the appearance of wrinkles and pigmentation spots. Photography is less compromising: knowing none of this will survive, it makes its best attempt at preservation.

I'm talking about a particular kind of photography here. It's no coincidence that it's the most widespread, tracing its chalk circle around both professional photojournalists, amateurs with their mobile phones, and much that lies between these extremes. These photographers (and their viewers) are united by an unwavering belief in the photograph as document, witnessing reality, grasping it as it really is, without any kind of literary ornamentation: a rose is a rose is a rose. Art photography, in its aim to bend and reconstruct the visible world in the name of individual perception, interests me only at those points when reality unintentionally overcomes intent, flattering the viewer who notices the seam: the rough boots peering out from underneath the carnival silk.

The claims, if not the actual possibilities, of documentary photography are extraordinary: to see and hold the existing and what has existed—a task perhaps reserved for the Being who *conservat omnia*, as it says on the gates of Fontanny Dom in St. Petersburg. Still technology makes its best efforts; it shaves off time's natural build-up of lint—and there are *many mansions* in its virtual house.

*

Many of the qualities of the camera induce a sense of dumb-foundedness. You might say it gives us a reason to quote a person, an animal, or an object as a single entity, as a unit of text—stripping reality of its little halo of signifiers, and at the same time ignoring the signified entirely. The camera places an equals sign between person and image for the first time—all that's needed is enough images to complete the outline.

A century or so ago, the portrait was exhaustive proof of a person's life, and with a few exceptions, the only thing you left behind. The portrait was the event of a lifetime, its focal point, and the very nature of the craft demanded the participation of both artist and sitter. The phrase "everyone has the face they deserve" was a literal truth in the age of painting; and for those whom class gave the right to be remembered as a singular face, that was the face of their portrait.

Or perhaps, even more importantly, the face on their correspondence. The greatest part of any legacy was textual: diaries, letters, memoirs, and the balance between the textual and the visual shifted only from the mid-nineteenth century onward, as the pile of photographs accumulated. These presented themselves to the memory not as "me, as I am," but "me on Saturday in my black riding habit." The number of photographs a family owned depended solely on their financial means and their social position, but even my grandmother's nanny, Mikhailovna, had three photos in her keeping.

The old lady of painting (for brevity's sake that's what I've named the ability to depict the living, by one's own hand, in any medium) is haunted by the impossibility of resemblance, and yet she becomes increasingly obsessed by the task of producing an exhaustive image, but a single image; an exact image, but an image that does not resemble the sitter; to present to the sitter in his concentrated form, not him-now, but him-forever, a bouillon cube of his vital parts. This is what lies behind the stories about Gertrude Stein becoming with the years more and more like her portrait by Picasso, or the story about Oskar Kokoschka's subject, who (it is said) subsequently went mad and came to look exactly like his image.

We are the permanent subject of the old lady's interest, and we know all too well that in place of resemblance she sells us a horoscope: a template interpretation, and we can either agree with it—the mirror flatters me—or refuse it. Once the photographic image appears, Madame Bovary is free to say *c'est moi* for the first time, as she picks out the most attractive of the thirty-six negatives. Life offers her a new mirror and it reflects fervently, demanding nothing, insisting on nothing.

Painting and photography go their separate ways at this point. One rushes to its inevitable end, its dispersal, and the other toward its vast proliferation. When the inheritance is divided up, one gets the house and garden, the other gets a pig in a poke. Martha takes reality, Mary is left to talk in the language of abstraction and installations.

*

With the invention of digital photography, yesterday and today have coexisted with unprecedented intensity. It's as if the waste chute in a building has been blocked off and all the trash just keeps piling up forever. There's no need to save film, just press the shutter release, even the deleted pictures remain in the computer's long memory. Oblivion, the copycat of nonexistence, has a new twin brother: the dead memory of the collector. We look through a family album with a sense of affection—it contains a little, perhaps just what remains. But what should we do with an album containing everything, without exception, the whole disproportionate volume of the past? Photography is directed at an endpoint, where the volume of life fixed in images is equal to the actual length of life. The printing press keeps turning, but there are no readers left.

I imagine the piles of images. Huge diggers shovel at them, scooping all the waste into their buckets: the underexposed pictures, the duplicates and triplicates, the tail of an out-of-frame dog, a picture of a café ceiling taken by mistake. We get a vague sense of the vast mass from social media, where thousands of mediocre pictures are posted, pinned like butterflies with "tags." For these images the future is just one more cemetery, a huge archive of human bodies we know nothing about for the most part, except that they existed.

This immortality is terrifying, but even more terrifying is the fact that it is imposed on you. What photography now registers is nothing other than the body of death: the part of me that has no personal will or choice, which anyone can claim, which is fixed and preserved without effort. It is the part that dies, and not the part that remains.

In the past immortality was a matter of choice, though you could reject it and choose what everyone was offered as a matter of course: "to be laid in a narrow cell forever." Now that forever narrow cell of "Gray's Elegy" has been withdrawn and we have accepted the impossibility of simply disappearing. Whether you want it or not, you are facing the strange extension of your existence, your outward form preserved for all time. All that disappears is what made you yourself.

It is a luxury permitted to very few to vanish entirely, to disappear from the radar.

You step into another photograph, it is as inevitable as stepping out into sudden summer rain. Who will actually look at all these images and when will they do it? Our outward form is scratched from us by a thousand CCTV cameras at stations, streetcar stops, in shops and underpasses—like the fingerprints left everywhere by humanity before forensics were invented. It has no alphabet, only the new (old) multitudinous nature of leaves in a forest.

Since we began recording and archiving sound, the unreproducible has disappeared from life. How Mademoiselle George acted on the stage and how Angiolina Bosio sang was described to us, and demanded time and passion of the curious: you had to imagine, flesh it out, recreate something in your head. Now there is nothing between you and what has been. The longer we keep recording the more people will fall into the zone of the undead. Their physical form keeps on walking and talking, their earthly voice resounds whenever you want it to. They still have it within their power to charm, to arouse desire, or to disgust (the body and the name separate, like film credits). The culmination of this is pornography from the distant past, nameless dead bodies performing their mechanical duties long after their owners are ashes and dust.

Still, the physical body cannot be handed down in this way— it carries no caption with its name and description. It has no distinguishing features. It is divested of all memory retrospectively, of any trace of what has happened to it: its history, its biography, its death. This divestment makes it obscenely contemporary. The more naked it is, the nearer it is to us, and the further from human memory. We know only two things about these people: that they are dead and that they had no interest in bequeathing their bodies to eternity. What once had a basic function, like the sparkwheel of a cigarette lighter, rotating between desire and satisfaction without any wish to become yet another memento mori, continues to function like a mechanism. But on this occasion, for me at least, it is a mechanism for compassion.

All the laws laid out by Barthes and Kracauer are in operation here. The *punctum* (a reproduction hanging over the bed, long black socks drawn up the skinny calves of a man) wants to be an alphabet, wants to turn events into a history—in this case to recount how time is constructed, its tastes and its sensitivity. But in fact all we see is the nakedness, which unexpectedly proved to be their last nakedness: these people, their thighs and potbellies, the mustaches and hair fringes of a time when *they* were contemporary, are left to the mercy of the viewer. They have no names, no future. All of it came to an end in the twenties-thirties-forties, those decades that still lie ahead of them. We can stop them in their tracks, speed them up, make them start over with their simple activities, again and again they'll lift their former legs and arms, and lock the door as if they were all alone and still alive.

*

A Russian collector bought a box of family photographs in Sri Lanka; they impressed her in some way, so much so that a year later she returned to buy the whole archive, and began a search for the vanished family. She even found documentary traces of them, although none of them had lived into the new century. She then did everything she could to give them the strange immortality sometimes possessed by objects that have lost their owners. What was it about the photographs that made them stand out from the common crowd? Perhaps that which sets the museum exhibit apart from its more ordinary siblings, a subtle quality that gives it the right to preferential attention. None of the photographs in the archive (the father Julian Rast was a professional photographer) serve the utilitarian purpose of the mere preservation of existence. A visual perfection gives each image the magnetic and enchanting sheen of an exhibit: a family in the snow under the pine fronds; a child on a sledge with a baby faun; bathers; horse riders; German shepherd dogs. All the pictures look just like film stills and the viewer is drawn in, waiting for the scene to change and new scenes to appear, he needs to find out what happened to the subjects of the photos.

There is such injustice in the way that people and their portraits cannot escape an immediate and basic inequality: the difference between the interesting and the not so interesting, between what draws our attention and what doesn't. Everything is in silent sympathy with the tyranny of choice, always on the side of the beautiful and the charismatic (to the detriment of everything that has no claim on our attention and so remains on the dark side of this world), especially our bodies with their entirely pragmatic agenda. Our preferences have nothing to do with age or upbringing, even three-month-old babies vote for beauty, health, and symmetry.

And this is unjust. Just as the dictatorship of the viewer or "watcher," with his unfounded demands on the image, is an unjust one. The word "watcher" in Russian has a second, less obvious meaning. In the language of prisons, camps, and the criminal underworld, known by a significant proportion of all Russian-speakers, the watcher is the one who sets the rules and makes sure the others follow them.

So perhaps we could characterize the relationship between the watcher and the photograph, the reader and the text, and the viewer and the film as small episodes of power, like ticket sellers in the museum halls of random access memory. Both the rules and how they are followed depend on this relationship, but let's not pretend that the "watcher" is a righteous judge. His rules and his choices are not God-given, they are human. Worse than that, they are criminal. He is intent on the acquisition/absorption of the foreign body: his taste is based on the rights of the strong when surrounded by the weak, or the living when surrounded by the dead (who are deliberately denied all their rights).

Maybe that's why I love photographs that need no interlocutor and have no desire to engage with me. They are, in their own way, rehearsals for nonexistence, for life without us, for the time when the room is no longer ours to enter. A family is drinking tea, the children are playing chess; the general bends over the map; the baker's assistant lays out the cakes—and we can satisfy our ancient and enduring desire to gaze into every one of the windows of the house of a thousand windows. The point of this dream is surely to be someone completely different for a short while, to escape ourselves. Most old photographs can't answer this need—all they can do is insist upon their own integral selves. Their identity is theirs, but this world is ours.

Photographs that failed to live up to the photographer's hopes are the unrealized scraps from a manufacturing process: a running dog, blurred to an unending streak, someone's shoes on a wet pavement, a chance passerby in the frame. All this waste was filtered out and destroyed in the age of printing on paper. But now these very pictures have a special attraction because they were not intended for us (or for anyone). They belong to no one and so they belong to me—these moments that survived by accident and are freed from all obligation, stolen from life by life itself. These images of people are utterly impersonal and this is their advantage: they relieve the viewer of the burden of succession, historical memory, bad conscience, and a sense of indebtedness toward the dead. In return they offer a sequence of images of the past and future, the more random the better. These pictures are not of Ivan and Mary, they are of contingent beings, him and her, her and her, light and no one. Freedom from meaning gives us the opportunity to add in our own meaning, freedom from interpretation makes a mirror of the image, a square pool in which we can immerse any version of events we please. "Photos trouvées," little foundlings, useful in their very readiness to become an object and abandon their past as someone else's subjectivity. To bury their dead: both the photographer and the photographed. They have no wish to look us in the eyes.

Not-A-Chapter
Leonid Gurevich, 1942 or 1943

My grandfather's letter can be dated by its content to 1942–3. He is thirty and has been sent back from the rear guard to a Moscow hospital for an urgent operation, as a special expert, essential to the war effort. His wife, mother, and baby daughter are all in evacuation in the Siberian town of Yalutorovsk.

On coarse buff paper, in violet ink that has seeped through to the back of the paper:

Dearest Lyolechka,

I received your letter (and you know I'm not sentimental), and once I'd read it through a few times I put it in my notebook where I keep Baby Natasha and your photographs, I haven't been parted from them since I left, and now I can add a second photo of Natasha. Your letter touched me very deeply and left me thinking on a great many things.

Now the doctors have told me that I am well on the way to recovery, and since I do honestly feel this to be the case, I can tell you some things about myself I didn't want to write before.

At one point I was very sick. I hardly thought I would survive.

The doctors wouldn't confirm this, however ... they allowed me visitors at any time of the day (and they only do that for the most serious of cases). And when they found out I had no relatives in Moscow at the time they noted down your address in Yalutorovsk. I knew what all that meant, of course.

But I fought back. In the hardest moments, please forgive me my honesty, I thought only about Natasha, and I felt better.

When it had passed I was so weak, and I know you know this, the worst thing for me is helplessness.

I got slowly stronger, I kept going. But I put up with a great deal (you can't imagine what terrible headaches I had, my darling, the worst thing was how they never let up), and then suddenly I couldn't bear it any longer and I gave in to my emotions.

So many thoughts came rushing into my head and (I had plenty of time to indulge them) I saw my unhappy life pass before my eyes, and … well, I indulged in the writing of some pretty bad poetry. I sought oblivion, wanted to drown out this storm of emotions.

I wrote an awful lot of drivel (I can't even explain how now, but it all came easily and freely to me), and even a long poem, on a very difficult subject matter, but I didn't finish it.

But something had a very strong effect on me (my nerves were extremely strained and even the tiniest inconvenience made me suffer terribly). There was a patient in the ward with me, an accountant from the Moscow Meat Processing Plant, his name was Teselko and he was 54. He had a brain tumor and he'd undergone a complicated operation, but it had been a success, and he was in recovery. His wife was four years younger than him, such a gentle woman.

You just can't imagine how she cared for him, the love and the tenderness of her touch during her daily visits. There was so much love, intimacy, and friendship between them (everyone in the ward, even the most curmudgeonly patient, felt it). After his illness he had become anxious, fickle, querulous, at times coarse and cruel, even toward his wife. But she understood this and forgave him and he felt her forgiveness and appreciated it.

She's a good wife to you, I said once, and he answered, yes, and said nothing more. Then we both retreated into our own thoughts.

I was thinking how they were older than us, but that they were still living and feeling far more fully than us, the younger generation. And how we could be living, if only we loved life and knew how to love as devotedly and boundlessly as they did, as our parents did.

[two lines crossed out with thick marks]

I've been thinking a lot, Lyolya. I've been analyzing my life, my past actions. I've been trying to understand things from your point of view and I've decided to change. I don't mean in terms of my love for you, not that. I love you now just as I loved you before, with a strong devotion. But considering the flaws in your character, your tricky personality, I want to try to understand you in all your actions, and to yield to you. When you think about it, all our arguments grew out of silly misunderstandings, and it was only because neither of us would give way that they turned into nasty rows.

Making this decision has forced me to grow up, to pull myself together and get a hold of myself, in a way I never have before. These last few weeks, I've felt quite different, I've felt sure that I have the strength to claim my proper place in life, to fight for it, to live and to be happy! [crossings out] *I know now that life and happiness are in our hands and when we find happiness for ourselves we find it for those around us.*

And then I received your letter. It seemed like a continuation of my own thoughts and hopes.

I answered you in my head. I said: forgive me. And at that moment I was desperate to be with you, if only for a minute, so I could take you by the hand, take the hand of my wife and my friend.

This letter is clumsy, poorly expressed, I know it is, but I mean it, I mean it with all my heart. I know you'll understand what I am going through.

I took all my driveling poetry and ceremonially, without an ounce of self-pity, burned it all in the stove on the ward, along with those dreadful poems I got rid of some very unhealthy urges.

Your letter taught me a great deal, it gave me so much hope and love. Thank you for it.

And to my dearest wife
I give thanks and love
For the daughter, and the son

We will one day have.
I imagine you before me
Embarrassed by my emotion
But things are quite decided
And not open to discussion.
I remain, deeply in love,
Your only Leonid.

I couldn't resist it after all—I lapsed into poetry! Thank you thank
you for Natasha's photo. Kiss her from me.

5. Aleph and Where It Led Me

I am talking far too much about objects, and perhaps it is inevitable. The people I wrote this book for died long before I started writing it, and objects were the only permissible replacements. They are just as dear to me as some strangers in a photo album: a brooch with my great-grandmother's monogram; my great-grandfather's prayer shawl; and the armchairs that miraculously survived their owners, two centuries and two homes. Their promise of knowledge is a false one, but all the same they radiate the stove-warmth of uninterrupted time. Here I remember Aunt Galya with the stack of newspapers she couldn't be parted from, and the piles of diaries, and I have the sudden realization that nothing can be preserved.

Tove Jansson has a story about a Fillyjonk who lives in continual fear of a terrible disaster. She arranges all her furniture and gets out the silver cream jug and the iced cakes, she even washes her best carpet in the sea, and she waits and waits, and is terrified she will lose it all. When the tornado comes (and they always do), it takes with it her house and all her knickknacks: tray cloths and photo frames and tea cozies and grandma's silver cream jug. All the past is carried off into oblivion, and it leaves a clear space for the future. The Fillyjonk is left playing in the shallows with her carpet, finally happy, "Never in her life had she had such fun."

I remembered Janet Malcolm and the house with the cluttered interior, the *aleph* of her book, when I was in Vienna, as there was something like it on every street corner. The building I stayed in was built in 1880 (and in the yard a smaller building, enwombed like a matryoshka doll: a house with white shutters, built in 1905 when the family had grown up). The owner of the house, anywhere between seventy and ninety, had high cheek-bones, architectural eyebrows, and a voice of otherworldly depth with which she told me, at the end of our conversation, that she'd always lived there—ever since returning in 1948. To read her history correctly I'd need to have known when she left the house, but our polite conversation didn't stretch this far. A handsome family genealogy book, published in 1918, lay neglected by the TV remote control. She rented her apartment to me with its two hundred years of tat and old trinkets, with apparently barely a thought for the preservation of these things: porcelain objects crowded the shelves, as tightly packed as books; boxes were bent by their weight of silverware; oil paintings hung on the walls; and ancient matchboxes lay on the tables and coffee tables. Gift messages decorated the albums (a Christmas card from 1941, slipped between the pages of an album, made her family history a little clearer). This white, tall-windowed house with its grand staircases resembled a huge store cupboard where the odd rental tenant might go unnoticed. At night everything in the building creaked and groaned and twitched. I came to the conclusion that the owner had crammed it full with the layers of unwanted history that kept her from sleep—and then emigrated into her own life: the little house on the other side of the lawn, her medical practice and garden chairs.

I found out quite by chance—by flipping open a guidebook to a random page in a museum shop—that the oldest Jewish cemetery in Vienna was close to where I worked. The cemetery was first used in 1540 or thereabouts, and had been razed to the ground by the Nazis. Later, after some time had passed, the decision was taken to restore it. The gravestones hadn't gone anywhere: they lay under the soil, they'd simply gone underground, so they were brought back to the light and arranged around the wide, grassy garden of an old people's home that had sprung up in the cemetery's absence.

There was a chill in the air that day, the sort that catches us unaware, a presentiment of winter. The street slowly narrowed; on its left-hand side the old people's home: a two-story house of the sort you might see in London, perhaps adorned with a couple of blue plaques. But there were no plaques here, and no people on the street. It grew colder still, a few very frail old men stood in the entrance hall, sheltering from the wind. They must have been at least a hundred years old, I guessed, using my landlady's appearance as a yardstick, and their emaciated forms gave them the appearance of happy, withered little shrimps. They inched about the hall in wheelchairs or on foot and held on to each other's sharp elbows with trembling tenderness. When they approached the nurse it was with the same faint smile, looking up into her face to ask or answer a question. I approached her in turn, and she pointed out the way to me.

A long, wide balcony ran the length of the building and faced a walled garden. The ground was a few meters lower here and a fierce wind bent the grass flat. The balcony was kept at the height required for the present to be able to say with certainty that the past was past: it had been tamed, restored, and fenced off. It wasn't even possible to enter the garden below, where the grass was being whipped by the wind. An unambiguous iron padlock hung on the door to a metal ladder descending from the balcony.

But there was something going on down in the garden. A tent-like awning with long green ramps hid the farthest part of the garden and two people were busying themselves around graves in the corner of the tent. The graves stood facing me, they were nothing like the cozy, almost armchair-like memorials I was used to. These were like gates, portals for transportations to the void—in some of them I could even sense the shape of an archway. In the cemetery in Würzburg, where my mother is buried, you can sometimes detect some little figurative elements, nods to the people left behind: a simple little emblem of a flame or two hands blessing the Star of David. Here, there was nothing of that sort, only letters, text. The cemetery could have been read like a book stitched from scattered sheets. On one stone the script rose in a crescent arc. A single decorative image, a horse that faintly resembled a hare, raced from right to left across the stone.

Meanwhile the old men had disappeared out of the frame of the lit glass, and I could see a girl in white carefully wiping the tables down in the dining hall. There was no one out here on the balcony with me, no one by the ashtray or by the muttering fountain a little farther on, where plastic ducks floated upside down in the black water. I'd read they'd found two or three hundred tombstones but it looked from here as if there were hardly any.

The grass was long, not like grass on city lawns, but the harsh grass of the plain, and the wind blew it into furious waves.

A few days later I was told about a very particular grave in the cemetery. My Viennese friend asked me whether I'd seen the fish: what looked like a heap of cobblestones was in fact a stone fish, coiled into a ring. There was a story attached to the fish: a man named Simeon bought himself a fish for supper and was about to prepare it for cooking when right there on the kitchen table, under the carving knife, the fish opened its mouth and spoke: "*Shema Yisrael*," the words a Jew says before death, and it might have said something more, but it was too late, the knife came down and severed the fish's head. The Rabbi said that the business smacked of a dybbuk, a wandering soul separated from its body, so they buried the fish just as they would a person in the cemetery. Sometimes I feel just like that fish, or the householder hiring men at the eleventh hour, or even like a conscript in the last wave of conscription at the height of war—managing to say and do what must be done, but only just, in the nick of time.

The museums in Vienna all reflected my own preoccupations, albeit each in their own way. In the Museum of Applied Art, I wandered into a Valhalla for furniture, a room filled with ghosts, the long shadows of Thonet chairs in bentwood cast across a white screen. In the same room you could read a list of the names of rocking chairs and armchairs and they sounded like human names: Heinrich and Max, whose wicker forms reminded me of our three-legged basketwork chair, which had hobbled its way into the twenty-first century. Nearby, an ancient forest of feathery, spidery lace lay draped on black velvet, composed of tiny holes and tears, just as my story is composed of silences and rents in the fabric.

Blinds were drawn over the windows of the Natural History Museum and I looked out at Vienna as if through a layer of ash. Lamarck's spiral staircase of evolution twisted backward through the reassuringly old-fashioned twilight of the museum's rooms. All the subjects of nature's experiments were on display: bears, both large and small; a host of spotted cats; a game park with deer and antelope, all necks and antlers; giraffes and the rest of the beasts, some of them surprisingly like cultural artifacts, speckled like clay pots. Even less life remained in the shrunken stuffed birds, despite their still-bright plumage. Beyond them the dreadful serried ranks of glass jars with a collection of bony parts connected with the production of sound, taken from the voice boxes of birds. Somewhere among the parrots and the corvidae was a small gray bird, round and fluffed up with a strange red brow and splashes of red around its tail, *aegintha temporalis*, and I nodded to it as if we were family, as I myself am *temporalis*, on my way to the barnacles and the segmented worms, and the fish in methylated spirits, standing on their tails.

Karl Kraus wrote "Immer passt alles zu allem" ("Everything fits with everything else")—or, in Tsvetaeva's words: "Everything rhymes." Every exhibit in the long suite of rooms provided another metaphor, explained another element in my history. It preoccupied me, but didn't change anything, since I knew that the real *aleph* of my story lay in my pocket already.

This *aleph* was a tiny white china figurine, about three centimeters tall. A very approximately molded naked little boy with curly hair, who could have passed for Cupid if it hadn't been for his long socks. I bought him from a stall in a Moscow flea market,

70

where one or two things could still be picked up very cheaply, and in a tray of paste jewelery I found a box containing a heap of these little white boys. It seemed strange to me that not a single one was intact, each differently mutilated, missing a leg or a face, and all the faces were scarred and chipped. I spent a while sorting through, looking for the most presentable, and eventually found him: nearly whole, he still had his curls and dimples, his ribbed socks, and he shone with a winsome gift-gleam—even the dark stain on his back and his lack of arms didn't spoil my admiration.

I asked the shop owner, just in case, if she had any figures in a better state, and she told me such an odd story I felt the need to find out more. The little figures were made in a German town from the 1880s onward, she said. They were sold everywhere, in groceries and hardware stores, but actually their main function was as packaging—dirt cheap, they were heaped up as loose fill around goods, so that heavy things didn't rub together or dent each other in the darkness. The little figures were in fact made to be chipped. Just before the war the factory closed and ware-houses, filled to the roof with boxes of the tiny figures, stood locked until they were bombed. A few years later, when the boxes were opened, all that remained were splinters of china.

I bought my little china boy without noting the name of the factory or the stallholder's telephone number, although I already knew that I was carrying the end of my book in my pocket, the hidden answer to a riddle in a puzzle book. My china boy seemed to embody the way no story reaches us without having its heels chipped off or its face scratched away. And how lacunae and gaps are the constant companions of survival, its hidden engine, fueling its acceleration. How only trauma makes individuals— singly and unambiguously *us*—from the mass product. And yes, finally, the way in which I am the little boy, the product of mass manufacturing and also of the collective catastrophe of the last century, the survivor and unwitting beneficiary, here by some miracle.

The china figure I chose was not the unluckiest: the headless ones remained in their box. In some contexts, or so the Vienna School of Art History proclaimed a hundred years ago, only the "new" and the "unimpaired" can be considered beautiful, whereas the pale, faded, and fragmentary can only be considered "ugly." An object's dignity, its starched collar, comes from its state of preservation. The poorly preserved object loses its right to human interaction.

And so it was: although I was thinking about the fragmentary and flawed state of any surviving witness, all the same in my soul I craved the whole, the inviolate. The little china boy's wounds could not be too extreme, to put it bluntly—I wanted him pleasant to look at. Half-destroyed a century ago, he nevertheless had to look new.

I remembered, as I took my purchase home, that I had read about these figurines in *My Pushkin*, a memoir of childhood by the poet Marina Tsvetaeva. She remembers her strolls as a child along the Tverskoy Boulevard in Moscow toward the Pushkin Memorial:

> There was another special game I played with the Pushkin
> Memorial, it was my game, and it was this: I'd place a tiny
> white china doll, the size of a little finger, a child's little finger,
> on the pedestal. You could buy these dolls in the china shops
> that appeared in Moscow at the end of the century, little gnomes
> under mushrooms and children holding umbrellas. I'd place a
> tiny figure on the gigantic pedestal and slowly lift my gaze up
> the sheer granite face until I thought my head would fall off
> comparing the sizes. [...] The Pushkin Memorial, with me
> under it, and with the tiny figure under me, was my first proper
> lesson in hierarchy, too. I was a giant next to the china figure,
> but next to Pushkin, I was—myself. A little girl. But one who
> would grow bigger. And I was the same for the tiny figure as the
> Pushkin Memorial was for me. But then what was the Pushkin

Memorial for the tiny figure? And after some hard thinking it
suddenly dawned upon me: The Memorial was so enormous
that the figure simply couldn't see it. I thought it was a big house,
or a rumble of thunder. And the china figure was so tiny that the
Pushkin Memorial couldn't see it either. It thought it was just a
flea. But it saw me! Because I was big and plump. And I would
soon grow bigger.

Over the years the little figure didn't stop giving lessons (Tsvetaeva counts these lessons in numbers, in scale and materials, in numbers and hierarchy, and in thinking). It's hardly surprising that the subject of her studies changed. I thought about it as I carried the little china boy in my pocket along this or that *strasse*, stroking his invisible back with my finger and imagining how he would look on the cover of a book about memory. His lack of arms made him look taller than he was, he looked straight ahead like a curly-haired figurehead, he wore old-fashioned knee-high socks, and he gleamed white. One rainy evening he fell out of my pocket and smashed on the tiled floor of the old house.

The boy broke into three pieces: his stockinged feet slipped under the bath's deep belly, his body lay severed from his head. What had struggled to symbolize wholeness in my own and my family's history had, in one fell swoop, become an allegory: the impossibility of telling these histories, the impossibility of saving anything at all, and my inability to gather myself up from the splinters of someone else's past, or even to take it on as my own convincingly. I picked up what I could from the ground and placed the pieces on the desk like jigsaw pieces. It was beyond repair.

6. A Love Interest

On my last day in Vienna I went back to two different places, both terribly alike, both models of preservation, storage devices designed for the remnants of human existence, for what will be left when we are no longer.

In the Michaelerkirche's crypt, human bones were arranged and inventoried in a beautifully clear system. The bones had collected over hundreds of years under the church, and someone had organized them by type and size, tibia to fibula, laid in neat heaps like firewood. Smooth skulls were heaped elsewhere. The guide had the terrifying cheerfulness of a scout leader, she pushed us this way, then that, she made jokes about the transience of earthy existence, she pointed out the fantastically preserved little shoes and the silk corset of a pregnant woman with a dark tuber of a face, exhibited for all to see in a special coffin. *Wie hübsch!* she exclaimed enthusiastically, really very sweet! And it was true, that there was a kind of hierarchical coziness in her underground realm: whatever hadn't quite lost its tangibility, and remained more or less undissipated, was laid out for public view. The rest had been dismantled into spare parts and pushed out of sight, to the periphery of oblivion.

My next stop was the Josephinum, a museum of human anatomy, or at least how they conceived of anatomy in the nineteenth century: the body a temple, eager to display its inner sanctum to the enlightened visitor. The Josephinum is a museum of medical science and my visit was by way of a bow to the complicated art of medical science, and also to my great-grandmother Sarra and her Bulgarian lover, who received his medical diploma in Vienna. What was once the gleaming pinnacle of medical knowledge, the last word in technical achievement and the object of professorial pride, looks much like a cabinet of curiosities now, a monument to ancient arts practiced by starched nurses and doctors with mustaches. Pipes and tiny hammers lay idle alongside surgical instruments, clamps and scissors and iron-beaked microscopes— all of it useless. Without their owners the objects took on the air of curios and lay under the glass like the rattles and swaddling of a profession that has long since grown up. The only things that hadn't grown old were the bodies, so to speak.

The bodies in the Josephinum had not aged like their corruptible counterparts. They were made of pure beeswax to celebrate the Enlightenment, the rational mind, and the benefit of teaching aids—a whole regiment of them, more than a thousand anatomical models, commissioned by Emperor Joseph II and manufactured in Florence under the watchful eye of Paolo Mascagni, philosopher and free thinker and the author of the *Treatise of Anatomy*. The models were then transported across the Alps on mules, just as France, aroused from Grenoble to Toulouse, tossed and turned on its bed of revolution. Then they were floated down the Danube to be exhibited in the interests of science, and here they all are, alive and proud as athletes on the podium in their boxes of tulipwood and glass.

Rational man is served up like a dish in this museum, his belly sliced open and his waxy organs laid out like a plat du jour: a varnished liver; testicles swinging comically on their little ropes. Some of the waxworks are resting on their elbows, some sprawled out, naked to their skeletons, or, wearing their red flesh in bundles tied with veins, they show off their ribbed muscle fiber, fatty tissue, the nifty combs of bone in foot and hand. Marquesses have their curly heads tipped back so the wriggling pipework of the neck is visible. All of it is haunted by the indifference of immortality: the crotch's cradle, the pearl on an untouched neck, the body's workings laid bare like a music box.

The Josephinum felt like another response to the question I

had been turning over in my mind. These beautiful inanimate bodies had lost their reason for being (teaching aids, witnesses, explications) and were empty shells, like the carriages and coffee pots in other museums. Objects falling out of currency slowly lose their defining qualities and turn a new nonhuman face toward us. They return to the materials from whence they came, wax, paint, and clay. The past rewilds itself, oblivion springs up out of it like a forest.

*

Eight years ago a friend was putting together a book of interviews with writers. In these interviews the writers were encouraged to talk about themselves, their childhood, early years, the friendships and conflicts that defined them, their early and not-so-early work. It was a marvelous book. My interview wasn't included. We made two attempts, with two years in between the attempts, but nothing worked. There was something extraordinary about the recorded interviews, but they were of no use for the book. Both of the recordings were like two peas in the pod: they made the same key points, the conversations climbed a route scattered with the same anecdotes—and they revealed nothing at all about me. It was almost funny how absent I was. Over the many pages of typescript I scrutinized my family legacy, jumped through the branches of the family tree, and made a virtuoso performance of avoiding any mention of myself. I answered direct questions, of course, but my answers were so drab and reluctant: born here, studied there, read and wrote this and that ... But what delight I took in somersaulting in midair and diving deep into the free waters of the lives of my unknown ancestors! As a result of this reticence about my own practice, nothing of the interviews could be used. I kept the recordings like the X-rays of a fracture, just in case, and a few years later they actually did come in handy.

I was reading Marianne Hirsch's classic work, *The Generation of Postmemory*, as if it were a travel guide to my own head. I knew everything she described immediately and intimately: the cease-less fascination with one's family's past (and, beyond this, with the densely populated human context for these lives, the thick undercoat of sounds and smells, the coincidences and concur-rences, the synchronized turning of the wheels of history) and the clinical boredom with which I roll my own contemporary world backward to that past, back to them, and feel quite certain, in-my-gut certain, of how it was back then, the streetcar routes, the stockings that sagged around the knees, the music from the loudspeaker. Any story about myself became a story about my ancestors. There they were behind me like an opera chorus en-couraging my aria—only the music was written seventy years ago. The structures that emerged from the black waters of history fought shy of linearity, their natural state was copresence, the simultaneous sounding of voices from the past, contradicting the obvious: time and slow disintegration.

The work of postmemory is an attempt to animate these structures, to give them body and voice, to revitalize them in accordance with one's own experience and understanding. This is how Odysseus called forth the souls of the dead, and they flew down in clouds, crying out like birds at the smell of sacrificial blood. He chased them off, allowing only the ones he wished to talk with to come near to the fire. The blood was a prerequisite, no conversation could happen without it. Now to make the dead speak we have to give them space in our own bodies and minds, carry them inside us like the unborn. And yet the burden of post-memory is placed on children's shoulders: the second and third generations of those who survived and who allow themselves to look back.

Hirsch sets the boundaries of postmemory with deliberate rigor. The term itself was invented for and applied within the field of Holocaust studies, the funneling space that was left in the aftermath of catastrophe. The reality she describes is taken directly from her own personal experience, which continually informs her approach. It's the day-to-day experience of those whose parents and grandparents measured their history from the catastrophe of European Jewry as once history was calculated from the flood. It can't be reckoned with, or pushed aside, because it will always be the starting point, the inescapable pretext for their existence. The need to constantly bring forth the memory of events (remembrance as the highest form of posthumous justice) has a particular quality. This knowledge, both inexplicable and unbearable, blinds like a flash of light whichever way you turn away from it. In its glare anything that has no direct relationship with *then* loses its significance: it has failed the test of the ultimate experience of injustice.

From here comes the unrelenting and troubled magnification of the past in the consciousness of those who are still within its grip. Perhaps those who were allowed to escape their fate feel this more acutely, those who did not pass through the extermination camps, but who were, in Hirsch's words: "survivors of persecution, ghettoization, and displacement." The survivor's situation leads to its own ethical quandary. It's hard not to feel that the place you occupy in this world could be filled by another, and by rights it should be filled by this destroyed and unfulfilled other life. In *The Drowned and the Saved* Primo Levi tells us with absolute candor: "The worst survived, that is, the fittest; the best all died."

Those who weren't "the best," those who benefited from geographic and biographical chance, the luck of the draw (as far as luck was possible, then or now), are forced to act according to an invisible imperative. This is not only to strive to be better than you were cut out to be, it has something to do with the constant sense of the world as an apartment that has just been abandoned. The owners are gone and we are left sitting on their orphaned divans, under photographs of strangers, learning to call them family without really having the right to do so.

This unchanging angle of vision, whereby the past inhabits the present, is a particular sort of enchanted state. It has such a powerful effect, like a light filter or sunglasses, sometimes obliterating the present day, sometimes tinting it. The impossibility of saving the already perished makes the gaze particularly intense—if not Medusa, whose stare petrified the disappearing world, turning it into a monument, then Orpheus's arresting gaze, momentary, photographic, tipping inanimate into animate.

Many people are now occupied by attempts to draw memory out from its hiding places, from the womb-like darkness of "personal history," and to make it seen and heard. Judging by the numbers of films and books appearing, it's a comprehensive salvaging operation. Even private love stories have become something like a collective project. Its aim is akin to Hannah Arendt's description of the difference between the warm accumulation of communities cast out of the world into nonexistence, and the lit public space where the world began. Hirsch describes postmemory not as a project or even a particular type of contemporary sensibility, but as something far broader: "It's not a movement, method or idea; I see it, rather, as a *structure* of inter- and transgenerational transmission of traumatic knowledge and experience. It is a *consequence* of traumatic recall but (unlike posttraumatic stress disorder) at a generational remove."

Postmemory, then, is a kind of internal language, establishing horizontal and vertical lines of transmission (and cutting out those who have no right to speak it). It is, besides this, a petri dish in which reality itself is transformed, changing its colors and its usual affinities. Susan Sontag once described photography in a similar way: "Photography is not, to begin with, an art form at all. Like language, it is a medium in which works of art (among other things) are made." Like language, like photography, postmemory is far more than its obvious function. It doesn't just show us the past, but changes the present, because the past is the key to everything that occurs daily in the present.

The circle of those who are involved in the heat transfer between past and present is much wider than those who feel a link with the history of Europe's Jews, or with the trauma wound, which makes a tear in time's matter at the point of no return, the border between then and now. This border, as depicted by familial memory, spoken memory, is too much like the border between the time of innocence and the time of—let's call it the twilit time. Grandmother's memories, great-grandmother's memoirs, great-grandfather's photographs—all are witnesses of "then," of the inviolate world, when everything was in its place, and might have remained so if darkness had not descended. In this respect, postmemory is ahistorical, but the very dichotomy of memory and history lives in the air we breathe, and it has become fashionable to prefer one over the other.

*

Memory is handed down, history is written down; memory is concerned with justice, history with preciseness; memory moralizes, history tallies and corrects; memory is personal, history dreams of objectivity; memory is based not on knowledge, but on experience: compassion with, sympathy for a desperate pain demanding immediate involvement. At the same time the landscape of memory is strewn with projections, fantasies, and misrepresentations—the ghosts of today, with their faces turned to the past. Hirsch writes:

> The images already imprinted on our brains, the tropes and structures we bring from the present to the past, hoping to find them there and to have our questions answered, may be screen memories—screens on which we project present, or timeless, needs and desires and which thus mask other images and other, as yet unthought or unthinkable concerns.

In some senses postmemory treats the past as raw material, destined for editing. "Invariably, archival photographic images appear in postmemorial texts in altered form: they are cropped, enlarged, projected onto other images; they are reframed and de- or recontextualized; they are embedded in new narratives, new texts; they are surrounded by new frames." (Hirsch). In their original form they are akin to food it would be unthinkable to eat raw, before the necessary, complicated, and careful preparation.

The problem is that the petri dish of postmemory—or new memory—is far larger than the circle of things and phenomena informing Hirsch's work. Because twentieth-century history spread its cataclysms liberally around the globe, most people alive can consider themselves survivors to some extent, the result of a traumatic shift, its victims and the bearers of its legacy, people with something to remember and to call back to life at the expense of their own today. And perhaps also because the world of the living and the world of the dead coexist in exactly this way: we live in their houses, we eat from their plates, but we forget these previous owners, we throw out their fragile reality, putting our own thoughts and hopes in its place, editing and abridging as we see fit, until time sweeps us into that corner where we ourselves become the past.

Each of us is in fact a witness to and participant of a lasting catastrophe. Our desire to shore up the past against rapid dissolution, and to keep it intact like the gold reserve, can easily become a fetish of sorts, something we can all sign up to, a zone of unspoken consensus. Events of the past hundred years have not made humanity more resilient, but they have made us think of the past like a refugee's suitcase, in which the dearest items of a life have been lovingly packed away. Its real value means nothing now, it has been multiplied by the consciousness so many times, because it's all we have left. One of the characters in Nabokov's novel *The Gift* describes "a picture of flight during an invasion or an earthquake, when the escapers carry away with them everything that they can lay hands on, someone being sure to burden himself with a large, framed portrait of some long-forgotten relatives" and the general indignation when "somebody suddenly confiscated the portrait." In the petri dish of memory things and events from the old world have become survivors themselves, saved by a miracle, their presence invaluable simply because they have reached us.

Tsvetan Todorov talks somewhere about how memory is becoming a new cult, an object of mass veneration. The more I consider it, the more I think that the global obsession with memory is simply the foundation, the essential precondition for a different cult: the religion of the past, as we knew it in olden times; a little splinter of the golden age, proof of the fact "that things were better back then." The subjectivity and selectiveness of the memory means we can fix on a historical "excerpt" that has nothing in common with history itself—there will be people out there for whom the 1930s were a lost paradise of innocence and permanence. Especially during times dominated by the dull fear of the unknown. In comparison with a future we don't want to inhabit, what has already happened feels domesticated—practically bearable.

This cult has its double, they reflect each other's symmetry like the points on a horseshoe and between them the self-doubting contemporary world lies unmoving. Childhood is the second object of our guilty love. This love, too, feels doomed, because childhood comes to an end and its supposed innocence should be preserved, cherished, defended at all cost. Both the past and childhood are perceived as stasis, a permanently threatened balance—and both are most venerated by societies in which the past is misrepresented and childhood is abused with impunity.

The whole contemporary world breathes the air of postmemory with its conservative reconstructions: make a country *great again*, return its former fabulous order. The screen has two sides and it isn't just those clinging to the sides of the funnel who can project their hopes, fears, and histories onto it—the grandchildren and great-grandchildren of the silent majority are also waiting for their moment to resurrect their own version of past events. In Russia, where violence circulated ceaselessly, society passing from one space of tragedy to the next as if it were a suite of rooms, a suite of traumas, from war to revolution, to famine and mass persecution, and on to new wars, new persecutions— the territory for this hybrid memory formed earlier than in other countries: spiraling, multiplying versions of what has happened to us over the last hundred years, dimpled with inconsistencies, like a sheet of opaque paper blocking out the light of the present.

At home we had a file of clippings from that once-fashionable Soviet literary magazine *Yunost,* and I spent many happy hours in my childhood poring over it. The poems, prose, and caricatures seemed to come from a different reality, similar to one I knew, but somehow removed, illuminated. Today, those clippings I loved look even stranger: the sense of a beginning, everyone looking forward, in love with the future. Everything was about newness. A story about a box of oranges on a Siberian construction site in the Far East, poems that interchanged "heroine" and "heroin," and a picture of a comic pair of *stilyagi* (him in a beard, her with a heavy fringe) changing an old table with a lace cover for a modern table on three skinny legs. The point of the image was that they were replacing like with like, the Soviet spirit demanded from its citizens indifference to bourgeois delights. From today's perspective, sharp with longing for a disappeared world, the caricature looks more depressing than it was intended to be. Those young people were voluntarily casting out the old world with its carved legs and reliable oaken gravitas. And that is how it was. In 1960s and 1970s Moscow the dumps overflowed with antique furniture: our own four-meter-high sideboard with its colored glass was left in the communal apartment when we moved. There was no room for it in the new modern apartment with its low ceilings.

No one would have reproached my parents for this—a complete and utter indifference to this kind of loss reigned. Besides, there was a youthful audacity in their irrational behavior: their readiness to part with intact, robust, and fit-for-purpose furniture thirty years after the war showed their belief in the permanence of their new existence. Other homes kept hold of their block of housemaid's soap, and grain and sugar and cardboard tubs of tooth powder in case of a rainy day.

7. Injustice and its Different Facets

Many years ago the stepfather of a friend of mine was in the hospital with very little time to live, perhaps no more than a week. He was a war veteran, a mathematician, and a fine man. One morning he asked my friend with some urgency to come back to hospital that evening with her mother. Something had happened to him a long time ago and he'd spent his whole life thinking about it without ever telling a single soul. Although he'd never spoken about it, clearly he had witnessed a miracle, something incredible, something he couldn't have raised in the normal way. But now he was afraid he was running out of time, and he wanted to tell his closest family. When they got there that evening he didn't have the strength to speak, and by the next morning he had lost consciousness. He died a few days later, without having told them anything. This story, like the very possibility-impossibility of finding out something important, lifesaving, hung over me like a cloud for many years, constantly shifting in its significance. Often I drew a simple moral from the story, something along the lines of always speaking out, always saying things before it's too late. At other times it seemed to me that in certain situations life itself enters and turns out the light, to relieve the distress of those left behind.

"How very strange," I said to my friend, not long ago. "You never did find out what he wanted to say. I often think about what might have happened to him, and when. It would've been during the war, I suppose."

My friend was politely surprised. She asked me what I meant, as if she didn't quite believe what she'd heard, but didn't want to doubt my sincerity. Then she said gently that nothing like that had ever happened. Was I sure that it was their family? Perhaps I'd misremembered.

We never spoke of it again.

Memory brings the past and present into confrontation in the search for justice. This passion for justice, like the obsessive scratching of a rash, tears any system from the inside, forcing us to seek and demand retribution, especially on behalf of the dead—for who will defend them, if not us?

Death is the primary injustice and the most extreme manifestation of the system's (and for "system" read "world order") disregard for human life. Death dismantles the border (between me and nonexistence), reassigns values and makes judgments without asking for permission, denies me my right to take part in any human gathering (apart from that multitudinous assembly of the disappeared), and reduces existence to nothing. The heart hates injustice, it seeks victory over death, it pushes back against this fundamental injustice. For centuries this pushback was the Christian promise of salvation, both indiscriminate and individual at once: resurrection for all.

Salvation only works when one condition is met: somewhere near us, and beyond us, there must exist another, wiser memory that is able to hold in its cupped hand everyone and everything; those who have already lived and those who are yet to come. The purpose of funeral rites and the hope of all who hear them are drawn together in the Orthodox prayer to God asking for "memory eternal" for the dead. Here, "salvation" and "conservation" mean the same thing.

Secular society takes the idea of salvation out of the equation, and in one stroke the whole construction loses its balance. Without a belief in salvation, "conservation" becomes no more than an institutional archive: a museum, a library, a warehouse, allowing a sort of conditional and limited immortality—a greatly extended single day, the only version of *eternal life* that is possible in the emancipated new world. Technological revolutions, one after another, have made vast digital warehouses possible, and "possible" in the human tongue means "indispensable."

Long ago, the memory of a person was passed into the hands of God, and any extra efforts to preserve her memory might have been considered excessive, perhaps pointless. Being long remembered was the preserve of those few who understood how to achieve it, or wanted it very much, and you could quite happily die and be resurrected without this, as the task of remembering everyone had been delegated upward, to the highest level.

Any attempt to fix a memory, to give it body, usually meant a list of wonderful attributes. In Plato's dialogue *Phaedrus*, there is contempt for the written memory:

> *Their trust in writing, produced by external characters which are no part of themselves, will discourage the use of their own memory within them. You have invented an elixir not of memory, but of reminding; and you offer your pupils the appearance of wisdom, not true wisdom, for they will read many things without instruction and will therefore seem to know many things, when they are for the most part ignorant and hard to get along with, since they are not wise, but only appear wise.*

By the nineteenth century and its technological revolutions, remembrance suddenly becomes democratic practice, and archiving a matter of general importance. It's called something different and it's thought of differently, but it manifests as an urgent desire to obtain photographs of all one's family. At first the disembodied voice provokes fear and recoil, then slowly the horned head of the gramophone is domesticated, and Moscow dachas ring to the sound of mezzo-soprano Vyaltseva. Change happens slowly, and at first the whole process seems to fit well within the ancient tradition of collecting the best and most representative things: Caruso's voice is recorded, a speech by the Kaiser.

Cinema appears—it too has a purely functional use, as another way to retell history. But now from the viewing platform of hindsight, you realize that something else entirely was intended (by whom?), leading directly to the high point of all human progress: the selfie stick. The home movie. Giving everyone the opportunity to retain everything forever. Immortality, as we understand it, is a kind of trick: the complete and total disappearance of any one of us can be hidden, like a grave, under a scattering of little deceptions that give the illusion of presence. And the bigger the pile of tiny deceptions (saved moments, little speeches, photographs), the more bearable the nonexistence of oneself and others. The daily visual and verbal debris is suddenly made respectable, it's no longer swept under the carpet, but carefully put away for rainier days.

You'd think that in order to become a whole archaeological strata (and lift the ground under our feet a meter or so), the rituals and materials of our life would have to be obsolescent, used up, detritus, like everything created by humans until now. But it's a strange thing: since the invention of photography and sound recording these rituals and materials have forgotten the art of decomposition, just like today's plastic waste. They won't be returned to earth and dust—they pile up higher and higher. They are of no use for the future. Anything that cannot adapt and change is fruitless and surely must be doomed.

In the apartments of the early twentieth century it was still fashionable to display stuffed creatures of various size and shape—from the stags' and boars' heads on the wall to the tiny birds, stuffed so delicately with sawdust that they looked alert and alive, frozen in the act of bathing their feathers. We often read of the elderly ladies who had generations of pets stuffed, to the point where any house with heavy curtains and fire screens went to auction with a dozen dusty terriers. There were other, more radical methods of conserving one's nearest and dearest: at Gabriele D'Annunzio's villa you can still see the souvenir made from the shell of his beloved tortoise. Fed to giant proportions, it is said the tortoise could barely crawl from room to room or along the avenues of the estate with its victorious-sounding title: "Vittoriale degli Italiana." When she died from overeating, her body was scooped out of its horned case and the case made into a dish, an elegant tortoise tureen, to decorate the table and remind the poet's guests of better days.

The difficult, fragile status of the dead in the age of mechanical reproduction made their very existence a task: if we can no longer hope for a new meeting, the joyful dawn of resurrection, then we need to do everything possible to put what remains of the dead to good use. This conviction resulted in a surge of funereal souvenirs: locks of hair with the beloved's initials bound in, photographs of the dead in which they look far brighter than the living—the long exposure of the studio photographer blurred the twitching features and tiny movements of the grief-stricken to unrecognizable emptiness, so it was immediately clear who, in the decorously dressed group, was the much-missed corpse.

By the middle of the twentieth century the process had been taken to its "logical extreme," however you want to understand that euphemism: the rouged face of a political leader lying in state in a crystal coffin on a main square, or millions of unknown bodies, seen only as a repository of raw material or spare parts. What began as the Russian "antideath" philosopher Nikolai Fedorov's obsession to give life to the dead, to drag them from their oak coffins so they walked and talked again; what began as an attempt to resurrect the old world with the power of words—to make a glass of tilleul tea and use it as an elixir of life—hit against a living wall of the drowned and the lost, against the simple impossibility of remembering and calling the dead by their names.

This tidal wave has rolled on for two centuries and is finally at our heels—but instead of the resurrection of the past we have artisans, the production of perfect casts, and taxidermy. The dead have learned to speak with the living: their letters, their voicemails, their posts on social media, all of this can be broken into its tiny elements. There's even an app that uses the words of dead people to compose answers to questions put to them. For several years now this app, available in the Apple Store, has allowed us the peculiar indulgence of chatting with someone as famous as Prince or as unknown as the unfortunate twenty-six-year-old Roman Mazurenko, who was hit by a car. If you type into the chat box the words, "Where are you now?" Mazurenko answers, "I love New York." There is no sense of awkwardness in all this. The seams all meet in the middle, the window doesn't suddenly blow open, there is no cold wind to send a shiver down your spine.

The digital creators of these verbal phantoms (made in the image of a friend) had plenty of material to work from as nothing is ever wiped in the digital age. Instead of one, *the only*, photograph, there are hundreds. No one, not even the photographer, manages to look at every snap: it would take years. But it doesn't matter, the important thing is to store all these many moments, to keep them safe for the Great Looking, the Grand Viewer who has all the time and attention in the world, more than would fit in any lifetime, and who will draw all that has happened into one line of events. There is no one else to do it.

Digital storage gives us a whole range of possibilities, and it affects how we see things: history, biography, one's own or another's text—nothing is seen as a linear sequence unrolling in time, glued with the wallpaper paste of cause and effect. In one sense this is pleasing, since no one feels unloved in this new world. There is space for everyone in the boundless world of the hoarder. On the other hand, the old world of hierarchies and bardic stories worked on the principle of selection: not quite saying everything; sometimes holding back. In some senses, when the necessity of choice is removed (between good and bad, for example), then the very notion of good and evil disappears. All that is left is a mosaic of facts—and points of view, which are mistaken for facts.

The past is now "pasts": a coexisting layering of versions, often with only one or two points of contact. Hard facts soften to modeling clay and can be molded into a shape. The desire to remember, to recreate and fix in place, goes hand in hand with incomplete knowledge and partial understanding of events. Units of information can be lined up in any formation, any order, like in a children's game, and the direction of play will utterly change their significance. My linguist friends, Americans, Germans, Russians, all tell me that their students are brilliant at finding subtexts and hidden meanings, but can't, or don't want to, talk about the text as a whole entity. I suggested asking the students to retell a poem, line by line, describing only what was going on. But I was told that this wasn't possible, *they simply weren't able.* The banal debt to the obvious, along with the need to tell a story, has been thrown overboard, lost in the detail, broken into a thousand bite-size quotes.

*

On May 30, 2015, I left my apartment on Banny Pereulok in Moscow, where I had spent a biblical two score years and one, amazed even myself at the length of time I'd spent here. All my friends had moved about from one place to another, and even from one country to another, and only I had stayed put like some ancient Aunt Charlotte on her country estate, living in the rooms my grandmother and mother had inhabited, with empty sky through the window where once there were tall white poplars, like in Odessa, planted by her grandfather. The rooms were repainted, but even the new decor had begun to look shabby. The furniture was long used to standing in a different formation, so when you shut your eyes at night, the rooms of the empty apartment became ghostlike and all the furniture returned to its original places in the darkness: the bed where I lay was itself overlaid with the shape of the writing desk that had once stood there. Its lid covered my head and shoulders, and above me hung the shelf with the three porcelain monkeys refusing to see, hear, or speak, and in the other room the heavy orange curtains were back, and the lamp stand covered in a silk shawl, and the big old photographs.

None of this remained, there wasn't even a chair to sit on, the apartment had become no more than a series of empty boxes, workboxes of odd buttons or spools of thread. The chairs and divans had departed for different homes, in the farthest room an anxious light burned, even though it was day, and the doors were already thrown back wide as if to welcome new owners. The keys were handed over, dropped from one palm into another, I took a last look at the pale sky over the balcony—and then life suddenly sped up, moving faster than ever before. The book about the past wrote itself while I was traveling from place to place, counting up my memories, just like the children's poem about the lady and her luggage: "a punnet, a pug, a painting, a jug ..." And off I went on my wanderings to Berlin, where the book stopped, held its breath—and so did I.

I found a home in a beautiful old part of Berlin, which had once been considered a Russian area, and had always been associated with literature. The streets seemed familiar, Nabokov had lived in the house opposite, and two houses down, a person who had, by mutual and loving consent, eaten a man alive. In the little square yard a dozen bikes gathered like horses at a watering trough. Everything was underpinned by a feeling of durability and presence, but a strange sort of presence when you remembered that this city had for years been known for its wastelands and its yawning voids, rather than the buildings constructed on these empty spaces. I enjoyed the thought that some of my notes about the impossibility of remembrance would be written within another impossibility: in a city where history is an open wound, no longer able to mend itself with the scar tissue of oblivion.

It was as if the city had unlearned the skill of coziness, and the city's inhabitants respected this quality of bareness. Here and there construction sites opened the wound further, streets were barred with red-and-white barriers, the asphalt was cut open to reveal its granular earthen heart, and the wind whistled, clearing the space for new wastelands. By every entranceway little bronze plaques in the paving stones told a familiar story, even if you didn't stop to read the names and count the years to see how old they were when they were taken from these elegant houses with their high ceilings to Theresienstadt or Auschwitz.

I managed nothing of the work I had planned in Berlin, in my cheerful little apartment with its Mettlach-tiled stove. Once I had arranged my life there, laid out my books and photographs, signed up at a library and been given a library card with a grinning stranger's face on it, I quickly resigned all my energies to a gnawing unending anxiety, which turned its toothed cogs in my stomach. I don't remember how I spent the days. I think I spent more and more time wandering from room to room until I realized that the only thing I could actually do well was move from place to place. Movement was forgiving, the thought of un-achieved work was pushed out of my head by the number of steps taken in a day, the physical shape of my achievements. I had a bike. An old Dutch beast with a bent frame and a yellow lamp on its forehead. Once it had been painted white, and at a good trot it made a snuffling-grinding sound, as if its last ounces of strength were being squeezed out of it by contact with the air. It braked with a ticking noise. An old German novel that my mother had loved featured a car called Karl, "the ghost of the road," and there was something similar and ghostly in the way my bicycle and I blended in to the hidden underpasses, slipping between people and traffic, leaving no trace of ourselves, not in their memory, and not in mine.

Riding a bike in Berlin was a new and unfamiliar experience. The whole city lived on its wheels, pushing the pedals round diligently but with ease, as if there was nothing untoward in this behavior in a grown-up person. In the evenings a quiet chirruping and a flicker of light were the only trail we left behind us, and it was transparently clear that the city had been built for this constant falling through the absences without noticing, like in that Kafka text where the horseman rides across the steppe, his stirrups gone, his bridle gone, his horse gone, and even he himself no longer there. The streets seemed to give way obligingly when a cyclist came through, offering themselves up as flatness, so the ride cost no energy and the rider hardly realized she was flying somewhere beyond. The lightness of travel allowed a feeling of safety—the shop windows, the passersby and their little dogs were not even beyond a thin glass screen, but speed and the insect rustling of the bike made everything around untouchable, slightly blurred, as if I were as invincible as the air passing through my fingers.

I wondered then if the people who were destined sooner or later to be air and smoke remembered this sense of invisibility and invincibility and longed for it when they were condemned to walk on the ground on May 5, 1936, losing their right to own and ride a bike. In the laws that came later it became clear they would always remain on the unshaded side of the street, never able to slip among the shadows, or allowing themselves the luxury of freewheeling without obstacle. When public transport was forbidden to them it was as if someone had had the explicit task of reminding them that their body was the only property left to them and they should rely on that alone.

On a rainy October evening, when all the passersby walked at an angle better suited to trees in the wind, I turned the corner (from Knesebeck Strasse onto Mommsen Strasse and only from Mommsen Strasse onto Wieland Strasse, as Sebald might have written) onto the street where Charlotte Salomon once lived. Salomon who, for a number of reasons, felt almost like a relative to me. She lived from her birth until 1939 in the house on this street, only leaving when she was fetched and sent to France in haste to be saved from the common fate. The worst stories of flight and salvation are the ones with a twist in the tale, the ones where right after the miraculous escape death pounces anyhow, grown thickly shaggy while waiting. That is what happened to Charlotte. But this Berlin house took a gentle leave of its child, except for perhaps the crowds of protesters she happened to see from the window with their crooked canvas banners. Back then you still could have seen such things through any window, and those fine art nouveau frames with their excellent proportions were simply doing their job. On this evening the rain was getting heavier, and a faint light could be seen inside, not lighting the whole huge apártment, just one of the rooms, and the others in a sort of twilight, so I could only really guess at the height of the ceilings and the stucco. In a scene from a book I hadn't read since childhood, a painting in a gilded frame hung at an exhibition. In the painting was a snow-covered town, a recognizable street corner, windows lit warmly—the resemblance took my breath away—and then a sudden trick: a horse cab traveling from one side of the picture to the other, a shadow, shape-shifting. There was a movement above me on the dark balcony, a cigarette burnt bright, a wisp of smoke. It startled me, although I don't know why.

I came to love the U-Bahn and the S-Bahn, the over- and underground railways, the orphaned smells of sweet rolls and rubber wheels, the spiderlike map of lines and connections. The glass dovecots of stations with their arched roofs seemed to suggest that you could hide under them but to me they looked temporary, untrustworthy. All the same I always relaxed when the train I was on entered the iron womb of the Hauptbahnhof as if its see-through helmet guaranteed me a moment to catch breath, a sudden eclipse before departing again into the light. There was always a crowd moving on the platform, the carriage filled instantly until no one else could get on: someone carried a bike, someone carried an impossibly huge double bass in a fu-neral-black case, someone had a little dog that sat so obediently it might have been posing for a black-and-white photograph. Even back then it seemed to me that all of this was happening in a past that had long ago departed, and was only now in reach if you stretched out a hand right out. Sometimes I found myself looking at the lit carriage, and me inside it as if at a distance, as if it were a model railway with tiny plastic figures sitting on the seats. The wet city circled in the window like a Ferris wheel on its side, and in it mostly the bits in between: the wastelands, underexposed scenes, and sometimes something more real and present—a column, a cupola, a cube, or a globe.

During that stagnant period in my life, everything felt close enough to touch, especially when we passed places I had once known, forgotten, and seen anew—these places gave me a brief sense of warmth. In one place I'd spent a few days in a hotel, where the guests were entertained in the oddest manner. The long narrow entrance hall was uplit with turquoise light, it was like walking down a plastic straw. At the end of the hall, where the glum residents congregated, there was a hearth with a fire burning brightly, giving off a visible heat. It was only when you reached the reception desk that you realized it was a deception: the fire burnt across the full width of a TV screen on the wall, crackling and creating an apparition of real coziness. Together with my plastic key card I was given two turquoise boiled sweets like cough drops, and I took them upstairs to the little bed-shaped room, with its basin-in-a-cupboard arrangement. The wall opposite the bed was empty of pictures and photos, there was nothing to distract from the main show: yes, there in the room a smaller but otherwise identical screen with a burning fire. The creaking and champing of the flames could be heard from the door, and, as soon as I entered, I sat down on the turquoise bedspread, as I was clearly meant to do, and looked the fire in the teeth.

In the middle of the night, still unable to find the off switch for the screen, I began to understand the little lesson the hotel's owners had provided for their guests as a sort of undemanding but compulsory entertainment, like the poems used as decorative inscriptions on soft furnishings, or embroidered proverbs in a frame: "The early bird catches the worm." The single screen, standing upright like a young conscript, was touched by a tiny flame, a halo at the very edge of the screen first, the forewarning of a future martyrdom. The fire grew stronger, seeming to reach out and touch my face, the flames unfurled, droning and subsiding before reaching the very top of the screen, where the bee whispering grew thicker. Then gradually the intensity dropped and the screen grew darker and then gasped softly and disintegrated into ashes and cinders. A short darkness followed, then the picture momentarily shuddered, straightened, and before me again the quick lithe fire, the resurrected image, as if nothing had ever happened to it. The whole business repeated itself over and over (the recording seemed ever more horrible, the longer it went on), and I followed it more and more attentively, as if I was trying to make out some variation, however small. Again and again the darkness gave way to the wood, repeatedly resurrecting itself from the dead.

Not-A-Chapter
Nikolai Stepanov, 1930

Fragile, crumbling gray paper, typed text. My grandparents' marriage was only registered in the early 1940s.

To Whom it May Concern
Rzhev Registry Office
From N. G. Stepanov
Citizen of Tver

I request the Rzhev registry office to register me as the father of the child born to Dora Zalmanovna Akselrod. I sent my identity documents as requested.

According to my information the child has not yet been registered by the registry office and this is only because I am not yet officially (please see the empty pages of my identity documents) registered as married to D. Z. Akselrod. But this is not correct.

There are no illegitimate children in a Soviet country, they are not possible. Therefore the nonregistration of my marriage cannot result in the nonregistration of my child in my name.

I am not currently able to travel to Rzhev so I am asking the registry office to fulfill my request, that is, to register me as the father of the girl, born to my wife, on the identity document I have sent you and not to delay with the official registration of the child's birth.

Signed here:
N. Stepanov

Stamp Tver Local Council (All-Union Communist Party (Bolsheviks))

Signed and witnessed by member of the Tver Local Council (All-Union Communist Party (Bolsheviks)) Comrade Stepanov

Added by hand: if the child is already registered but not in my name, in accordance with all laws I insist that the child is reregistered to me. I have no interest in simply agreeing to what suits you. N. Stepanov.

8. Rents in the Fabric, and Diversions

Every now and then a friend will send you some startling image of a face on a postcard or via an internet link. To them the face seemed to resemble yours, the features, the expression, hair, eyes, nose. When you put all such pictures side by side they suddenly reveal themselves to have nothing in common, apart from their likeness to you, the common denominator. As they say in film credits, any resemblance is purely coincidental.

But perhaps this is not true? Why do these apparent resemblances excite both sender and recipient of the postcard, as if something really important had been revealed, some secret mechanism? It's tempting to see them as an expression of another order: a selection based not on family resemblance or proximity, but design, by mirroring a pattern you don't know. It's hard to resist evidence of hidden rhythms in the world order, and writers from Nabokov to Sebald have taken pleasure in the ringing of signal bells to mark coincidences: such as finding your birthday is the date of death on a stranger's gravestone, or wearing a certain color for luck, or when a resemblance with Botticelli's Zipporah or someone's great-grandchild becomes the cause of passion. Such coincidences seem to confirm that we aren't chance presences in the world, that everything is interrelated, woven into a warm nest of twigs, excrement, and fluff: people were here before you and they will still be here after you are gone.

And yet this isn't the only version of events. The anthropologist Bronisław Malinowski described the way that classic observations along the lines of "doesn't he look like his grandmother" were met with unease and horror in societies constructed to a different model. "I was then told by my confidential informants that I had committed a breach of custom," writes Malinowski of the Trobrianders in Papua New Guinea, "that I had perpetrated what is called "taputaki migila," a technical expression referring only to this act, which might be translated as "to defile by comparing to a kinsman his face." Pointing out a family resemblance was seen as an insult: an individual was like no other person, he was without copy, he was the first of his sort to appear on the earth, and he only represented himself. To deny that was to doubt a person's existence. To quote the poet Mandelstam: "do not compare: the living are beyond comparison."

There's a short film by Helga Landauer, made in 2009. I have it on my computer and I watch it again and again, as you might read and reread a book. It's called *Diversions*, and the title could refer to many things: an entertainment; a distraction; a turning aside or deviation from the route; or even a tactic designed to draw your enemy's defense away from the main attack. In place of instructions, I, the viewer, am given a sequence of waymarks, each pointing in a different direction. Not a map or a route—more like a swinging weather vane. Something very similar happens on the screen as well:

People in absurd pith helmets crowding in the shallows, a rowboat is about to set off. The bare-legged sailors carry them out to the boat on their backs, like luggage. Parasols rock over their heads.

Hanging lace sways in a draft.

A dark mass of leaves, a parasol over an artist's easel, a dim rain-filled light.

Children, like deer, peering out from behind trees.

An oar slices through the shining water, a long ripple runs across it. Sunshine. You can't see who is rowing.

A woman lifts a fishing rod out of the water, her smile stretches from ear to ear, like a skull's.

The victorious bustle of ladies' hats and their fur, feathers, wings, fearsome excess.

A mass of leaves, the wind troubles the leaves, children run across the image from corner to corner like little beasts.

Tall flowers in a white vase standing on a table, almost invisible, like everything that is not important.

The whiskers and biceps of an athlete.

The whiskers and bowler hats of passersby. One sees us and lifts his hat.

Bicycles and boaters, walking sticks and briefcases.

The pine tree bends forward. Someone wearing black wanders along the shoreline, only his back is visible.

People pass by, more and more people.

Funny little miniature trains trundle through parks. The passengers wave.

Children peep through branches like gophers.

Dead trees lie alongside the roads.

A man in a workman's suit cups water in his hands, and offers it to a small dog to drink.

Pigeons come to rest on a path through a park.

A little girl with a parasol searches for her family in a crowd.

Montgolfier balloons, round, satin-sided, rise into the air.

Two people, one anxious, the other reassuring.

Women in long skirts race little balloons along the ground, waving them on with fans.

An embarrassed, gentle smile beginning in the left-hand corner as if a light had been turned on.

Rowers hurrying down to a pier, carrying long, flipper-like oars.

Water rushes up a beach, then recedes, exposing the loose pebbles.

Picnic chairs cast their shadows across the wet sand.

A pure white sky above a concert and musicians.

Skirts fly out in a dance.

A little boy selling violets.

Glasses of water and newspapers on a table, a packet of Chesterfields on a saucer. A newspaper headline: Buffalo Bill.

A brick wall lit by the sun.

A sign saying *Dancing tous les soirs*.

Flashing legs of a horse.

Boxes full of grapes, shall I wrap them for you?

Lacemakers bend over their bobbins.

Two hands linked.

A tired, soiled collar at the end of the day.

A hat brim shading the eyes.

A car turns a corner.

Accordion buttons.

The swallows were smaller back then and the roses were larger.

Men in caps watch some men in hats passing by.

A bride's veil is adjusted.

A spoon lies face down on the edge of a coffee saucer.

People in bathing suits crowding in the gray sea.

Grass and fallen trees behind a garden fence.

Striped beach umbrellas, striped beach tents, and striped summer dresses.

A wheelbarrow, its handles pointing up to the sky.

Flags flutter.

A dog runs across the sand.

The round shadow of a table on wooden floorboards.

It's easy to see the white blouses and dark skirts, lacemakers at their work, men sitting outside cafes and clinking glasses, as memory's errand boys, fulfilling one (obvious to me) task. The film is composed of old documentary material, it can be seen as a requiem to the Old World (or one of its sections at least: as far as I remember it covers decades and is barely broken into individual voices). The film's final credits are a long list of names, finishing with a single line by the film's writer: "The last scenes were filmed on the coast of Europe in late August of 1939."

There is so much documentary cinema occupied with this archaeology, that any scene, even any face, looks instantly familiar: crowds brought together at random by the cinecamera, divested of their names, their fates, doomed forever to scatter across the street in front of the oncoming streetcar, and to illustrate any historical situation: "Citizens of Vienna Welcome Anschluss," "Love and Honor," "We'll All Be Dead Soon." The ancient division between important and unimportant is everywhere: the hero speaks, the girl eats ice cream, the crowd loiters as crowds do. We requisition this found footage as we might the goods in a warehouse: there is so much of it that we can select what we want. The author tells a story, and passersby illustrate that story. It's never about them, they are cutaway scenes (to use the filmmaking term), they fill the pauses, delight the eye, and don't distract from the general idea.

It never occurs to anyone to set these people free, to give them one last opportunity to be themselves and not just typical representatives of the 1920s. Yet this is what Helga Landauer does, without taking away a second of their screen time—everyone gets as much time and space as the cameraman originally allotted them. A kind of freedom that is usually inherent to life rather than to art makes *Diversions* a refuge for the lost and forgotten, a paradise of democracy in which everyone is visible. A long-awaited equality between people, objects, and trees is achieved in the film, with each given its position as a representative of *what has been*. In some senses the convention established here is the equivalent of emancipating the serfs. The past is relieved of its feudal duties to the present, to us. It can walk freely.

Only now do I notice that every one of these people at some point lifts his or her eyes and looks into the camera, looks at me, at us, and this is one of the extraordinary things about this film: that gaze into the lens never finds its addressee. And this to such an extent that in ten or twelve viewings I have never been aware of meeting any eye: meetings have been replaced by nonmeetings, which may be more important. The people and objects depicted radiate the unbroken peace of a memorial and that makes this fifteen-minute film persuasive: where else (or where still) do they not know about suffering, where still (or where else) is there no place for it? The gaze stares out and through me, without leaving any trace or impression. It has no direction, no aim, no addressee, it is as if a landscape lies before this gaze and it can be entered and exited at will. In the lens's eye, all causal relationships are gone: they lie beyond judgment or interpretation. Every time I watch it the order of the episodes seems to change, as if they had been given permission to stand up and wander at will.

This is the great gift: to explain nothing, to imply nothing; a woman in polished boots riding a horse, perhaps through the Bois de Boulogne, she's in a hurry, she lights a cigarette, she poses, she lowers her new jacket with a languid gesture, she likes that jacket, she smiles as a person might smile when someone else is gazing at them appraisingly. In the film's space she is free of all appraisal, like an animal in a zoo—what is the point in comparing a lion with a toucan, or a walrus with a bear, or me with not-me?

*

The Russian poet Mikhail Kuzmin has a short story about an English governess who lived in Russia. She hadn't heard from her brother for a while, and when the First World War started she went to the cinema to watch the news, short reports on how conscripts in uniform were being sent off to the front, and she sat running her eyes over the lines of troops, their faces and sleeves, hoping for the unthinkable. And her faith triumphed—she recognized her brother. The miracle happened. But just like the oldest stories, she didn't recognize him by his face but by what made him stand out from all the others: a hole in his trousers. I think this may be one of the very first texts of the century in which people find each other through loss and damage: holes, rents in the fabric, participants in a common fate.

There is too much past, and everyone knows it: the excess (which is continually being compared to a flood) oppresses, the force of its surge crashes against the bulwark of any amount of consciousness, it is beyond control and beyond description. So it is driven between banks, simplified, straightened out, chased still-living into the channels of narrative. The quantity and variety of *sources*, those babbling rivulets to the left and right, bring on a strange queasy feeling, rather like the perplexed anxiety a city dweller has when confronted by nature in its rawest state, free of its straitjacket.

Unlike nature, past lives are endlessly submissive, allowing us to do whatever we may decide to do with them. They reject no interpretation, endure any amount of humiliation, exist outside the rule of law or any notion of fair play. Culture treats the past as a state treats its mineral wealth, mining it for all its worth; this parasitical relationship with the dead is a profitable industry.

The dead agree to everything we do with them, and with such compliance that it provokes the living to do ever more. There is something horrible about the new fashion of purses and note-pads decorated with faces staring out from old photographs, whose names and fates are long lost. And there is something offensive about the way "authentic lives" are sent to stroll the pleasure grounds of historical romances, as if the text would be lifeless without a drop of real blood in the mixture. These are all manifestations of some strange perversion, which leads only to the dehumanization of our own ancestors. We attribute our own weaknesses and passions to them, our amusements, our optical instruments, pushing them slowly out of the world, dressing up in their clothes as if they'd been made for us.

The past lies before us, like a huge planet waiting to be colonized: first the raiding parties, and then the slow modification process. It looks like all culture has been mobilized to preserve the little that remains; any effort at memorialization is an excuse for complacency. More and more silences rise up out of the abyss, people forgotten by their own time and discovered like islands: pioneers of street photography, music hall singers, war journalists. How easy it is to be thrilled by the jubilation, the opening of the stores where you can purchase any colonial souvenir from the past and interpret it as you see fit, without even considering what the mask or the rattle meant in its own time and place. The present is so certain that it owns the past, just as once "both th'Indias" were owned. The present knows as much about the past, as Donne did "th'India," and barely notices the ghosts that float back and forth, ignoring state boundaries.

*

Walking through the Jewish cemetery in Würzburg where my mother is buried, past the gray backs of tombstones and glancing about as I walk, I start to remember her neighbors, those lying beside her, by the emblems which are hidden in their names: rose wood and rose hills, stars, deer, people of love, freedom, Würzburg's men and women, Swabians, the lonely Miron Isaakovich Sosnovich (the totemic tree of his name—*sosna* is Russian for pine tree—goes unheard in these parts) from Baku (but born

in Białystok, the tombstone adds helpfully), those killed in the
First World War, those killed in Theresienstadt, those who died
in good time, that is, before anything happened, in 1920, 1880,
1846. They have become my family, because we share the same
ground, but their emblem-names are all I know about these new
relatives.

There is a room in the Berlin Jewish Museum put aside for
what is called family histories: children's photos, the teacups and
violins of those who didn't manage to escape. On a screen facing
me a homemade cinefilm plays on a loop, the sort of thing that
everyone produced in the age of early home video, but back then
a cinecamera was a signifier of wealth, along with ski lifts and
summer evenings at the dacha.

In this film, as in *Diversions*, the foreign past is given the freedom to speak about what was, and to remain silent about how it
ended. In this case we know a few of the circumstances, and we
have an eye to the likely outcome. One jolting characteristic of
film is very clear: unlike an old text, which goes to lengths to un-
derline and shade in the differences between then and now, video
insists on similarities, on the joined-upness of time, on how there
is no difference between then and now. Streetcars and trains still
clatter past, the S-Bahn above ground, the U-Bahn below, women
lean over cots and coo. No hesitations, no moments of awkwardness: someone simply disappears from the frame, and that is all.

And then there is all of *this*: a dog bounding joyfully in a heap
of snow; the dog's cheery owners, their ski trousers bobbled with
snow; an unsuccessful attempt to negotiate the nursery slopes
without falling; skis going their separate ways; barn doors, the
family porch and the tiled roof of another house, a child, waving
its arms from an old-fashioned deep pram, a Sunday morning
street, looking much like a street today, filled with people in their
Sunday best, cloaks, nuns; pools or lakes, a rowboat, children
growing up in front of us, winter again and long-distance skaters
are clearing the ice in front of them. 1933 or 1934, the film is now

in reverse and a moon-colored little boy flies up out of the black water back-first onto the planks. When I'd watched the montage to the end I waited for the credits to see the family's name. Their surname was Ascher. I stood by the screen where once again they were checking their skis, the half-transparent family plumping down in the snow. I know how this story ended. The surname spoke for itself. The daughter (who was in the films) had given the museum these films in 2004, but there was no mention of what had happened to her parents, the boat, or the dog.

All war films look the same if you take away their captions: a dead man lies on the ground and it could be Donetsk, Phnom Penh, or Aleppo. We are simply presented with the face of misfortune, which is always the same, a hole that can open up in any place. Children's photos are also all the same (the smile, the teddy bear, the little dress), as are fashion shots (monochrome backdrop, taken looking up from below, arms outstretched), or old photographs (mustache, buttons, eyes; puffed sleeves, hat, and lips). All that remains of *The Iliad* is a catalog of ships.

When I watch the homemade cinefilm of the Ascher family, skiing in 1934, the dark ski tracks in the snow and the lit-up window, the film is just a conduit for the preexisting knowledge of what happened back then to people who looked like them. Dust to dust, ashen snow to ashen snow, the collective fate of the unlucky ones: the trajectory is so very clear that any diversion from it shocks, like a divine apparition. Half an hour's internet research tells me that both parents and children, with their skis and boats, belonged to the small number of those who survived. They left in 1939, settled in Palestine, then moved to America. They managed to escape the common fate. It's a shame that the people in the film don't yet know that their film has a happy end. None of the rents in the fabric suggest it.

Not-A-Chapter
Lyolya (Olga) Fridman, 1934

My grandmother was barely eighteen. My grandfather Leonid (Lyonya) was older than her by four years. They met at a party of architecture students at a dacha, but they only married after a few years: Lyolya's mother, Sarra Ginzburg, insisted that she finished her degree in medicine first, and wouldn't allow Lyolya to drop her studies.

1.

November 25, 1934. On a lined sheet of exercise paper.

Moscow, 27 Krasin Street, apartment 33.
To Leonid Gurevich

A tear, my darling, a single tear, has turned all my thinking on its head. A tiny, tiny tear rolled out of your eye and conquered everything. It defeated all my stupid doubts, my fear, shame, everything that stood in the way of your happiness.

That little point of shining light seemed to enchant me, it filled me with a real and bright happiness.

You know, my love, I never imagined that the suffering and grief of another could give me so much happiness. Now I understand your desire to see my tears, and I forgive you for all the suffering you forced me to endure.

I've never felt such blessedness. To see a person who is endlessly dear to you suffering terribly, simply to avoid causing you suffering, to feel how dear and necessary you are to that person—my darling, that is happiness!

It's both a painful and blessed feeling. A special joy, one I don't fully understand.

Really, I can't even quite explain to myself how I felt at the moment when that magic jewel of a tear—a single tear for all your months of suffering—forced me to finally overturn my inner self. I've never had to watch people suffer, I've always felt as if it's only me who suffers so deeply, but how can what I feel be compared to the depths of your suffering? It can't! Only now I've realized what it means to feel, only now I've realized where what is called "desire" resides. I didn't see you for a day and I was heartbroken, I didn't know where to put myself, but I didn't ring you or tell you how my heart was feeling. I was held back by my doubts, my fear, I thought it would divide us, I thought that I shouldn't be in the grip of my desires to such an extent, I thought … I couldn't stop thinking … But I'm used to being reserved, not giving in to impetuosity, and my reserve saved me.

Still, you, my darling, you are impetuous in your passion, and today I realized what it has cost you to keep your desire under control. And my own sufferings seemed so little in comparison, and I even had the brief fleeting thought that perhaps I'm not worthy of you.

I don't want you to think that my feelings are shallower than yours, or that I'm more superficial. That isn't the case. Please don't misunderstand me. But you seem so much finer in your feelings, so much finer … No, that can't be right! I can't have you think that you love me more than I love you! That would be a lie!

But you're spoiled, you've never had to deal with difficulties, or withstand your desires. And I've always had to do it. You're egotistical, you think only of yourself, and most of all you have never had to choose between two things, both equally desired, even if they are loved very differently, and share between them what you are desperate to give up to only one.

Think about it, my little boy, think how hard it is to love like that, and maybe my suffering will give you even more spirit for the fight, for the wait.

I didn't want to tell you all this, I didn't want to cause you pain, not on my account. I'll admit it ...

But today was enough to convince me.

I have always put my own needs second. Recently I decided to live a little, for myself, without taking anyone else into account. But I have realized that this is a mistake, a cruel mistake, or perhaps an insubstantial dream, because living just for myself and making my beloved suffer—well I just can't do it! I realized today that I no longer exist as an individual, I have merged with you, I am dissolving into you, and I had already decided, my darling, to be all yours, but when I came home I met mother, all agitated and upset, and felt a huge pain, a burning pain in my heart. I had decided, but mother's troubled, suffering expression said, "You must wait."

How could I forget her, even for a moment?

Mother has seen so little happiness, she's known such hard times, she has endured so very much on my account and she is still suffering and I don't think I can hurt her even more. I'm her only family. I've got you. Your mother still has a husband, but mine has no one. For me she gave up her chance of happiness as a young woman and sacrificed her whole life and because of me she didn't remarry and brought me up all by herself. Quite alone.

I know what it cost her. I can feel just what a sacrifice it was, I just know, although mother has never ever spoken of it, not even a hint or a faint gesture. Oh, she's a rock! All her suffering and pain will be buried with her, not a single soul will guess how she suffered. To suffer so and to hide it—only she could do that.

My darling, mother is so frightened of losing me, and has been since I grew up, not even losing me, just letting me go into the world naive and unprepared, she considers me a child, and the idea that I could get married before becoming an educated, independent woman causes her so much pain. She doesn't speak of it, occasionally she hints at it in jest, but I know, I know that if that happened it would be the last straw for her.

So you see, I'm in such pain too, but I can't do what I read in your eyes today. How complicated it all is! Harder than you could ever know!

A long time ago, when mother destroyed her own life for me, when she turned down her beloved at my request, I made a promise on father's grave: I promised that I would make her no less of a sacrifice in my turn.

That time has come. I'm telling you to wait, my darling, just as mother once said to her own beloved, "Let's wait until Lyolya is quite grown up."

Please don't tell me that I don't understand how difficult it all is. I understand it only too well ...

I sent you that letter because otherwise I would have had to send today's letter. I didn't realize how deep your suffering was.

I'm so sorry!!

If I'd known I would never have been so cruel.

And then today I had to tell you what I never wanted to have to tell you.

I'm so sorry about that, too!

I underestimated your feelings, I was scared to share what belonged to me. But your tear taught me that I don't exist anymore, there is only "us" and we have to get through difficult times, full of self-denial, and we have to repay the sacrifice to a person who gave up so much for one of us. This is the only way out I can see, my darling. Will you be able to do this, my sweetheart? Will you have enough strength and resolution? Please decide. From today onward I will be absolutely open with you. You must understand absolutely what I am asking of you.

It may be that our sacrifice will help us look into the future with joy, perhaps by supporting each other we will be able to get through those dark hours. Perhaps the inescapable nature of our situation will make us stronger.

I can't bear to think of a different outcome. I'm sure you will support me, after all how could I lose you now that you've become so close and dear to me? I can't!

Please promise me that you will help me carry out what I have always considered to be my sacred duty. Promise me that your love is deep enough, and I will be so very happy. I will feel renewed certainty that I made the right choice in you ...

I promise in return that I will lighten the heavy burden of your daily troubles with my gratitude and loving attention, because I value your sacrifice very highly. That tear, your tear has done so much good, my love.

Your loving Olya

2.
Undated.

My dearest
How endlessly slowly the days are passing, how depressingly slowly.

These last three days have seemed an eternity.

I'm out of sorts, I can't do anything. I want to be with you, to bear your troubles with you, although, thank God [crossed out], they are behind you now, but that only gives me a little relief, mostly my mood is desolate.

I sit and read your letters and I realize once again just how good you are.

My sweet friend!

How can I tell you what I've suffered and what I've thought over these last long days, how can I tell you about all the terrible sadness, how my soul ached. My dearest, I hope our life together will be lit by the love and tenderness I feel in your letters.

So much has been left unsaid. But I have no words! I'm no good at sharing confidences.

On the other side of the paper:
I want our happiness to be enveloped in the new feelings you have

woken in me. I want our relationship to be one of tender touch and attentions, and for the bitterness to remain undisturbed deep in our hearts, the angry words to remain unspoken. Even our thoughts should be constantly occupied with each other's happiness.

I am changed ...

Farther down, in my grandfather's large handwriting:
My darling

These few words will tell you everything I am thinking, everything I desire and dream of, more than if I wrote a hundred words, because you would still have to read between the lines to understand what I want to tell you. It can't be expressed in words because words only convey my thinking, and not my feelings. My darling, be happy!

9. The Problem of Choice

"All the earth is a sacred tomb, the ashes of our fathers and brothers are everywhere" is a line from the Orthodox Burial Service. Since there is only one earth (and we are its only human dwellers), the meeting place between the quick and the dead, traditionally the cemetery, could be in fact any scrap of land under our feet. But the cemetery still works for us, in fact it has even too many functions. In eighteenth-century Venice, monasteries had special reception rooms where the secular and worldly could come to make music, play dominoes, chat among themselves, drink coffee, and (almost incidentally) visit their dead. The monks and novices sat separated from them by an iron grille, nodding at their conversations, but leaving back into their own very different lives. Over the last two or three hundred years the cemetery has become such a zone of one-way conversation, like a visiting room in a monastery or a prison camp, always fragmentary, always partial. But the cemetery has other, far more ancient preoccupations: it is also the place of letters, of inscribed witness.

The cemetery as address book for all humanity sets out everything we need to know with concision. In effect it comes down to names and dates—we don't need to know any more. We read and remember at most two or three familiar names, for who could fix all its thousands of pages in the mind? But supposing those who lie there have an interest in whether they are remembered? All they can hope for is a chance passerby to stop and read; a stranger, filled with an age-old curiosity about life before he appeared in the world, who will pick out their grave from all others, and stand and remark on it. This belief in the redemptive regard of a stranger—in his eyes, flickering between the stone-carved lines of text, from letter to letter, imbuing each with temporary life and teleological warmth—makes orphans of the tombstones without inscriptions, or the stones with such worn faces they can no longer be read. A tombstone might seem almost pointless, functioning merely as a road sign (Here Lies a Person!). After all, the important stuff is under the tombstone and not on it, and people know their own dead, don't they? Still, for some reason, the inscription, what the person under the gravestone was called and how old they were, is essential to us. Why it is so is another matter entirely.

This need is very ancient, far older than Christianity and its belief in resurrection for all. In *Economy of the Unlost* Anne Carson offers a careful and surprising comparison between two bodies of work (by Paul Celan and Simonides of Keos), and maintains that it is on the burial mound, where there is only a stranger's death, a stone, and the need for a clarifying text, that poetry emerges from its shell of sound and comes into its own as a written art, aimed at the one looking at the tomb, and his ability to do what the words cut into the stone ask of him: to use his memory and its "sense of order." The epitaph is the first written poetic genre, the subject of the contract between living and dead, a pact of mutual redemption. The living offer the dead a place in their memories, and they believe, to use the poet and songwriter Vladimir Vysotsky's words, "the dead won't leave us in our hour of need."

The poet, whoever he might be, is quite essential: he carries out the task of redemption, makes a life "portable," decouples the sign from the body and the memory from the place where that body lies. Once read, the epitaph takes wing: a vehicle, a right of passage, giving the dead a new verbal existence, unlimited movement within the internal and external space of memory, in the anthologies of world poetry and the corridors of our minds. Still, what do the dead care for our anthologies?

"The responsibility of the living to the dead is not simple," writes Carson. "It is we who let them go, for we do not accompany them. It is we who hold them here—deny them their nothingness—by naming their names. Out of these two wrongs come the writing of epitaphs." Poetry as an epistolary form, a letter intended for a recipient, begins with the attempt to right the wrong inherent in the idea of choice, which divides the human population into two categories, the interesting and the less interesting, those who are fit for retelling, and those who are only fit for oblivion.

A cemetery doesn't make that choice: it attempts to remember everyone. That must be why they have been pushed out to the very edges of our towns, to the periphery of vision and consciousness, as if the volume of life lived by others, as well as the quantity of these others, is simply too much to contain in the mind. Our daily lives are surrounded by the displaced peoples of human history, the agitated sea of the dead, who have been crossed off the list and denied every right, except the right to an inscription and the occasional posy of flowers. There are rare times when they become more visible, and at these moments reality distorts, breaks down into its separate layers, and as my little boat makes its way across the black surface of the water, pale faces rise from the depths. I can make out each of them clearly, I regard them, I can put my hand out to them and pull them into the spotlight.

Yet how to choose and whom to choose? Between the clear necessity of saving everyone indiscriminately, and the desire, equally human and obvious, involuntary as a muscle spasm, to choose from the multitudes the *very one*, the only one, there is no space for a correct decision. This is a zone of infernal wrongness, run through with one's own and others' suffering, warped by a general helplessness, shot through with an electric arc, welding past and present until both are burnt out. Any text, any speech rooted in the impossibility of choice flares up and burns, without answering its own questions. Perhaps it is best not to choose? To reel off names one after another until the pages run out? Or limit oneself to what (who) is closest? Or to find something that answers to a single vaguely formulated principle and pull it loose, like a colored thread running through the fabric of time? Or maybe it is simpler just to close your eyes and fall backward, as if you knew familiar arms would be waiting to catch you?

*

The Great Hall of the State Archives, with its bright, full-length windows, was packed with readers, and the whisper of page-flicking echoed in the air. The information I needed was scattered throughout the various collections. I had inventory numbers and inscrutable references, but slowly the contour of a possible request took shape, like the spine of a large fish glimpsed in the murk of a lake. The unremarkable names of my relatives, all those Ginzburgs, Stepanovs, and Gurevichs, lengthened the process; I was showered with pellets of time-hardened information, like mothballs from an attic, none of which pertained to my family's history, but were in their own way peepholes into other lives, wriggling beyond my reach.

There was, for example, an official report written in 1891 concerning a Gurevich, who was not a relative, but who had reached a high rank despite his Jewishness, and had become the Governor of the Odessa Prison Fortress. In Russia's South that was briefly possible, especially in Odessa, with its magnificent disdain for the thin partition walls of nationality. Close to Odessa, in Kherson, his namesake, my great-grandfather, was building his first factory. But this unknown Gurevich was having troubles, and one hundred and twenty years later I sat reading, line by line, an account of his downfall.

The report was addressed to Mikhail Nikolaevich Galkin-Vrasky, the Head of the recently founded Central Prison Service:

In the past year, during a visit to Odessa, Your Excellency observed the local Prison Fortress and was much pleased with the order found there. He was moved to intercede on behalf of the prison's management, for their diligence and special efforts. As a result the Prison Governor Court Councillor Gurevich, among others, was, by Royal Assent, granted the Order of St. Anna, Second Class. Unfortunately a few recent occurrences in the prison have shown Gurevich's lack of competence for this position, which requires, above all, unceasing vigilance, an ability to grasp a situation rapidly, and to take the correct measures. These qualities are especially necessary in the Governor of Odessa's Prison Fortress, which houses a significant number of hard labor convicts. Without appropriate and careful supervision, these convicts have a deleterious influence on the other prisoners, who become their obedient servants and help them attack the prison systems. Gurevich does nothing to counteract this, and it now appears that he frequently places hardened criminals in the same cells as petty offenders and as a result the latter become quickly demoralized and find it hard to submit to the demands of prison discipline. If that weren't enough, observation of Gurevich has revealed that he often allows himself to grant indulgences and permits small lapses in discipline for the hardened criminals, simply to curry favor with them. A cowardly man, timid, weak of character, and underhand, Gurevich is not only unable to keep control himself, he also hinders the efforts of his assistants and the prison guards, and prevents them using the prerequisite energy to rein in the prisoners. As a result the smallest upset in prison life becomes a notable event, and any real trouble quickly escalates into serious rioting.

I do not consider it excessive to list the following examples from the life in Odessa Prison Fortress as evidence of the above claims:

1. Prisoner Chubchik, notorious for his brutal murders, burglaries and banditry, and sentenced to indefinite hard labor, boasted more than once that he could escape while incarcerated in Odessa Prison, and despite this he remained almost unsupervised. Chubchik and two of his comrades, also sentenced to hard labor, used the excuse of laundry washing to leave their cells several times a day and spend

time in the latrines, where they managed to saw off an iron bar from the window bars using a thin metal file they had on their person, then to tie together sheets and towels to make a rope, and Chubchik even managed to take off the manacles he wears at night and drop down through the hole in the window into the prison yard, where he made his way to the fence. Luckily he was noticed and apprehended in time.

2. […] There are regular roll calls of the prisoners at named hours and senior members of prison staff are often absent at these roll calls, so the prison guards conduct them. Against prison rules bedding rolls are often carried out of the cells, not just by the prisoners on cleaning duty, but by every prisoner, and last year a hard labor prisoner in transit named Kuznetsov carried out his bed with the others and took it to the tower corridor, where he hanged himself with his own belt without being noticed.

3. […] cards, dominoes, bones, tobacco, and various metal objects were found on the men, and this was noted in the prison records. When Prison Inspector Eversman commented on this Gurevich replied with utter naivety that "you can't do anything with these men, when the guards try to search them they bandy blows!"

In the round of the peephole I can see Chubchik serenely playing dominoes with the other prisoners, but I can't make out the fate of the timid Gurevich. Other reports from later years are attached to the case file and it is clear that things didn't change in the Odessa Fortress even under a new governor, who also went on to be sacked. The images proceeding before my eyes as I read these papers are suffused with a peculiar and terrible reality, far more real than my great-grandmother's yellowing spiderweb-lace dickey. Not intended for the eyes of others, nor for long life, the archived papers are illuminated on a first reading, as if they had been waiting for your attention—the unfortunate Kuznetsov at the moment of his death in the corridor, mentioned only once, but forever before my eyes, as if there were no one else to remember him and call him by his name—and I suppose there isn't.

*

In Leningrad in 1930 an intriguing book was published with the title *How We Write*. Well-known authors, from Gorky to Zoshchenko and Andrei Bely (and a certain number of representatives of Communist Party–approved literature, whose thinking was exactly what you might expect) contributed essays about their writing process, how the cogs of idea and execution meshed together. The writers also included the aristocrat Alexei Tolstoy, a man who had returned to the USSR from emigration to occupy the absurd but privileged position of the acceptable aristocrat, *The Red Count*. His prose is among the most remarkable in this altogether fascinating book.

Tolstoy writes with unambiguous rapture about the texts that became both templates and sources of inspiration for him: seventeenth-century confessions under torture, extracted with the aid of pincers, clubs, and brands, written up by anonymous functionaries, deacons, and servants, in the presence of the victim. Tolstoy admired their ability to get to the heart of the matter, "preserving the particular nature of the torture victim's speech," "exact and concise," so the reader can see and feel the language, its musculature. "... Here I saw the Russian language in all its purity, not spoiled by the dead form of Church Slavonic, nor translated under duress [...] into a fake literary language. Here was the language Russians have spoken for a thousand years, but no one ever wrote down."

Tolstoy's text is very talented, arranged (with the help of many tiny literary maneuvers) to give his interest the appearance of respectability, something along the lines of an ethically sprung mattress, allowing the author to recoil from the reader's enjoyment, and avoid falling into the black hole that yawns before the reader as soon as he even begins to concern himself with what is actually happening (and will continue to happen as long as the text lives) to the person whose Russian language you are tasting in your own mouth. Tolstoy's *taste* has an invisible subtext. The political trials, exiling, and sentencing hadn't yet reached their heights in 1930, but just beyond the world of his writing desk, too close for comfort, were the mass roundups by the OGPU, the Shakhty trial, and the recent execution of fellow writer Sillov. Pasternak wrote about the last of these in a letter to his father, saying "I will never be free of the effect of this act." The Russian "records of proceedings," as Tolstoy called them, with their sequence of confessions tortured out of the victims over the centuries, were clearly an invaluable source—but what end did they serve?

What Tolstoy doesn't say is that the attraction of these testimonies, what makes their syntax so lively and the choice of words so exact, lies in their forcedness. They are not the product of free will—they result from pain. The Russian language of the accused and the tortured is the child of a terrible conjoining, quite literally torn from you by another's hands. It's without internal compulsion, it isn't a drawing, but an imprint, the raw (as meat is raw) tracing of events. The words of the victim are without design, they have no interlocutor, and we can be sure that the victim never wanted them to be voiced. It is the most extreme example of what Rancière called the "monument"—a message that is entirely matched to its reason for being and has no desire for a long life, a listener, or even understanding. Speech is tied up, naked, in the last stages of pain and humiliation, on the brink of collapse.

Like everything that is not intended for the inadvertent gaze, the words of an arrested person under interrogation, the words of an informant and of a witness, have a particular direct quality. We see the *prohibited*, that is, we see what we shouldn't see under any circumstances, and it blows a shell hole in the mind, like Arlette Farge's "tear in the fabric of time." It happens outside the normal way of things, the usual framework, when the gaze settles on an object it wasn't expecting.

The language of document circulation and court proceeding is a revelation, but not because it lacks literature's glossy veneer, the desire to "say it well." It is perhaps more the case that this speech and its subject have no subjunctive mood. They have no past, they've already been torn from it; they have no future, you can't see any future for them. Archival documents exist entirely in the present, and they see nothing more than themselves, their own *process*, their own result. This is life buttoned up wrongly; these are the ones who will never exist again, dragged out of the darkness into the sudden random light, and then deposited back into darkness.

In Farge's book about the poetics and the practice of archival work the light is dimmed, as if we are discussing the negotiation of catacombs. She continually describes the darkness and the difficulty of movement; she talks about the density of archives as one might talk about a rock in which we discern different scattered metals. As I read I imagine how the underground life of data congeals into one collective mass over the centuries, similar in form to the body of the earth itself—the thickening mass of millions of lives, freed of their past significance, lying side by side, without a hope of being recognized or seen for themselves.

History, in contrast to the archive with its "overabundance of life," has a narrow throat: it only has need of one or two examples, two or three enlarged details. The archive returns us to the single unit, the one-off nature of every unfamiliar event. But strange things happen—the general begins to stratify, to decompose into the constituent particles of individual existences; parts of the whole rise like bread dough; the rules pretend to be exceptions. The darkness of the past becomes a stationary screen, made of nearly transparent film that hangs before the eyes continuously, changing the proportions and the relationships between objects. Paul Celan, in his "Conversation in the

Mountains," speaks of this when he writes: "No sooner does an image go in than it catches a web, and right away there's a thread spinning there, it spins itself around the image, a thread in the veil; spins around the image and spawns a child with it, half image and half veil."

*

It was a July day. The heat was terrible, the city was filled to the brim with sticky warmth, and I was sitting in a small room in the Kherson State Archive reading the documents of the revolutionary committee. On one of the six tables, which looked more like school desks, was spread the blueprint of a factory of agricultural implements. The factory was enormous, and the blueprint barely fit across the table, with its sheds and outhouses, some of which hung down over the sides—I couldn't inspect them properly. I had just finished reading the local sanitary health commission report, where I learned that in 1905 "the pink sago from Ioffe's Stores was discovered to be colored with aniline and one and a half pounds were destroyed" and "in all the shops serving beer a jug of water is used to wash glasses. It is suggested that a tap and supply of water is used instead." Alongside such hygiene measures were the orders issued to residents to clean and tidy their yards, privies, and dumps. Among the offenders the residents of Potemkin Street: Savuskan, Tikhonov, Spivak, Kotlyarsky, Falts-Fein, Gurevich. Whenever I stumble across my great-grandfather's surname, especially in such unforeseen and even unfavorable associations, I feel the prick of sudden proximity, as if a pointed instrument had pierced a hole in the text of the report, and my eye had peered through and wandered the trash-filled yards in search of food.

But there was nothing more for me in the yards and shops. The Kherson Revolutionary Committee file, swollen with typewritten and handwritten papers, orders, reports, and demands from that terrible civil war year of 1920 had nothing more for me either. There were no more Gurevichs on the lists of those who had made efforts on behalf of relatives, who had been left without housing or employment or who had asked for their requisitioned piano to be returned. I leafed through to the end, and then back to the beginning, I couldn't stop reading. "I am applying for the advance payment of sixty (60) thousand rubles for the creation and establishment of the Kherson Criminal Investigation Unit, which has been trusted to me." "I confirm that Citizen Pritzker is the father of Maria Pritzker, a *bor'bist* who escaped the persecution of the White Army. Citizen Pritzker was arrested and robbed, in place of his daughter. It is essential we provide support." "Urgent information required as to who was given order to search and requisition property of the former bishop of Troitsky Monastery. This information needed for an urgent report to the Area Military Committee."

It looked as if no one had held these documents in their hands for seventy years—there were no names on the list of readers, the list of robbed *bor'bists* (the name for members of the left-wing Ukrainian Socialist Revolutionary party) and former bishops was barely discernible against the stationary screen. Editorial staff at the closed local paper *Our Land* asked to be allowed to continue their work; Comrade Olshvang, dealer and repairer of typewriters, offered the Revolutionary Committee "typewriter ribbon, used, 800 rubles."

In some places what seemed like a choir was divided into individual voices, and the text expanded with the rising bubbles of literature. "The countless relocations of the Office of Management (four moves in a week) has left its nomadic imprint on staff and visitors to the Office. Everyone is rushing around, moving from office to office, and it's a waste of energy," wrote the Assistant Director of the Office, Comrade Fisak, who noted the importance of "girding our loins and finding a permanent location for the Office with enough (eleven) rooms." And a St. Petersburg theater company, trying to move to the nearby town of

Kakhovka, explained their desire to move because there were too many theaters in Kherson, the theater public had had enough, and the company had nothing to live on.

It was as if I was traveling over the turbid dark waters of a lake in a flimsy little vessel, leaning down to the lip of the water, and the waxen rounds of heads were rising up from the depths to meet me. They increased in number, floating up like *pelmeni* do, bobbing at the edges of the pan of boiling water. I could hardly make out their faces, I had to pull those closest to me with a heavy boat hook, twisting them round, peering at them without recognizing them. Their lips moved, but they made no sound, and none of *mine* were among them. Almost no space was left in the boat, the hull was piled high with sacks of some nameless ballast. There was no end to this sequence, as there often isn't in dreams, just the quiet unrelenting motion, the constant inescapable fact that you can never take anyone with you, or perhaps you can take this one, or this one. You can shine a torch into the blackness of a half-opened mouth and try to make out what he or she is saying, but to choose—is it possible to choose?

Perhaps there is no greater lie than the feeling that someone else's prolonged daylight depends on you, their chance to flounder for a while longer on the surface, to appear briefly once more in the light before yielding to the complete and total darkness. All the same, I sat at the little plywood desk in the archive and wrote down someone else's words, the captive tongue of our general history, as another might root around in the earth looking for last year's rotten potatoes, trying not to change a single word.

To the War Comisar of Kherson

You comrade comisar sacked the head baker that saboter and theef and snak in the grass and White scowndrel. Also a specolater and a lot of others things besides but still living in the army house by the fotress and using the kindnes of the peepol and spiting in their faces. I says to you wot write does he have that eneme of the peepol and the

sovietts. I a working man protest and ask you comrade comisar to
chayse him out to a place where he deservs to be

The same note is written in red pencil above this text, and typed in blue ink below: "By order of the War Committee: Forwarded for information."

PART TWO

And you see only those who stand in the light
While those in the darkness nobody can see.

— Bertolt Brecht

1. The Jewboy Hides From View

My great-grandmother's postcard correspondence (dozens of cards that had winged their way across the prewar borders of France, Germany, and Russia) has survived by some miracle, but its incompleteness intrigues me. The correspondents constantly refer to letters written and received and they are always promising to write more, in more detail. But none of these letters have survived, though doubtless they did once exist, and the explanation for this is almost too obvious: our continuing love affair with the visual. When, in my childhood, I leafed through the two stuffed postcard albums, I noted the skeleton embracing a marble-skinned girl, and the lights of Nice shining by night, but I never thought to turn the cards over, to where handwriting and postmarks jostled against each other—there was no need. The family knows everything about itself that needs to be known.

I began reading the cards a century after they'd been written, and, as I read, events lined up obediently. It became slowly clearer who was answering whom, and in what order. Apart from the main topics of conversation and the very few details in passing, one thing struck me: in all this correspondence there was not one reference to Jewishness, however superficial. And beyond this absence (of festivals, rituals, anything connected with the observance of tradition), lay another: Yiddish, the language of exile and humiliation, was never spoken.

There were flashes of Latin, the professional language of diagnosis and assessment, and tiny scatterings of French and German. But words from the language of home, words that could have served as little shared call signs or beacons of understanding, seemed to have been excluded from daily use, forbidden for conversation. Only once, when the discussion focused on family matters and summer examinations, my future great-grandfather suddenly reached for a phrase from this hidden register: «(«эс редцех а зай!»)» written just like that, with the double quote marks and the brackets, as if the phrase had been placed under the glass of a museum case. The meaning of the phrase "*es redt zich azoi*" is remarkable, literally "it is indeed so," but the actual sense is the exact opposite: "it is supposed to be so, but I don't believe a word of it." What did hiding it in its punctuation mean? It seems obvious now: it was a form of distancing from the people who spoke "like that," an attempt to define a common ground with a correspondent who lay outside the sphere of Jewishness, its general opinions, its intonations. That was how their childhood spoke: loudly, incorrectly, without brackets or quote marks. That—according to observers from outside—was how they were supposed to speak.

In the 1930s the poet Osip Mandelstam read a description of himself in an emigrant poet's memoirs. The author considered Mandelstam's face so *characteristic* that he must remind even the old shopkeepers of their grandsons, "some little Yankel or Osip." The same half-insulting, half-sentimental tone is heard in the late notes of another poet and critic, printed in a journal that had once published Mandelstam. These notes adroitly turn past events into little anecdotes, which is to say that they attempt to pass off the singular as typical. Among them is a description of the young Mandelstam visiting the journal's editorial office with his mother, Flora Osipovna Verblovskaya, whom the author insultingly calls "mamasha" in the memoirs. Her speech is carefully stylized and even accented (and this was probably even clearer for the contemporary reader, more sensitive to the "deviant" in speech): the hilariously plain dealing appeal of the foreigner, "You tell me what to do with him. We're in trade, the leather business. But all the boy can think about are his poems!"

You could say that what is being sent up here is class, and not race, but it is Jewish identity (not poverty, nor a comic combination of insistence and uncertainty, and hardly even his poetry) that defines how Mandelstam is seen from the very outset in the literary circles of the early twentieth century. His identity was considered exotic then, to such an extent that it overshadowed everything else. Most of the documents relating to his first literary steps openly mention his "roots," and the tone of these mentions is shocking today. Mandelstam first appears in Mikhail Kuzmin's diaries without a name: "Zinaida's little jewboy." The writer Zinaida Gippius's letter recommending the young poet to the influential Valery Bryusov had this to say: "A certain nervy young Jew, who was tied to his mother's apron strings only two years ago, has come on tremendously recently and even writes a good line from time to time." In the papers of the famous *Bashnya* literary salon in St. Petersburg, where attendance was meticulously recorded, especially of writers, Mandelstam is repeatedly called Mendelson. Because what difference does it really make?

On October 18, 1911, the poet Andrei Bely wrote to Alexander Blok: "You mustn't think I've become a *chernosotenets* [member of the ultranationalist and anti-Semitic 'Black Hundreds' movement]. But through both city noise and rural dreaminess I can hear louder and louder the future movement of race." Blok was also listening to the underground rumblings: he was preoccupied with the relationship between Aryanism and Jewry, and the difference between *yids* (dirty, illiterate, incomprehensible) and the more acceptable *Jews*. Ten days later he wrote in his diary: "Had tea at Kvisisan this evening, Pyast, me, and Mandelstam (the eternal)." The shadow of the half-mentioned Eternal Jew stretches forward into the 1920s, when an offended fellow poet wrote an article in which Mandelstam is mentioned as a Jew ("hungry wanderer, Ahasverus") and then given the epithet of "the Khlestakov of Russian poetry," after Gogol's comic impostor. As predictable as a menu: the mention of tribe and race as a starter, followed by the main course of personal slur. In Blok's own words, from notes in his diary, written many years later, when he had more time for Mandelstam's poetry: "You gradually get used to him, the jewboy hides from view and you can see the artist."

In order to get noticed, the "jewboy," whoever he was, had to hide himself away: purge and recast himself, improve himself and destroy all traces of family, race, or tribe, or adherence to place. In 1904 Thomas Mann wrote approvingly about the family of his future wife: "One has no thought of Jewishness; in regard to these people, one senses only culture."

It was understood that belonging wholeheartedly to the world of culture meant rejecting your Jewishness. To insist on Jewishness seemed almost old-fashioned, "as if nations still existed after the fall of the Roman Empire, and it was possible to build a culture on the raw idea of nation" wrote Boris Pasternak. It's worth noting that in all the general excitement about national heritage and folk arts and crafts, the flourishing of the Viennese movement in art and the Abramtsevo artists' colony, the patterns and the firebirds, there is only one national identity left out of the party. At the turn of the century, enlightened, educated, secular European Jews felt no kinship with their relatives in the *galut*, with their accents, their chickens, their cozy inseparableness— and the cumbersome load of their religion. No lyric memoirs— for those who had the opportunity or the inclination to assimilate, everything that reminded them of the musk of Judaism was perceived as ugly atavism, the fish's tail dragging the lucky survivor ashore. This lasted for decades: in Isaiah Berlin's *Personal Impressions*, he describes a meeting with Pasternak in 1945: "He was unwilling to discuss the subject—he was not embarrassed by it, but he disliked it: he wished the Jews to assimilate, to disappear as a people. [...] If I mentioned Jews or Palestine, this, I observed, caused him visible distress."

The children of the turn of the century had three choices before them, and they all looked much the same. Revolution, assimilation and Zionism: there they were, like three allegorical figures spaced apart on the colonnade of a deserted building. Herzl's dream of a Jewish state, conceived only a short while before, had not yet taken full shape. Yiddish or Hebrew? The choice of language was the subject of many heated discussions, and even back then Hebrew was the preferred choice: the language of denial of the current "self" (victim, exile, refugee) in favor of the ancient and original "self." Assimilation, the voluntary immersion into the powerful river of another culture, happened gradually and naturally with a certain level of education and wealth. The archaic religiosity of parents faded before the eyes, and revolution (with its obligatory equality and brotherhood) was even more tempting because it knocked the barriers of nationality and social standing off the table with one sweep of the hand. On October 17, 1905, my great-grandmother joined street protests, arm-in-arm with half acquaintances and strangers, each of whom felt like a family member—and it felt natural because they had come together to build a new and better world, based on the stable foundations of reason and justice. This new sense of community had something in common with traveling: you suddenly found yourself a thousand miles from everything you knew and, as if floating on air, you felt yourself to be better than before, brighter, more beautiful, capable of greater depths of both good and evil. The leaflets she handed out in the town's barracks talked of a reality very far from her own experiences in childhood and early womanhood, and so it was even more important to communicate their message to others. It was, even to her ears, a new message—those concepts had not existed in the language of her household.

The other thing I noticed while reading the postcards, which danced back and forth between 1907 and 1908, was the warm, unquestioning sympathy the correspondence radiated. Alongside this warmth was the very thing an external world noted and attributed to *us*: the bonds of family, the inseparable clan, the continual care for every cell of the living organism, which drew into itself family, friends, relatives, acquaintances, the acquaintances of acquaintances. This was how Jews were represented in jokes and on cheap broadsheets—they knew their kind, they helped their own, they supported each other. There were a lot of them, and they kept to themselves. It's hardly surprising when you realize the level of loneliness they felt, the wasteland surrounding them—these people who had taken a tentative step away from tradition were outsiders, with nothing and no one, apart from themselves.

Where's Katya? Fanya is in Naples; I haven't got Vera's address, but Fanya's is below. Ida Shlyummer was asking after you. I'm sending Fanya's address again. Did you see your family? They wanted to send a telegram. If you go to Lausanne please give my best wishes to the Vigdorchik sisters.

What looks from outside like a comic scrabbling (soon to be captured in countless caricatures of Jews, like cockroaches, skittering away into nooks and crannies—fetch the insect powder!) is in fact the safety net of recognition and familiarity under the high wire. Even this becomes tiresome—not just for those looking on, but for the Jews themselves. The logic of assimilation, with its belief in progress and its basis in the sentiment that "not everyone will be taken into the future," required of people that they admit (in their heart of hearts) that not all Jews are alike. So the enlightened residents of Vienna suffered terribly at the inpouring of their *Eastern* kin, with their mispronunciations, their inability to acclimatize to city life; so the secular inhabitants of Odessa took against the new Rabbi, brought from Lithuania, with his exalted ways and silly strictures.

*

Proust's narrator observes with curiosity the eccentricities of his friend Bloch, a caricature of a Jew, armed with a host of carefully chosen mannerisms (like that other stereotypical character, the gay Baron de Charlus). One of his traits is a declarative anti-Semitism, loud and affected diatribes against the excessive numbers of Jews, quite literally everywhere, with their opinions and their noses!

One day when we were sitting on the sands, Saint-Loup and I, we heard issuing from a canvas tent against which we were leaning a torrent of imprecation against the swarm of Israelites that infested Balbec. "You can't go a yard without meeting them," said the voice. "I am not in principle irremediably hostile to the Jewish nation, but here there is a plethora of them. You hear nothing but, 'I thay, Apraham, I've chust theen Chacop.' You would think you were in the Rue d'Abou-kir." The man who thus inveighed against Israel emerged at last from the tent; we raised our eyes to behold this anti-Semite. It was my old friend Bloch.

This episode has a tragicomic Russian counterpart—a quote from a letter by Boris Pasternak, written in 1926, "Everywhere you look, a mass of yids, and—this has to be heard—it's almost as if they deliberately want to make themselves into caricatures, or they're writing their own denunciations: they haven't even a shadow of aesthetic feeling."

Unlike Proust himself, the narrator is not burdened by his Jewish or homosexual identity. He was created by the author in the role of an observer, a piece of clear glass, whose gaze would be unaffected by the shameful diseases of the century, one of which Proust considered to be assimilated Jewishness, not knowing himself what was harder to forgive: being different, or wishing to be like everyone else. In his opinion this wish was doomed to failure. In a later episode with Bloch there is an impromptu parade of "the unwelcome" across the Balbec beach, whose main failings are the peculiarities of their breed, which can't be drowned out, or polished out of them:

Always together, with no blend of any other element, when the cousins and uncles of Bloch or their coreligionists male or female repaired to the Casino, the ladies to dance, the gentlemen branching off toward the baccarat tables, they formed a solid troop, homogeneous within itself, and utterly dissimilar to the people who watched them go past and found them there again every year without ever exchanging a word or a sign with them, whether these were on the Cambremers' list, or the presiding magistrate's little group, professional or "business" people, or even simple corn dealers from Paris, whose daughters, handsome, proud, derisive and French as the statues at Rheims, would not care to mix with that horde of ill-bred tomboys, who carried their zeal for "seaside fashions" so far as to be always apparently on their way home from shrimping or out to dance the tango. As for the men, despite the brilliance of their dinner jackets and patent-leather shoes, the exaggeration of their type made one think of what people call the "intelligent research" of painters who, having to illustrate the Gospels or the Arabian Nights, consider the country in which the scenes are laid, and give to Saint Peter or to Ali-Baba the identical features of the heaviest "punter" at the Balbec tables.

It isn't altogether clear on first reading who would not care to mix with whom: the "solid troop" or those who watch them pass. Of course, people of the Orient, as E.T.A. Hofmann described them a century before, could certainly be ill-educated and ridiculous: this is often the preserve of those who have had to arm themselves against constant suffering and who mistrust sudden good fortune. Jewish children of the Belle Époque were the first or second generation to have a secular education; they were the product of a series of decisions, each of which drew them further out from under the protecting roof of tradition. Hundreds of new concepts, of shifts of behavior and changes to everyday ritual, entered their lives together with education, and all these needed to be invented from scratch, based on this novel object, *culture,* to which they now had a right. It is somewhat comparable to the early post-Soviet experience as I remember it twenty years later, now life has more or less straightened itself out: the new words have found homes, and what was once clumsy mimicry seems to have become the reality.

In the 1900s the new language, spoken with an unaccustomed awkwardness, began on the beaches, in artistic salons, in rooms misted with cigarette smoke where young medical students gathered. The first attempts to talk about the world as if it now also belonged to them had a parodic quality. They were overly demonstrative, the outsider's uneasy connoisseurship, trying to create the impression that "we Jews" have occupied such armchairs forever, that there is not a restaurant, a wagon-lit, a lift that could surprise us, that we have the right to admire ourselves in the plate glass mirrors of civilization. This is where Mandelstam's famous "yearning for world culture" originates—it is nothing to do with the literary movement Acmeism, a short-lived Russian phenomenon. Mandelstam clutched to the memory of world culture as he did to the life buoy of friendship, but his longing for conversation as equals was more ancient and more pained.

In Proust's novel the young writer Bloch describes going to Venice to "sip iced drinks with the pretty ladies," and he says of the resort hotel: "As I cannot endure to be kept waiting among all the false splendor of these great caravansaries, and the Hungarian band would make me ill, you must tell the 'lighft-boy' to make them shut up, and to let you know at once." In a letter written in 1909, eighteen-year-old Mandelstam also makes colossal efforts to write in keeping with the European tone of his addressee, the poet Vyacheslav Ivanov:

I have strange taste: I love flashes of electricity over the surface of Lake Geneva, respectful footmen, the silent flights of lifts, the marble entrance halls to hotels, and English girls playing Mozart to one or two listeners in a dimly lit salon. I love bourgeois, European comfort and I have a sentimental attachment to it, as well as a physical one. Perhaps my weak health is to blame for this? I never ask myself if it's a good thing.

This is a touching and convincing imitation of what will later be the theme of Nabokov's opening chapters in *Speak, Memory*: the comforting presence (and, later, the utter absence) of Swiss hotels, English collapsible tubs, and gleaming Pullman cars. Yet something almost imperceptible in the intonation gives the impression of a tiny gap between the author and his bourgeois comfort. Mandelstam's family fell into rapid decline and this was his last visit abroad, and to Europe. He would remind himself of it all his life, up until the point when his memory is compressed into his late, great poems in the 1930s.

In the year after the Revolution, in the St. Petersburg Writers' House an evening of new poetry was announced. Somewhere in the Writers' House there was a bust of the poet Nadson, who had died young. He had been incredibly famous at the end of the nineteenth century and was now all but forgotten, twenty years later. His friend, the elderly Maria Dmitrievna Vatson, said of the bust to Anna Akhmatova, "I want to get him out of there, because he might get hurt otherwise."

I am so scared of hurting these people, even more so because I feel it in myself, this sense of hurt, a blood link and a proximity with each of them, all those who hid their Jewishness like an embarrassing defect, or paraded it like a cockade in full view of everyone. Very soon even that choice became a fictitious one: whatever a Jew did—with his seed, his immortal soul, his corrupting flesh—he could not alter the contract drawn up with the external world, as the twentieth century demonstrated. Even the right to weakness (to treason and denial) would be withdrawn with the other rights, as even atheists and converts were drawn into the extermination camps.

On April 20, 1933, Thomas Mann wrote in his diary: "I could

have a certain amount of understanding for the rebellion against the Jewish element ..." He was writing about the recently introduced law forbidding Jews to work for the Civil Service, the first of dozens of carefully planned restrictions intended to set into motion the engine of regression in the *Jewish element*, their thorough and meticulous distancing from civilization, and its capacity to make life bearable. Step by step their existence was reduced to the bare biological minimum. Among all the various prohibitions (visiting swimming pools, public parks, stations, concert halls, traveling around Germany, buying newspapers, meat, milk, tobacco, owning woolen goods or pets) there was one stipulation: after August 1938 every Jew whose name did not unambiguously indicate Jewish heritage had to add "Israel" or "Sarra" to his or her name: Maria Sarra Stepanova, for example.

At the beginning of the 1950s my twelve-year-old mother walked to her old Moscow school one morning, with its wide parade staircase, the polished banister rails rising in caressing curves. From above, on the top landing, Vitya, my mother's neighbor, hung over the rails and shouted down: "Gureeevich! What's your grandmother's name?" Both my mother and Vitya knew full well that grandmother was called Sarra Abramovna— just Sarra alone was putting the knife in, but Sarra Abramovna ... It was a doubled roar, like two rampant lions, shamelessly unambiguous, SARRAABRAMOVNA! It stood out like a sore thumb: living with a name like that was really just hysterically silly.

Not-A-Chapter
Sarra Ginzburg, 1905–1915

1.

Aleksandr to Sarra Ginzburg in Pochinky, December 24, 1905

Next to grandmother on the photograph we used to call "Babushka on the Barricades" there is a person whose face will appear from time to time in the archive. His full name isn't ever given in the correspondence. Grandmother's girlfriends mockingly called him *Sancho Pancho*, in reference to Don Quixote's companion with his undying devotion.

This postcard has a stormy seascape on the front by the painter Aivazovsky, a picture that graced the walls of Russian living rooms and community halls for decades: the soapy-green underside of the sea, a huge wave cresting over the shattered remains of a mast to which the drowning seafarers are clutching. A boat is sinking in the distance. Above the picture someone has added by hand: *Greetings from Nizhny!*

Sara,

You wrote and told us to send word of how things are and what we are up to. I think it would be better if you came to see us as soon as possible. You'd see what we are up to for yourself and you could also join in the heated political discussions we are having here. Haven't you had enough of being fattened up by your family? I'm slightly annoyed that my throat doesn't hurt any more, I'd like someone to look after me again.

Aleksandr

What were they arguing about with the Socialist Revolutionaries that December? And who was arguing? Judging by Great-Grandmother's circle of acquaintances, Sancho, like her other friends, was close to the Bolsheviks, and it seems likely they were discussing the necessity of revolutionary terrorism. Just before that, after the October Manifesto in 1905, the Socialist Revolutionary Party announced its own Combat Organization. The Bolsheviks insisted that an increase in terrorism and expropriation was essential; the SRs felt differently. But the Bolsheviks pressed ahead without them and between Autumn 1905 and Autumn 1906, 3611 civil servants were assassinated.

Sarra used to go home from school for the holidays to Pochinky, to her father and sisters "to be fattened up." She was a student in Nizhny Novgorod, at the best gymnasium in the town, and her friends also studied there. This particular new friend made the classic mistake in writing her name: Sara, instead of Sarra. But it seems she did travel to see him and stood next to him on the Barricades, with her black eye and her absurd bonnet in disarray on the side of her head. The day Aleksandr sent her this postcard there was rioting at the Sormovsky Factory and the snowy streets were blocked with whatever came to hand—wooden boxes, office cabinets. The Governor of Nizhny had already sent an urgent message to the capital: "Dangerous situation in the town. There could be trouble tomorrow. We have no troops." On December 29, the date on the Pochinky postmark, the protesters were already shooting from cannons.

2.

Platon to Sarra Ginzburg (in prison), February 9, 1907

A barefoot harpist with burning eyes and a mane of black hair sits on a deserted and melancholy shoreline. A text reads: *N. Zikhel, Solace in Music.*

Hallo, Comrade Sarra! I'm no musician and a very poor singer, but music and poetry have always brought me great consolation and delight. I know from "Little Sarra" that you sing and love poetry so I'm sending this postcard to you in your fortress. I like the execution of the picture and I like its subject. This embodiment of beauty speaks to the bruised soul, and perhaps it will find a place in yours. I do believe, despite everything, that you won't be held for long, and although we hardly live in a time of fairy tales, there is still hope! The leftists and the opposition have sustained a victory in the Duma. This speaks of a victory over those dark forces and perhaps we won't have to wait long for the "dawn of enchanting happiness."

> *Comrade, have faith—dawn will break*
> *A dawn of enchanting joy,"*
> *Russia will shake itself awake*
> *And on the broken pieces of tyranny*
> *Your names will be shaped!"*
>
> *Pushkin**

Tyranny = suffering in the name of Russia's new dawn. The future is bright, comrade!
> *Be of joyful faith, and bear your part bravely.*
> *I shake your hand. Platon.*

Two years had passed. Sarra Ginzburg had been arrested for handing out illegal literature and she was in prison in the Peter and Paul Fortress in St. Petersburg. "Little Sarra" must be

---

* From "To Chaadaev" by Aleksandr Pushkin, written in 1818 and addressed to Pushkin's friend Pyotr Yakovlevich Chaadaev—one of the poems that contributed to Pushkin's disgrace and exile. In this version the writer has replaced "a star" with the revolutionary commonplace of "dawn" in the first line of the excerpt, and "our names" with "your names" in the last line.

Great-Grandmother's lifelong close friend, Sarra Sverdlova, who was also the sister of the ruthless Communist Yakov Sverdlov.

Platon was the party nickname for a rather brilliant man, Ivan Adolfovich Teodorovich, the son and grandson of Polish political rebels, a professional revolutionary, Lenin's friend and advisor, and a member of the Central Committee of the Russian Social Democratic Labor Party. Ten years after this he became the first Soviet People's Commissar for Manufacturing, and then almost immediately left the Soviet People's Commissariat as a protest against War Communism. Thirty years later, on September 20, 1937, he was shot, after being sentenced to death by the Military Collegium of the Supreme Court.

The Second State Duma had just been elected, the first had lasted a mere seventy-two days. The second unhappy attempt at Russian parliament lasted for thirty days longer before being disbanded. There genuinely were a lot of leftists in the parliament, making up more than a third. It's a strange experience to read the lists of deputies from that Second Duma: they include a huge number of peasants (169), 35 laborers, and only 6 manufacturers, 20 priests, 38 teachers, and even a single poet, Eduard Treimanis-Zvargul, who lived in Riga and wrote in Latvian. Comrade Platon had also put himself up for election, but hadn't been elected.

3.
Aleksandr to Sarra Ginzburg, August 12, 1907. Portrait of a Woman.

Dearest Sara, isn't she a beauty! Just like you! When I look at such a beautiful face I realize what a powerful force women are, especially in our male lives. Just for her, just for one of her smiles, we would go into any battle, we'd undergo torture and death. She is the Tsaritsa, the ruler of life and everything in it; the best and most wonderful things in life belong to women, because women are the most wonderful and beautiful of all nature's creations! What utter joy to be the man who

makes her wonderful eyes light up with the fire of passion, or glitter
with mad merriment and intoxicating beauty … Even the Gods would
envy that man. I want to be that man, I want that so desperately …
  Aleksandr

4.
Aleksandr to Sarra Ginzburg, October 17, 1907
  The postcard has the caption *Don't go!* and shows a woman
seeing off a revolutionary in an astrakhan cap. He has a mustache
and carries a revolver. In the background, snowy roofs and a little
onion dome. Above the image someone has added by hand: *you*
would have told me to go!

Sarra, this morning I sent you a letter, but I forgot that today is Octo-
ber 17 and so I didn't mention it. You know that this day will always
be dear to me and not just because it's a national celebration, but
because on this day two years ago we went to our first street protest,
and we took each other's hands. We hardly knew each other back
then, and how could I have known that the black-eyed girl walking
beside me, whose hand I held so tightly, would become so dear to me
and would even agree to marry me? October 17 made us comrades
and brought us together. How I love this day!
  Your Aleksandr
  Say hallo to Katya

October 17, 1905, was the day the October Manifesto was published, in which the Tsar promised the people of Russia civil
liberties and the creation of a State Duma.

5.
Mikhail Fridman to Sarra Ginzburg, December 26, 1909
  A girl with large yearning eyes and hair loose over her shoulders, sitting by a window, her hands placed uselessly on her
knees. Caption: *Richon. If only I were a bird!*

My dear Sarra! I didn't send you my greetings for the New Year. I didn't know where you would be, as I heard you'd left Montpellier. But then I found out that you were only away for a short while, so in the hope you will receive this I send you all the very best for the New Year. I hope you will never lose your faith in the future, and that all your endeavors will be crowned with success and you will be able to build a life for yourself that meets your ideals as far as possible.

I also hope we will see each other again.

Your loving Mikhail

6.

Dmitrii Khadji-Genchev to Sarra Ginzburg, Montpellier, December 29, 1909

The letter is entirely preoccupied with arrangements, the tiny cramped handwriting fills a page from top to bottom, the shifts from French to a deformed Russian look like mistakes born of haste and agitation. Two days until the New Year. Sarra is just about to return to Montpellier.

Sarrka, I right in hast, reply to you card which I just receive. I wrote day before yestday that it is better you leave Lausanne in morning and arrive here in bonne heure. Best variant is you travel at 5:45 early morning. In Lyon the train arrives at 10:13, 10:45 dep, Tarascone apresmidi in Montpellier at 7 in the evening. Another good train, but arrive late in Montpellier is at 9:17, Lyon will be at 4:05 apresmidi, depart Lyon at 5:53 arrive Tarascone at 10:23 and Montpellier 12:23 in nigt. Third variant but don't know if there is 3 Class, is best at 12:10 at noon, arrive Lyon 4:34 apresmidi, leave Lyon at 5:53 and arrive Montpellier as last a minuit. Check this one, says it is best and with 3 Class. Please take this if you cannot take train at early morning. Then look, do as the plan says, and make sure you little head is out of window at all station and you look for me also. Otherwise we may risk not seeing each other. But we will definitely see each other on Montp station if not before. We'll see how it is. I have decided I come

to Tarascone. *So you look for me there. If I don't see you Tarascone I go to Nime, and if not there I come back to Montpellier and wait all night but I will find you. Write Ida about envelopes. Buy me I need for visite de [Nrzb], don't depart Lausanne this apresmidi or you have all night in train.*
    Warmest greetings, your MG

7.
Aleksandr to Sarra Ginzburg, January 4, 1910
    A German postcard with a Berlin postmark. Two peasant lovers are kissing in the rye, he has a flaxen mustache, she wears a brightly colored skirt. To the side a little ditty concerning *Liebesgedanken.*

"Die Liebe bleibt immer gleich" … whether you are in Paris or Berlin. I've been wandering around looking at Berlin for two days now. It's an interesting place. If I didn't already have a ticket to St. Petersburg I'd have stayed around and tried to find some work. And then I'd have found a pretty little face like the one pressed to the young plowboy's on this card, and found some respite from the torment of the black eyes of a Hebrewess.
    Greetings, Aleksandr

8.
Dmitrii Khadji-Genchev to Sarra Ginzburg, July 27, 1912 (translated from French)

Dearest Sarra, I just received your card from Sofia. I passed my state exam a while ago. It wasn't easy, but I passed. You know me, things work out for me from time to time.
    I'm spending another two or three days here and then I'll go to another town to take up a post as a military doctor in an army hospital. The worst part will be the lack of money, the work itself, the

professional side won't be hard. I had my first patient yesterday. They only paid two francs. I spent it all the same day. Things aren't easy for me at the moment and all because I've no money. I haven't got married and I'll probably never get married. No one loves me, no one wants to marry me. Sarra, why don't you write more about your past life and your future to me—I hardly know anything about you.

On the other side:

Sarra, dearest, come and live at the dacha in Dryanovo with me. It's so nice here, so good, so free—no one around, just chickens and pigs. I shake your hand. Goodbye.

9.
Dmitrii Khadji-Genchev to Sarra Ginzburg, Tyrnovo, October 29, 1912

Greetings from the ancient capital of Bulgaria. Tomorrow I'll be checked over and approuvé as a soldier by the conscription service. I'll be back in Dryanovo tomorrow night and I'll write more. My brother came to stay three days ago (back from war). He had an injury in his right arm (1/3 moyen du bras, Humerus intact). Salut [...]

War on European soil began two years before the outbreak of the First World War. The First Balkan War was already underway in 1912.

10.
Sarra Ginzburg to Mikhail Fridman, November 1913

Paris, 15 novembre
   Misha, you are quite the limit, your Sarra goes away, and you

vanish from the face of the earth. I know one shouldn't ask lawyers questions, but even so! I was taken to a tavern yesterday (I complained that I wasn't getting to see much), so today I want to sleep and my head is ringing. What news have you got? How is work, what's the mood like after the "Beilis" affair? Write and let me know or I won't write to you either.

A jury had just vindicated Menachem Beilis, a Jewish man accused of the ritual murder of a twelve-year-old boy from Kiev; the notorious trial was often compared to the Dreyfus affair.

11.
Sarra Ginzburg to Mikhail Fridman, Paris, February 18, 1914

You're right to say that I haven't been writing. I've been conscious of it, but fleetingly, and just now when I read your postcard I realized how little I've been in touch. You are partly to blame. Although, no, I don't really think that. It's just I've had a lot to deal with, and it would have been hard if not impossible to tell you about it. You are too far away, things are too different there for me to be able to make it as simple and clear for you as it is for me here. But I was so much in its grip that everything else seemed remote and I was quite alone. Yes, I understand your predicament, Misha, I really do. So much effort for such little money. As for me ... I've got such a long time to go! For a start my time here has been extended and I won't finish before Easter, and once in Paris you can't ever tell when exactly you will finish. God alone knows. I haven't managed to have a photo done, in answer to your question. But then you also promised, so send yours. All the best, Misha. Send more news about yourself. S
    P.S. I found these two postcards of old women among my papers, I've had them for two weeks without sending them. + aren't they crazily old?

12.

Sarra Ginzburg to Mikhail Fridman, March 29, 1914

Misha, you should see the Spring we've been having!

It was an incredible morning today, I couldn't tear myself away from the streets, the sunlight was pouring down, nor from the bright, laughing springtime faces I passed. I want to be one of those smiling faces, I want to leave the town and go somewhere where there are meadows, the first spring flowers, gather a huge pile of them and breathe in that uncomplicated and unbelievably fresh scent of meadow—don't you? I feel very cheerful today, I have heaps of energy and I'll try to use it well. I'm just starting my studies.

13.

Sarra Ginzburg to Mikhail Fridman, May 8, 1914

Just back from my exam. I'm quite shattered. Incredible how my nerves are on edge and no physical effort can hold them in check. The nervous reaction dominates everything. Everything went well, but I have another exam tomorrow—on birth and midwifery. If it goes well I can rest a while.

Write and tell me your news.

Sarra

14.

Sarra Ginzburg to Mikhail Fridman, October 1914

This postcard is sent from within Russia, on the front a view of the Anichkov Bridge. The First World War began in July, three months earlier.

I am incensed by your careless indifference to me. Not a word in reply to my letters. S

15.

Mikhail Fridman to Sarra Ginzburg in Petrograd, October 1914

A drawing by Leonid Pasternak: an injured sailor leans against a wall, red paint on his face to make it look flushed. A handwritten note reads: *This is the last sketch from contemporary life by Leonid Pasternak. Isn't it true to life? Misha*

Sarra, I only received your letter and your request to go into the university the day before I was due to travel to Voronezh, so I wasn't able to do as you asked. But I think it's pointless to make inquiries, it will be the same in Saratov as it is everywhere else. The declaration of war with Turkey is hardly going to change the situation. They'll need doctors, and there are bound to be additional exams. But even if there are more exams, don't let it upset you. When you finished in Paris you thought you would have to take an exam, so there's no need to despair now. All the best, Misha

16.

Sarra Ginzburg to Mikhail Fridman, November 1914

2 o'clock at night

I'm alone now. I saw Olya and Sanka off a short while ago. I turned down my bed a truly luxurious one by Russian standards (the landlady spent some time abroad and knows what the bedlinen is like there, so she made up a bed for me in the same way). I was just about to go to bed, and I suddenly looked around my room and saw how cozy it all was. The white flowers that Polya brought are in the corner, it's clean everywhere, and pretty, an electric lamp casts a soft glow, and I started to feel sad that you left without coming here. I wanted to send my greetings at least, as I can't do anything else. Olya brought the postcard, my sadness is about the view, and not about you. Night night. Write soon.

17.
Sarra Ginzburg to Mikhail Fridman, December 4, 1914

The days last forever, and the nights even longer. How long will I have to wait for a letter from you. Can you feel my need, enough to answer me, enough to write to me right now? I'm cheerful though, so don't be sad, Misha. S

18.
Mikhail Fridman to Sarra Ginzburg, April 10, 1915

I haven't written for a while, Sarra. It's all been a bit much recently. I'm sick of the endless grind. I would love to rest from all the worry and bother and live without a care in the world. But it hardly looks likely. I've been traveling every day to Tambov and Razskazovo— they had some unfortunate regulation issues there and it put me in a difficult position. Not that I really give a damn. I'll go one more time and put an end to the whole business. Write to me in Saratov. My regards to your friends. Misha.

*

Sarra and Mikhail's *ketubah*, their prenuptial agreement, written in Hebrew, was signed a year later in April 1916. My grandmother Olga (Lyolya) Fridman was born a few weeks later.

2. Selfies and their Consequences

Moving through the rooms of a gallery from portrait to portrait it becomes abundantly clear, and you'd think obvious, that the various ways of preserving the "I"—canvas and oils, pastels and paper and all the rest—come down to the single basic formula $x=y$. At a specific moment in a person's continuing presence, that person hands over the right of posthumous representation to the portrait. The job of the portrait is to draw together and condense everything that makes you what you are now and will become, your past and future, and to sort all this into a fixed shape that is no longer subject to the laws of time. This process bears a direct relation to the old adage "the best words in the best order," only the conditions are more stringent, and the order lays claim to being the single, decisive summing up. In a sense every portrait wants to be a Fayum Mummy portrait, to be shown like a passport as you cross the border between living and dead; when the work is at an end, you come to an end yourself. For this reason no person needs more than one portrait, one is enough, all the other portraits of Philip IV of Spain are like zeros lined up after a four, multiplying the distinctness of his features, tallying them up.

Photography casts even this principle into doubt, to the extent that it is now possible to believe that the identity of a portrait's subject can and should be made up of a dozen different jigsaw pieces, selected from a range of various and sometimes not even acquainted versions of the "I." A selfie (the most extreme manifestation of the belief in mutability) is born of the need to fix the image in place, and the conviction that the face of today and the face of tomorrow are infinitely different. Developing this principle leads us down the way of cinematography, a road composed of a thousand momentary prints. This might be a good point to remind ourselves of Aristotle's definition of memory as the imprint of a seal. He goes on to talk about states of mind that are incompatible with memory, like passion, age, youth, describing them as a flood of raw unorganized movement: "Both the very old and the very young are defective in memory. They are in a state of flux." A precise impression is not possible, instead the shape of a movement is left on the surface of the mind, like a half-erased tire mark on a road.

A portrait of movement—this is exactly how we see ourselves now, presenting our faces daily to the camera, or changing our social media avatar. Social media play this game with enthusiasm, constantly inventing new ways to arrange images: "my face five years ago," "my photos with this or that friend," "last year in pictures," presented so they appear to be the turning pages of a book, or grandly as "a film." It's not even that Facebook helpfully remembers (chooses what to remember and what to forget) for me and on my behalf that I find so fascinating—it's that the never-ending nature of the flow seems to oblige me to feed it with new photographs. Your own face needs constant updating or you'll forget how it used to look.

Each new face casts off and cancels the ones before. It reminds me of the way a space rocket releases each stage, one after the other, in order to pick up speed. Elena Shvarts describes in a poem a room in which all her past, worn-out, and cast-off selves are "crowds /Of the dwindling, clothed, unclothed / Of the raging, and joyful, and sorrowing," among whom the soul runs like the flame along a safety fuse. Charlotte Salomon draws her subjects in much the same way. Here's a woman leaving her home on her way to end her life. Eighteen little figures repeating across the page in different phases of movement, a little like a corridor with *intention* moving down it. Each following figure confirms the decision of the one before, each new figure moves a step closer to the hole in the ice.

*

Rembrandt's younger contemporaries, Von Sandrart, Houbraken, Baldinucci, all wrote studies of his life. These were not motivated by a love of his pictures, but were rather an attempt to depict a curious instance, an example of "how not to go about it." The list of his crimes was long, but the complaints against him were all strangely similar—along with his "ugly plebeian face" and the crooked letters of his signature, he was accused of what must surely follow from these basic flaws: a crooked sense of taste. A predilection for the creased, the wrinkled, and the dog-eared, the bedsore, the mark of a tightened belt on the skin, for anything that bore on it the imprint of life.

For his first biographers, Rembrandt's unwillingness or inability to derive contentment from the best, the select, the exemplary—to know how "to distinguish and to choose from life the most beautiful of the beautiful" was a serious failing. It had to be explained in some way, best of all by his background, his education, and his resulting pigheadedness. The biographers (including Von Sandrart, who knew Rembrandt in life) also insist on his desire to model from nature, and as any event back then needed a precedent, they nod to Caravaggio, who was at the time the archsinner in this worship of nature.

I don't know that it's worth taking this too seriously: you don't need much of a pretext if you're bent on studying with nature, at her school of lifelong disintegration. However, in the Kunsthistorisches Museum in Vienna there's a work by Caravaggio that sends me straight back to Rembrandt, although the connection between them is a half rhyme at best. This work is "David with the Head of Goliath": the fiery brightness of what stands out from the surrounding gloom only makes the arc of the composition more visible. The adolescent boy with his childishly plump cheeks balances the weight of the huge head of his vanquished foe. The color is already draining from the head, the jaw hangs slack, a tooth gleams in the light, and the eyes have neither light nor expression. The boy's yellow trousers and white linen shirt are the same shades of color as the clothes in the famous 1658 self-portrait by Rembrandt, the cane in Rembrandt's left hand is tipped with the same dull metal as the sword David rests across his shoulders. A yellow jerkin encloses Rembrandt's chest like a cuirass and the folds of his shirt are escaping from under it, his heavy paunch is girdled with red, and the same red in the Caravaggio picture colors the strands of flesh that dangle from the dead man's neck.

If you stare at David and his trophy for long enough, at the balance between the killer and the killed, the tender and the stiffening, the dimmed and the illuminated, between what you might simply call the rotting and the blooming, you discover that there is no difference between victor and vanquished. You might think that the whole and calculated construct of the painting is about this, but it is suddenly brought dramatically into focus when you realize that the living boy and the dead giant have the same face, that they are different stages of the same process, and a graphic example of all those "before and after" comparisons we are so used to seeing. It is thought that Goliath's face is that of Caravaggio himself, and it becomes even more fascinating when you look across at the child and it occurs to you that it is in fact a double self-portrait.

At this moment the triangle (the two protagonists and you, the viewer) bends, breaks apart, becoming open-ended like a horseshoe: all the ages and changes in this face as it travels from beginning to end are compressed, hammered into its invisible curve. What I see is the literal expression of the classic perspective of "souls looking down at the body they have left behind." The author (who offers for our view not a body, but bodies, the estranged and cooling *corpus* of a whole lived life) is in a strange place, equidistant from everything, and this position excludes him from any reckoning or choice. This might be the first example I know of an artist's subject becoming not just the "I" as a result, but the "I" as a movement.

Art historians believe around eighty of Rembrandt's self-portraits to be authentic (that is, attributed to Rembrandt, though occasionally with the assistance of members of his workshop), and fifty-five of these, or so I believe, are oil on canvas. This is a lot: a tenth of his whole prodigious output. Some of them are painted over other works in the absence of a ready canvas, forming a second layer of paint over the initial image. The already painted canvases were not necessarily Rembrandt's own. This was recycling in its purest form and everything was reused— other people's work, his own failed pictures and drafts, expressive little "tronies," little genre paintings. Among the canvases were the portraits his patrons didn't want. On their surfaces the artist himself appeared, his face momentary, one-off.

But only *his* face. The used canvases became a kind of drafting space or a sketchbook for the artist, where he could react fast, perhaps because his patrons paid for canvases or gave them to him for their own portraits. The self-portraits, arranged in a long line, examined consecutively, make a kind of catalog, a selection of snatched reflections, that very same following after nature. "After Nature," as Sebald's first book was called.

It seems that the speed with which an image was transferred to the canvas was important to Rembrandt. More important than other circumstances or obligations.

It once happened that his pet monkey died suddenly when he was halfway through painting a large portrait of a man, his wife and children. Having no other prepared canvas available he painted the dead monkey into the picture. The people objected strongly to this, not willing that their portraits should be arrayed alongside a disgusting dead ape. But no, he was so enamored of that study of the dead monkey that he chose to leave the picture unfinished and keep it as his own rather than please them by painting it out; and that is what happened. The picture in question eventually served as a partition for his students.

In the authoritative series *A Corpus of Rembrandt Paintings*, published by the Rembrandt Research Project, the self-portraits are given their own thick volume. Despite this, one of the main purposes of the accompanying editorial is to warn the reader from seeing the portraits as a special category. We shouldn't see them as a distinct project or subproject, a lyric diary lasting years, a Montaigne-style inquiry into the self.

The editor of the volume is engaged in a polemic against something even greater than the human tendency to retell the past with a contemporary vocabulary and to present Rembrandt's works as a quest for identity (or a search for an interior reality, opening up the space for introspection). This is not about a conflict of methodology, nor the extent to which we can eradicate the sin of anachronism—a sin inherent in any attempt to read a text that has moved a good way along the timescale. It's more likely that his is just one more attempt to *kick against the pricks*, to preserve the dignity of the past, and the rights of knowledge—the first of which is an immunity to ready-made concepts and imported frames of reference. There is no longer any escape from these: the agitated search for connection is in the air itself, the air a society breathes in an age of decline in the absence of common lines and unambiguous answers.

When the foundations of our day-to-day life subside and shift, hindering any attempt at systematic interpretation, we begin to search out handrails, and to welcome even the merest hint of structure. You begin to see order in any sequentiality, trusting chance and coincidence as if they demonstrated an intrinsic connection between things. There are a number of texts dedicated to Rembrandt's project, and each of them says more about us than it does about him, just like the first biographies. And yet there is something vaguely troubling about the optics that make us see the self-portraits as if through a microscope, the "interior world of their author" magnified, each movement of spirit, dark corner of the soul, or grief-marking laid bare for the purposes of study. I can't help thinking that the meaning of the many-headed multitude of sketched Rembrandts (their actual *face value*) is in fact in limiting them to exteriority, to the Aristotelean imprint of today. This is enough in any case: they give far more than we ask of them.

In some sense the self-portraits are close to the fashionable teaching aids of the time, which set out for future artists the permissible limits of bodily expression for suffering, astonishment, horror, and joy. This logic (based on an ancient faith in "characters," a range of types explaining human variety with a few templates) predetermines the further splitting of movements of spirit into a series of consecutive emotions, each one of which is a separate capsule, insisting on its own existence. These are universal, each has its own facial expression, meaning that what has been observed once can be applied many times, like a mathematical formula or a prayer.

Houbraken, the most lenient of Rembrandt's ill-wishers, saw in his work above all a carelessness of approach, something akin to crossing the road at a red light.

Many of the manifestations of emotion are ephemeral. Facial expressions rapidly change their appearance on the least prompting so that there is scarcely time to sketch them, let alone paint them. Consequently no other means can be imagined by which an artist could help themselves using this method other than fixing the idea in their mind by means of catching hold of a momentary particular. On the other hand, one might avail oneself of the genius of such men who, by means of established rules and the elements of art have, for the instruction of eager students, communicated to the world each particular expression of emotion in print: such as that invaluable book Discours Académique, *dedicated to Monsieur Colbert by the masters of the Royal Academy in Paris, following which example we also have provided samples of that kind, among other borrowed materials, and placed them in the second volume of Philaléthes's Letters.*

What is interesting here is not Houbraken's faith in ready templates, but the belief that the emotions exist as separate zones (just like the human types), and that they can be carefully delineated. Anger and pity are thought of as static states, like phases in a process, yet the point where they mix is not thought of as a separate space because there is an intangible line between them. In his comparison of the work Rembrandt and Montaigne made on the subject of themselves cultural historian Andrew Small refers to Foucault and *The Order of Things*, which concludes that despite the chains of vital resemblances, a person is imprisoned and limited by the parameters that describe her borders and leave the center untouched.

Rembrandt's contemporaries and detractors all reproached him for exactly this: a disrespect for borders—or his lack of ability to draw a line between one thing and another, between light and dark (a draftsman's chief asset). On this matter they all agree, finding the very manner of drawing unacceptable, "without contour or definition by means of inner and outer lines, but consisted entirely of violent and repeated strokes." "Clean outlines ought really to be drawn in their proper place and in order to conceal the danger [of this lack] in his works, he filled his paintings with pitch-black; and so it was that he demanded nothing from his pictures as long as they maintained a universal harmony." "... The other figures could scarcely be distinguished one from another, in spite of their being all closely studied from life." The attempt to resist what Pushkin called "the mixing up of everything" with a whole variety of rational arguments looks both touching and futile in hindsight, if only because Rembrandt doesn't impose change, he changes the system from within: he stretches it out to its full extent until it gives under the strain.

In his world there are no precisely drawn borderlines between figure and background, color and blackness, or, to extend the thought, between the self-portrait and the "tronie" nonportrait. It's as if the corpus of self-portraits rethinks the ruled line of ready-made states, while asserting the presence of another line where states are countless and flowing, like shades on a spectrum, but still held in an arrangement moving toward a clear and distinct end: a sequence of facial developments, along which change flickers without altering the overall reckoning. The task of *emulatio* (imitation, meaning not just the copying of the original, but the exceeding of it) is embedded in the nature of the genre—and one's own body becomes an artist's model, the ideal, unpaid model, over which ripples of emotion, age, phases of life play: a sequence of emblems. Alienation, the constant companion of observation, is essential here, as well as precision in the reproduction of what is seen.

*

A commentator has likened the relationship between Rembrandt and his own images to a trial of the self. Wouldn't it be more exact to call them "a refutation of the self" (however what happened between mirror and canvas was translated into the language of the seventeenth century): the alienation from, and shearing off of a whole phase of life, together with the one who has just lived it. For this to happen the artist has to very literally come out of himself, to be exteriorized to the point where he no longer sees the difference between himself and any one of his patrons (or, as in the Dresden self-portrait, between his young, pink-cheeked self and the dead bittern this self holds by the legs).

All the phases of this process are simultaneously discrete and unending. We see before us not inquiry (with its implied result), but fixation, a diary of observations from nature. There is not a single retrospective self-portrait—each new day is fixed and immediately exhausted, cast off, a *waste product*. In this respect it's important to look at the self-portraits in order, one after the other, as on their own they have the quality of scientific observation: another notch in the doorjamb marking a new height and age. It is not introspection, but rather the refusal to indulge in introspection; the externalizing and separating of the passing minute. Not autobiography, but autoepitaph.

Often a single portrait is repeated a few times, sometimes with variations and sometimes almost without, in different materials, oil, engravings, by the artist himself or his students. It's very clear that the concerns of the post-Romantic era, the necessity of avoiding repeats, the whole search for the new and uncaptured, all lie outside Rembrandt's circle of interests. Add to these the logic of self-knowledge, which is far too easy to impute to anyone found to be interested in their own persona. Perhaps the intention (however it was formulated back then) was not to acknowledge the opening curve of a new segment of life, but to fix the typical, to pin it down. I was this. I will never be this again.

The "selfie" genre operates in exactly this way. It is concerned with the contemporary: the search for variation has been replaced by the production of repeat images. Anyone on social media knows how often pictures appear in little clusters, a few self-portraits all taken in the same place and presented to the world one after the other, out of the sheer impossibility of choice. A number of tools have been developed in order to give the appearance of variety to these clusters: filters that refashion a picture in the manner of an artistic system, in the style of Munch, Klimt, Kandinsky, leaving the core of the self untouched.

It's this core we're concerned with. As usual all questions asking "how" are simply a way of answering the fundamental question of "who." Rembrandt experts all tell of the incredible variety of media for the age, the different ways of applying paint, the brushwork. In this sense Rembrandt has no "signature," no authorial manner, nothing of what was valued by the art of a new age obsessed with the personal. Or rather, he has too many of them. For each new task he develops a new technical approach, which you could call a filter. It's a little like our photographs, with their pretense at variety. The difference is first and foremost in what's present in every Rembrandt portrait, glancing out like the skull beneath the skin, in every fold of flesh—and what the poetics of the selfie eschews at all costs. Facebook photos, like the fairy-tale mirror on the wall, seek to persuade us of our invulnerability. As they dispassionately record each new wrinkle they insist that the face in the mirror is still ours, still the fairest of them all, hardly changed from the day before yesterday.

Jean Cocteau said that cinema is the only art form that records death at work. Rembrandt's self-portraits are solely occupied with recording death, and lined up together they make a sort of protofilm—whereas the kilometers of selfies, taken and uploaded for communal access, look like the exact opposite to me: the chronicle of death as it walks among us, no longer of any interest to anyone.

Even stronger then is the temptation to see the sequence of Rembrandt's oil paintings as a narrative arc, a kind of graphic novel, with *the face* as hero. All of the events and adventures happen to the face, as if it were a character you could manipulate at will, allowing for distortion or dislocation. And these distortions happen of course, although they have little to do with the subject. That is, yes, the metamorphoses of the face are accompanied by changes in the entourage: a little further to the left or right, but you're still the hero, the emperor, the unfortunate, the old man, no one, yourself. Sometimes this "I" is more successful than in real life, appearing in the clothes and the pose of the princes of this world. Often, the subjects insist on their just deserts—appearing with a gold chain over the chest, the sign of an artist's success. Rembrandt never received such a reward in life, but the portraits set this to rights. Most of all the artist is quite literally testing the model for durability, for its ability to reinvent itself.

The quality of loving-kindness is intimately connected with the work of the hands, with the touch of the brush on the canvas, stroke by stroke. Here it is conjoined with the powerful energy of alienation, or distance, to put it simply. The painted Rembrandt changes from canvas to canvas, but retains an unchanging presence—almost like the protagonist of a comic or cartoon, Tintin or Betty Boop, whose depictions have become a symbol, a few oversized characteristics grouped around an empty space. The mathematical constant, along with the constant of the subject, have been canceled out. Sometimes the portrait necessitates smaller eyes, sometimes larger, sometimes they are apart, sometimes closer-set. The chin, too, gets longer and then shorter again. The nose however remains unchanged—if you think of the features of a face as a collection of personalities then the comic stubborn nose, with its bulbous tip would be the main character, the hero of the tale.

Then there's the ear with its fleshy lobe. There's an apocryphal tale that Rembrandt deliberately darkened the wonderfully painted Cleopatra in order to make the single pearl stand out. Cleopatra, if she ever existed, has not been preserved. In an early self-portrait from 1628, with its captivating combination of rosiness and red hair, transparent shadows and flickering surfaces, Rembrandt's ear is that single pearl. The lighting is what you might call "dimmed houselights": that melancholy half light that rescues any photograph or film, imparting to it a sudden perfection. The face is immersed in darkness, and only the very button of the nose is illuminated. Part of the neck, the soft cheek with its downy hair and a corner of the white collar appear almost gilded with the light of the disappearing sun, and a ring of hairs on his nape are lit like wires. The center of the composition has followed the light and shifted to the left, and the crimson earlobe (disproportionately puffy, as if he'd just had it pierced and it was still stinging and swollen) is suddenly everything: the sunset, an expensive earring, an unseeing and flesh-covered third eye.

Consider the "Portrait of a Young Woman with a Fan," dated 1633 (its pendant, showing a bearded man, rising from his armchair to greet someone, is now somewhere in Cincinnati). It's a virtuosic work, a demonstration of mastery: thick scalloped lace, the black and wine-red fabrics, the earrings and necklace all appear to hold symbolic meaning that might be deciphered like a rebus. But none of it bears any relation to the face, which is wide and flat as a tray. No message plays across its surface, merely the smooth evenness of the concentrating listener. Something in it looks familiar though, like a fin emerging from the waves and then disappearing again, and it unsettles and distracts from the task, which the artist has so marvelously fulfilled. The young woman has neither name nor biography, giving rise to the suggestion that she never existed, and that both works were calling cards, painted to show the artist at his best and attract new patrons. Something in her figure and the turn of her shoulder, in the way her sleeve is tucked up and her large hand rests on the arm of the chair is in vague contradiction with the silk and gold of the artist's task. Her eyes are wide apart (a slight skin fold in one eyelid) and she has a broad forehead, an inelegant nose (the bulbous tip is tinged with red) and the expression on her face combines a high level of attentiveness with a little boy's excited readiness. I can't rid myself of the thought that Rembrandt liked the idea of painting a female version of himself, just another of the many possible-impossible forms of being — especially handy if a portrait of an unknown woman was suddenly needed.

The heavy-browed, the surprised, the smirking, contented, and self-satisfied, the suspicious, despairing, and desperate, the slicked-back and curly-haired likenesses of Rembrandt formed their own scale, they were a school unto themselves. The face seems to be able to teach itself to meet every given standard — and at the same time to refute it. The Dresden "Self-portrait with a Dead Bittern" with its mustache, the feather in his cap, the extended hand holding the bird like Goliath's head, has its echo in the victorious Samson, standing with his hand on his hip at his father-in-law's gate.

The comparatively spare late self-portraits, with their dark hats and white linen caps, are even more economical, a serial testing of the faces of acceptance, despair, mockery. They have something in common, it seems, a particular quality to the gaze, although it's easier to define in an apophatic sense, to note what is absent. They are missing the integral attribute of the genre: an attempt to penetrate. The portrait with its fist of meanings, an embodied demand for attention, a place in the sun, tries to break open your head like a door, to enter in and make itself at home. It has the intensity of a message in a bottle, a voicemail—a letter that sooner or later will become the very last letter.

Rembrandt's self-portraits are beings of a different type. They don't demand attention, but with all imaginable generosity they offer up to you their own attention. The internal space of the portraits is given over to this, the gaze we meet at the threshold opens up to us, allows us in, creates a soft indent for our momentary stay, a womb-like hollow, deliberately intended for partings. What is parting from what here? What is ending, which is hardly begun? If we remember that we are looking (even in the same portrait with the yellow jerkin), in the most literal way, with Rembrandt's eyes, and through his mind, as if it were a coin-operated telescope presenting a segment of distant reality to us up close, then at this very moment, we are able to cast off our own selves with a mixture of tenderness and gratitude. What happens then is the simultaneous disappearance of both pans on the scales, both parts of the equation, the y and the x. In the hollow, in the deserted meeting place, only its permanent resident is left: the invisible dead monkey.

3. Goldchain Adds Up, Woodman Takes Away

In W. G. Sebald's *Austerlitz* there is a long list—a page or more—of confiscated goods taken from the flat of Prague Jews after they have been dispatched. Everything is itemized, down to the jars of strawberry jam with their conserved summer light. Sometimes we can trace the objects' journey (I almost added "posthumous"), and there are even photographs of the warehouses where the confiscated goods were stored—a little like transit camps, barracks for captive objects. Long tables, as if in preparation for a wedding feast, are stacked high with orphaned china and crockery, terrible in their ornate nakedness; wooden shelves like bunks, inhabited by pots and pans, sauce boats and teapots, forced to rub along. It's as if someone's cupboards had been sliced open like a belly and the contents had slithered out—and this is in effect what happened. There are whole rooms of polished wooden cupboards and cupboards of neatly piled, cold-to-the-touch bedlinen, ancient pillows and duvet covers. These warehouses were closed distribution points, places where the privileged could come and be presented with a gift from someone else's halted life. The same warehouses existed in Soviet Russia—the furs and furniture of the spoiled bourgeoisie were handed out to the victorious, the people of a new Social formation.

In contemporary Europe, with its barely healed wounds, black holes, and traces of displacement, a well-preserved family archive is a rarity. A set of furniture and china that has come together over decades, inherited from aunts and grandmothers and once thought of as an ancient burden, now deserves its own special memorial. Those who were forced to flee (it hardly matters from whom they fled) burned documents, shredded photographs, cut off everything below the chin—officer epaulets, army greatcoats, civil service uniforms—and left their papers with other people. By the end of the journey very little is left for the memory to cling to, and to set sail on.

Exercises in bringing the past closer to understand it remind me of those school tests where you are asked to tell a story based on a picture, or to draw a picture based on a few existing elements: nose, tail, and paw. Whether you like it or not, you are simply more visible than those who came before you. And we have nothing to lay our foundations on—like most of the people who escaped from the black ink of the twentieth century, taking only what they could.

What can you do when your imagined subject's possessions amount to almost nothing: a postcard and five photographs that have survived by accident? The imagination bodies forth, the objects acquire mass and the links between them, both past and invented, and smeared thickly with *a priori* knowledge of that object, establish their own order. But objects from the long distant past look as if they've been caught in the headlights, they're awkward, embarrassingly naked. It's as if they had nothing left to do. Their previous owners and functions are gone and they are doomed to aimless existence. It is much like retiring from work and finding yourself unable to build a new life. The list of clothing I took to pioneer camp as a ten-year-old (three white t-shirts, blue shorts, a pioneer cap), is hardly different from the lists of property that were so lovingly drawn up in the seventeenth century, the frock coats, garters, and breeches. They slowly grow cold in the absence of human touch, of being spoken of and remembered, and each item is suffused with a touching glow when it is brought briefly back out of oblivion. Together with a white cloth of silver doublet and another black silk doublet we find: *five East Indian wicker baskets, a green armosin sash, six hair wigs, a cane, being a walking stick with an ivory knob,* and *a Turkish tobacco pipe.* This comes from a list of items belonging to Lodewijk van der Helst, drawn up in Amsterdam on January 7, 1671, on the occasion of moving to his mother's. It's a long list and nothing is left out, down to the "various silks and other textiles of "antique" clothes and what belongs to it, as part of the art of painting." We know almost nothing about the artist Edo Quitter, except that he died in 1694 and all that remains is a list of his still-living possessions, drawn up December 10:

> *Three old black hats*
> *A red Polish hat*
> *A red leather belt for the waist*
> *Two black sleeves*
> *Two pairs of old shoes*
> *A silver signet ring*
> *A pair of purple slippers*

*

Rafael Goldchain's book *I Am My Family: Photographic Memories and Fictions* might be described as an album or a catalog, the paper equivalent of a completed art project. This extraordinary book's concern is memory and the vanity of memory.

Goldchain was born in Chile in 1953. He is what is known as a second-generation survivor, a son and grandson of those who managed to escape.

From the early 1920s until the eve of World War Two, most of my family members emigrated from Poland to Venezuela, Costa Rica, Brazil, Argentina, or Chile. A few others sought a new life in the United States or Canada. Some left Poland intending to come back with funds to help their families but were prevented by the outbreak of the war. All of my extended family members who remained in Europe after the beginning of World War Two perished in the Shoah.

The project (I don't know how else to describe it) begins like other such projects: the father tells the son a story, and as the story continues the father becomes more deeply immersed in it. It seems Goldchain wasn't very interested in his own family history until he became a parent himself. No one spoke of the past in his home, the silence was sealed tight, much like a message in a bottle, not yet ready to be opened. This is usual: "we didn't speak of those things," "he kept his silence," "she never wanted to talk about it"—the grandchildren and great-grandchildren of survivors quote the same phrases. Goldchain lived in various places: Jerusalem, Mexico, Toronto, and it was only when he was close to forty and his first son was born that he realized he was the same age as his grandparents on the eve of the Second World War, and that he knew nothing about them, or even about those he had lived with his whole life.

There comes a day when the scattered pieces of knowledge need to be fixed in a transmission line. It's a truism that the "dough" of comprehension only rises to its shape in the moment of telling, and in this telling it then sags and subsides. Here's the emblematic account, a picture from the golden library of generalized experience: a mother or father is recounting family history to the child, passing it from one mouth to another. This is how Art Spiegelman begins *Maus*, the classic work about the Holocaust and how it is spoken of; this is how hundreds of other works begin:

> A lad comes to his father's side
> And asks, this little lad:
> Tell me, Daddy, what is good
> And tell me what is bad?

When the listener is a child, simplicity isn't just appropriate— it's essential. The sharp corners round themselves, the lacunae quietly disappear. The tale of the past constantly risks becoming a tale of the future. We have to make the knowledge bearable, skirt the painful, repair connections—or the world will fall apart.

Only a few photographs remain of the huge clan of Goldchains living in Poland a century ago, and they are all reproduced at the end of the book in an appendix. The book begins with an introduction, and then a warning by the author, and only then the real meat of the book: eighty-four photographs recreating the body of the family. Each is presented like a studio photograph on a monochrome background, the portrait extending downward to the chest. They include men and women in hats, heavy-boned women with piercing gazes, little jug-eared yeshiva students, peasants from the shtetl, imposing gentlemen to whom the respectable labels "Don Moses" or "Don Samuel" adhere as a matter of course. There's no sleight of hand about it, and I won't try to pretend that there is. You can see immediately that despite the different ages and genders, the face is the same—we are following the family resemblance down a mirrored corridor. The Goldchain family album is a collection of self-portraits, made in an attempt to resurrect a lost connection, to find oneself in the features of another.

My first ancestor self-portrait—based on my maternal grandfather, Don Moises Rubinstein Krongold, who had lived in our house from 1964 until 1978—was motivated by the desire to create an image purely out of memory that could be thought of as defining my life in a foundational way, an image that I could point to and say, "This is where I came from."

The Soviet poet Gennady Aygi has a book in which he translates into words the first months of his daughter's life with a deep attentiveness, silence by silence. He describes what he calls the "period of likenesses," a short period of time during which familiar and unfamiliar faces and expressions flit across the baby's face like passing clouds, as if the fretful ancestors looked down at the mirror-face of the child, both recognizing it and impressing on it their own. Goldchain says something similar when he describes his working process as being a spiritual medium: ghostlike shapes swim up from the depths of the image, but only briefly; the likenesses are not perfect, they can't be held fast.

From the first glimpse the imagined photographs of an imagined family (what it might have been, what it never did become) shock with their abundance. There's a plethora of types of person, as if they were competing for places on the ark. It reminded me of the parade of professions in August Sander's photographs, although in this case all the subjects are members of the same family—as if the Goldchains had been chosen to settle a new world and had to be prepared for all eventualities. There are peasants and city dwellers, two chefs, and the author appears to lose his mind over the family musicians: violinist, saxophonist, accordionist, drummer, another violinist, a tuba player. It's like some Kafkaesque trade fair, where one and the same person sits at every stand, and peers out from every barrel. The wider the selection of professions, the more we peer straight to the depths and the differences vanish before our eyes. All that is left is typology: profession, age, costume, and the quality of the costume, the frame of the *formulaic*, which the author will stick his head into, for example "a middle-aged, stylish woman, suffering from chronic, mild depression—there is one in every family."

There are family members about whom nothing is known except for the name, and the lifesaving operation demands the invention of clothes and an exterior appearance. Sometimes the self-portrait doesn't work, Goldstein simply isn't able to catch the likeness with a "real-life cut out." But these also come in useful: names are made up for them, the family grows larger. A "Naftuli Goldszajn" appears in the world, whose nonexistence up to that point was only a matter of chance. As it says in the introduction "... we are faced with a black-and-white image of a man who might have lived in Poland sometime after the 1830s. He must be a Goldchain, since he looks like all the others."

For Goldchain, the attempt to tell his son about his heritage becomes a journey into the Kingdom of the Dead: to become each of them, to stand in their places, to allow them to look out through him like a window. The author becomes a way out, the bottleneck of the family story, the only way and the only material for saying all that can be said. You can call the result of this anything you like, but you couldn't call it a family history. The brevity of the descriptions, their feathery-perfunctory quality (well-dressed, distinguished-looking, in a hat, with a bird) become clearer with each photograph: in this thoughtful, subtle project a whole tribe and an entire world appears on a single face, and the result is strange and unsettling. The problem with memory (its unrecognizable, rainy darkness, lit with the sharp flashes of guesswork) is removed at once: the entire tribe, three or thirty generations back, is me, all me, me with a mustache, me in a bonnet, me in a cradle, me in the grave, indivisible, irrevocable. Once again the past gives way to the present.

The structure of the book tells us a great deal about the mechanism of authorial view: after the introductions, the portraits, the laconic notes on the characters/types, there are some diary jottings from years before the project was being prepared: everything that could be gathered together, including guesses, fantasies, a few *real* photographs. Among these, an old woman with a wonderful face, who would have been quite impossible to impersonate. The notes are handwritten and you have to make an effort to decipher them, becoming a textual critic in the process—this moment of resistance makes the material irresistible. Here Goldchain and I are as one: the bare threads of knowledge give us wings. The text includes some "ready-mades," everyday objects, fragments of authentic letters and documents and although they don't amount to much, by some authorial magic they are transformed and rendered compelling.

Such magic is rare, which is why I am picking through different approaches to the past, as one might pick through dried peas, in the search of one that might work. Anna Akhmatova once said that there is nothing more tedious than someone else's dreams or someone else's fornication—but other people's family histories also leave unwanted traces of dust and whitewash on your hands. There are very few ways to flick the switch and turn the uninteresting into the enticing corridor of new experience, and people seldom succeed. Rafael Goldchain's approach was to create for himself and his son the illusion of continuity; to add to his own family a chorus of imaginary figures who shared his own features and his gaze. This is the world of compensation where the lost is returned in triplicate, where Job's children and flocks increase in number and the unexpected is canceled out.

The catastrophe is displaced, the hole is resealed, things find their places once again, everyone is alive, there are no omissions, no silences. It is, in its own way, Paradise before the Fall (there are far too many people now who think that Europe in 1929 or Russia in 1913 were such paradises). We long to have our pictures taken before such a backdrop: I was there. But "there" does not exist. The oath of fidelity to family history becomes its destruction, a parody of the resurrection of the dead: another is replaced by oneself, the known world is squeezed out by the invented world, *hell is other people* becomes the family album where everyone is in their rightful place, pretending to be alive. Ideally they would also talk—but in your voice, like an answering machine gone rogue.

*

In the Holocaust Memorial Museum in Washington there's a whole type of exhibit that is displayed so it can't be seen unless the visitor makes a conscious choice to view it: usually this constitutes video materials or photographic sequences, which are just terrifying—how might one describe such things more exactly? These images are even less reconcilable with life than the rest of the exhibits. The viewer is kept apart from them by a low barrier, so to see the actual images you have to stand up close. The intention here seems to be that viewers can then half-close their eyes and deliberately protect themselves—not from knowledge of what happened, because that is always there inside, descending lump-like from the throat to the stomach; not from the actual *details*, after all you don't have to look at the layers of slowly rotting bodies, one on top of another, or the murderers being washed with hoses to cool them down, or a bulky old woman trying to hide a naked little girl behind her. No, you don't need to get too close to those screens.

Sometimes it rather seems to me that the pictures need protecting from us: so that the nakedness of the dying and dead remains their business and illustrates nothing, invokes nothing, serves neither as a basis for conclusions nor identifications after the event. It isn't about the fact that this turning of a life inside out, in as little time as it takes to show a film clip, to show its seams and fibrous lining, is a type of the deformed experience described by Varlam Shalamov: it has no meaning, no use, it cannot be applied, nor can it be unseen. All it can do is destroy you from the inside out. And this isn't simply because all one's systems of self-defense strive to neutralize the images into mere "pictures," screens that are estranged from real life for the purpose of terrifying and titillating us.

The further the contemporary world wades into the past (up to the knees, the waist, the chest, by stages transformed to marble, like the character in Carlo Gozzi's *The Raven*) the louder the conversation about who owns it: the right to this or that scrap of the old world—and who has no such right to the past. Usually the inheritors and defenders are those who are closer by dint of knowledge or birth, scholars, family, associates. After them come all those who consider the dead to be their own property. It's fascinating to watch when a stranger is drawn to this fenced-off property: someone from outside, someone who has not worked off their debt to this common ground. Events mostly unfold with the logic of a fight over an inheritance—and the first accusation flung at the outsider is his or her *I*. Someone like him or her has no business to be sniffing round such things, and so must be driven by self-interest, or worse, unfounded interest—overwrought, chance, without *roots*. Here the metaphors of agriculture and vegetable growth work best: blood-and-soil hums under our feet. So, even posthumously (which gives an especially morbid quality to the affair), the fair-haired Sylvia Plath was accused of the appropriation of images of Jews and ovens in the poems she wrote in the last months of her life. Accusations of exploitation hang in the air above the fields of memory, over the bent spines of her workers, her households, her underground streams, and the tips of her arrows.

*

There are those who manage to work in the past's territories (to use the poet Dmitri Prigov's expression: "to bide there, and yet to emerge dry"), as if without noticing where they are. In the (very short) history of Francesca Woodman there is nothing that speaks of the past's vulnerability, or even shows particular interest in the old world. The daughter and the sister of an artist, she began photography at thirteen. When she died at twenty-two she left behind a body of prints, a few videos, and a large number of negatives, all connected by a rare sense of unity, not of method, but of approach. What preoccupies her—that is, the subject of her compulsively perfectionist art—is hard to formulate, not least for her. Her typed letters (written in a rush, so the words are often begun, then left unfinished, then a space, then she starts the word again, very much in the manner of the piping voice we heard on her videos) hardly try to explain the tasks she has set herself. The letters might be described as the bubbling surface of a river, flexing itself over rocks.

There are two types of writing about Francesca Woodman, and they might be characterized as biographical and formal. Interest in her work grows in both camps: the character of her work and her early death combine to give her a special sort of fame, she very quickly became an icon for the unhappy young; another divinity in the post-Romantic pantheon; a highly prized incompatibility with life. In Woodman's case, because her favored material was the female body, it is easy to read her subject as the impossibility of living in a male world, under the male gaze, or the hopeless attempt to avoid this gaze by hiding or pretending to be someone else. Rosalind E. Krauss interprets Woodman's message this way in one of the first articles about the photographer, written at the beginning of the 1980s. Krauss's article lays the foundations for the perception of the work as the chronicle of a disappearance, a commentary on Woodman's own future death. As this version gained popularity, the most frequently used word in any discussion about Woodman became "haunted," spoken with the kind of comfortable horror we reserve for ghost stories. If we adhere to this interpretation of Woodman's output then our role is to witness the fair-haired girl disappearing underwater, or lost in the roots of a tree, or flickering behind tattered wallpaper, extenuated, finally fading out, and yet ceaselessly documenting all this for our entertainment and edification, in the best traditions of confessional lyric.

The photographs certainly allow this interpretation, alongside many others. Their natural environment is the smoky light of metamorphosis, of various kinds of transformation and distortion, which do not permit a perception of the self as a thing of wonder, or even an anomaly: in Woodman's world this is just the natural order of things. Seen from the outside Woodman's subjects fit in a tradition of homemade Victorian shadow theaters: fluttering ghosts strolling with lost maidens.

Seventeen-, eighteen- and twenty-year-old Francesca enjoyed dressing up. She loved and wore old clothing, what we'd now call vintage, flowery dresses, woolly tights, Mary Jane shoes. At school she told the girl who shared her room that she hated contemporary music and had never watched television in her life. It seems she was telling the truth. The documentary *The Woodmans* gives at least some insight into her upbringing, the right art school, the uncompromising exclusion of anything her parents thought unworthy. At some point Francesca's father notes in passing that if his daughter had been interested in her girlfriends rather than in photographic angles and the specifics of lighting, then he would have had nothing to say to her. This seems to have been the truth, and I can only pity the child. The "fabricated" quality of Woodman's person and her work resembles an integrated and successful project—the clarity of the handwriting and decision-making, the consistency and the ambition of every move—and this is yet another reason to think of her as a victim: of the times, of circumstances, of parental ambition. The expectation of success, the drive to success (and the inability to adapt to the inevitable delays and obstacles) is familiar to all children of professionals, the young musicians and ballerinas, in whom far too much effort and faith is placed, and it adds something to our understanding of her life and death. What it doesn't explain is the more than eight hundred photographs taken by Woodman in her hope of creating something of her own.

"No live organism can continue for long to exist sanely under conditions of absolute reality; even larks and katydids are supposed, by some, to dream." This is the opening of Shirley Jackson's *The Haunting of Hill House*, written in 1958, the year of Francesca Woodman's birth and one of the best books on the relationship between the human and the uncanny, when the uncanny itself takes a sudden interest in the human. The book's heroine is forced to convince herself of her own materiality by carefully noting each action: drinking a cup of coffee, buying a red sweater against her family's better judgment, a victory, a beginning to life; but as the book progresses she blends more and more into the cursed house.

A few quotes, taken at random, from writing about how

Francesca is disembodied in her own photographs: "her own body becomes transparent, strangely weightless, almost fleshless, blurring the boundaries between the human body and its surroundings," "her body, caught in movement by the camera like a dark haze, as if she were as unbodied and unhuman as the air surrounding her," "a ghost in the house of the woman artist." Francesca Woodman took her own life, the result of a long depression, and as is so often the case, a fatal concurrence of the absurd and the hurtful: her bicycle was stolen; she didn't get a grant; she had relationship troubles.

Suicide shines on any fate like the most powerful spotlight: it conspires to make the shadows deeper and the failures sharper. But Woodman's family and friends collectively and convincingly refute the biographical interpretation of her work, drawing attention to another formal side of her work, the planned brilliance of these little shots, their particular humor, the language of coincidence and chance, the visual rhythms, the shadows of André Breton and Man Ray, the lifted hands metamorphosing into birch branches, branches voting with a lifted hand. They are irritated by the critics' insistence on the theme of disappearance, but when you look at these pictures it is hard not to feel an answering desire to dissolve, to allow oneself to flow into the frame, the interior or the landscape. Or flow together with the author to the point where you become indistinguishable: The cliche of Woodman as a genius at self-portraiture nearly obscures the fact that many of the bodies, and even the faces we interpret as *the confessional self* belong to other women.

These women were friends, models, people she knew. Sometimes we see their faces, sometimes they resemble each other to a strange degree, sometimes they are shielded from view by mute objects: plates, black lace, even photographs of Francesca herself. Sometimes they are completely faceless, unpossessed to the point of dereliction, severed from us by the edge of a print, or parts of the body: someone's legs in stockings, breasts and col larbones (in another picture), a hand emerging from a wall, the body of a woman in flight, a leap, blurred. None of this belongs to anyone—it is quite literally nobody's: like a black umbrella or a crumpled stocking, it is simply part of the location, the interior of whatever abandoned house Woodman had chosen (for she only used such interiors). If we ask ourselves who all these orphaned arms, legs, shoulder blades belong to, what sort of a creature it could be (what species of being), then we might guess that all these constituent parts make up a single entity, something like a collective body—the body of death, or more precisely, the body of the past.

Woodman titled one of her photographs a portrait of "legs—and time" in her journal. She wrote of the objects featured in a late series of works, which went into her artist book before her death (the photographs are pasted on the pages of an old geometry primer, *be fire with fire*, I suppose, the new order prevailing over the old): "These things arrived from my grandmother's they make me think about where I fit in the odd geometry of time." The geometry of time is indivisible from its texture, which is constantly transforming itself, crumbling, breaking apart, evaporating, and then reforming in the vapor, ruled by the laws of the organic world. The phrase "body of work" takes on a living, almost medical sense: these photographs register the body of the world as a physical entity, with its pile, its skin, the dirt that eats into the pores, its twitching extremities, its ceaselessly shifting surfaces.

The eroticism of the images takes us a long way from the straight and narrow of human desire; it's the crushed white fabric, barely touched by the sun, that seeks a meeting/illumination, far more than the bare shoulder of a woman does. Woodman's interiors and landscapes are filled with naked bodies, bride-white Wilis trembling like water reeds. Never sated, they stare wolfishly into the forest of further possibilities. Their zone of interest passes along the boundary of their own skin and no external touch can compare with the drive for adventure already set in motion within them. In this sense the ghosts are harmless: they are entirely focused on themselves and what has happened to them. The fact that Woodman called her photographs "ghost pictures" is telling. All her ghostly images—a cloud of human form condensed around a tombstone or someone's face peering out of the wardrobe, legs hanging out of another wardrobe, doors taken off their hinges and hung at a strange angle—are stages in a process, and the meaning of this process lies beyond the photograph, somewhere in time. The long exposure, the incredibly slow shutter speed and darkroom techniques reveal particular qualities in the person, an ability to be anything at all—a movement, an erosion, a whirlpool. Although she is more vulnerable and less lasting than, say, a floral-patterned tile, a person suddenly discovers she can walk through walls, cover objects with a fine layer of dust, rise out of nowhere, be air and fire. "And then I flew," as the woman in Tarkovsky's *Mirror* says.

The body, one's own or another's, is the essential material, the modeling clay, must be tested simultaneously for strength and fragility. In one of her self-portraits, a transparent telephone cord stretches from Woodman's mouth as if she were vomiting a chain of soap bubbles. In other pictures shards of mirror press into the flesh of the stomach or thighs; breasts and sides are covered in pegs, hanging from the skin like beaks. Here is time passing, the human is washed away but objects keep their outlines; there is no difference between oneself and others, just an unending impersonal tender love. This is the pure matter of oblivion—an ocean without a window, as Mandelstam wrote—forever scattering, drawing itself together, then shrinking away; saving face, then suddenly removing it, ripping it off. Sometimes, not always, very seldom in fact, a ripple appears on the surface of the watery flow, something that presses from inside comes into focus, swelling, rising up, crystallizing, almost against its will. This is how the past rises up into the contemporary world, like a drowned man from the murky waters. This is how Francesca's body rises from the floral patterns and chipped whitewash, not disappearing or fading into the background, but coming into focus, sharpening, print after print. In one of the videos she is folded into paper, writing her name on it, letter by letter—and then she rips the paper from inside and emerges into the light.

4. Mandelstam Rejects and Sebald Collects

"I've never seen Moscow look so calm, so rich, so peaceful and cheerful. Even I've felt its calming effect …"

In December 1935 Nadezhda Mandelstam traveled to Moscow from Voronezh to manage the affairs of her exiled husband. Being in Moscow was good for her: the mood of celebration in the city, the brightness and certainty of its own righteousness and its place at the center of the world, all had a calming effect—the word "calm" appears twice in two sentences, as if she needed to stress it.

The spirit of the Soviet thirties is immediately recognizable in her letters to her husband, just as it is in the cheerily urban paintings of Yury Pimenov, or Bulgakov's late prose: a funny and terrifying world that never tires of insisting on its overwhelming sense of cheerful completeness. The daytime city (dresses, factories, parks) is all the harder and smoother for the existence of a nighttime city that is better left unmentioned. The presence of terror even seems to invigorate. It forces its way into the reality of the scurrying ant's nest, imparting a very particular jittery sensation, bubbling like seltzer, a fresh breeze over the river, the morning lightness of those who survived the night:

> It smells of postal glue over the Moscow River
> Schubert sounds from the loudspeakers' cones
> Thin trickles of water, and the air is more tender
> Than the frog-pocked skin of silken balloons

Impossible for me to forget that we are the direct offspring of this ant heap of the celebratory and the disappearing; flower sellers, cab drivers' backsides, people clinging on to the hand rails on the outside of busy streetcars—or that my own twenty-year-old grandmother was among them on the Moscow "A" streetcar, fondly called "Annushka"; part of the crowd, part of this movement, part of this language.

The wide arc of the thirties is so colored by its time, its canvases and texts mingle together in the air over their authors' heads. Dates and places of birth are more important than direct relationships. These works have their own elusive common denominator: the sudden return of cozy domesticity, life's comforting thickness giving people, with their spindly civic rights and short memories, a false sense of being rooted in the present. This new coziness knew what to promise (as Pasternak wrote: "In the Spring we'll add to our living space, / I'll take on my brother's room"). Life was becoming more enjoyable, in 1935 citizens were given permission to celebrate New Year and a "pact on general work and collective celebration" was sealed with Christmas tree resin.

Mandelstam's new poems written in exile in Voronezh on how "we are full of life to the highest degree" weren't simply contributions to this new collective effort, brilliant as lectures on physics, proof that he could measure time in five-year plans, measure time like everyone else, like Pasternak—no, these poems had far bigger concerns. They laid no claim to the recent past, nor the palpably accessible present, but tried to cut a large crooked piece out of the future with tailor's shears, to run ahead and begin to speak in a universal language that did not yet exist. And they succeeded in this.

The work done by these poems was, according to Mandelstam, of the highest significance—so obviously important—and it needed to be delivered to Moscow like a nugget of precious metal or a gigantic ear of corn, like an agricultural or scientific achievement. This was the reason for Nadezhda Mandelstam's trip to Moscow in that winter of 1935: it was clear to both of them that the literary world only had to see these poems and they would take their rightful place under the glass sun of the near future—*what I say now, every schoolchild will learn.*

Their confidence in the poems' urgency and significance made them hurry, and so speeded up the inevitable disaster.

"Overall I'm pleased with myself—I have done and am doing everything I can. And after this we wait for the inevitable. [...] we mustn't go anywhere, or ask for anything, or do anything [...] I've never felt so intensely that we mustn't act, we mustn't make a noise or give them the runaround."

But they could do no differently.

*

A decade earlier, in 1926, Marina Tsvetaeva went to London for the first and last time in her life: "I am going to London for ten days where I will have, for the first time in eight years (four Soviet, four in emigration) some TIME. (I am traveling alone)."

She would spend that miraculous uppercase TIME unexpectedly and not at all as a tourist. In the space of a few days and with unwavering determination, she would write a furious article that she was not able to publish in her lifetime. The article was called "My answer to Osip Mandelstam." A London friend and critic, a great fan of Mandelstam's prose, showed her Mandelstam's book of essays, *Noise of Time*, published in Leningrad. Tsvetaeva couldn't hold back, she thought the book despicable. Mandelstam had written about Feodosiya in the Crimea in 1919, when it was held by the White Army, and Tsvetaeva absolutely refused to accept the tone of comic admiration Mandelstam adopted to speak about their mutual friend, a volunteer White Army colonel with his poems and his illusions ... a man on the losing side, in other words.

Tsvetaeva's sense of outrage was very personal, perhaps too much so. The matters discussed in the chapters about Feodosiya had direct relevance to her own home and poetic affairs, and she wrote about these in a very different tonal range. Tsvetaeva's husband Sergei Efron had been a volunteer in the White Army, and volunteering was for her a pure and heroic gesture of self-sacrifice; perhaps more importantly her old friends were the inspiration for the official portrait, the template of a "noble life." The distorted and compressed style of Mandelstam's description was not, for her, a literary device, but simply mockery of those who couldn't defend themselves. Much of this is easier to understand with the distance of a century: for example, Mandelstam's phrase "nanny-colonel," which so upset Tsvetaeva, was in fact imbued with tenderness for Mandelstam—he signed his letters to his wife with the nickname "nanny."

Their optical systems were incompatible, and there is no reason why they should have been compatible. But Tsvetaeva's annoyance moves seamlessly from the chapters about the White Army in Feodosiya to Mandelstam's writing about the past, the heart of the book and its reason for being. Time passed, but the enmity remained. In 1931 Tsvetaeva wrote to a friend about "Mandelstam's stillborn prose, hateful to me, in *Noise of Time*, where the living are merely props, where everything alive is just an object."

A sense of bewilderment at *Noise of Time* seems to have united readers of very different mindsets. Nadezhda Mandelstam reported that "everyone refused to print the thing, as it had no subject and no plot, no class awareness or social significance." But Tsvetaeva saw *only* an attempt at class awareness, the fine trappings of the surrender and death of a Russian intellectual. In the same article she writes that *Noise of Time* is Mandelstam's gift to the authorities.

We should keep in mind the level of inflammation (all too easy to imagine today) in the reader's consciousness on both sides of the Soviet border. Both prose and poetry had a secondary— and at times primary—function, to witness an author's political choice (which flickered about like a cursor, depending on circumstances). The text served to answer the question of "which side is the author on," and only after that did it serve its more ordinary purposes. In Mandelstam's case, with his unavoidable postrevolutionary travels to Batumi and Kiev and everywhere in between, this question is on hold until the beginning of the 1920s, but by 1924, when *Noise of Time* was submitted for publication, it couldn't be put off any longer.

Mandelstam's paired poems "January 1, 1924" and "No, I was never anyone's contemporary ..." were written when time was out of joint: the old world was giving way to the new, but they were written, and this is important, *from* the new world. The old carriage was still rocking forward, carts were still creaking past at midnight, nothing had come to a standstill, but there was no way back. No return. A pact with the future had been signed simply by the act of moving forward, by being drawn into the general mêlée. For Mandelstam, as for many others, this seduction by what he called the "twilight of freedom" was tinged with unambiguous ecstasy, and his New Year's poem about the change of fate, written against the backdrop of *Noise of Time*, wasn't just an attempt at farewell, but a rebuttal of the past.

*

How quickly they took to reminiscing, as if the past, crumbling to dust in front of them, needed fixing in the mind before it was blown away by the wind. Clattering along, heaped untidily high like a barrow of old possessions, the twenties unexpectedly became a time of memoirs. A lid was slammed shut over the old world, and all available memory, all abolished knowledge remained under it. Pasternak's autobiographical work *Safe Conduct* and Andrei Bely's memoirs were fixated on Moscow student conversations *at the break of the centuries*, like archaeologists poring over excavations: these conversations were data that needed reanimating, deciphering, presenting to the contemporary world.

Noise of Time was one of the first such texts, written in 1923, when the new world had barely set fast. It immediately fell out of line and spent a century looking as ill-fitting as *The Good Soldier Švejk* on the parade ground of the twentieth century's big memoir projects, although it initially seemed to resemble these. The century of Kafka and Platonov, which began with a powerful surge toward change, collective utopia, and a global yearning for the new, very quickly shifted into an awareness of itself as a space for retrospection. As the Modernist era drew to a close, memory and memory's half brother, the document, came to be something of a fetish, perhaps because they hint gently at the reversible and inconclusive nature of loss, even in a world that is constantly changing its order.

What began with Proust continued with Nabokov's *Speak, Memory* and ended with Sebald's prose. Between these points are the pages and pages of connective tissue: other texts without any claim to literary status but brought together with an *a priori* and unquestioning belief in the value of everything lost and the necessity of resurrecting it simply because it isn't there any longer.

Against a backdrop of the memoir canon's tower blocks and skyscrapers, Mandelstam's prose stands apart as a little remote building in a district preoccupied with other business. *Noise of Time* reacts warily to any potential reader, and not just because of the mystically dim light of Mandelstam's mode of thinking—"in dropped stitches" as he describes it. In any case, after a century of careful reading that light is now brighter. I believe the difficulty lies in the text's own pragmatics, the task the author has set it.

The purpose of these strange memoirs is to nail down the pine coffin lid on lost time, drive in the aspenwood stake, and turn on one's heel. It is hardly surprising then that the author has few allies in this task, so very few that it's almost easier not to notice what is going on and why. This is despite the fact that Mandelstam describes the purpose of his efforts of memory with absolute precision. This passage, so often cited by those who have written about his prose, repeats his message, with its stress on the repeated word "inimical":

My memory is inimical to everything personal. If it were up to me I would only scowl when I recalled the past. I could never understand those writers, Tolstoy, Aksakov, Bagrov's Grandson, in love with their family archives with their epics of household reminiscences. I say again that my memory is not loved by me, it is inimical to me, and it works not to reproduce the past, but to make it strange.

This is a surprising conceptual frame for a writer who is intending to do just that—recall the past—and to do it at thirty-two, hardly the ripest age for such an occupation. He was one of the first, if not the very first, of his generation to do this: *before it sets fast.* The prose is concerned with the bodily and intimate, the domestic world, its sounds and smells, with the way that a madeleine dipped in tea, and a tender (hope-filled) melancholy, can be converted into a viable currency. His mother and father, a bookcase behind green taffeta, the dachas in Finland, violin concerts, walks with nanny and so on and so forth, all details for a cozy account of his childhood, which appears to have been a huge influence on his later life, demanding great efforts on his part to tear himself free.

The result is a very peculiar text, peculiar firstly in the degree of compression with which units of tactile, auditory, and olfactory information are concentrated into a dark mass, shot through with veins and clots of amber, or into mineral seams, only visible in the beam of a miner's headlamp. There is no place to pitch your tent among the formulae opening like flower heads; every phrase is the sealed door to a corridor. The past is described like a landscape, perhaps even a geological case with its own history and methodology. A tale of childhood is transformed into a scientific text.

It seems to me that the logic is this: the author is the cartographer of a place he does not wish to return to. So right away and insofar as he can, he subtracts the human factor, the little pilot light of tenderness that's nearly always present in any discussion of the remembered past. The text spreads out before us from one winter to the next: in frost, clouds of steam, and the rustle of fur coats. Room temperature would be the most unimaginable luxury—the natural climate for this prose is freezing weather. In the language of cinematography, a freeze-frame is a static shot, and in some ways *Noise of Time* is constructed like a camera, describing the circles that surround such freeze-frames, shots of moving shapes without their teleological warmth (or with it hidden away down their furry sleeves). This is what Tsvetaeva means when she says, so unjustly, but so exactly: "Your book is a nature morte. [...] without a heartbeat, without a heart, bloodless—just eyes, a sense of smell, hearing."

The function of a historical nature morte, as Mandelstam conceived of it, runs counter to childhood and familial tenderness to give a precise diagram, an adaptable formula for the past. It works like a military parade, in a procession of rows and geometric shapes: puffed sleeves reflected in the glass dome of the Pavlovsk Station; the vast volume of squares and streets filled with a mass of people; architecture and music together as one. But any geometric construct is undermined by the guttering, smoking little flame of the 1890s, the musky, fur-clad world of Judaism. Literature (its wispy icon lamp, its teachers and family members) has the dark warm taste of the family affair; Jewishness is either climbing up out of the chaos, or growing its shaggy runic coat anew. In the presence of both, the picture is blackened with soot, retreating back into the black earthen mass of its cultural layer. Lucky then that architecture and music have an older brother in logic: the Marxist class system.

I'm not talking here about the usual demonstration of Tsarist excesses justifying a speedy revolution: that's how Tsvetaeva read *Noise of Time*, seeing it as a desire to please the authorities. In fact there are little signposts scattered with a child's slyness throughout the work, pointing the way to a more precise science, gathering all the disparate narratives into one. Of course it's likely that a childish political pragmatism also affects the work: many writers were scrambling to show their undying support for the changes. But Mandelstam's adolescent Marxism, past or actual, had a serious, structuring intent: it was like an arrow, its flight directed at the final break, the "full screeching turn of the cumbersome steering wheel" as he described it, toward a clear, fully articulated here and now that somehow needed to come about.

From this here and now Mandelstam looked back at the burial of a century, just as a few years later he would look down on Lamarck's "staircase" and the constant temptation of disintegration, that indiscriminate green tomb. A shuddering affection for the near past characterizes Mandelstam's prose and sets it apart from its other simpler brethren. Memory is not sentimental, it is functional, it works as an accelerator. Its job is not to explain the author's origin to him, nor to reproduce the infant's cradle in order to rock it. Memory works on behalf of separation, it prepares for the break, without which the self cannot emerge. Shove the past away like ballast so we can be propelled forward. No speed, no future.

In light of what came later it might seem that this separation was pointless. There was Mandelstam squirming, squealing his starling song, demanding this and that, living on the hoof, always passing over the present in favor of the unfulfilled promise. "Making a noise and giving them the runaround," as Nadezhda Mandelstam put it. But where did it lead? The new, the turn of the wheel, was paid for with the good old currency of collective fate, mass slaughter, labor camp dust, and labor camp death. And there was Tsvetaeva, with her unwavering trust in the past, her magnificent dismissal of news and newspaper truths. We know only too well that their disagreement, that ancient meeting of past and future, ended in nothing, in the most literal sense of the word: in dust, in two unmarked graves at different ends of the million-headed cemetery. No one won that argument. Everyone lost.

*

In a late interview on the subject of history, W. G. Sebald described an experiment: a rat was placed in a tank of water and observed to see how long it could swim. It lasted a short while, perhaps a minute, and then it died—its heart stopped. Some rats were given the unexpected opportunity of climbing out—just as their strength was leaving them a hatch opened in the wall of the tank, and through it shone the blinding light of freedom. When the rats were thrown back into the tank, those who had experienced this miracle of salvation behaved differently: they swam and swam along the walls of the tank until they died of exhaustion.

None of Sebald's books can be read as a consolation, whichever way we understand that word. There is no provision for the version of events where a hand is stretched out to life as it chokes and splutters in the watery darkness. He skirts any matter bordering on the divine with a long-held polite disbelief. It is quite pointless to treat his prose as a source of biographical material, but in the second part of *The Emigrants,* the section titled "Paul Bereyter," there is a passage about the divinity classes, which irritate and upset in equal measure the hero of the story, the schoolteacher, and the schoolboy who is the narrator of the story. A child growing up in postwar Germany could end up with the most upended view of the world order: back then, one of the main attributes of the big town, distinguishing it from the frivolous village, were the spaces between buildings, filled with rubble and clinker, heaps of bricks, wastelands. Sebald absolutely refused to consider himself a thematic writer, of the catastrophe of European Jewry (he felt the same solidarity with all the annihilated, even the trees and buildings, and I wouldn't say that people were more important to him than the rest). In the lectures he gave in 1997, later published in English as *On the Natural History of Destruction,* he spoke about a different sort of memory: about

195

the carpet bombing of German cities in the last years of the war
and the amnesia it had produced in those who had survived it:

*From what we now know about the ruin of this city it seems unlikely
that anyone who then stood on the Brühl Terrace, with the air full of
flying sparks, and saw the conflagration all around can have escaped
with an undisturbed mind. The apparently unimpaired ability—
shown in most of the eyewitness reports—of everyday language to go
on functioning as usual raises doubts of the authenticity of the experiences they record. The death by fire within a few hours of an entire
city, with all its buildings and its trees, its inhabitants, its domestic
pets, its fixtures and fittings of every kind, must inevitably have led to
overload, to paralysis of the capacity to think and feel in those who
succeeded in escaping.*

Sebald uses a few German sources and accounts by Allied pilots
and journalists who witnessed the bombardment for his description of the fires that rose some two thousand meters into the air,
so that even the cockpits of the bombers above were warmed by
the flames; the scalding water in canals; and the corpses lying in
puddles of their own fat. In the logic of Sebald's lists, whatever
else there might be place for, there is none for theodicy: the space
in which one might turn to God with a question or a reproach on
one's lips is utterly filled, like the ark, with all those who didn't
escape.

In this sense Sebald didn't need to choose between the
drowned and the saved, or the perished and those who still await
death. The feeling of comradeship in the face of our common
fate, just like in a town under siege or a sinking ship, makes his
approach universal and all-embracing. There is no miracle. Everything we see before us, including ourselves, will disappear,
and it won't take long. So there is no choice: any object or fate
or person or name board deserves to be remembered, to flicker
once again in the light before all is finally dark.

This lens, this way of looking at the world as if through a film of ash, through Celan's stationary screen, is particularly persuasive when you realize that the author will be with you until the end, that he is himself already on the other side, and is stretching out his hand to you from over there. In Marina Tsvetaeva's terrifying poem "Pity..." a woman stops by the unknown dead ("Not your husband? No. // Do you believe in the soul's resurrection? No.") hardly herself understanding why, until at the end:

Let me oh let me lay by him
Nail—down—the—lid!

But Sebald's speech doesn't just follow the departed. It is as if he has fastened himself to their slant rain-like structure, actually becoming one of those moving along the road toward the past. The narrator of his documentary fictions occasionally inhabits the contours of the author: he has the same history, a few friends among the living, the mustache and passport photograph of Sebald, but a strange transparent quality stops us from thinking of him as real. We follow everything this person does—his movement, which resembles a person driven along by a gust of wind; his hours of work and leisure, which do not coincide with ours; his chronicles of journeys and transfers, of bus routes and long-past hotels, where he watches a woman busying herself at a rolltop desk, as if the forces of gravity still acted on her as they had in life, and there was no point in hurrying on. The listing of street names and railway stations, as if the author doesn't quite trust his own memory and preferred to note everything down with the greatest care, attaching restaurant receipts and hotel bills. And the photographs that are embedded into the text serve to identify Sebald's work as accurately as a set of fingerprints. When the photos were being prepared for print Sebald would devote long hours to making them indistinct, as muddily unclear and homogeneous as he could.

Mandelstam pushed the past away, shoved it aside, compressing it into hard matter. But Sebaldian time is constructed quite differently—it has a porous, interstitial structure, like the monasteries in cliff faces, each cell in the rock still maintaining its parallel existence.

When we get close to these texts the problem of their authenticity comes to the fore. It's as if in working out the relationship between invention and truth, we make a decision on whether or not we can trust the author. This is how you might choose a guide through mountainous territory where every mistake could mean death. It's almost touching, how pragmatism shapes our persistent interest in the documentary carcass, in the prototype for this or that character and to what degree they are acquainted with or related to the author. Whether the boy on the cover is a real image of the boy inside—*what if none of these people are actually real?* Critics of Sebald sometimes cast him in the role of a museum curator or a park guard, wrapping the statues to protect them against the frost and checking the glass in the orangery windows: that role is redundant. If we bear in mind that there are no windows and there is no orangery then the function of this prose becomes clearer: it provides the illumination needed for a few things to become discernible. In *Austerlitz* he describes it like this: "... the longer I think about it the more it seems to me that we who are still alive are unreal in the eyes of the dead, that only occasionally, in certain lights and atmospheric conditions, do we appear in their field of vision."

I am so very in favor of any combining of the real and imaginary past, the documentary and fictitious, which allows Sebald to set his light machine in motion so the transparent discs of the past move, overlapping each other, filtering the light from one to the next, so that when a real event unexpectedly manifests itself (a real uncle from the family album, an original picture) I am strangely troubled, as if the chosen prototype had unexpectedly turned out to be a special case. I feel this particularly when Sebald is writing about images.

The last part of *The Emigrants* ends with an extraordinary fragment of memoir. When I haven't read the book for a while I remember this passage as an enormous text, almost infinitely extending, making up at least half of the entire book. But when I reread *The Emigrants* I am shocked to find it painfully short, no more than twenty pages. And I think to myself that I don't really want to know who wrote it. Is it the real woman with a name that begins with the letter L, who decides to think about her childhood, only her childhood, on the very threshold of death: her mother's books, roses, the road into town? Or is it Sebald himself, speaking in the woman's voice? Whichever it is, the fragment breaks off suddenly and the book ends with a cinematic darkening of the scene. And then the author tells the story of a photograph he once saw by chance.

Photographs are reproduced throughout the pages of Sebald's work, scattered like the breadcrumbs Hansel and Gretel plan to use to find their way home. But this image is not shown, merely described, and I have this description before my eyes, always. It is a workshop of some sort in the Łódź Ghetto, dimly lit, in half darkness. Three women bend over the diamonds and triangles of a woven carpet. One of them, says Sebald, has blonde hair and the air of a bride. The second woman's eyes are in shadow and can't be made out. The third weaver is looking at me with so steady and relentless a gaze that I cannot meet it for long.

I never thought I would ever see this photograph. Like the well-known portrait of Barthes's mother in a winter garden, which is described but doesn't appear in his great book, I thought of this photo as simultaneously real and nonexistent. How strange it was therefore to find that it fits the description absolutely. The picture of the three women was taken by a man named Genewein, a Nazi, the chief bookkeeper of the Łódź Ghetto. In his spare time he documented the hard work being done in the workshops under his charge with a confiscated Movex 12. The collection of pictures includes color images: a group of children dressed in various shades of brown with their caps to one side of their heads. The picture with the carpet and the three weavers is black-and-white, and, unlike the others, when you see it you don't immediately go cold with horror—the scene imitates life so closely, the calmly seated subjects in front of the camera, the light from a window in the background falling on them, touching their shoulders and hair as if nothing much is happening. This is exactly how it is described in *The Emigrants*, but with one important omission. In the softly lit air between us (between the women and the camera, between them and me) something that looks a little like a frame hangs at an angle, made from many vertical threads pulled tight. The carpet is rising slowly up this loom and it will soon obscure the room and all those in it. Strange that Sebald didn't notice this rising veil of carpet. Perhaps it wasn't there when he looked at the picture.

Not-A-Chapter
Lyolya (Olga) Gurevich, 1947

Undated, written after 1944 and the return from evacuation.
Addressed to Berta Leontyevna Gurevich, her mother-in-law
(the mother of Lyonya), who lives separately from them.

Dear Berta Leontyevna,
I came to see you, but Lyonya doesn't know this and I would prefer
it if it stayed between us.
It was very hard for me to come here, as you know I have my pride,
but I have been thinking a great deal over these last few days and I
decided that I had to do this. I came to see you with pure intentions.
I felt very bad that I was the cause of our appalling conversation. I
didn't mean to hurt your feelings, it's just that I haven't been well
recently, my nerves are in a terrible state and I was hurt that Lyonya
didn't consult me. Well, it doesn't matter now. I'm ashamed that such
a trivial thing has caused us to exchange bitter (and I think, on both
sides, undeserved) reproaches.
I have forgotten everything you said to me and I beg you to forget
everything I said, too. Life is hard enough as it is without making it
harder with unnecessary rows.
You have a son and a granddaughter, and I have a husband and
a daughter and I think that the purpose of life is, in the end, to bring
joy to those close to us.
I came to see you to make it up with you, to put our differences
aside. I hope you will understand why I came and that you will be
able to feel warmly toward me.
Sadly you were out when I came round, so I've had to use your

writing paper. I won't write more, I am leaving with the hope that you will be with us for the New Year.

    Allow me to kiss you.

    Lyolya.

5. On One Side and on the Other

Obverse:

Painted porcelain boys and girls of various sizes, with bright mouths and caps of black or yellow hair. Other cheaper versions, plain basic-white. All are bisque dolls manufactured in Germany for decades from the 1840s. In the small town of Köppelsdorf, in the oak land of Thuringia, whole factories produced nothing but dolls. Most of them were large and expensive with real hair, bodies of kidskin, and flushed porcelain cheeks, but there were other simpler figures. In Ernst Heubach's furnaces thousands of tiny dolls were fired, on sale for pfennigs and sold everywhere, like boiled sweets or soap. They looked like lost stubs of soaps, stiff little hands slightly in front of them, motionless legs in tiny socks, and because they were hollow and only their faces were varnished to save money, they could be put in the bath and they would float, little and modest, on their painted fronts.

There are many tales of these dolls as possessions. Apart from their obvious occupations (born "for the roll of a fist, for the life in a pocket" or the work of the tiniest units of humanity, as in the Tsvetaeva essay "My Pushkin"), they were placed on the shelves of dolls houses, hidden in Epiphany pastries to bring luck to the finder, and even, if it is to be believed, dropped into cups of tea instead of ice. I can't find any confirmation or rebuttal of the story that the broken dolls were used as packaging chips for transported goods, but it is clear that they were the foot soldiers of the toy world, ephemeral, easily replaceable and multipurpose.

The lion's share of this clay army was sold outside Germany. The tiniest were thumb-height and cost next to nothing. The bigger dolls were thirty to forty centimeters tall and were more prized by shopkeepers and their owners. Their export only stopped during the First World War, when selling dolls to the enemy began to feel awkward, and enterprising Japanese manufacturers took the place of the Germans. The Japanese dolls were made to the same model but using cheaper materials and only fired once. They smashed more easily, too. Lonely, valueless dolls crushed under the weight of time, like bird skulls crushed underfoot, they reappeared without limbs, black holes in place of joints. Some even returned from the earth, soil ground into the bisque, piles of broken dolls dug up from factory land. Years later their scarred white bodies were once again salable commodities, like everything from the past, sold as virtual lots on eBay, regiments of them, in sixes, tens, dozens. They are grouped carefully, or so it seems to me, with one or two near perfect specimens, victorious in the battle against time. An overfired back or a broken wrist hardly matters to these heroes, their heads are thrown back proudly, and their cheeks are round and glistening. The rest hardly aspire to being anything beyond splinters. This heap of survivors has only one name in the English-speaking world: frozen Charlottes.

Reverse:
   Charlotte is one of the classic names of the Germanosphere, where the number of blonde little Lottes nearly outnumbers the contingent of Margaretes or Gretchens. Lotte, the cause of Werther's suicide, with her apples and Brötchen, a pink band round her white dress—and before you know it she's back as Thomas Mann's muse. Goethe's Lotte, who came involuntarily to mind in 1939 when the old world crumbled under the jackboots of the new. Despite this, the German dolls were only called "Charlottes" in America.
   On February 8, 1840, the *New York Observer* reported: "A young woman, whose name is given as Miss _____, froze to death while riding twenty miles to a ball on the eve of January

1, 1840." A Portland journalist, Seba Smith, known for his love of maudlin subject matter, used the story as the basis for a ballad, which had some success: a few years later the "blind Homer of Benson, Vermont," William Lorenzo Carter, set it to music as "Young (or Fair) Charlotte." The 1840s was a time of snow fascination, the romance of the blizzard and frost. In the early 1840s Hans Christian Andersen published his "Snow Queen": "She was fair and beautiful, but made of ice — shining and glittering ice. Still she was alive and her eyes sparkled like bright stars, but there was neither peace nor rest in their glance. She nodded toward the window and waved her hand." Seba Smith wrote a second snowy ballad in the early 1840s "The Snow Storm," in which a young mother perished to save her baby, but the success of this fell far short of his "Young Charlotte."

"Young" or "Fair" — the song was sung with interchangeable epithets to suit sentiment across ten US states, and its story is both like and unlike the version of Hans Christian Andersen's "The Red Shoes," where the girl's terrible vanity is the cause of her undoing and amputation. But there is no morality, no anguish in "Young Charlotte," the text has the marmoreal balance of an antique frieze. A beauty rides to a ball with her intended, on a winter's night, desiring to be "seen," and so they drive across the snowy hills to the sound of horses' hooves and merry bells and all she wears is a silken coat and a silken scarf. The sleigh's speed increases with every verse of the ballad ("Young Charlotte said with a trembling voice: I am growing warmer now"), the stars shine coldly and the ballroom grows closer and closer. But when they arrive the heroine is cold and hard as stone. One of the less polite names for this song was "A Corpse Going to a Ball." The young man dies of a broken heart and is buried alongside his love.

The little china figurines crossing the Atlantic from Europe would soon be known as "frozen Charlottes" because of their rigid little bodies. To this day they are known by the same name, it's become a shorthand for these creatures of horror, the tiny white people of nightmares, and without a voice they are unable to object. The male figurines rapidly became known as frozen Charlies and they were no more able to object. Their curls their socks and their spectral whiteness makes them look like the small gods of a less ancient pantheon. Unlike the Greco-Roman Gods, who lost their color together with their power, there was never enough paint to go round for all the frozen Charlottes.

Obverse:

Arthur Rimbaud was interested in new technologies. He sent his family long lists of essential items, dictionaries, reference books, tools, and equipment to be delivered to him (no easy task) in Abyssinia. The parcels arrived in Harar. There was always something missing, but his camera at least arrived safely. Seven of the photos Rimbaud took have survived. In a letter to his mother and sister, written on May 6, 1883, he describes three self-portraits, including one "les bras croisés dans un jardin de bananes." In another he stands by a low fence, which looks like a cartoon railway track. Beyond the fence there is nothing. Uninterrupted desert, filling the whole print. You might think you can see a point where the gray of the land washes into the gray of the sky but it's unlikely. If we believe his account, Rimbaud the entrepreneur, in his white trousers, was photographed in "un jardin de café" and "sur une terrasse de la maison," but it would be hard to imagine anything less like a garden. Although we can only really guess at what we are seeing because something in the developing or printing of the pictures went wrong. All the photographs Rimbaud took—the market square with its awnings, the tiny building with a many-sided cupola, a man sitting in the shade of a column with bowls and gourds laid out in front of him—are fading to white, and there is no way this process can be stopped. The photographs are disappearing before our eyes, slowly, imperceptibly, like the ring of moisture left by a glass on a table.

Reverse:

Google Maps makes efforts to renew its satellite photographs as often as possible, but not always and not everywhere. Many towns, with their boulevards, tourist information offices, and unattractive monuments have a reliably unchanging profile for months, if not years: if you zoom in on Moscow on a snowy evening you see summer roofs and green spaces. Nearer the center of the earth, or wherever the program considers that to be, the changes happen faster—but even so they aren't fast enough. A woman leaves her lover, he smashes up the car and it goes to the scrapyard. He leaves town, she unfriends him on Facebook, but on Google Maps the colorless box of the car is still parked outside her door.

Obverse:

In his documentary tales of Istanbul, Orhan Pamuk describes a particular variety of local misery called *hüzün*, very different from European notions of melancholy, which arise from an awareness of the shortness of life. *Hüzün*, on the other hand, is not directed at the future and the sense of life passing, but at what has already passed and yet still suffuses our daily lives with its soft glimmer. The sensation is brought on by the counterpointing of past greatness with present wretchedness and mediocrity. For Pamuk it is based on a classic "before and after," what was and what has come to be, his bifocals allowing him to keep both the created model and its destruction (the ruin and its former glory) in focus. He remembers Ruskin in a passage where he talks about the chance nature of the picturesque, about how we find a visual pleasure in decay and dissolution, a pleasure that no urban architect has ever intended us to feel, in the deserted yards and marble flagstones overgrown with grass. A new building becomes picturesque "after history has endowed it with accidental beauty." In other words, after history has chewed it up and spat it out, unrecognizable.

Pamuk also quotes Walter Benjamin's phrase about the exotic and picturesque features of a city being of more interest to those who do not live there. When you think about it, the phrase applies equally to different forms of the past, not just its visibly aging stone skin of towers and turrets—but all the other boxes and cases in which a person packs and unpacks herself. Houses, beds, clothes, shoes, and hats—anything abandoned by its owner that hasn't yet quite fallen apart is suddenly filled with a new posthumous brightness. Our delight in vintage, as we call it now, comes precisely from entering a past life not as equals, but like a little girl in her mother's wardrobe, knowing full well we are trying on someone else's belongings.

The more the contemporary world plays at *olden days*, the further those days recede, spinning slowly down to the murky depths where nothing can be made out. The impossibility of exact knowledge is in the physical disintegration which protects the past from our trespasses; it forms a hygiene barrier against mixing with us, the present. For us, this impossibility is an advantage. The owners have left the house, they've gone away, and there is no one to see how we are dividing up all their many goods. For the full enjoyment of those *olden days* we need those who once peopled them to die—then we can begin the yearning process, trying out the role of rightful heirs. The heaped mass of witness accounts only teases us in our hunger: rifle through the bank of pictures, enlarge them, bring them up close to your eyes, spend a lifetime gazing at a single iconic image. It's all pointless: scoop it all out, to the very bottom of the cup, its tin walls, you can walk in to the house of the past, but you can't penetrate it, nor will it enter you, like the chill slick of a ghost that appears out of nowhere in the warm twilight of a July evening.

Obverse:

... and then I suggested to myself that I divide memory into its three types.

The memory of what is lost, inconsolable, melancholy, keeping tally of these losses while knowing that nothing can be returned.

The memory of what has been received: sated after-dinner memory, contented with one's lot.

The memory of what has never been—seeding ghosts in place of the real. Like the magic comb of Russian fairy tale: a deep dark wood springs up where the comb is thrown down and helps the hero to escape pursuit. The phantom memory does much the same for whole communities, protecting them from naked reality and its drafts.

The object of remembrance can be the same in all cases. In fact, it is always the same.

Reverse:

My fear of forgetting, of allowing anything to escape my hold—my mind—from the still-warm past, was justified and even extolled in the Old Testament. What is more, the people of the Old Testament were obliged to remember, and any failure to do so led to certain death. The chapters of Deuteronomy insist repeatedly on the remembrance of God: "Beware that thou forget not the Lord thy God, in not keeping his commandments, and his judgments, and his statutes, which I command thee this day." The scholar of Jewish history Yosef Hayim Yerushalmi recounts in his book (itself called *Zakhor*, the Hebrew imperative "remember!") how this powerful drive to remember lasted all the centuries of exile and diaspora. It was memory that demanded the scrupulous adherence to laws, to the achieving and the preservation of perfection—not by the individual, or the family, but by a whole people taken as one. A pure, holy life became the pledge that ensured survival, and no single detail could be lost or omitted.

Unusual historical events, understood to be without precedent, gave rise to the fear of forgetting. The prohibitions and obligations of Jewish faith were in some ways the result of these events, their imprint left on the mutable human wax. For many generations there was no further attempt in Jewish tradition to chronicle what had happened to the Chosen People, as if the Torah was the last word on the subject and nothing more was needed. It's said that the Russian futurist poet Velimir Khlebnikov quickly lost interest when reading out his own poems and would break off with "and so on and so forth ..." Yerushalmi describes something similar in *Zakhor*, but with different words: "Perhaps they already knew of history what they needed to know. Perhaps they were even wary of it."

It wasn't that *they* went into a new age utterly unaware of the discipline of history: there are plenty of examples in the texts and missives circulating around medieval Europe showing that the dates and markers of an unwritten history were well within the field of vision for Jewish scholars. They noticed these events, but nothing had the necessary magnitude to become part of the holy tradition. All the major events were long behind them as they'd happened at the very beginning. In a world dominated by precedent, when the destruction of the First and Second Temple was one single event, and the difference between Babylon and Rome was insignificant in the face of perpetual catastrophe, all the assaults and pogroms of the new wave of persecution (in France, Germany, and Spain) were simply continuations on a theme. The epitome of this approach to the past is Megillat Ta'anit (the scroll of fasting), which also sets out the red letter days in the calendar, the days for feasting, rather than mourning and fasting. These were the dates of feats and celebrations, recorded from pre-Maccabean times and up to the destruction of the Second Temple. A Scholion or commentary gives the dates of events separately. The scroll is not an effort to make history, but has a very different task: structured around the turning of the seasons it lists the days and months and not the years. In a later incarnation it becomes the Christian liturgical year. In the Jewish tradition there is no difference between the recent and far past, just as there is no difference between past and present.

In this way the Judaic memory is free from the need to commit everything in history to memory, free to choose the significant and essential, to cut away the inessential. The limitations were of a different kind; the imperative not to forget fitted well with the duty to focus—on one's own history among other things—when multifarious details threatened to overwhelm the fundamental truths. Jewish historiography (which barely existed before the Enlightenment and which suddenly blossomed in conditions of assimilation, departing from tradition for the simple reason that there was no real tradition; even the first persuasive history of the Jewish people was written by a gentile) seemed an unnecessary science; everything one needed to know was stored on a different shelf. Yerushalmi quotes Franz Rosenzweig's *Star of Redemption,* in which Rosenzweig maintained that the meaning of Jewishness lies in its ahistoricity: the Jewish people stood outside the general current of time and had even achieved a desired stasis through their observance of an unchanging law. Rosenzweig's work was published in 1921. Twenty years later the current once again washed against their shore. History claimed its own.

Even the Nazi imagination worked as if from inside the logic of the Jewish world, as if they desperately wanted to confirm or deny a thesis, to test the strength of the contract the Jewish people had with their God. Acts of punishment were meted out in accordance with their foreign calendar, although without discerning between days of mourning and days of feasting. The massacre of Jews at Babi Yar took place on Erev Yom Kippur and the destruction of the Minsk Ghetto was timed to coincide with Simchat Torah. The clearing of the Warsaw Ghetto began at Passover. Even such violent plungings into the black hole of catastrophic knowledge can be considered a sort of confirmation. The impossibility of forgetting searches out its own markers, its own mounds, familiar stones, or ravines and *refuses to be comforted for its children, for they were not.* Yerushalmi's *Zakhor* is a book about memory as the highest of all the virtues, and yet it ends with a near prayer for oblivion: that it might cease to be a sin, that all the rips and tears might be left in peace, to be themselves, untroubled.

Obverse:

Dybbuk means "cleaving to" or "clinging to"; the description often involves the sense of grafting, like a gardener experimenting by splicing a pear shoot to an apple tree, or a briar rose to a garden rose. The restless soul of Ashkenazi legend cannot be parted from this world, either because the weight of sin is too heavy upon it, or it has simply got stuck staring at something living, and can no longer trace the way home. A soul whose death was terrible or shameful, or who won't be divested of earthly joys, wanders from door to door looking for a crack to force themselves through, a person who can be inhabited like a tidy, well-swept house. It might be an old man, weakened by illness and no longer able to pinch tight the corners of his own body, or a woman tormented by waiting, or a person whose own soul is not stationary, but wanders back and forth like a pendulum. Clinging to this person, the dybbuk worms his way in, puts down roots — this home is warm and raw. Ten men wearing burial shrouds and blowing on a shofar (ram's horn) must beg the evil spirit to leave the body, but are not always successful in talking it round. It cries pitifully and begs its tormentors in many different voices, calling them by their names and listing the sins they have until now kept private, and their birthmarks and their childhood nicknames ...

This is just like the past when it won't leave. It cleaves to the present, burrows under its skin, leaving its spores there and talking in tongues and ringing its bells, so there is no greater joy for a person than listening and remembering what has never happened to him, crying for those he never knew, calling by name those he never saw.

Reverse:

I once read a book on the ghosts of birds that described the relationship between an Indigenous tribe and its dead ancestors. It was laid out very precisely, like diplomatic protocol, and based on a complicated system of agreements and indulgences. Its descriptions of protocol included chance meetings—that awkward moment when you walk into a dead person on a dark road, like a pillar of icy air. I'd like to quote from the book but I can't—I picked it up and read from it in an overseas bookshop, and I'm afraid I will misremember the text. In many ways this resembles my negotiations with the past, which are based on hard facts, like the hard cover of a book, but I have to resurrect them from thin air and resign myself to the inevitable inaccuracies: in the same way they draw the image of a bird from just its claw or its feather, once it has become a shade.

It's no secret that the people of the past are easily and quickly transformed into something unrecognizable and often nonhuman. In "The Arm," a short story by Ludmilla Petrushevskaya, a dead pilot drags a burnt log from his cockpit with the words: "This is my navigator." This fictional account has its nonfictional doppelgänger in a dream the prose writer Vsevolod Ivanov had just before his death. He dreamed that he was with Anna Akhmatova at a World Congress of Writers, in Greece of all places (at the time it was easier for a citizen of the USSR to cross the Lethe than an international border). This fantastical trip, the dream of a Soviet writer in hospital in the summer of 1963, had a distinctly paradisiacal nature. "In the morning I went downstairs and I saw a woman sitting at the table and weeping. Anna Andreevna, I said to her, Anna, why are you crying? And she answered that she had seen her son in the table, only her son was pink, and the table was black marble."

The records of dreams are inaccurate in an unintentional way: did the oneiric Akhmatova see the face of her son (who was brought up by strangers a long way away from her, arrested, rearrested, and rendered unrecognizable by labor camps) in the polished marble surface? Or was the table actually her child in the dream, like the burned log of the navigator: a four-legged marble child, black instead of pink, her little Lev, found by her in the unattainable and paradisiacal Greece? Her table son, upon whom the dead are laid out to be dressed for the grave, like the rock where Jesus was laid to be washed and anointed. In "Requiem," Akhmatova compares her still-living son with the crucified Christ, and her suffering with the suffering of the Mother of God. Years later he returned from the camps and was rearrested, as if these passages into the world of the dead and back again were quite normal.

The philosopher Yakov Druskin was a member of the Chinarei, a group of Leningrad poets and philosophers who had formed a very close circle in the thirties and who were slowly squeezed out of existence by Soviet reality. They were excluded from official writing structures (by their own choice and also because the radical nature of their texts hardly met the expectations placed upon "fellow travelers," those writers who weren't currently aligned with official party policy, but were "catching up"). For a while they flourished in their modest way, working for children's magazines, writing virtuosic poems and short stories, playing cards and spot-the-difference, going to the races and sunbathing on the thin strip of Neva sand by the Peter and Paul Fortress. Little by little their untroubled and dimly lit patch of shade shrunk in size, and they became more and more conspicuous. Members of the circle were arrested, exiled to other towns, or they lost their work, but they kept coming back, as if unaware how transparent their spare little existence had become. In his diaries Daniil Kharms, perhaps the best known of all the Chinarei, interspersed prayers, metaphysical problems, and longings for female folds and smells with the odd note that he had no money, nowhere to get money, and was growing hungry. Kharms did indeed die of hunger in an NKVD jail in the terrible winter of 1942, during the Siege of Leningrad. Aleksandr Vvedensky died in a freight car during his enforced evacuation from Leningrad in December 1941. Leonid Lipavsky went missing in action in September 1941. Nikolai Oleinikov didn't last as long as his friends—he was executed in 1937.

Druskin alone survived, hardly understanding himself why he had been spared. He never once ceased his conversation with the dead. More and more space in his philosophy notebooks is given over to writing out dreams in which he sees his dead friends and tries to make certain that it is really them, that they have returned at last. He can't be certain; the experiment is fruitless. Druskin and his friends are cutting open the chest of a person they believe to be Lipavsky "to see whether this is a dream or not" but they immediately forget what they are trying to prove. One of his ghosts doesn't want to acknowledge him, another is transformed so he looks like a Soviet writer (just as he might a log of wood or a marble table or a wardrobe). On April 11, 1942, Druskin writes up yet another dream meeting with his dead friends. He dreams of them all the time, he sees them more now than when they were alive:

We all gathered, I prepared some refreshment, some fizzy water. We looked at each other and laughed. Who had we come to look like? Lipavsky, for instance, he and I, we've changed more than the rest. But L is utterly unlike himself. And the third L—well I would never have taken him for L. A. D. I. [Kharms?] *I would barely have recognized him. And perhaps it isn't him, although it should be. And there were some others around, one of them was Shura (Vvedensky), but which one? And there was a Pulkanov there. With a different surname.*

Pulkanov is not a common surname. No one in Druskin's circle had that name. The dream had fitted the name over someone like a cloak and masked that person, hidden him so well we don't even know who he was. Perhaps he was the dreamer.

6. Charlotte, or Acts of Insubordination

I love books, films, and stories that begin like this: a person arrives at a small home in a remote part of let's say France, opens the windows, goes out onto the balcony, moves the furniture around. She lays out her books, crawls under the table to plug in her computer, studies the contents of an unfamiliar kitchen cupboard and chooses the mug she will use. She walks to the village for the first time and buys tomatoes and cheese. Sits down at a table in the only local café and drinks coffee or wine. She wrinkles her eyes in the bright sun and returns to the house. She watches the television, looks out of the window, up at the ceiling. If she's a writer (let's say) then she starts work earlier in the morning.

Usually this moment of unspoiled happiness, work that has at last found its proper space and time, blessed utter peacefulness, is interrupted by some unasked-for act. In Islamic texts there is a euphemism for death—"the destroyer of pleasure, disbander of gatherings"—and this seems to me to be the perfect description of the storytelling dynamic, which has the task of pitching the peaceful prehistory at such an angle that everything is set in motion and the hero begins the slow roll down the slope, arousing both the reader's sympathy and irritation. We know and dread what literature and history offers us in this situation. The heroine will never finish the page she is writing because uninvited guests will arrive. The hero has no time on his own because a murder happens nearby. The resurrection is halted because a war has just begun.

At the end of 1941, twenty-four-year-old Charlotte Salomon did something rather odd. She left Villefranche-sur-Mer, a villa with a view over the Côte d'Azur where she had been staying with her grandparents. Things were different now: the money had run out, her grandmother had died, and they were relying on the pity or the whim of their hosts. Like many other German Jews, they had once been respectable, but hardly knew where to turn now. Charlotte left abruptly, in the manner of a person suddenly standing up and leaving a room. She took lodgings in nearby Saint-Jean-Cap-Ferrat and stopped seeing friends. It isn't clear what she lived on, but we know where she lived, in a tiny hotel with the age-old name "La Belle Aurore." She spent six months there, quite alone, working on what would be her great work, *Life? Or Theater?*, a sequence of 769 gouache pictures in which images are interspersed with text and musical phrase. There are also a number of pages of material that didn't make it into the main body of the piece: all in all she painted 1326 gouaches. When she ran out of paper she painted on the other side of the rejected sheets, and toward the end of the process she painted on both sides of every sheet.

The gouaches were painted on sheets of A4 paper in such terrible haste that she had to hang them around the walls of her little room so they would dry quicker. They were overlaid with tracing paper on which phrases, "stage directions," and what might be termed "instructions" were written to tell the viewers what musical phrase they should have in their head when looking at the picture. Sometimes this could be complicated: the melody itself had another text attached, a bitter little street ditty to the tune of the "Horst-Wessel-Lied" or "Habanera." Music was an intrinsic part of the narrative. The pages themselves are ordered in three parts with a prologue and epilogue and even a defined genre: a "Dreifarben Singespiel," a three-color singspiel—the phrase should instantly bring to mind *The Magic Flute*, the most popular singspiel in the German canon, and also Brecht and Weill's *Die Dreigroschenoper*, banned only a short time before, but still resounding in everyone's ears.

The music Charlotte (or CS as she signs her work) incorporates into the work is hardly esoteric. It's the music of the period, the music the people of her world had in their shopping baskets, from Mahler to Bach and back again, from the music halls to Schubert's Miller song cycle. She wanted to remind people of the familiar (and to parody it), but eighty years later there is practically no one left who could instantly recognize these tunes. The sound element no longer resonates, it is merely suggested and is, in its own way, like memory itself, with its inevitable dark spots and corrections. To quote Salomon:

Since I myself needed a year to discover the significance of this strange work, many of the texts and tunes, particularly in the first paintings, elude my memory and must—like the creation as a whole so it seems to me—remain shrouded in darkness.

The high register, quickly supplanted by mocking tongue twisters and the many-voiced dialogues interrupting the authorial voice all make perfect sense if we think of it as theater, with the opening sheet as the cover of program notes or a play text, with curly scripts and theatrical flourishes and a cast list. Just like traditional theater, the Prologue and Epilogue come out center stage to deliver their explanations and warnings. Yet *Life? Or Theater?* doesn't unfold neatly like a play. Nor is it a guide to be slipped in a pocket—it is so big you can barely pick it up. To read it from beginning to end would be a real undertaking, requiring both time and willpower.

It is also extraordinarily hard to exhibit the work properly, and not only because of the vast space you would need to do it thoughtfully, in narrative order. The images themselves seem to demand more—they want to be a book, the pages interleaved with transparent overlay so the text interacts with the image showing through, and we can lift the curtain and look at the naked image beneath, without its veil of text. There is a complex balance between the out-of-frame voice of the handwritten text (which changes color for certain key words and phrases, sometimes several times on a page) and the *live transmission* of the reportage-style images: this balance doesn't just suggest a rhythm for reading/looking, it insists on one. What we see needs to be treated like "temporary art," in the same category as cinema or opera. To do this through museum exhibition seems impossible—the full work is never on display and so the very first graphic novel never looks anything more than a series of talented sketches.

In the Amsterdam Jewish Cultural Quarter, where the Salomon archive is kept, there is a single case where (of 1300 gouaches) a mere eight pages are displayed. The work is damaged by exposure to light, so the display is limited and continuously changed. Displaying them in book form would be even more damaging, as it is said every single touch would cause irreparable damage. *Life? Or Theater?* has become something like holy writ—never seen, known only by reproduction and hearsay. It can be quoted or interpreted or called upon, but never just read in the order intended.

About her work, Salomon wrote:

The creation of the following paintings is to be imagined as follows: a person is sitting beside the sea. He is painting. A tune suddenly enters his mind. As he starts to hum it, he notices that the tune exactly matches what he is trying to commit to paper. A text forms in his head, and he starts to sing the tune, with his own words, over and over again in a loud voice until the painting seems complete. Frequently, several texts take shape, and the result is a duet, or it even happens that each character has to sing a different text, resulting in a chorus. [...] The author has tried—as is apparent perhaps most clearly in the Main Section—to go completely out of herself and to allow the characters to sing or speak in their own voices. In order to

achieve this, many artistic values had to be renounced, but I hope
that, in view of the soul-penetrating nature of the work, this will be
forgiven.

*

"Soul-penetrating" is a sly self-ironizing, but when we consider
Life? Or Theater? it isn't really an overexaggeration, more of a
diagnosis. The narrative has all the qualities of sensationalist fic-
tion: it can't be put down, it breathes fire and frost. The narrator,
named simply "the author," lays before the reader a story that
spans generations, includes eight suicides, two wars, several love
stories, and the victorious onslaught of Nazism. Anyone who
knows that it closely follows the real history of Charlotte's family
(and there's a long tradition of understanding the "three-colored
singspiel" as a purely autobiographical work), also knows how
the story ends. In September 1943 the Nazis conducted what they
called the "cleansing of Jews" in the Côte d'Azur—the efforts
of Vichy France seemed to them, and probably were, lacking
in assiduousness, and tens of thousands of refugees were quietly minding their own business down by the Mediterranean.
By then the rhetoric of Jews as insects, bedbugs, cockroaches,
as constant as the sound of running water, had hardened to become perceived reality, and it was time to "take back control."
A man called Alois Brunner was put in charge of the operation
and it was effective: a villa owned by an American woman in
Villefranche-sur-Mer was one of many "decontaminated." The
villa was called L'Ermitage and a Jewish couple lived there pretty
openly: Charlotte and her husband of only a few months. They
were taken at night, their neighbors heard screams. On October
10, a freight transport (with x number of freight "units," as they
wrote in the consignment notes) arrived at Auschwitz. On the
same day, just arrived, twenty-six-year-old Charlotte Salomon
was put into a group destined for immediate destruction. This

was unusual: a young woman, full of energy and able to draw as well, had an increased chance of surviving longer. But Charlotte was visibly pregnant. Clearly that decided her fate.

The horror reflex, the onrush of pity when we face such information is overwhelming, it shapes our understanding: a long history of critical inertia mean that we see in Salomon's work the spontaneous (and artless, in the face of her silence) expression of a pure heart. Any story of a victim is doomed to be emblematic— an arrow pointing toward a collective fate, a collective death. Charlotte Salomon's life story tends to be thought of as typical: the result of layers, one forming on top of another, of political and cultural conditions, of terrible and immutable patterns. But it was against all of this that she rebelled, and I think she felt herself to be victorious. *Life? Or Theater?* isn't the witnessing of a victory, but the victory itself, the battlefield, the captured castle, and a declaration of intent on 769 sheets of paper. All the same, it is often treated not as an object, but as material (as *raw* material from which fragments can be taken, and the excess discarded), and not as an artistic achievement but as an act of witnessing (which can be used in different generalizing contexts), not as a result but as an unfulfilled promise—a human document, in short. This interpretation could not be further from the truth.

Almost everyone writing about Charlotte in the last few years has cautioned against the obvious danger of seeing the work as an account of death told by a victim. This singspiel in pictures, written on the Côte d'Azur just before the world ended, is not a tale of the Holocaust (although unlike its author it has, against the odds, become a survivor). But it takes special effort from the viewer to stand in front of these works and simultaneously remember and forget, to know and not to know about Auschwitz at the end of the tunnel. The pages of *Life? Or Theater?* are overlaid with tracing paper and through it we see the image, but at any moment we can remove this filter to find ourselves alone with pure color.

In the summer of 1941 Charlotte Salomon had a stroke of luck that overwhelmed her and made her life feel charmed: rounded up and imprisoned, she was one of very few who were released and managed to escape disaster and death. In her text, alongside the initial "The action takes place in 1913–1940 in Germany and later in Nice, France," she writes "Or between heaven and earth beyond our era in the year I of the new salvation." So Noah might have described himself with his sons, or Lot's daughters, and that is how Charlotte saw herself and her situation: the known world had ended, together with everyone she had loved or hated. They had died, disappeared, or been dispersed to other places. She was much like the first person in a new world, the recipient of unexpected and indescribable largesse — she had been given a renewed and redeemed world: "Foam, dreams — my dreams on a blue surface. What makes you shape and reshape yourselves so brightly from so much pain and suffering? Who gave you the right? Dream, speak to me — whose lackey are you? Why are you rescuing me?"

Straight after the war, when Charlotte's father and stepmother were finally able to come to Villefranche-sur-Mer to search for her — for anything, traces, tokens, tales — they were handed a file that Charlotte had left with an acquaintance with the words: "This is all my life." The logic of the "typical" that I spoke of earlier pushes us to search out analogies, and in this case an analogy was waiting in the wings: in exactly the same way Miep Gies gave Otto Frank a bundle of papers, including Anne Frank's diary, when he returned from concentration camp. There is, astonishingly, a very real connection between these stories in that Albert Salomon and his wife hid in Amsterdam, not far from the Franks, and Otto Frank chose to show them Anne's diary before anyone else. A little later they decided together with Otto what to do with Charlotte's drawings. I have an idea of them in the fifties and sixties, parents who had lost their children, sitting together and arranging their children's posthumous fate. The first publication of

Salomon's work appeared in 1963 and the quality of its reproductions remains thrilling. Eighty of the thousand-plus gouaches are included and the book is called *Charlotte: A Diary in Pictures*. "In pictures"—as if we are talking about a little girl, Anne Frank's age or even younger. The diary is a traditionally female genre, a sort of mirror-mirror-on-the-wall: the spontaneous and unadorned voice of the feelings. The joy of the genre is in its very immediacy and simplicity. Anne Frank's diary was carefully edited to make it a text of consolation rather than horror, and was already making headlines all around the world, it had become the most influential text about the Holocaust, a way of thinking about it without thinking about railway lines, pits, and corpses, pushing all these horrors back to the epilogue: *and then they all died*. Whether consciously or not, Anne Frank's diary became a model for the first publishers of Salomon's work, who insisted on the convergence of Charlotte the author and Charlotte Kann, the fictional heroine of the work, young victim, so very promising, so little fulfilled.

The tradition set by the family both elides author and heroine, and yet suggests at the same time that actually "things happened quite differently." Whatever the reality was, we only know how Charlotte had wanted to tell the story at any cost. It's hard to distort the carefully constructed *Life? Or Theater?*, the editing principle already lay at the heart of its structure and the 500 rejected drawings testify to this—but the first publishers' impulse to "tidy the story up" meant they didn't stop at cutting the images, presenting fragments from the carefully composed whole image without indicating they were fragments, and crossing out or rewriting phrases. They had a harder job than the editors of the Anne Frank diary, where only very particular elements of the text were censored: anti-German outbursts, hurtful things about Anne's mother, chat about contraceptives, shocking for the time—and, more interestingly, any reference to the everyday Jewish experience, like Yom Kippur, which would be inaccessible to a wider readership.

The editorial changes to Salomon's singspiel ran counter to everything, foremost actual authorial intent: Salomon had shaped the work like the film of a family's history, run from beginning to end as if everyone was dead and gone, including her, and nothing could touch her anymore. Everything that happened from the 1880s onward was subject to revision, to satire and distancing: deaths, marriages, meetings and new marriages, career hopes, the love of art. That sort of chronicle, describing lives over several generations as the movement toward an inevitable endpoint, won Thomas Mann the Nobel Prize. But then his work was far more conservative.

*

You could, I suppose, tell it like this: an old, honorable, and assimilated Jewish family, oil paintings on the wall, a summer house in Italy, candles on the Christmas tree, breaking into "Deutschland über Alles" at moments of national fervor. And far too many suicides. We'll skip the brothers and other relatives and begin with one of the daughters, the more melancholy daughter, who leaves the house one November evening and drowns herself in a lake. A few years later the second daughter, the happier one, gets married. Eight years later, after promising her own daughter she will send her a letter from heaven, she jumps to her death from a window. The daughter is never told how her mother died: she thinks she died of flu.

New governesses, trips to Italy, the little girl grows up. She is called Charlotte after her dead aunt and her living grandmother—as if the line of Charlottes can't be broken. One day her workaholic father ("And I will be Professor. Don't disturb, please don't disturb me.") meets that peak of refinement, a blonde woman who sings Bach. In *Life? Or Theater?* she has the clown-like name Paulinka Bimbam. I should add here that for one reason or another all the characters with some connection with the stage have operetta-style names with jester's bells attached: Bimbam, Klingklang, Singsang. These masked players have double names to match their own comic duality. Bimbam's real name was Paula Lindberg, but even that was not her real name: she was the daughter of a rabbi, and her real name was Levi. She was Jewish like everyone else in Charlotte's life. Ten years later Charlotte wrote about her family that one should remember they lived in a society consisting entirely of Jews.

The marriage of science and art (medicine and music, of Albert Salomon and Paula Lindberg) pleased fourteen-year-old Charlotte more than anyone. Her relationship with her stepmother can only be described as passionate, and as time passed this passion became weighted with its attendant sentiments: jealousy, misery, exigency. Lindberg wanted to be a mother to the orphan, but instead she became embroiled in a white-hot crush friendship, a pleasure and a torment to them both. Our only clear source for this is *Life? Or Theater?* where much of the information may be deliberately or involuntarily distorted—but what can't be mistaken is the level of attention directed at the heroine of the novel (or the operetta?), Paula. There are hundreds of portraits of Paula and they reproduce with terrifying precision the expressions and movements of Paula's face (in a video interview with Paula, made decades later, it's these expressions you recognize first—the face is old, but the mannerisms are unchanged). There's a page filled entirely with the bodies and the faces of Paulinka: sullen, passionate, animated, downcast, detached. In the center, her official portrait on a playbill with a list of the towns where she had sung to great acclaim. Only the character of the singspiel, Amadeus Daberlohn (Alfred Wolfson) takes up more space in the narrative.

The many pages of "drawn" writing stand outside the main body of the text. This writing was intended as an epilogue, but constantly strives to become a letter to an addressee, Wolfson, whose fate Charlotte did not know. Parts of this "letter" are online at the Jewish Cultural Quarter Museum in Amsterdam. It has been excerpted and quoted, but never published in its entirety. At one stage in the composition of *Life? Or Theater?* the artist thought of the whole work as a speech in a dialogue with Wolfson, a way of proving to him her own ability to regenerate. The work has an addressee who is the person Charlotte Salomon considered or wanted to consider her beloved, and in dozens of scenes she rehearses the notion of inseparability, from embrace to complete union.

This can perhaps be explained by the fact that the gouaches depicting Paulinka are lit with erotic energy, but they never cross the line into the territory of love: the narrator deliberately holds the narrative on the brink, hinting and never clarifying ("our lovers have made it up again"). This page is a rapid burst of images of the two women moving toward each other, the little girl in her blue bedroom, stepmother by her bed, their embrace caught in nine frames, Paulinka bending down, her stepdaughter moving toward her, suddenly tiny, a babe in her mother's arms. The embrace is full, Paulinka's face is pressed against Charlotte's breast, the white sheets blossom pinkly. In the last image at the bottom of the page the childish blue pajamas are gone, and instead we see the naked shoulders and arms of both women. Charlotte's eyes are screwed up and the sheet is now a crimson wave. The explicit nature of the drawings has no textual equivalent—if a thing is left unnamed, does it exist?

The relationship between Daberlohn and Paulinka is never elucidated, either. It remains a matter of projection and guesswork. It's vitally important for the text and the narrator that the relationship be presented as a triangle with Charlotte forming the third side: the grown-up and equal rival. The singing teacher who has promised Paulinka Bimbam that he can perfect her singing cannot avoid falling in love with the singer because in the world of the singspiel she is irresistible, as any indifferent divinity should be, and because his passion is the fuel for her flight. He still finds time to pay attention to the little girl and her drawings, and even to have a separate love affair with her, taking walks and talking with her, and this doesn't seem to surprise her in the least. She rather feels a deep sense of gratitude. He is writing a book and she illustrates it: their relationship is shaped so it can be grown into, and it gives a purpose to her existence. She remembers his theories, she inhabits them; his theory that one cannot begin a life without the experience of going through death (and the need to "go out of oneself," the cinema as a machine invented in order to leave one's "I" behind) becomes the hull of the enormous ship *Life? Or Theater?* Their meetings in the station café (Jews are prohibited from going to other cafés) and on park benches (also prohibited, but they risk it) are placed right at the center of the text, along with hundreds of pictures of Daberlohn's face, framed in his own rather simpleminded sermons.

Everything takes place against a backdrop of passing crowds, mouths stretched into cries, children boasting about their ballpoint pens requisitioned from Jewish shops. On one of the sheets, depicting Berlin at the time of Kristallnacht, Salomon distinctly appears among the names of looted shops (Selig and Cohn). To describe what is happening at that point among her circle of acquaintances she invents the word combination *menschlich-jüdisch*: she speaks of these human-Jewish souls as if she were speaking of some strange wild hybrid that needed to be observed and studied. And that is more or less how it was.

In 1936 the Jew Charlotte Salomon won a place at the Berlin Academy of the Arts, an impossibility, according to the laws of the time, and perhaps only because the Academy was overwhelmed by Charlotte's uncommon bravery and doggedness. The Academy was later forced to explain their behavior, and it's worth noting how they did this: Charlotte was allowed to study because of her asexuality, as someone who was clearly not capable of exciting male Aryan students. In *Life? Or Theater?* Charlotte writes up a dialogue from the entrance interview: "But do you accept Jews?"—"You probably aren't Jewish."—"I am a Jew, of course I am." — "Well, never mind." A fellow student, featured in a few of Charlotte's gouache drawings, remembers her as an outsider, dressed in gray, like a somber November sky.

Three years later Charlotte was dispatched against her will to France to live with her grandparents. They were by then impoverished, but somehow contrived to live much as they always had. In a publication of *Life? Or Theater?* published in 1969, the picture of her saying farewell to Daberlohn (one of many silent embraces owing something to Klimt) is titled "a fantasy." Paula Lindberg insisted till her dying day that the love triangle embodied in the singspiel was teenage invention and that it had never happened. In the images on the following pages we see a general farewell at the station: Charlotte's stooped father, who has just been released from Sachsenhausen concentration camp; her stepmother in a mink coat; Daberlohn's round glasses.

*

As for the "soul-penetrating nature of the work," Salomon encouraged the reader to see a lyrical shape in the work, something along the lines of a love story. A "romance," to employ that useful term, which holds within itself both the kernel of narrative and a system of nuance underpinning everything in the book, and most importantly the love interest. It's a word Freud uses in his important 1909 article "Familienroman der Neurotiker," which is traditionally translated as "Family Romances." In the article, Freud describes a particular stage of development when the child begins to consider how he, such a "special" child, could be born to such ordinary parents, and so he invents new parents: spies, aristocrats, divine presences invented in his likeness. He thinks of himself as a victim of circumstance, kidnappings, fraudulence: a Romantic hero imprisoned in the fortress of dramatic realism. Pasternak writes of this with understanding in an early poem, the inevitable experience of "dreaming that your mother is not your mother, that you are not you, that your home is a foreign land."

The subject of *Life? Or Theater?*, with its suicidal angels, fairy-godmother stepmother, and magical teachers is apparently such a "romance" and I occasionally catch myself on the word, as if I were considering it a "he-loves-me-he-loves-me-not" tale. It is of course nothing of the sort—nothing could be further from the virtuous stepdaughter trope, like *Cinderella* or *Snow White*. The work has both the structure and the sweep of an epic. It's a wake for the disappearing world. Charlotte Salomon is writing—with precision and complete self-awareness—the decline and destruction of her class, the only one she ever happened to know. The days were numbered for the enlightened, lofty Jewish bourgeoisie with its refined taste, expensive habits, and little sermons on positivism. (Life must go on, says Charlotte's rather sinister grandfather after the suicide of his daughter. You can't get around what you are, he pronounces in 1939 as the shadows are gathering. Everything natural is holy, he repeats.) The family had become a relic, a people of the past, living by inertia and dying by their own will. Charlotte Salomon became the dining-table chronicler of this age of decline, bewilderment, and pitiful efforts to keep one's dignity intact.

Without meaning to, Charlotte's hateful grandfather gave his granddaughter an unbelievable, albeit rather depressing, gift by offering her the possibility of a new life. At an opportune moment he told her the whole family history, and he gave it to her pretty straight: the eight suicides lined up in a row looked like an invitation: you're next. But the knowledge of what had happened, once laid bare, had the opposite effect. In one of the gouaches Charlotte, bent over the pans on a stove, says approximately this: "What a wonderful thing is life! I believe in it! I'll live for each and every one of them!"

So the colossal system of *Life? Or Theater?* begins to unfold from the tiny speck of an unexpected revelation. The story of a tribe, seen from the outside, by a person who has lost their connection with the old world.

*My life began when my grandmother wanted to commit suicide ...
when I learned that my mother had also taken her own life ... It was
as if the whole world, in its depth and terror opened up like an abyss
in front of me. [...] Then when it was over with my grandmother and
I stood alone in front of her bleeding corpse, when I saw her little foot
that still moved in the air and twitched in automatic reflex ... when
I then threw a white sheet over her and I heard my grandfather say
"She did do it after all," [at that moment] I knew that I had a task,
and that no power in the world may stop me from carrying it out.*

*

The director of the Jewish Cultural Quarter Museum in Amsterdam once commented that the problem with *Life? Or Theater?*
was that there was nothing to compare it with—in the whole of
world art there was nothing that stood alongside it. Its loneliness
coincides rather strangely with the massive wave of interest in the
history captured in the work. The artist has become yet another
icon of collective suffering, an *important figure,* the synopsis for
a Hollywood film, not because of what *she* did, but because of
what *they* did to her.

I want to write about the singspiel itself, and its wondrous
complexity, as if it weren't connected with the fate of its maker—
but it doesn't seem possible. There's something in the character
of the work that makes us want to lay a filter over our reading to
ease it, and then to throw the same filter aside in irritation. This
is not autobiography, although it is incredibly similar. Neither is
it an exercise in self-help therapy that we are witnessing, nor an
effort to contain trauma (although Charlotte herself tells us more
than once that the work is not an end but a means). It's not even
an anti-Nazi text—the Nazis in *Life? Or Theater?* are not more
comic or frightening than any of the other protagonists. "I was
each of them," states the author.

This is not true either. Both named and unnamed are present
in the work: the text about trauma, what one might term "fe-

male optics," the sign of the Catastrophe, the magic of childish thought: *if I draw it, that's how it will come to be.* All these readings are rational and justifiable in themselves; it's the incongruity between the scale of the singspiel and its reception that hurts. It's as if we rummaged through the archives of the male art world and found that the whole body of textual interpretation of Proust's *In Search of Lost Time* was based on Proust's biography: Proust and Jewishness, Proust and homosexuality, Proust and tuberculosis. This *thing* Charlotte Salomon invented and made is far more than its own reflections.

I keep wanting to discuss Salomon's singspiel, with its carefully conceived theatrical frame, as if it were literature. I keep using the words "text," "book," and "read." Perhaps this is because its drifting space has the contours of the classic nineteenth-century novel, the sort her grandparents might have read, the tradition continued by Proust, Mann, and Musil. But I'm wrong—as far as I know there are no references to literature or to writers in the work, although there are dozens of direct and indirect references to the musical and visual arts. Literature was invisible, but you could feel it in the air you breathed during adult conversations. Operetta is the younger sister of the Dombeys, the Karenins, and is occupied with the same immutable concerns: that thematic high road of "the disappearing world." Charlotte Salomon serves up the institution of the bourgeois family; a torture chamber, with the caressing instruments of pressure and exclusion. Since the object of her observation is her own history, it is harder to see the shadowy model for her text: the nineteenth-century novel, where everything is both symptom and verdict.

She is fighting a world order, and what angers her most is that it's doomed and yet won't put up a fight: it would rather delude itself and clutch at straws. Sitting by the hospital bed of the dying century, she isn't quite sure whether to love or hate it, save it or put it to death—and she makes the decision to disown it, curse it and give away its terrible secrets. You could compare *Life? Or*

Theater? with the comics in vogue at the time, or today's graphic novel, but neither would be exact comparisons: the images in comics and graphic novels are shaped both by their chronological sequencing, and by the borders between each frame. These borders chart a route through a selection of images, they help the reader negotiate that route and protect her from misunderstanding and loss of focus.

In Salomon's work all the borders are removed and every sheet can be gazed at infinitely, like a figure eight or a Möbius strip, where everything happens simultaneously. The same character makes a series of movements, each hardly differing from the next, as if the author is hoping to preserve the most minute phases of that character's movement for all eternity. We can only guess how much time passes between each phase. Perhaps minutes, or perhaps months—it could well be either. The coexistence of different layers of time in the singspiel makes it unique, perhaps resembling only the calcified time of the poem, which is temporally and rhythmically defined by the reader's breath. What Charlotte depicts, the absolute past and its capsule of color, is a place so remote that everything happens simultaneously there, both recent and long past; the phrase begins again before you have finished saying it.

This place, this world, is very tightly packed; the people, both the familiar and the unnamed masses, swarm and multiply. Although the actual cast list is short, we have the sensation of being on a crowded station concourse or a beach at high season. Here the measure of time is very clearly shown: its repetitiveness, its monotony, its transparent sack filled with bodies, gestures and conversations. All this space is filled with intense and powerful color—red, blue, yellow, and all of their combinations. Griselda Pollock has produced very detailed work on the function of color in Salomon's universe—every character is given not only a musical phrase but a color code:

blue for the mother; yellow for the diva, the golden voiced woman [...] and red for the voluble, fantastic, imaginative, crazy prophet who preached how to live after having been, like Orpheus, through hell to death and back. Red tinged with yellow would also be the threat of death and madness.

But the power of the work resides in its ability to resist any interpretation, especially that of its own narrator, who quotes the theory of her hero as if it is holy scripture—the same hero who presses her against the wall in a dark corridor a few pages later with the words: "What a lovely neck you have, child. Let me kiss it. Won't your mother be home soon?"

It does seem as if one of the main drivers of the drawn text and the "talking pictures" is the refusal to pass judgment. Every point of view is understood to come from outside the text, and no motivation or explanation is provided for anything; it is all treated with the same icy malice. If Charlotte really ascribed a magical function to her work, then she was not wrong to do so. She succeeded in locking the past away in a room, and we can still hear it restlessly pacing, and beating at the walls.

The German word "Erinnerung" (memory) has a distant echo in the Russian ear: the flight of the Erinyes (or Furies), those vengeful divinities who remembered and pursued the guilty to the corners of the earth, however they tried to remain hidden. The extent of memory, its ability to catch those who try to evade it, depends directly on whether we can turn and meet it head-on. This is exactly what the heroine of *Life? Or Theater?* does when she faces her decision: to take her life or to embark on something really quite mad. That is, to become everyone she ever knew, to speak with the voices of the living and the dead. At this point between her and the author there is no border.

Not-A-Chapter
The Stepanovs, 1980, 1982, 1983, 1985

1.

Addressed to my grandfather, Nikolai Stepanov, from his niece. The letter is undated, but appears to be from June 1980. My little round big-eyed grandmother Dora Zalmanovna Stepanova (maiden name: Akselrod) died in May 1980. She and my grandfather were the same age, both born in 1906. He outlived her by five years.

Galina is the daughter of Grandfather's much-loved sister, Masha. She lived near her mother in the village of Ushakovo in Kalinin District. Up till then they had been used to corresponding frequently but that summer Grandfather broke off correspondence for a long while.

Dear Uncle Nikolai,

Your letter arrived. We found out about Auntie Dora from your letter to Mother. It was so unexpected. Just before that mother received a letter which seemed very hopeful—and then suddenly this. We were very upset, especially because the letter took a long time to reach us and it's strange you chose to tell us by letter. We're family after all. We've known Auntie Dora for so long and we would have liked to give her a Christian send-off. I can't believe that Auntie Dora is gone. Although I haven't seen her in a long while, I remember her clearly, looking after everyone, very caring. I wrote straightaway, Uncle Nikolai, but then I ripped up the letter. I'm not good at offering comfort. Words seem so pointless, so empty, at times like these. And just knowing that she is gone forever, for all time, kills me. I had my first close encounter with the word "death" in 1948. I knew that it was possible to die in the abstract, that people died of old age and in wars. But my own sister, eighteen years old, so close to me, so warmly alive, and suddenly not there—I couldn't begin to come to terms with it, I ran out of the village to the scrubland and I wept and cried and scratched the earth and prayed to God that He would bring Lusya back to life. I never spoke her name aloud, but day and night it was all I could see. At night I mostly cried, but very, very quietly so no one could hear, and then worn out by weeping I would fall into a heavy sleep. I was a shy child anyway, but after this I withdrew even further into myself and perhaps no one except my father understood me, but we kept out of each other's way and we carried our burdens alone. I was in torment, or perhaps I was scalded by a sense of shame—I don't know how to describe the feeling—that she had died and not me. And more than once the terrifying and unchildlike thought of dying came to me, into my young head, but when I was ready to take the step I suddenly felt sorry for my parents. If we'd all mourned together, wept together, then perhaps it would have been easier. But we all withdrew and carried these hellish torments, the suppressed cries, the tears and the unhappiness in our souls. And then 1960, 1963, and 1966. Irreparable losses, beyond any comprehension. I can't offer you any comfort, Uncle. I am only writing because I know the cost of such losses and I have no words of consolation, I am just mourning together with you, I understand your grief.

Those who are dear to use are shaped forever in the heart's memory, as long as we are alive, and the grief, the pain and the loss are with us, too. Come and visit us, perhaps you'll find some respite being with others, do come.

Love, Galina.

2.

From my grandfather, in reply to his niece, Galina. Unfinished draft. June 1980. My fifty-year-old aunt Galya was dealing with grief in her own way. She and her father, my grandfather, who was unyielding in his demands and his assessments of others, didn't get along, and months passed before they could find a way of living together harmoniously.

Galina, you wrote that your first brush with death was in 1948, when Lusya, if I'm not mistaken, died. Dora and I happily kept our distance from death until May 1980. I remember how it all happened, but I won't go into details. Masha's family has had a few funerals to cope with over the last thirty or so years. Maybe less. There's been a series of them to get over. Leastways, the ones I know about. They were heavy losses indeed. We were fortunate and never had such losses. No one died until this year. Everyone present and correct. So this loss was all the heavier, all the more painful. The first twenty-three days since Dora's death have passed in spring sunshine. I just can't get used to it. I'm a healthy person, but morning till night I pace the empty flat, I'm beside myself. Up till then, wherever I was, whatever I was doing, I knew that someone would be waiting for me at home and the sooner I could get back there, the better. And now there's no need to hurry because there's no one there anyway. It's so hard, Galina, I can't tell you how hard it is. And I feel much the same as you, why her and not me. She was the mother, the grandmother, all the young ones needed her, not me. But as much as I might have wanted to, I couldn't take her place.

Still, even with all these feelings and in this mood, life goes on. One other important thing to mention is that when Dora was alive I didn't have much of a relationship with my daughter Galya. I often used to point out to her how she didn't help her mother much, how she didn't help with the housework or the cooking and of course that didn't help matters. She's a tricky girl, she's withdrawn, very close to her brother, always has been. I didn't share her casual attitude to housework, but her mother protected her and did everything herself, as she thought Galya got tired at work and on her long commute on the metro. But now all of that means we are not close.

Once when I went to hospital to see Dora she told me straight out all her wishes for after she was gone. She said, "Just in case. Who knows how this operation will go and I'd like you to know my wishes. Look after Galya. She's all you've got. She's an introverted girl, she won't come begging. You take the lead. She has a difficult life as it is." And when I replied, "What are you talking about, it'll all be fine, and you'll be back home with us soon," she answered that she didn't know what the outcome of the operation would be, but she had at least told me her dying wish.

3.

Undated, but clear from the content that this is July 1980. Father and I were traveling and staying by a lake, Galka was in a sanatorium. On two scraps of writing paper, paper-clipped together, my grandfather has written in his firm hand: "Page from diary." He is writing here (as it later becomes clear) about my mother.

I am a person with quite a developed sense of personal responsibility so I was working hard until four o'clock in the morning to make the apartment look presentable for someone I'd describe as being very close to me. And today I continued the work, so I could receive her without embarrassment, despite being a man, and not a woman with all the experience and skills in household matters. It took up all my time and energy, but I was sure it would all be worth it and I wouldn't be ashamed to have her in the house.

So the job was done. But all in vain.

She didn't come.

I waited so long, I did all that running around, I made such an effort so the meeting would take place in the best possible circumstances...

But she didn't come, despite telling me that Monday was a day when she could do as she wished...

She didn't come.

Clearly she just doesn't want to admit to a mutual relationship—between a woman who loves the revolutionary "Gadfly" and her just-

a-good-friend, who is like the character of the doctor in the book ...
who loved her and cared for her, never asking for anything in return.
And she knew it and was a friend to him, a comrade ... and was
even grateful

4.
Nikolai Stepanov to Natalia Stepanova
Grandfather is writing here to my mother in Mishor, the
Crimean resort where we were holidaying in 1983. It's possible
he didn't send the letter. This is a draft and I couldn't find a clean
copy in my mother's papers.

Moscow, June 5, 1983
   My dearest Southern Belles, Masha and Natasha,
   Thank you so much for the letter which I received last night from
my southern belles! Thank you. Please believe me when I say that I
heaved a huge sigh of relief on receiving it. The weight on my heart,
the anxiety which had burrowed deep into me, all was removed by
your warmth and kindness ... and I felt young again! Thank you,
thank you, Natasha, for recovering my heart's balance. If I were a be-
liever I would say "may god give you and all your dear ones immense
joy." Thank you. All my gratitude.
   That Crimean landscape, the nature, the sea ... I remember well
how Dora and I once spent a holiday there back in the good old
days, and we stayed in a little privately owned house belonging to
a Ukrainian woman, very neat and tidy, very welcoming and kind.
That was a long time ago, in those precious days of youth, when two
young people still had everything ahead of them—still free, nothing
to tie them down. And those were simpler times. We were still in the
Komsomol youth movement, no children, no cares, nothing to make
our lives harder. We were just starting our family life together. And
yesterday your little postcard nudged my memory and your letter
made me feel livelier and I couldn't get to sleep for ages for the mem-
ories, I was transported to the past, to our youth together. Just for

this—not to mention that you are there, in the South surrounded by all that wonderful nature, and yet you didn't forget that somewhere in the world, in one of the world's great cities, there's a person called Nikolai, who is also known as "Grandpa Kolya," and for that, Natasha, dearest girl, I send you all my gratitude. But I also want to say that I appreciate your straightforwardness and your warmth, and that you exist and that you are mother to my (Dora would have joined me in this, I am sure) our very first grandchild. They used to say about Vladimir Ilich Lenin that he was "simple as truth" and I believe this to be one of the best qualities in a person.

Everything I have written here is true. I have the most ordinary personality. Russian, but with some particular qualities. These are not just to do with my simplicity and openness, but to do with the fact that anyone I have a spiritual connection with I open my heart to, and I trust that person absolutely. And so I wanted to say that your postcard delighted me, that simple little message, but I was also delighted that I hadn't been deceived in your friendship. In these difficult times there aren't many people one can rely on and trust. I'm happy you are who you are! Looking back I can see that I always felt close to serious women and girls, with whom I could have fun, but also talk about the serious things, the real things. Who made me feel trust, and also, no less important, respect for them. I am sorry to say that these days there are many young people of both sexes, who are indiscriminate, who aren't able to blush or feel any kind of shame.

Well. There we are, Natasha. Dearest mother to my very first granddaughter.

5.
A draft of a letter from Grandfather to his own sister. It is undated but I think it is from 1984 or even 1985, when Grandfather was fast losing his memory and becoming sadder and more remote.

Moscow. Sunday the 16th.
  I send my greetings and best wishes to you, Masha, my dear sister!

How are you? How are you getting along? How's your health been? And—once a teacher, always a teacher—I want to know how your pupils are getting along and what successes you've had with them. What classes are you taking in school? How many teachers are there in the school and what have they done in the past? Are there any you can fully rely on in school as well as in life? Does the school have its own party organization or are your communist teachers registered elsewhere? Who is running the school: a nonparty-affiliated person or a communist and what sort of relationship have you got with that person in school and outside school? I'm full of shame that I haven't seen you for so long, and I can hardly imagine you alive, and working hard. As a teacher and school leader of old I'm interested in the conflicts and where they come from. And one last question: is everyone friendly toward each other? Do you work a single or a double shift? Oh yes! I meant to ask how many teachers there are, and whether there are more men or more women. And the main question: how does everyone get on? Do they get on with each other? And with the school leadership?

And my last question is to you personally. Why haven't you written to your brother since the beginning of the school year? I thought long and hard about that and couldn't find an answer. Surely after the death of our mother you had someone you could write to in the immediate family. Surely you didn't suspect us all

7. Yakov's Voice and Isav's Photograph

When you start sorting through the things and concepts of the past you can tell instantly which are still wearable, like old clothes, and which have shrunk, faded, like a jumper that's been through the wrong wash. Those yellowing suede gloves, like plate armor in a museum, look as if they belong to a schoolgirl or a doll. They seem to belong with certain intonations, certain opinions; they're smaller than we imagine humans to be—if you look at them through the wrong end of the telescope, they have an ant-like precision; yet they are very far away. Sebald describes an empty house with its dusty carpets, a stuffed polar bear, and "golf clubs, billiard cues, and tennis rackets, most of them so small they might have been intended for children, or have shrunk in the course of the years …" Sometimes everything in the past (untranslatable, unusable, barely meeting today's needs) seems child-sized, to be treated with the fond condescension of those who have left childhood behind. The simplicity and naivety of the past is habitually overstated, and this has gone on for centuries.

The once-acclaimed novel *Trilby* graced my parents' shelves like a living presence, its spine still hard, the golden letters gleaming. The Russian edition was published in some haste in 1896, by then George du Maurier's tale had been published in America and Britain in unprecedented print runs of hundreds of thousands of copies. The only picture in the Russian edition was on the cover, a tall woman in an infantryman's greatcoat, caught around the waist by a belt, standing determined on a small rise, bare white legs, one hand held out, holding a cigarette, her hair loose on her shoulders. Despite all this she resembles nothing more than a milkmaid. She has a purposeful straightforward air, as if to quash any ideas of silliness, and this impression is borne out when you read the book.

The story of *Trilby* follows an artist's model, posing "for the altogether" in Parisian art studios. She makes friends with some jolly English artists whose odd habits include daily ablutions in hip baths, then falls in love with one of them but gives him up, convinced he is destined for a better woman. All of this is very sweet, especially the heroine with her wide-eyed loving-kindness and her tuneless singing. The softhearted Trilby suffers from neuralgia and the only person who can help her is a man named Svengali, a rogue, a hypnotizer, a great musician, and a dirty Jew. Dirty in the most literal sense—the cleanliness of others merely makes him laugh uncontrollably. He has bony fingers and a "long, thick, shapely Hebrew nose"; "he would either fawn or bully, and could be grossly impertinent."

At the beginning of the twentieth century the "Svengali" became a phenomenon in and of itself: not the name of a literary hero but a term to describe someone exerting a mysterious force on others. The Merriam-Webster Dictionary dryly defines a "Svengali" as a person who "manipulates or exerts excessive control over another." The Oxford English Dictionary adds the words "mesmeric" and "for some sinister purpose." The inexplicable ability to control another, to turn that person on and off like a desk lamp according to your will, so intrigued readers that the story, rather than falling into obscurity, lived on in a whole series of screen versions. Most of these were no longer named after the novel: from the end of the 1920s the novel became indistinguishable from the magnetic "Svengali, Svengali, Svengali."

Neither author nor reader would have had cause to reflect much on this matter-of-course anti-Semitism. It was as natural as birdsong; simply another feature of Du Maurier's book, as much as the constant jokes at the expense of the Germans or the discussions of women's beauty (a "deformed" woman, a "squinting dwarf" will only "inflict on his descendants a wrong that nothing will ever redeem"). But the difference is that, unlike all the prejudices expressed en passant, the Jewishness of Svengali seems to fascinate the narrator. He returns again and again to the theme, picking through a fairly standard selection of descriptives: greasy hair, bold and brilliant eyes, a comic aspect, a cruel sense of humor, physical and moral uncleanliness. And there is his great talent, which for a time even allays the disgust of the hearty, hygienic heroes with their drooping whiskers: "There was nothing so humble, so base even, but that his magic could transform it into the rarest beauty without altering a note. This seems impossible, I know. But if it didn't, where would the magic come in?"

Du Maurier's *Trilby* is entertaining and good-natured, uniting both author and reader in a rare feeling of satisfaction, even self-satisfaction: "and they would try and express themselves to the effect that life was uncommonly well worth living in that particular city at that particular time of the day and year and century, at that particular epoch of their own mortal and uncertain lives." The action of the novel takes place toward the end of the 1850s, and everything is retrospectively gilded with the spirit of the Belle Époque: the three Baudelairean flaneurs taking their strolls down the "crowded, well-lighted boulevards, and a bock at the café there, at a little three-legged marble table right out on the genial asphalt pavement"; and enjoying more traditional amusements, like donkey rides and hide-and-seek in the Bois de Boulogne. The suspension springs of progress are well-oiled: these children of civilization laugh at prejudice, and even illegitimate love engenders sympathetic respect in them. The horror and the repulsion they feel for Svengali is all the more striking against the backdrop of this Great Exhibition of modern virtues. It feels as if it has something to do with the rasping friction between two extremes: a superhuman ability and what seems *subhuman* to the author.

This ancient combination presents itself as a threat once again in the post-Romantic age, the source of a scandal that might blow up at any moment. The raw element of virtuosity, born of the gutter, the dirt, and the dust, stooping at nothing, in the hands of the "foreign"—Jews, gypsies, mediums—is balanced by the presence of standards, the flowering of complete ordinariness that knows its boundaries and is pleased with this knowledge. The cheerful little Parisian art studios are pleasurable forays into the life of a Bohemian. With the same cozy pleasure the novel's heroes perform Romantic and realist roles, drawing toreadors and coal miners. Painting in Du Maurier's novel belongs to the decent world—but music is to be avoided at all cost.

George du Maurier himself drew cartoons for *Punch* for several decades, caricaturing modern aesthetics, the emancipation of women, the mass enthusiasm for china. He was especially excited by the comic potential in technological progress: *"Please look a little pleasant, Miss. I know it's hard; but it's only for a moment!"* says a photographer to a young woman. Elderly parents sit by an enormous plasma screen, called the "telephonoscope," and watch their offspring play lawn tennis. A housewife gaily operates dozens of levers: pull one and you hear an opera transmission from Bayreuth, turn another and it's from St. James's Hall. One hundred and fifty years later the jokes aren't so very funny, the problems they face are pint-size ("doll-like, puppetlike" as the poet Elena Shvarts writes), but one of the drawings from 1878, a year after the phonograph was invented, is incredibly touching.

A woman in a housecoat and a man in a jacket and hat stand studying the contents of a wine cellar. They have already chosen a few bottles and they are intently looking round at the shelves, but the bottles contain voices, and not wine. The long caption (all Du Maurier's captions are long) reads:

By the telephone sound is converted into electricity, and then, by completing the circuit, back into sound again. Jones converts all the pretty music he hears during the season into electricity, bottles it, and puts it away into bins for his winter parties. All he has to do, when his guests arrive, is to select, uncork, and then complete the circuit; and there you are!

On the wine cellar's shelves are Rubinstein, Tosti, all the musical hits of the period, long since scattered and vanished; opera stars whose voices we have been told about but will never hear. Perhaps only Adelina Patti, recorded later, at the beginning of the twentieth century, can still be heard, although it's a strange sensation, the voice barely emerges from the bottle throat, and the 1904 coloratura sends shivers down the spine, as if a ghost were tickling you. The other inhabitants of the wine cellar were not so lucky. The more famous ones look down at us from old photographs: garlanded, bright-eyed, monochrome. One or two didn't even have this honor, just a name, a few mentions: "never made gramophone recordings of her voice"; date of death unknown. Sometimes the picture ripples, there is the flicker of an anecdote: St. Petersburg students once lay in the February snow so Christina Nilsson could walk across them to her coach. In another story she's taking aim in a damp, cold wood and firing— and the bear drops down to the ground, flat as a bearskin rug. Here's another: the graduates of West Point each cut a golden button from their dress coat and make from the buttons a heavy golden wreath to lay on the singer's shoulders as a souvenir of her audience. The aria swells, but we can't hear a single note. The "great Trebelli," as Joyce called her, putting on her men's clothes to play the role of Gounod's Siébel: white stockings, ruffled sleeves, and a white feather. Another diva signed her name on the wall of a London restaurant where they served borscht on a Sunday: blue curtains, light-blue wallpaper, and the autographs of the habitués preserved under a piece of glass.

Somewhere in the lowest drawers of my parents' polished cabinet were deposits of sheet music. There was no one with any musical skill left in the family to sort through the scores. When we moved to a new apartment in 1974, the piano that had stood for seventy years in the old apartment was on the list of *essentials*, what needed to be taken up into the new life. The millipede-like dining table that could seat twenty, the huge carved sideboard that looked like a house, the rocking chair and the chandelier with its serried rows of crystals—all remained in the old life. But the "musical instrument," like the portrait of a half-forgotten relative, took up its position against the wall and stood patiently, putting up with my reluctant scales, studies, and Old French chansons until they dried up of their own accord.

The pages of music were a different matter. The jumbled sheets were marked with little blackberry stains of sound I couldn't decipher, but they were interesting for other reasons: their names written in a spidery script, running from beat to beat, syllable to syllable, with my finger following. These had nothing in common with the everyday Soviet world: "Lit-tle-black-boy-Tom, in-Alger-ia-born, where none-fear-death and love-is-strong." Sometimes a piece of music would be illustrated. I have a dim memory of the cover of "The Salon Waltz: A Dream of Love after the Ball," cherubs teeming under the sleeping debutante, the silky puff of her gown, her tiny slippers on the carpet. All this seemed ancient, and not because of its remoteness in time— at that point, the 1920s felt like yesterday. Then and now were completely irreconcilable. We had our own intimate pleasures, but they were from an entirely different songbook with different lyrics: the wooden seats on the train to the dacha and the noisy blue-tinged counters at the grocery shop, with their alkaline tang and sour-cream smell. Next door in the hardware store the wooden drawers held oily mounds of nails of differing sizes and shapes; at the market black-eared rabbits were sold alongside poorly gilded wooden angels; farther on, a line for liters of fermented *kvas* stretched as far as the telephone box.

The music my relatives bought over the years was not complicated, it was meant to be played at family gatherings: waltzes, foxtrots, and tangos to dance to at home; Tchaikovsky romances, "We will be silent, you and I"; and a Technicolor range of hit parade numbers for singsongs. On the back of the sheets the names of other songs were pressed together in a list, a hundred or more on each sheet. The sight of them gave me to understand the volume of sound that had been lost and gone underground, pushed out beyond the periphery of the known world.

None of this can be reproduced, least of all the kinds of feelings brought on by "Romances and Songs from Gypsy Life": the endless *sweet friends,* the stars and the sunsets, the misty morns and gray dawns, dark nights and sleigh bells, the perfumed white acacia and the roses, the "sweet scent of you"; when the lilac blossoms, and countless "I want to love!" and "I don't want to forget!" It's hard to imagine all this being sung, murmured, and squawked by a million voices all at once: voices in tenements and rented rooms, in offices and on dacha verandas, over keyboards and to gramophone records. It poured from open windows like water from a watering can until it had flooded all Russia. Even when it began to disappear it still buzzed like a spinning top as it soaked into the ground. The simple quantity of music held in the airwaves back then, a time still unused to other joys, was enormous: it swelled in vast rainclouds, forever promising rain.

Du Maurier's cartoon advised bottling what had already been conserved, wound onto black shellac records. When sound was first recorded, the many imitators of Adelina Patti, pouring their own more modest voices into the romances and arias of Glinka, were out of a job. Caruso and Chaliapin now strode into the family parlor. In the new century people didn't sing, they sang along and they knew the music not from the page, but from the voice, the raw and irresistible original. Fewer people now played music, and more listened to it; music imperceptibly ceased being a domestic affair at about the same time as domesticity itself began to reveal its ephemeral quality. Pillowcase-size, light as a feather, it could be folded into a traveling case. Music, like much else, became an instance of deferring to authority, *his master's voice*. Listeners gathered around the communal radio, they swapped gramophone records, they rushed to the cinema to hear the jazz recordings played before the feature.

*

As the dead get more distant, their black-and-white features look ever nobler and finer. When I was younger people still used to say of prerevolutionary photographs: "What wonderful faces, you don't see faces like that anymore!" Now we say that about the faces of Second World War soldiers, or students in the sixties. And it's quite true: you don't see faces like that anymore. We aren't them. They aren't us. A picture cunningly replaces this terribly obvious fact with simple parallels. They are holding a child, and we sometimes do that, too. That girl looks just like me apart from her long skirts and squashed hat. Grandmother is drinking from my cup, I am wearing her ring. Them too. Us as well.

However effortlessly convincing the (full and exhaustive) knowledge offered by the pictures seems, the words that accompany them, written *back then*, relocate us in our own time. The little beak of the punctum taps at the points of similarity; whereas the voice, reminding us of the real extension of time, can barely be heard from the other side of the abyss. Years ago, the vivacious eighty-year-old redhead Antonina Petrovna Gerburt-Geibovich, an older friend of my mothers, admitted shamefacedly that her mother-in-law had reproached her for her "officer's" tastes: "I love gladioli and champagne!" I was immediately aware that champagne and contemptible officer's tastes were very far from the world I inhabited, and even the ordinary gladioli couldn't bridge the gap. But Antonina had no regrets. She had come from a tiny shtetl in the middle of nowhere, was married for her looks and her boldness, could read in eight languages and used to recount, laughing, how her gallant Polish father-in-law said to her before the wedding: "I am so very glad of this infusion of young Jewish blood into our wilting dynastic line."

The Gerburt coat of arms (an apple on a red background, pierced through by three gold swords, two from the upper corners of the shield, and the third from below) and its dynastic history barely interested her. Jewishness excited her far more, and in her lonely little apartment she would passionately relive the successes and failures of those who shared her "young Jewish blood." Around the age of twelve I used to visit her and she would treat me with volumes of ancient Greek literature and *kovrizhka* with nuts. Once, I left her apartment with a feeling of intense embarrassment, hardly able to explain this feeling to myself. On that particular day she had taken out a battered volume of poetry and read an old and sentimental poem. As she finished the poem, I noticed in horror that she was crying.

Only photography shows the flow of time as if it had never existed: just the length of women's skirts sliding up and down. Text is a different matter: it consists entirely of time, which opens the little windows of vowels and shakes out the mothlike consonants, filling the gaps between paragraphs and haughtily displaying the full range of our differences. When you look at the page of an old newspaper, the first thing you feel is its hopeless remoteness. There is a strange stylistic kinship between texts of the same moment, written in the same cross section of time, but it has nothing to do with authorial intention and can only be seen in hindsight. With a distance of twenty or thirty years it's hard not to notice the single intonation, the common denominator welding together newspaper, shop sign, poem read from the stage at the all-women college, the conversation on the way home. It is as if every age produces its own particular dust that settles on every surface and in every corner. Even those who behave as if they stood outside the idea of the "typical" suddenly make a linguistic gesture that's common to their contemporaries, without even noticing it, as if they were unaware of the pull of gravity on them.

There were plenty of other entertainments besides *Trilby* in the 1890s, many of them relating to science. The century saw itself as enlightened (and in a sense it was): a little hill onto which humanity had climbed and was now happily looking back over the ground traversed. Behind it lay much to learn from: prejudices overcome, wars that could never be repeated, religious extremism, the depths of poverty; all of this, to be sure, had taken watchfulness but it had yielded to rationalism. Civilization had reached into the furthest parts of the globe and was busy gathering its unusual souvenirs. The World Exhibitions and their many clones presented to the public the highest achievements of humanity, but the audience also wanted to hear about its darker corners, remained curious about the strange nations at the earth's rim, doomed by fate to be the comic sidekick to the victorious and favored children of progress. This natural-historical curiosity needed feeding.

In April 1901 a daily paper in Moscow reported to the educated public that an all-female troupe of Dahomey Amazons, who could be seen in the Manezh, were "more curious than any 'blacks' who had come to Moscow before. They demonstrate some interesting dances and military formations." The Amazons soon transferred to a more appropriate venue. "Yesterday at the Zoological Gardens the Dahomey Amazons began their performances of dancing and military moves. These will take place three times a day on weekdays and five times a day on holidays."

It hardly raised eyebrows, this idea of adding to the exotic fauna of the zoo with enclosures for rational man in his natural surroundings. What became known as a human zoo—Laplanders, Indians, Nubian villages "with live inhabitants" dressed in traditional costume, holding naked live babies—was an everyday reality in American and European zoos by the mid-1870s. Public morality at the time demanded that "natives" be dressed decently and sometimes public taste demanded quite the opposite: the clothing didn't seem "revealing" enough, nakedness befitted the savage man. The exhibits wove their mats and smoked their pipes, demonstrated their bows and arrows and the now unnecessary accoutrements of labor. Sometimes they died, sometimes they revolted. Between the exhibits and the millions of spectators there was nearly always a barrier or a fence to illustrate the boundary between humanity's past and its much-improved present.

In 1878, when the couple in Du Maurier's drawing were busy inspecting the bottles of stoppered music, the Exposition Universelle in Paris featured alongside the megaphones and phonographs a "Negro Village" with around 400 inhabitants. Twenty-five years later, at an even more visually arresting exhibition, the representatives of the "lesser races" were confined in cages. At the St. Louis World's Fair in 1904 the crowds streamed to view the primitive nations. On that occasion, the evolution of man had been illustrated carefully with a line that ran from "primates to pygmies" ("Cannibals Will Dance and Sing!") to Filipinos, Native Americans, and on, at last, to the happy visitors to the Fair. Racial theories prevalent at the time embodied the competitive system, and white man's victory was a plain indication of his superiority.

The Amazons came in handy: they were more interesting to look at than the glum Inuits with their shaggy dogs. They offered an almost real threat. These female warriors who had been defending the Dahomey throne for two hundred years still had terrible strength and were the stuff of legend, potboilers, and wet dreams. The war between Dahomey and the French dragged on until the army of Amazons was decisively routed. Their weapons (machetes, and something resembling an ax) were no match for bullets, and long bayonets gave Europeans the advantage in hand-to-hand combat. But even a year before, a troupe of "tame" Amazons had visited Paris to demonstrate their fighting techniques. They were dressed in the wildest of outfits: to survive one has to fit in with other people's preconceptions.

An eleven-year-old boy was taken to see such a demonstration of fighting techniques in Moscow. Later in his life Boris Pasternak would remember how

in Spring 1891 they showed a regiment of Dahomey Amazons in the Zoological Gardens. How my first impressions of woman were linked forever with that naked line, the closed ranks of suffering, the tropical parade to the beat of a drum. How I became a captive to form earlier than I should have been, because I saw the form of captivity on them.

*

I look at the words and the possessions of the dead, laid out for us in the cabinets of literary museums, or ready for printing, or lovingly conserved, and I feel more and more as if I were looking into an enclosure containing the silent and closed ranks of the "exhibited." When you spend a long time with what the old inventories called "linen belonging to the deceased," the bars of the cage start to come into focus more sharply, and what lies behind recedes from view.

The letters of my grandmother written in her girlhood, which I transcribe, line by line; the Soviet songs Aunt Galya wrote up; the letters of a philosopher, the diaries of a machine worker—all of this reminds me more and more of the brain, pelvis, and sexual organs of Saartjie Baartman. The Hottentot Venus, as they loved to call her, was a much-favored object of scientific interest at the beginning of the nineteenth century. The shape of her body, the diameter of her nipples, and the line of her buttocks were living proof for various different types of evolutionary theory and formed the basis for boldly sexual prepositions. The well-known naturalist Dr. Georges Cuvier paid particular attention to the length of her labia. She was exhibited to medical students, enlightened amateurs, and crowds at freak shows. On occasion you were allowed to poke her. Her service to "humanity" did not end with her death: for one hundred and fifty years her remains were exhibited in museums in France and only reluctantly withdrawn from view in 1974. We, the people of the past and the present, are endlessly vulnerable, desperately interesting, utterly defenseless. Especially after we are gone.

8. Lyodik, or Silence

In Spring 1942, in the Leningrad Region, lines of soldiers walked through the twilight, one behind the other, holding on to each other as tightly as they could. They were usually led by the soldier with the best sense of direction. With a stick he felt for potholes and the bodies of people and horses, and the chain of the unseeing followed him and tried their best to wind their way around obstacles. Nyctalopia is the Greek name for a condition that begins in the following way: the sufferer stops being able to tell blue and yellow apart, the field of vision narrows, and on entering a lit space he sees colored spots in front of his eyes. Its name among the people is "moon blink." It is caused by the long winter, a lack of vitamin A, and extreme fatigue. I once read this description of it in a memoir: "I could only see two small stretches of land and they were directly in front of me. Everything else was hidden in darkness."

Leonid Gimmelfarb, my grandfather's nineteen-year-old cousin, was somewhere in the marshes and forests in this district: his 994th Rifle Regiment had held its position since the autumn, during which time the regiment had completely replaced its personnel as well as its commanding officers several times. Lyodik, as he was called at home, wrote regularly to his mother who had been evacuated to the faraway Siberian town of Yalutorovsk. He'd been in these parts before: he'd sent his first letters to his mother from training camps in the region in May the previous year. In one letter, he wrote that he'd gone to Leningrad to apply to the college of aviation, "although of course I wasn't accepted, they said I wasn't right."

On September 1, 1939, the first day of the Second World War, a conscription act was passed in the USSR, leading to mass conscription. The children and grandchildren of all those of doubtful lineage (aristocrats, factory owners, merchants, officers in the Tsarist army, priests, richer peasants) were also included, although they had to serve as infantrymen without hope of promotion—the military academies and colleges remained closed to them as they had been before. The new act seemed fair on the whole, since it was based on a need for equality, though it lowered the conscription age quite considerably, from twenty-one to nineteen, and even eighteen for those who had left school early. Lyodik wrote that it was warm and comfortable in his tent, which slept ten recruits. They'd built a bench and a table and even decorated it a bit, and he'd set himself the challenge of learning to play chess better. New regulations had come in and now instead of a kilo of bread they each received 800g. There was a "vegetarian day," when they ate cheese instead of meat, and even if it wasn't exactly fun, at least they understood what was going on, and it kept them busy.

In my mother's papers there was a special bundle with Lyodik's letters and childhood postcards. The little boy, standing in his felt boots with shining galoshes and his lambskin cap pulled down over his eyes, was an important part of her own childhood—his absence made him almost her contemporary, and the fact that he was fated to die at the terribly young age of twenty was overwhelming. When Lyodik's mother, the wizened, gray-haired Auntie Verochka, died and was buried somewhere along the wall of the Donsky Crematorium, all that remained of her worldly possessions was this little bundle. The death notice, and strips of army paper with numbers on and little notes: "greetings from the front," "all my love," "P.S. I am alive and well." "Alive and well" was pretty much all Lyodik's letters amounted to, although he used every possible occasion to send word. "Nothing much to report" was the mantra, and it filled the sheets of paper—whatever was going on around him was by now beyond description.

What he couldn't quite suppress though was a strange ringing, it wasn't in the words themselves, but still it sounded in the background. Much as if a calm person were writing calming words, just as a tank rumbled down the street and all the china in the cupboards began to hum.

In pencil, on the lined sheet of an exercise book:

May 28, 41

Dearest Mother,

The day before yesterday I received a lot of correspondence: five letters, a postcard and two letters from you, one letter from everyone, and one from Father. You can probably imagine how pleased I was to receive these precious letters. I haven't written for a while because I wasn't able to send letters. Now our political officer is involved and the postal service is much improved. I'm moving around but the address is always the same.

I am in good health, feeling well and certain of our victory. I hope to be together with you for my twentieth birthday. I'm so proud of Father and his brothers. In a letter sent on May 6 he said that he had signed up as a Local Defense Volunteer and would make himself useful in the rear guard and on the front line. Uncle Filya and Uncle David are also joining up, Father writes. Auntie Beti's husband has been called up—he's a political officer. Father has found a placement from May 2. I'm so pleased for him.

Have you been troubled by air raids? As a soldier with some experience, I want to give you a little advice. It's best to find shelter in the metro if you are near a station, or in an air raid shelter. If you are a long way from both, then try to run to a low place, and don't stand at full height.

Many thanks for all the warm words from Auntie Beti, Lyonya, Lyolya. Congratulations to Lyonya on becoming a father, Lyolya on becoming a mother, and Beti and Sarra Abramovna on becoming grandmothers.

Did you receive the money back? If you didn't then there is no need

*to worry. I don't need any money at all at the moment. And anyway
I received twenty rubles in wages. How are you feeling, Mother? Is
your arm quite better now?*

*I'll finish now. I wish you health and happiness and I send you my
love. All my love to the family, especially Auntie Beti, Uncle Syoma,
Uncle Busya and Aunt Rosa, Lyonya and Lyolya.*

love,

Lyodik

Lyodik was mobilized straightaway and found himself in a war
that hadn't yet started. The letter above was written on his nineteenth birthday. German forces had already tightened their grip
on Leningrad. The 286th Division was put together hastily from
evacuees, boys barely out of their teens, local volunteers, whoever they could find. The 994th Rifle Regiment was part of this.
They were thrown straight into battle.

There is a small river, the Naziya, in the direction of Mga
Station, and all around, for up to twenty kilometers, spreads
endless forest and boggy ground. Kirill Meretskov, who was in
command of the Volkhovsky Front, and whose actions resulted
in the deaths of many hundreds of thousands of soldiers in this
area, wrote years later that "I have rarely been in an area less suit-
able for a military offensive. I will forever remember the endless
expanse of forest, the impenetrable marshes, the standing water
on peat bogs, the broken roads." The 994th Rifle Regiment survived among these peat bogs for three years, holding and losing
positions. It began in September 1941, when their troop train
arrived in the fog. The train didn't even reach the junction—the
Luftwaffe was overhead, and there were no Soviet planes around.
The soldiers disembarked under fire, slipping about, dragging
carts and weapons into copses. They could barely tug the carts
with their wooden axles to safety. Then there were weeks of
nonstop air raids. Along with the bombs, barrels fell from the
sky. The barrels had holes punched in them and as they fell they

made an unbearable screaming noise. Sometimes field kitchens went missing in the forests, because the staff were afraid to cross open ground, and the soldiers went hungry. They were armed with nothing more than rifles. On 11 September, when the Germans attacked in tanks close to the village of Voronovo there was panic. Soldiers dispersed across the marshes. After a few days the division had lost half its men and a large number of officers.

Astonishingly, it is possible to reconstruct the events of these days and weeks with a fair amount of detail. A number of texts, interviews, and letters belonging to those who survived have been preserved. The Battalion Commander of the nearby 996th Regiment remembered that there was no artillery support for two months: in addition to a rifle, every man was given a hand grenade and a bottle of incendiary liquid. It got colder. There was no bread, only dried crusts. There were no spirits either. The soldiers got hot food once a day. Some took the greatcoats off corpses and wore them over their own coats. They slipped and slid through the snow to HQ and back. They shared things between the different companies and boiled the meat from dead horses.

There was a day when we didn't receive any orders to attack. The Germans didn't bomb us either, or shell us. You couldn't even hear firing. There was a deep silence all down the line, through the Sinyavinsky marshes. Imagine that! A day of silence. After an hour or two the men were seized by panic, deep unease. [...] Some men were on the point of throwing down their rifles and running back to the rear ... We, the officers, walked the lines and calmed the men, for all the world as if we were facing German tanks.

In Lyodik's letters there is nothing about this, not even a hint. Almost all the letters had the "checked by military censor" stamp on them, but the censor would have found nothing to concern him in these letters. In one of the accounts of the Volkhovsky

Front there is a quote from a letter by a Lieutenant Vlasov written on October 27, 1941:

The first freezing temperatures and the snow is driving the Fascists mad. Especially when they look through their binoculars and see us with our padded clothes and our warm caps and a greatcoat over the top. We can see them, they're still in short jackets ... All I can tell you is that the military operations are currently going our way, and those officers of Hitler's won't be eating in the Hotel Astoria as they dreamed of doing.

I see this scene, the warm hats and snow drifts, as if through the same set of binoculars; the rather forced humor, the bravado, was usual for a commanding officer. Still, you might expect a lieutenant to be more open about the fact that he was actually "at war" in a letter to his wife.

This reluctance characterizes Lyodik Gimmelfarb's letters, too: he is absolutely intent on saying nothing about himself. He asks endless questions, mostly about his mother's health, which worries him terribly. Does she get tired at work? He asks her not to worry on his account, he is quite, quite well. If he is silent for longer than a month then it's only because of his "shocking laziness in writing letters." He is just as before. How are Lyonya? Lyolya? Their new baby? Sarra Abramovna? And how are Uncle Syoma and his wife? What has Uncle Busya written? How are you all, my dearest family? Please don't worry about me. It's completely unnecessary. Be happy, healthy. I have everything I need.

*

At the beginning of the war in Leningrad, Daniil Kharms and the artist Pavel Zaltsman met by chance at a friend's house. We can imagine what they spoke about, since neither had any illusions, and Kharms at some point during the meeting said about the imminent future: "We will be crawling away, without legs, holding onto the burning walls." Around the same time, in an air raid shelter on the Arbat in Moscow, Marina Tsvetaeva rocked to and fro, repeating to herself "and the enemy just keeps going …" Kharms's wife, another Marina, wrote, of the day before his arrest, that they had had to move a chair in the corridor, and Kharms was "afraid that misfortune would come upon them if they moved the chair." Kharms was arrested on August 23, 1941. Perhaps he could hear the muttering in the clear sky from his cell on September 8 as the planes flew overhead to bomb the Badayev food storage warehouses.

Many people remembered that sunny day. Nikolai Nikulin, an officer cadet at the time and future art historian, whose memoirs were published posthumously, watched the antiaircraft shells exploding in the blue sky like cotton wool clouds.

The antiaircraft guns fired a wild uncoordinated barrage, missing the bombers. The planes didn't even break formation, they flew on toward their target as if they barely felt the antiaircraft fire. […] It was very frightening and I suddenly found myself hiding under a piece of tarpaulin.

The incendiary bombs hissed and went out in the sand. When it was finally quiet a black cloud half-covered the sky over the city. Sixty-one-year-old artist and diarist Lyubov Shaporina looked out her window:

High in the air the white balls of explosions and the desperate antiaircraft fire. Suddenly a white cloud began growing up from behind the houses and roofs, bigger and bigger. Other white clouds piled up around it, lit golden in the sunset. They filled the whole sky, the clouds were bronze and a black stripe rose from below. It was so unlike smoke that for a long time I couldn't believe it was a fire. […] The picture was grandly, sublimely beautiful.

In the diaries and notes written during the Siege of Leningrad in the terrible winter of 1941 (known from then on as "The Terrible Winter"), there are often "zones" that are utterly different from the rest of the text. Resembling the bubbles forming under ice, these zones are the spaces set aside by different authors for the seeing and describing of beauty. The starving city was completely taken up with the business of survival, but from time to time it fell into deep contemplation, just as its people sometimes fell into deep sleep in the freezing cold, no longer afraid to die. The tempo of the writing changes: what had been a hasty noting down of details, conversations, anecdotes—chronicles of daily dehumanization undertaken in order to save these experiences from oblivion—suddenly changes the pace of its breathing and becomes a meditation on the clouds or the effects of light. This is even more striking when you consider how the writers of these texts were entirely occupied by the exhausting labor of survival. Their acts of witness are addressed to a future reader who will be able to grasp the situation in all its horror and shame, who will see the arrests and the exiling, the nightly air raids, the streetcars standing silent, the baths filled with frozen sewage, the fear and hatred felt by those standing in bread lines.

These extended passages have neither particular purpose nor direct meaning. I would call them "lyrical" if it wasn't for their strangely impersonal quality. The seeing eye feels detached, as if it belonged to no one, has no focus—it roams around the space that was once a home, a peaceful place to live, rest, and move about in, and is now transformed into a hard and impenetrable surface, nameless and beyond understanding. "It is as light as day outside. The moonlight is blinding. I don't think I've ever seen Ursa Major shine so brightly." It's as if the viewer herself disappears at these moments: the person who sees the changing earth and sky is no longer *me*, but someone else. The body aches, it itches, it is full of fear, it tries and fails to forget itself, but the beholding eye moves freely and without haste, as if it were the air itself with its unlimited reserves of time, looking at the river-banks and buildings.

In the memoirs of those who fought outside Leningrad during those months, and who saw with their own eyes the parachutes hanging like huge chandeliers over the icy beam of the spot-light, and the pulsing multicolored streams of fire lifting from the burning city, the narrative moves in the same way, with these trancelike pauses. It feels as if the front line and the besieged and dying city had suddenly become reflecting halves; as if there were no difference between them (780,000 people died in the first year of the Siege). Propagandists loved the phrase "Frontline City." It both elevated and explained the rebirth of the everyday experience as a strange offshoot of daily decline and disaster. The boundary between the everyday and the unthinkable dis-appeared. In the Leningrad Public Library the cold corpses of librarians lay on the floor, but you could still borrow a book.

The people who lived in the city and on the frontline changed themselves as fast as they changed their own understanding of what was possible and natural. Lydia Ginzburg's *Notes from the Blockade* describes with precision these stages of rebirth, which were above all physical, affecting personal hygiene and domestic tasks, manifesting as gray hairs and graying skin and crumbling teeth, displacing even the desire to read, but honing the instincts for adaptation and survival. In the summer of 1942, when the cold was gone and hunger no longer at its peak, this led to a new and unusual problem: a gap between this moment of rest and a hardwired fight for existence. A leather cushion on the arm-chair (a gift, a sweet memento from a past life) now merely gave rise to an intense sense of bewilderment: "the opportunity to return their original meanings to objects." But what to do with the books sitting on the shelves? They appeared to have crept their way back into view, though there was still no interest in lifting them off the shelves. The new skills of lighting the stove, dragging a bucket of water up the congealed ice on the staircase, balancing dishes and bags and ration books, and the terrible daily rituals of waking and getting ready to go out—all this belonged to someone new. It was better to leave that old "I" behind and not look back. Eventually everything around forgets its past and itself and mutates: vodka becomes bread, furniture becomes sugar. This is how Ginzburg described it: "They made cakes out of greens, and cutlets out of herrings." For her there was a clear lesson in this: "Every product had to cease being itself." And it goes without saying that this applied to people as well.

Nikolai Nikulin describes this process in himself. He was called up in 1941. By the end of that autumn he was a bewildered walking skeleton, but a sudden change came over him. Louse-ridden and weak, he spent a night in a shell hole, weeping with his misery and helplessness:

I found strength from somewhere. Toward dawn I crawled out of the hole and began skulking about in the empty German dug outs. I found a frozen potato, hard as a stone. I lit a fire. [...] This is the moment when I was reborn. I developed a defense mechanism, I found some energy, a sense of how I needed to act to survive, a new-found alertness. I started scavenging for food [...] I gathered up the dry crusts and ends of bread around the stores and canteens, I found food wherever I could. I started being taken up to the front lines.

The new man, the man who learns how to survive, is of use not just to himself, but to the state—he's effective, and in this there is no distinction between the frontline city and the line of fire. Ginzburg's texts from the besieged city are animated by the idea of "usefulness," which she understands in a surprising way. The Western world had proved itself powerless in the face of Hitler, she wrote, and the only thing that was capable of tackling him was the Soviet Leviathan: a corrupted and terrorizing system, which had dehumanized the individual to such an extent that he had learned to sacrifice himself without even realizing it. Meaning is given to the individual existence through the collective opposition to a clear evil—even as that existence disintegrates, frozen with horror, or behaves with repulsiveness or stupidity. From the womb of a dying city, from within the sacrifice, Ginzburg offers herself and her class of "intellectuals" a very different form of mobilization: refuting the personal and self-interested in the name of a form of austere citizenship, indifference to each individual fate, but salvation of the whole. This would have been impossible before the war, but the war had changed the old relationships. Where are the famous academics and intellectuals now, she asks? They stagger through the streets, their empty flats looted. The effective man is reborn in wartime, cleansed of his old habits. He has nothing left to weigh him down and is now useful to the collective effort.

As if in the same spirit of service, Lydia Ginzburg's prose is concise and workmanlike. The notes, which exist in a number of variations, are selected for their specific subject matter, from which a sense of the typical can be gleaned, observations that serve as a basis for conclusions. All personal matters are eschewed, as if the personal were considered to be dead already, a matter for study, evisceration, analysis; description, but only in order to pass general comment. Everything unnecessary (hedonistic accounts of the wondrous and beautiful) is shoved out. Although in the huge volume of her texts about the Siege of Leningrad there is one fragment (which feels almost ashamed of itself) in which the narrator almost imperceptibly falls into the familiar mode of trancelike contemplation:

People in cities often hardly realize that the moon doesn't just shine on the dacha, but on the city as well. We used to think it natural and obvious that it would be light on the streets at night. I remember how I felt it for the very first time. It was a pitch-black night, a November darkness. You could barely distinguish the black of the sky from the black of the buildings, which stood like huge blocks (a few tiny cracks of light from chinks here and there). The strange dark-blue streetcars looked like they were double-deck, as they cast a long shadow on the wet black asphalt.

Large pairs of lights from cars rose in the direction of Nevsky Prospect and drew closer. They were dark blue, or greenish or dirty-orange-colored, for some reason. The lights took on unprecedented significance. They passed in pairs (and in a chain sometimes) and they thrust their dense beam through the fog like a tusk.

The text, which has up till then operated somewhere between report and abstracted general experience, suddenly stops for a closer look, then brims over like water. The self is momentarily effaced and all circumstances and duties are forgotten. After a few lines the author comes to her senses, rushing to add that "for our contemporaries there is no mysticism, no Romanticism in this," only inconvenience—but the experience of her comrades in misfortune, who were also entranced by the nightscape and the light, suggests otherwise. The collective "us" of the city's inhabitants, which Ginzburg defined herself against, was nearly threadbare by then, so thin you could see the city's bridges and buildings through its fabric. It seems as if these shameful trance-like moments, where a person contemplated the existence of a world beyond her, were the only manifestations of Lydia Ginzburg's unrealizable dream of a shared space.

*

In mid-autumn the weather in the city was only just beginning to cool. People talked about the inevitable food shortages to come, but they were still serving food in the cafés. After the air raid they *filled the bath and washed the children,* but very soon the idea that you could turn on the tap and water would flow from it became inconceivable. The city was being bombed, the windows were taped over, and darkness filled the evenings, but the dark-blue streetcars continued to run until December. Food rations decreased. Instead of 600g of bread they now gave workers 200g. In September Lyubov Shaporina went shopping, got her bread ration, and stopped to read a newspaper board. Then she realized she'd forgotten to get the five eggs she was permitted. A few weeks later, the simple idea of forgetting to get one's ration was in itself unimaginable. One person wrote that they had been sleeping in their clothes for many days, ready to go down to the shelter at night. That Terrible Winter they slept in their icy apartments fully dressed, pulling any rags they could find over themselves (when spring came and Lydia Ginzburg had survived, she found it hard to make herself take off her felt boots and change back into shoes). Fuel supplies ran out in September and it was becoming colder. Everyone was sent to chop wood: teenagers, girls in thin coats and light shoes. Snow fell for the first time on the night of October 7. The following day Lyodik turned up in the besieged city.

Purple ink on a small sheet of paper
October 8, 1941
Dear Mother,
Please forgive me for not writing more often to let you know I'm fine. I keep meaning to but just don't get around to it. You do take things very hard, and there really isn't any need.
I'm writing this letter from Auntie Lizochka's house. I was close to Leningrad and thought I'd take the opportunity to go into the town. When I got to Auntie's house I found Auntie Soka and Lyusya at home. You can't imagine just how happy and pleased I was to see them!
They looked after me as if I'd been their own son. I was embarrassed. Lyusya sewed me a padded jacket I can wear under my coat.
Auntie Liza gave me some warm socks, gaiters, and handkerchiefs. All these things will come in so handy, I am very grateful to them. They put some good cigarettes in my pocket, so I'm a "rich man" now! But sadly this evening I have to leave them. I can't do anything about it, it's just how things are.

I received some postcards from you on the way and a few letters from Yalutorovsk. The last letter I received from you was written on September 25. I was very glad to hear you are doing well. I'm glad you've found work. It isn't so much the money, it's just you won't be at home with nothing to do anymore. It's wonderful news that Auntie Betya is staying.

I had a letter from Father, sent on September 27 from Moscow. He wrote that he would be called up soon. I have had nothing else from him. Has the new baby come yet? And if so, is it a boy or a girl? I wish you health and happiness. I send you all my love. Auntie Lizochka will write to you today.

> *Love from your*
> *Lyodik*

At the very same time Lyubov Shaporina was writing in her diary that the stewed cabbage cores she'd found outside the city were very good, and it would be worth stocking up on them. It was evening. Lyodik had already left his aunts and he was walking down the unlit streets, returning to his unit. By nightfall the clouds had parted and the stars were bright. Shaporina was waiting for "surprises"—her euphemism for air raids. "Marina Kharms came to see me. Daniil Ivanovich [Daniil Kharms] was arrested six weeks ago, the building next to theirs has been destroyed and their house has a crack running through it. All the windows have been blown out," she wrote. "Marina has nothing to live on, and her anguish over Daniil is killing her."

On the same day German intelligence reported back to the High Command for the 18th Army on morale in the besieged city, and recommended broadening the approach to propaganda: "It is essential to use leaflets as a medium which is both unexpected and can bring about confusion among the enemy, by suggesting that Soviet measures are in the German interest. For example: workers should not refuse to take up arms, as at the necessary moment they can turn these against their red masters." This is a strange echo of the words quoted in the case against Kharms. If we are to believe the unnamed secret police informant, Kharms once said: "If they force me to man a machine gun from the rooftops during street battles with Germans, then I will fire, not at the Germans, but at them."

Secret Police reports, quoted in a book about the Siege of Leningrad by historian Nikita Lomagin, kept a precise record of defeatist attitudes in the besieged city. In October there were 200–250 manifestations of "anti-Soviet sentiment" a day. By November it was 350. In the shops where bread lines began forming at 2:00–3:00 a.m., and flocks of teenagers came begging for crusts, conversations were all about how "the Germans would come and restore order." Shaporina wrote, and not unsympathetically, about a circulating myth: that special bombs would fall and cover the city with smoke, and when the smoke dispersed there would be a German policeman standing on every street corner.

I remember how in the first weeks of war Lev Rakov, the former lover of the poet Mikhail Kuzmin and a handsome scholar and Russian dandy, said reassuringly to a friend in a Leningrad café, still with all its windows sparkling and intact: "You worry too much. What if the Germans do invade. They won't stay for long. And then the English will come in their stead, and we'll all be reading Dickens. And anyone who doesn't want to won't have to."

For many, Dickens was a savior in the besieged city, he was medicine for the soul, and a source of warmth. People read and reread his novels, and read them aloud to children, particularly *Great Expectations* with its ice-cold house and its wedding cake overhung with cobwebs; in sixteen-year-old Misha Tikhomirov's diary he writes that he has kept for the evening's reading (for added sweetness) "three scraps of dried bread (very small), a piece of rusk, half a spoon of caramelized sugar."

Today I am rereading Lyodik's letter from that October, with the padded jacket and the handkerchiefs. I want this blissful scene from Dickens to go on forever: the aunts giving warmth and succor to the freezing, half-animal soldier, fussing around him, dressing him in anything they can find, happy that he is alive and they are alive, and feeding him with their very last (or nearly last) provisions. And all this in the worst hours of war, in a city that has gone black from the inside out, where soon no one will be able to help anyone; all this in an apartment with taped-up windows, shining on the inside like an amber lamp.

The letter was passed between relatives and not subject to the censor so Lyodik could have written as he pleased, but he didn't and wouldn't have written freely. On the Leningrad Front in Autumn 1941, letters were increasingly being stopped by the censor. In the city alone the censored letters numbered in the thousands. Even those that reached their destination were different from Lyodik's letters: most of all in their desire to share their experience of what was happening around them. Some ask for items of equipment or clothing or cigarettes; others describe the workings of gun batteries, or explain what a political officer's job is. Some promise to beat the enemy to the last, and describe how it is to be done ("Dear Manya, dear sister, I'm on sentry duty a lot and it's unbearable"). Leonid Gimmelfarb, Lyodik, is, as usual, very well, and the whole thing begins to seem more and more peculiar, especially after a month with no letters and then a new letter in which he mentions both his laziness and tonsillitis.

November 27, 1941

　Dear Mother,

　I just can't seem to get around to writing to you. The main reason has been my terrible laziness with regard to letters. I went back to Leningrad, and saw Auntie Liza, Soka and Lyusya again. They are all well and healthy. I was in Leningrad because I was back down with my old problem—tonsillitis—and I ended up in hospital, where they visited me. How are you though, Mother? How have you been? I beg you not to worry about me, there's nothing I need and I am doing well. I feel completely healthy.

I am very sorry that the things you sent didn't reach me, I've been away from my unit for over a month now. But I think you'll get them all back again. It really isn't worth sending me things, because I have everything I need.

I don't have any news. I don't have an address here yet. I'll write and tell you when I do. I wish you good health and happiness. All my love to Auntie Beti, Lyonya, Lyolya, Uncle Syoma, Rosalia Lvovna, and Sarra Abramovna.

Love from your
Lyodik

Impossible to verify this, but I can't dispel the thought that in those terrible weeks tonsillitis was hardly reason enough to leave the front line for a hospital, especially a hospital in Leningrad, which, to compound matters, would have been hard to reach. My immediate thought was that Lyodik had been injured and didn't want to tell his mother, and this seems both likely and unknowable. In Nikolai Nikulin's notes he says that no one got sick at the front: there was *nowhere to be* sick. They slept in the snow, and if anyone had a fever they simply walked it off. Nikulin remembers how the nails came away from his frostbitten fingers, and recalls a radio operator who spent a night on all fours because he was in constant pain from a stomach ulcer. Another witness wrote about the permanent hunger:

Many of the soldiers made their perilous way across no-man's-land and then lost their instinct for self-preservation and started looking for something to eat in the German lines. The Germans began shelling us straightaway and throwing grenades, so that anyone who survived had to make their way back to the Russian lines.

On November 16, the 994th Regiment held their position under artillery fire. A cold day, around minus twenty degrees. It was impossible to build any kind of concrete defense on the marshland, so the soldiers dug in as best they could. The Germans advanced to occupy a part of the Russian front line, but constant gunfire gave the Germans no opportunity to advance farther. On the following day the attack faltered, the Germans fell back. The ground was frozen, so they found pits that had been dug earlier in the autumn and threw four hundred bodies in them. The remaining dead, both German and Russian, were left lying in the battlefield. Soon the snow fell and covered their bodies as best it could.

Lyodik's letter was sent on November 27. It isn't clear where he was writing from, or what had happened to him. Why didn't the Leningrad relatives ever write to our side of the family to say that he had been ill? How did they make it to the hospital at a time when some people no longer had the energy to climb stairs? How did they get home afterward? On November 25, the bread rations were reduced again. Workers, children, and dependents now received 125 grams of bread a day. Hospital workers and the injured had it a little easier. Doctor Klavdiya Naumovna—I don't know her surname—(her diary notes are addressed to her evacuated son, "my golden boy Lesik," and the diary breaks off in 1942) writes,

My darling boy, we eat in the hospital and we have the following rations: in the morning I get gray macaroni, a piece of sugar and 50 grams of bread. For lunch we have soup (often very bad) and then either some more gray macaroni or buckwheat porridge, sometimes a piece of smoked sausage or meat, and 100 grams of bread. At dinner macaroni or porridge again, and 100 grams of bread. There is tea, but no sugar. It's a modest amount, as you'll see, but compared to how they eat in town, it's a banquet ...

At the beginning of December Shaporina noticed that people's bodies were beginning to bloat with starvation. Their faces had the yellow tinge of scurvy, "there were many like them in 1918 as well." She recalled someone saying they had seen two frozen corpses on the streets. During these weeks the presence of death swelled to occupy more and more space in the texts about the Siege. The authors described the lines for burial spaces, the sleighs and carts loaded with the newly dead, corpses lying on the streets, corpses scattering from the back of trucks. Toward the end of January this horror had become the ordinary state of things, along with the daily coexistence with death, taken for granted, barely worth mentioning. On the morning of January 1, 1942, the seventy-year-old artist Anna Ostroumova-Lebedeva noted down, not without pride, that she had eaten wood glue: "Never mind. A shudder of disgust ran through me from time to time, but I am sure that was simply just an excess of imagination. The jelly of it wasn't revolting, if you added cinnamon or a laurel leaf."

*

It was too easy to fall into thoughts about food, dangerous and inescapable thoughts, and then lose the will to keep moving— these thoughts made up the secret heart of life under siege. It was frighteningly tempting to talk about food, and people tried to avoid it, especially in company, or at work, or in places of public assembly. At home in the evenings, food was the only channel of conversation, spreading into the warm shallow waters of collective reminiscing: of dinners, of breakfasts, restaurant napkins, and little pools of yolk. Dreams about food to be enjoyed once the war was over were fantasies with a particular poisonous joy: they warmed the mother and daughter falling into sleep with visions—bread that didn't need to be measured out but could be ripped into hunks, sprinkled with sugar and doused in oil, blushing potatoes fried to perfection. The city's inhabitants considered it best to fend these mirages off, as they soon became the beginning of the end. In the same way they advised people not to stuff their bread ration in their mouth as they left the shop. Food had to be discussed carefully and selectively because any mistake could end in scenes of wild ferocity, terrible accusations. In the letters and diaries the least mention of food gave rise to a whole list of accounts of food, which few could refrain from: *Let me tell you all about the food we used to eat at a party!*

In Lyodik's letters no mention was ever made of food.

November 28, 1941

Dear Mother,

I've been writing all the while unable to send you a return address. Now I have that address, so you can send a letter back. A few days ago I was called in to our unit's HQ and they told me I was going to be sent for training. I had no say in the matter and I was put straight on a training course the next day. It's an officer training course. Because we are on active wartime service the course is much shorter, about two months. I want to know what you think about this. Will you write and tell me?

I haven't had a letter from you for a while, so I don't know any of your news or the family news. Please write and tell me all the news you know I'll be interested in. How are you? How's your work? What did Lyolya and Lyonya call their child? Auntie Beti is a grandmother now! She must be happy. Is it very cold with you there in Siberia? How upsetting that the things you send never reached me. I am sure you will get them back. I am dressed for winter now and keeping warm. You wrote that it's hard to get hold of cigarettes: is that still the case? Have you had any news from Father? I saw Yury Apelkhot and Aunts Lyusya, Soka and Lizochka a month ago. They all look fairly well. Yura is quite grown up now, he was in uniform. He's a military doctor. Well I think that's everything. Love to Aunt Beti, Lyonya, Lyolya, and the baby, Sarra Abramovna, Uncle, Syoma. Write back soon.

Love from your
Lyodik

My address: PPC 591, Officer Training, 2 Company.

This letter seems particular and strange, at a slant to the rest. The other letters always begin with a fountain of questions and end with a symmetrical collection of answers (the Aunts, baby, etc., etc., the order is pretty much the same always: from close family outward). The questions would seem formal if they weren't underpinned by melancholy. This melancholy is not in the words themselves but in the space behind them, and in the number of letters—have they reached their destination?—and in the insistence of the repeated phrasing. It's as if a person wanted desperately to send news, but was instead obliged to simply cover the whole surface of a piece of paper with one and the same question. The correspondence is the only way to reach out and touch his beloved family, but at the same time he can't let them know what is actually happening to him. Only very occasionally the seams come apart and you can see the padding inside. The summer before, Lyodik wrote to his aunt, my great-grandmother: "I am glad you've settled so well and you have your own smallholding and even chickens. You made me laugh when you said you'd be very glad to leave it all and go home. However good it is, home is better always. We don't need to hide this fact, right?"

The excerpt about training is one of the only places where the anxiety eating away at him is visible. The whole matter is squeezed into a few unsure sentences, and the "choice" made ("I had no say in the matter") seems not entirely fixed—it could possibly be undone. He wants to hear what his mother makes of it: "Will you write to me and tell me?"

There was a desperate shortage of officers of all ranks on the frontline. By January 1, the commanding officers on the Volkhovsky Front had been almost entirely replaced. On October 4,

1941, Order 85 was implemented to deal with this shortage, "On the Creation of Training Courses for Junior and Mid-ranking Officers in Every HQ and Division." Stalin himself amended the order, decreasing training times to match the situation: a month for those on frontline duties, two months for those stationed at bases. The latter applied directly to Lyodik, with his recently acquired military experience:

2. To create training courses for Junior Lieutenants to prepare them for the command of a platoon. Courses for up to 200 men. The combined courses to be attended by sergeants and the best lance corporals who have distinguished themselves in combat, including the lightly wounded after their rehabilitation. Course length: two months.

3. Trainers to be picked for the courses from the ranks of educated officers from unit HQs and other parts of the army.

There was an amendment in the third paragraph as well: Stalin changed the phrase "best officers" to the more realistic "educated" officers. There were extremely low demands placed on trainers, and the training itself was incredibly short. Officers were supposed to lead their soldiers into attack and so they fell first, dying in their thousands. The country needed ever more officers—it was hungry for them. They stood out more than the men they led, and could be blamed when the platoon retreated under heavy fire, or when a sentry left his post to warm up.

Daily food allowances for hungry frontline soldiers were far more generous than they were for recruits in the besieged city. Rations were constantly being reassessed and reduced in 1941, but all the same rations for soldiers on the frontline were unbelievably luxurious compared to allowances in the city just ten kilometers north. There was tobacco and 900 grams of bread, meat and cereal, onion and potato. Anyone with scurvy was given vitamin C tablets. The rations for the wounded in hospital were fairly generous, too. They got 600 grams of bread a day, meat, fish, but also milk and butter, juice or fruit extract. For those in recovery the bread ration rose to 800 grams. In comparison with this the life of a recruit was pared back to the minimum, and rumors about how bad life was reached the frontline.

Even if Lyodik hadn't been afraid of facing hunger on his training course, or if he hadn't seen with his own eyes what was going on in Leningrad, he still would've had grounds for anxiety. The conscription act had included those of "doubtful lineage" but only up to a limit: the children and grandchildren of priests, aristocrats, and merchants were fine for basic military service but they were not eligible for officer ranking. Lyodik (Leonid Gimmelfarb) had a complicated backstory: relatives abroad, whose new colored photographs were in the old albums, and grandfathers whose lineage and position were best left unmentioned on forms. Rising through the ranks made all that a little more visible as the forms were more scrutinized, one's position less secure. And perhaps there was also his shame at leaving his comrades on the frontline. Besides, Lyodik, with his dislike of melodrama, must have found the position of an officer repellent: controlling the circumstances of others, always in the wrong, dragged into the limelight against his will.

The frontline soldier Ivan Zykov describes officer training in Leningrad, though at a higher level: commanding officer of a battalion. The training took place in a former school on the outskirts of Leningrad, where they slept as well, with their revolvers under their pillows and their loaded rifles stacked in pyramids. They didn't once go into the city, because there was nothing to do in town but remember its prewar glory. There was no heating in the school—the water pipes had frozen back in November. They say that some theaters were still open, that the actors shuffled onstage with sunken faces to *act*.

Organizing food was tricky. The cooks were civilians and some of the men on duty were responsible for the chopping of wood and fetching buckets of water. We fetched water from the Neva several times a day in a big container on a sledge. About 400 meters from the school was an old wooden house and we demolished it for the wood. We'd heave a few logs back on our shoulders, saw them, chop them and take them to the kitchen so the cook could make porridge or soup. When food was ready, we weren't allowed into the dining room. We'd line up first for a mug of pine-needle infusion which we had to drink it to avoid getting scurvy, and only then were we allowed to eat.

The freezing weather lasted a very long time. "The snow fell, and fell, and fell. The square, the banks of the Neva, the peeling facade of the Winter Palace, the broken windows of the Hermitage—it all seems somehow distant and fantastical, a fairy tale of a dying city, where Chinese shadow puppets still move, hurrying about until they breathe their last." By February the constant talk was of cannibalism; dark rumors filled the pages of diaries. "Professor D, a pathologist, says that the liver of a person who has died of starvation has a bad taste, but when mixed with brains, is delicious. How on earth does he know???" These stories are relayed with the repeated refrain: "True or false?" The extreme naturalism of the description returns both the storyteller and the reader to their senses. Around this time Shaporina, who remained an objective and sober narrator, almost to the point of removing herself from the narrative, writes: "I have become a cave dweller." She received her ration of 450 grams of meat and "I didn't have the patience to cut it with a knife and fork, I picked it up in my hands and ate it."

May 17, 1942
  My dear family,
  I don't know where to begin. I'm alive and in good health and doing well. I wrote many times from the training camp but didn't receive a reply. I don't know why that is.
  I have a permanent address now and so I am writing again in the

hope of a reply. Please write and tell me how you all are, whether you are well? How are Mother, Auntie Beti, Lyonya, Lyolya, the baby, Sarra Abramovna? I'm worried that I haven't heard from you.

I was in Leningrad until March, so the food situation was fairly bad. At the end of February I went to Lake Ladoga, and the food got better immediately and I feel quite fit and well now.

Please write as much as possible about everyone and everything. I can't wait to hear. All my love to Mother, Auntie Beti, Lyonya, Lyolya, their baby and Sarra Abramovna.

My address: PPS 939,994, s/p 3 Battalion, 7 Company, Junior Lt Gimmelfarb L. M.

*

In Spring 1942, stiffly, almost unwillingly, life began returning to its former shape. Food supplies increased, a market opened, things could once again be bought for money. The city was coarser, in the sun it seemed almost rural—here and there patches of land appeared from under the snow, ready for sowing potatoes, cabbage, and cucumbers. In April the city's inhabitants came out onto the streets to clear them after the Terrible Winter. The Terrible Winter lived on of course, it seemed to breathe through every crack, but still the changes felt like heaven. This insubstantial, shaky euphoria (there was no faith in it, but still a desire to linger beneath a glassy sun) washes through the Siege diaries during these weeks and months. At the beginning of summer Klavdiya Naumovna writes to her son:

Things are happening again, life feels quite exhilarating, especially after the winter. People are washing themselves, they've started wearing their best dresses. The streetcars are running, shops are reopening. There are lines for perfume in the shops—they got perfume into Leningrad. It does cost 120 rubles a bottle, but people are buying it and I was even given some. I was so happy. I love perfume! I sprayed some on and I don't feel hungry at all, I feel as if I were just returning

*from the theater, or a concert or a café. This is especially how I feel
wearing "Red Moscow" scent.*

Shaporina confirms this, writing that the air was wonderful—
and how delicious the radish was. She didn't have much hope
left, but at least they were still alive.

Otter, Lydia Ginzburg's hero and alter ego, expresses the same
feeling of a suspicious absence of hunger, waking with a "wonderful, still undiminished lack of suffering." *Otter's Day*, from
which she later draws the perfectly constructed *Notes from the
Blockade*, was written with some distance in 1943 and 1944, but
the description of life returning to its former state, without apparent reason, seems very real in its unlikeliness. "The window
was open. He was neither hot nor cold. It was light all around.
And it would stay light the whole of the white night through. He
didn't even feel like eating. [...] Otter threw back the sheet and
exposed his body to the light, bright air, neither cold nor hot."

There was a welcome lull in hostilities on the Leningrad
Front. Nikulin wrote of the "layering of corpses" that had been
left over the winter and had reappeared when the snow melted:
the September dead in their light jackets and shoes, overlaid by
the marines in their felted peacoats, the Siberians in their short
fur jackets, and the city's volunteer defense forces. The roads
were wet and impassable, the dugouts filled with water. Spring
dried everything, made the earth even again, decorated it with
green, and disguised the graves. "The soldiers rested behind
their defenses. There were hardly any new dead or wounded.
Training began, they even started showing films [...] They built
bathhouses everywhere, and got rid of the lice." It was a sunny
summer: they slowly got ready for an offensive. Lyodik's mother
asked him if he was due leave and he replied that "no leave is
given in wartime. When the war is over then I hope to see you
all, my dearest ones." Singers came and gave concerts to the soldiers—the still-unknown Klavdiya Shulzhenko sang "The Blue

Scarf," which had been adapted for her and which would later become a wartime classic:

> When I receive your letters
> I hear your voice in my head
> And between the words, the bluest scarf
> Waves with what's unsaid.

*

July 5, 1942

Dear Mother,

I got a postcard from you yesterday and I was delighted. A little while ago I got another one. I was happy to know that you and all the family are in health and doing well. Did you get my letter where I wrote down everything in detail? On the same day I wrote to Father but I've had nothing back from him yet. I sent you 700 rubles, I wrote to you about this. Did you receive them?

Here everything is just as before, the days pass uneventfully. The weather is good. A few days ago we had a show: jazz, readings, two dancers, a singer and a baritone. I especially liked how they sang "Chelita" and "The Blue Scarf," and how they played Dunayevsky's jazz. For a long while I couldn't get the concert out of my head, because it was such a big luxury for me. Probably those despicable Germans heard the music as well, as it was put on not far from the front line.

I am doing well. I live in hope of seeing you, father and all our dear family very soon. I am so proud of Father that he has been promoted to a guardsman. I hope in my turn I can justify the faith placed in me by the nation as a Red Army Officer.

Mother, tell me everything, I want to know about everyone. I have one request. If possible could you send me envelopes as they are hard to come by here.

I wish you health and happiness. I send you all my love.

Love from your

Lyodik

Please give my love to everyone.
P.S. I met some soldiers from our part of Moscow. It was good to
talk to them. One of them lived and worked on our street.
Love again.
Lyodik

*

Before the war "The Blue Scarf" had seemed little more than a simple ditty, and the words were quite different. It was almost by chance that it became the hymn to the soldier's blues: another young lieutenant on the same Volkhovsky Front handed the singer, Shulzhenko, a piece of paper with his version of the lyrics, and they stuck:

> *For them, for her*
> *The one he did adore*
> *The gunner aims, the scarf is blue*
> *That his beloved wore*

Many of the popular songs of the period had similar fates. The fashionable "Chelita" was given new life by the Soviet music hall stars of the thirties. The Mexican original was more urgent and more sublime, but the Soviet version had some catchy lyrics and carefully managed class awareness: the Mexican *señores* may have promised her heaps of pearls, but the heroine only has eyes for the baker's boy under the midday sun. A famous Red Army song, "Boldly We Go Into Battle for the Soviets," has a White Army twin, "Boldly We Go Into Battle for Holy Rus," only the latter is sung in a slow deep voice, as if rising up from underground. Both versions have a common root (or branch) in the beautiful song "The Scented Buds of the White Acacia." Grandmother Dora, who remembered the Civil War well, used to sing a song about the Priamursky Partisans to me in my childhood, and only years later I found unexpectedly its perfect reverse, the same tune used for the war march of the opposing Siberian Infantry. Even the salon waltzes from the piles of old manuscripts have their strange echoes in Soviet propaganda songs.

The Second World War song "Katyusha," composed in Russian in 1939 by Matvei Blanter, was sung across the world—one of its incarnations was the hymn of the Spanish Blue Division, who fought on the Leningrad Front, but on the side of the Wehrmacht. In this version the singer sings of a spring without flowers, far away from a loved one, and the ignoble foe swimming in vodka. It's a sad song and it ends with the promise of a heroic end. In a single battle at Krasny Bor, over a thousand Spaniards were killed in only an hour.

There was death everywhere that summer. On the other side of no-man's-land Lyodik wrote to his cousin: "I think I will join the Party, so I can defeat the damned enemy in a Bolshevik spirit! Here's to victory! Here's to meeting again soon!"

July 26, 1942

Dear Mother,

I found out from Auntie Beti's letter that you received the money (700 rubles). I don't understand why you didn't write yourself. The last time I heard from you was the postcard with Lyonya's note on it. I really hope to get a letter from you soon. You asked me to send you a money order. I sent it and now you should receive the money every month from your local Military Office. I earn 750 rubles, but that's with field payments, my basic wage is 600 rubles. I can only send 75% of this amount by money order, so I've done this for 400 rubles. I'll send the rest in smaller amounts by mail. The money order is valid for a year from July 1943. You can get out money from August 1943. On July 23 I sent you 900 rubles. Please let me know you have received this. I wrote the address 13 ulitsa Lenina, Yalutorovsk on the money order because I couldn't send it poste restante. Please let me know if you live a long way away from Auntie Beti. If you need to you can put a different address on the order at your local military office.

How are you feeling, Mother? I hope you aren't getting too tired at work. Don't overdo it, please. I've already told you that I had a letter from Father, I replied straightaway, but I haven't had an answer yet. Did you get my last letter? I am in good health and doing well. In two days I'll be twenty. I hope that I'll be back with you and all our family by my next birthday. I wish you health and happiness. I send you all my love.

Your loving son,
Lyodik

Surprisingly, soldiers and officers still received a wage in wartime. In 1939, an infantryman received between 140 and 300 rubles a month, and artillerymen and tank crew received slightly more. Soldiers on active service received additional "field payments." For officers these payments were set at 25 percent of the basic wage. Junior Lieutenant Gimmelfarb was in command of a platoon and his minimum wage would have been 625 rubles. In the bundle with the papers that the beautiful Verochka Gimmelfarb left on her death were the yellow stubs of money transfer orders, on the back of each a few words including the unchanging "love, Lyodik."

August 10, 1942
Dear Mother,
I received a letter from you yesterday but when I opened the envelope there were just four more envelopes inside, and no note. Maybe the letter fell out, I don't know. I haven't had a letter from you for a long time and I am very worried about your health because Father wrote that you were complaining of exhaustion. Please write and send details, tell me how you are. The last letter I received was from Aunt Beti a while ago now, I answered it straightaway and included a note to you as well. I wrote out a money order for you, to Aunt Beti's address, as I couldn't send it poste restante. The order was for 400 rubles, I couldn't send any more. I'll send the rest poste restante.

Did you receive the 900 rubles I sent you a month ago? I got a letter from Father and a card from Uncle Fili. Father is well. Uncle Fili has been with the Pacific Fleet for nearly a year. His wife Tonya is working in a studio in Almaty. Uncle Fili promised to let me know everyone's addresses. He wrote to you as well, he got your address from Father. I am in good health and doing well. How is everyone? Write to me about everything. Only please don't worry about me, it's quite unnecessary. Be happy and healthy. I send you lots of love. Love to all the family.

    I look forward to your letter.

    Your loving son,

    Lyodik

This was his last letter. On August 25, Lyubov Shaporina, writing up conversations she'd had, noted in brackets: "(I'm writing and somewhere outside the city or on its outskirts there's prolonged gunfire, an artillery duel, the guns are muttering deep and low, threateningly, like a big storm approaching.)"

On August 27, the ill-fated Sinyavinsky Operation began. The offensive was intended to breach the Siege at its narrowest point, where besieged Soviet troops were only 16 kilometers away from the main Soviet army. But it was across an area of marshland and forest, which the Germans had reinforced with gun emplacements, dugouts, and minefields. Hundreds of meters of barbed wire, fences with gun slits surrounded by ditches of marsh water, "and the guns kept roaring and the radio plays a cheerful tune. It's rumored the offensive has begun," Shaporina wrote.

The 994th Rifle Regiment had been given orders to take the village of Voronovo and dig in there. Beyond a stream lay two half-destroyed hotel complexes held by the Germans. The Commanding Officer of the 1st Battalion described it all very carefully in his memoirs: the constant firing meant the infantry had to keep low to the ground, a few tanks breached the line and crossed a bridge only to find they were alone and exposed, five days of incessant and futile fighting, officers dying one after the other.

The Commanding Officer of the Third [Lyodik was in the Third Battalion] *was hit in the leg, my Commissar was hit in the shoulder, the Senior Battalion Commissar had both legs ripped off. A few people were killed outright, I was hit below the knee of my right leg. Shrapnel took the flesh off down to the bone. I had two fingers ripped off my right hand, two more injured. Three pieces of shrapnel in my hip on the right-hand side.* [...] *The blood is flowing, but for all these wounds we only have two bags of blood.*

The man who wrote this returned home crippled. Lyodik Gimmelfarb's mother received the standard notification of death. It says that her son was killed on August 27, on the very first day of the Operation. In the fog of mass slaughter, the dates and anniversaries of death could only be approximate since no one knew the actual dates. Aleksandr Gutman, who commanded a battalion in a neighboring regiment, said that they wrote "fell in battle" on all the notifications of death, as it wasn't always possible to rescue the bodies of comrades from the battlefield and the record of the dead was poorly kept. The last moment of clarity before the darkness descends is a few hours before the beginning of battle:

The objective was clear, everyone was ready for the offensive. We passed on our defensive area to the arriving unit. The regiment went to the point of assembly, ready for the offensive, or to put it another way, we took up our first position. We ate dinner in the woods, organized sentry, and lay down to sleep as best we could. For many this would be their last night alive, but no one thought about this, everyone was filled with a single thought: to be victorious and to survive. We slept, it was a little rough, but the night passed without incident.

*At six in the morning we ate breakfast, smoked a cigarette. Then
checked weapons, ammunition, bullets, gas masks, and rolled up our
greatcoats and fixed them onto our kit. Then we waited for the order.
At 8 exactly the artillery and mortars began firing along the whole
Sinyavinsky line of troops of the 54th army. At 9 the soldiers began
their ground offensive.*

*

*National Commissariat
Defense Union USSR
994th Rifle Regiment
September 16, 1942
№ 1058
PPS № 939
Death Notification*

*Your son, Lieutenant and Officer in the rifle platoon of the 7th front
line company, 994th Rifle Regiment, Leonid Mikhailovich Gimmelfarb, of Moscow Lenin District, was injured and died of his injuries
on August 27, 1942, in the battle for the Socialist homeland, true to
his oath and displaying courage and heroism.*

*He is buried in the village of Voronovo, Mginsky District, Lenin-
grad area.*

*This notification is needed to begin the process of applying for a
pension.*

Commanding Officer of the 994th Rifle Regiment, Lt Col Popov

*Military Commissar of the 994th Rifle Regiment, Commissar
Gus'kov*

Chief-of-Staff Capt Zhizhikov

*

*February 19, 1943
Dear Vera Leontevna*

I received a letter from your husband, Mikhail Gimmelfarb, who wanted to know about his dearly beloved son, Leonid. I can tell you that your son died the death of the Courageous, while defending Leningrad on August 27, 1942. He was a worthy son to the homeland. You should be proud to have brought up such a son. Of course it's a terrible shame, but what can we do. War is pitiless, it demands sacrifice. We must find joy in the fact that the blood spilled by the Russian nation was not in vain. We, the soldiers of the Red Army, will avenge your son's death. I am asking you as I don't know your husband's address and couldn't answer him personally.

I wish you good health and send you courage.

Deputy Commanding Officer. N Regiment

A. Ugolkov

*

April 1, 1944

Dear Comrade Begun,

In answer to your letter I would like to inform you that Mikhail Gimmelfarb was sent to serve in a military unit on February 10, 1944. On his way to his destination he was killed by enemy fire on February 11, 1944.

His death notification was sent by the same military unit to his home address.

Military Unit fieldpost address 24778 c

Lt V. Maratov

Lyodik always mentions the baby in his letters, still nameless and without gender. The baby has either appeared, or is just about to. This unborn child who was so important to him was my mother, Natasha Gurevich. She used to tell me all about Lyodik when I was small. She had chosen him in childhood to be her hero, making him the secret center of her little world, and she remembered him as long as she lived. The envelope of letters, photographs, and death notifications has her handwriting on it.

9. Joseph, or Obedience

In Würzburg there is a palace, the Würzburg Residence, and in it a fresco by Giovanni Battista Tiepolo that is unlike anything else in the whole wide universe. That's a silly thing to say, of course, because everything in the universe is like everything else; "everything rhymes," as Marina Tsvetaeva said. The fresco blushes pink the length of the ceiling, and is filled with the incredible creatures reality usually keeps hidden in the circus or the Hollywood costume department. But here they are all, gathered in a parade of the Four Continents. The Continents have detached themselves from their geographic positions, gathered their belongings, and made haste to join the celebrations in honor of the Prince-Bishop of Würzburg. The artist himself arrived at the party before anyone else, sitting out three years in the northern town—three whole years, while this phantasmagoria was appearing on the ceiling: parrots, monkeys, dwarfs and Indigenous peoples, serving girls, empresses, crocodiles, the white legs of heavenly creatures, half-dissolving in the rosy atmosphere. All of them angled to look down on our far thinner existence, like a lid on a boiling saucepan, hinting at the fact that reality can be far brighter and more fascinating than the version we have constructed for ourselves.

This rainbow apparition was nearly destroyed in the air raids during the Second World War, when over 900 tonnes of TNT was dropped on the town in just a few weeks. The square where they burned books on a spring evening in 1932 was unrecognizable by 1945; the adjoining residence a mere ghost. The palace no longer had a roof, and what hadn't been consumed by fire was spoiled by rain and soot. The pale white stucco ceiling in the

Throne Room had disappeared as if it had never existed—its painstaking relief had been more like the seabed than the ceiling of a place of pomp and splendor: the feathers and the flagpoles lay in patterns reminiscent of fish bones picked clean, and the spears gathered in sheaves could, without much effort, pass as the masts of shipwrecks.

Everything has been restored: the stucco and the mirrors, and the shifting tones of the room, where silver flows into green as if there were no difference between them. The huge fresco, with its varied wonders and crocodiles, shines as it always did. Roberto Calasso describes its rose-tinted luminosity as the last breath of happiness in Europe in his book about Tiepolo. Despite its teeming, multicolored crowds, he insists on apprehending it as a single spellbinding composition. "We are in the midst of a sample of humanity that is not yet exotic, but *not provincial.*" It is able to establish a "relationship of familiarity" with "every imaginable figure, human or semidivine, such as the Nymphs or other denizens of rivers and springs. For Tiepolo, the plumed Indian woman riding an alligator is no more singular than the European musicians who played at court." In this *peaceful demonstration* the real and the invented appear as equals; mysterious creatures and strange substances alongside the representatives of the familiar world, as if that were the only way. There is no image too banal, no novelty too shocking for these crowds. Tiepolo "invented something one might dream about to this day: a democracy leveled off toward the top, where aesthetic quality makes it possible to eliminate any divergence in status."

*

On the website of the Whitney Museum of American Art there's a description of a work of art that sounds a little like an inventory of someone's trouser pockets, a list Tom Sawyer might have aspired to. It reads: painted wood and printed paper, aperitif glasses, marbles, plaster head, painted cork ball, metal rods, brad nails, and painted glass. All this, collected into the cardboard term "assemblage," and kept in a specially made glass-fronted wooden box. We might think of it as a shopfront, or a jewelery box, or an icon surround, a suitcase with a transparent lid: in every case the essential attribute is that the contents are singled out, exposed and inviolable under their glass shroud (and perhaps they might even be invisible, living inside their own belly).

The artist Joseph Cornell is best known for his boxes. He made a huge quantity of these over his long life. At first he used ready-made boxes for his strange projects, and then he began making them himself in the basement of his little suburban home. There are dozens of these boxes: he gave some to people he admired. Occasionally his admiration cooled and he wrote to the recipient to ask for the return of the gift to its owner. In one way or another, they always remained his, his treasure, his *precious* ...

All Cornell's boxes are glass-fronted; there's a teasing element in this, as every little object seems intended to be touched, the colored sand run through your fingers, the marbles transferred from glass to pocket. Sealed shut, like museum cabinets, the boxes promise play and yet suggest that playtime is delayed indefinitely. The box's addressee is usually long gone; one of Cornell's most famous boxes is meant as a gift for a great ballerina who died in 1856. "Taglioni's Jewel Casket," lined in brown velvet and garlanded with a necklace of large gems, contains sixteen transparent cubes, like ice cubes, resting on blue glass and waiting for their owner. An inscription in the lid tells the story:

On a moonlit night in the winter of 1835 the carriage of Marie TA-GLIONI was halted by a Russian highwayman, and that enchanting creature commanded to dance for this audience of one upon a panther's skin spread over the snow beneath the stars. From this actuality arose the legend that to keep alive the memory of this adventure so precious to her, TAGLIONI formed the habit of placing a piece of artificial ice in her jewel casket or dressing table where, melting among

*the sparkling stones, there was evoked a hint of the atmosphere of the
starlit heavens over the ice-covered landscape.*

Taglioni only came to Russia in 1837; the fairly unlikely story
of the honorable highwayman is different in its original telling:
instead of a panther skin spread over the snow there's a carpet
spread over the wet slush, and there is no mention of the ice
cubes. The only "actuality," to use Cornell's word, is Cornell himself—and his ardent belief in the power of boxes and caskets.
His many closed chambers could be brought together to form
a doll's house, filled with priest holes and secret rooms, "Suitcases," "Soap Bubble Sets." Or perhaps a doll's town, complete
with "Hotels" and "Observatories," "Dovecotes," "Pharmacies,"
"Aviaries," "Sand Fountains." These are the titles of series, rather
than individual works, consisting of many variations, each leading to the next, like a suite of rooms.

Cornell died on December 29, 1972, a year before his seventi-
eth birthday. He would have enjoyed the date, placed in a celebratory box between Christmas and the New Year; he was born
on Christmas Eve as well. He spent almost all his life in the same
place, Utopia Parkway, 3708, in a modest suburban house, with
his elderly mother and his disabled brother Robert. His studio
was in the basement, where he kept tens of thousands of images
and photocopies ready for future works, boxes of essential objects
("best white boxes—Empty," "Plastic Shells new-1960"), files of
notes and clippings. His strange passions made him a specialist
in many niche areas, from ballet iconography to the history of
silent film, and even experts would sometimes turn to him for
advice. As he grew older he became increasingly impatient with
collectors and tried to avoid selling his work or even exhibiting
it. There was one sure way to get a hold of it, though—to visit
him at home in the company of a young ballerina or starlet, and
afterward buy up anything that the old man gave her as a gift.

After the death of his brother, Joseph Cornell often said that

Robert had been the better artist—Robert (as an acerbic critic once noted) mostly drew mice, and was seriously into model railways. A sequence of works was dedicated to his memory, signed "Joseph and Robert Cornell." The simple and rather sad mechanism, which stood behind this desire to bring the two names together, to make something together, was the main engine for Joseph's very many activities, it was what made him tick. Robert Cornell, Taglioni, Gérard de Nerval, and many others, each in their own way, all demanded love, little temples to the embodiment of memory. These usually took the form of the little boxes: memorials to a meeting, drafts of a space where a conversation might take place.

Over long years of rummaging in antique shops, Cornell perfected his complex system of internal rhyme to the point where he could couple anything together with little or no effort. In this lay his sense of secret delight. He considered his teachers to be Mallarmé and Baudelaire: both were informed by a sense of the "correspondences" riddling the world with their countless ant trails, but in Cornell's work this has the opposite effect. His objects learned a new obedience—each item considers for a moment, then lies down in its place and makes itself useful: all the objects became family. Every object has the chance to bask in the golden light of "being seen"; the wood shavings, the colored sand, and the cork balls exhibit a majesty and poise more befitting to ballerinas and poets. It seems as if the fact of future oblivion and decline was enough to make any object invaluable to Cornell. Every new work was constructed like Noah's Ark, with the intention of preservation at its heart.

*

Anyone who lived in 1970s Russia will recognize in Cornell's boxes the game of *sekretiki* or "little secrets"—the passion of my childhood. Nothing in the humdrum reality of this time could have explained the appearance of this game. Strictly speaking it was only a "game" in the sense that it had rules. *Sekretiki* wasn't just any activity, it was a secret that you shared only with your closest friends and it was like no other game played in the street or at school. It was "underground" in the most direct sense of the word because the little secrets were kept under the ground, like treasure or dead bodies. In the country, where people were always bent over the land, planting seeds or digging out food, there would have been nothing special in this, but we were children of the city who knew the way home from school by the cracks in the pavement, and we had no relationship with the black and granular earth that every Spring gave the acacia and the lilac its freedom.

To make a "little secret" you had to drop down and press yourself against the earth. Choose a place, dig a little hole, look around and check no one is watching, put in the precious object, cover it with a piece of scrubbed-clean glass and then pour the earth back over, tamp it down so it looks untouched. Now I realize that these tiny tombs, lined with foil and filled with a tiny supply of all the beauty in the world were very like ancient burial chambers, with their assortment of objects ready for the immortal life. Very special things were chosen for the "little secret," things that were few and far between: gold and silver paper, feathers, clippings from newspapers with a photograph of an actor or actress, precious beads or buttons, sometimes even tiny little dolls or figurines. The essential layer of glass turned the "little secret" into a shop window waiting for someone to come past and look in.

Like all buried treasure (X marks the spot), they weren't very reliable hiding places, and you could more or less forget about ever seeing your trove again. Very few people knew about the burial place, two or three trusted friends. But a few days later, when you checked back under the bush there was nothing there. The "little secret" had disappeared as if it'd never existed. Either some boys, who had followed your movements with a predatory eye, had dug it up, or a rival had found it and buried it somewhere else. Or perhaps you'd simply forgotten where to dig (all your little remembered coordinates proving false friends). Sometimes it felt as if the *sekretiki*, like underground rivers, or seams of gold, lived according to their own instinct and could even move from place to place.

There was nothing much for the *sekretiki* above ground. The aesthetic system of Soviet life was thorough and in its own way convincing, but it adhered to an unspoken bias toward understated, decent, cheerful modesty, with no pretense to the gaudy or extravagant. Some insignificant departures from the norm were acceptable, as long as these were only small steps out of line: sentimentality, the soft focus of tenderness or grief as a response to understandable and general feelings, like yearning for lost youth or love for one's children, or hope for something better. Anything suggesting equality or unity was acceptable, but eccentricity, standing out from the crowd without justification, was quite another thing. Anything that could be interpreted as outlandish behavior (even earrings in the ears of schoolgirls) was seen as an attempt to break into a space labeled "unacceptable exclusivity" and *that sort of thing*—opulence, plumes and tails, silk stockings and sparklers—was in danger of destroying the general equilibrium and had to be kept at bay. Perhaps that is why it now feels to me as if the "little secrets," filled with the "outlandish," a concentration of the burlesque, forbidden beauty, crystal beads, cut out paper roses, became political refuges, crossing both state and other boundaries.

At various moments in history, in the villages and the rural hamlets of this vast country, people hid sawn-off shotguns and Grandfather's revolver and even Tsarist gold coins. Nearer Moscow, in the gardens of summerhouses and allotments, anti-Soviet literature lay in the damp darkness—the seditious books and manuscripts that were too dangerous to keep even in the attic. Our apparently pointless little secret burials might have had a direct relationship with this history: we were hiding from chance view the beauty that was so lacking around us, and which we didn't want to share with anyone in our *sekretiki*.

Years later I came across the word in a book of memoirs. A short text, written in English in the 1950s, with nothing to do with the underground sparkle of foil and glass. The book described the period of pogroms in the south of Ukraine in 1919 through the eyes of a little girl, how the people in the village lay awake at night waiting for *them* to come, and then they did. It recounted how the women and children hid wherever they could, under fences and behind tree stumps, and then returned to their houses to wash and dress the murdered. The people living there had different ways of hiding, the hiding places necessary when flight is impossible: brick-lined secret rooms, underground holes, dugouts with whole families sheltering in them to sit out the pogrom. Sometimes they managed to escape notice. The memoir gave these hiding places a name. It was spelled with English letters, but the Cyrillic pulsed feverishly from within: *sekreten*.

*

In December 1936, in a New York gallery, Joseph Cornell showed his first film to a small audience. It was called *Rose Hobart* and it lasted about seventeen minutes. The lens of the projector was covered with blue glass that gave the image a lunar tint. The film was in slow motion and had no sound, as if the action was happening twenty years before, in the age of the silent movie.

The thirty-two-year old Salvador Dalí was in the audience. In the middle of the screening he jumped to his feet and shouted that Cornell had robbed him. He insisted that this idea had been in his subconscious, these had been his, Dalí's, dreams, and Cornell had no right to use them as he wished.

After Dalí and his wife and muse Gala had left the gallery, the film continued: dark-blue Indigenous people in light-blue loincloths chased crocodiles down to the river with poles, wind fluttered the palm fronds, a woman of exquisite beauty moved toward something and looked at it closely, and then did this another few times. The sun was eclipsed, a bubble appeared on the surface of the water, round as an eye. A woman played with a monkey. Cornell showed none of his films after this one, although in some ways it had fulfilled its function, even on its own.

It's curious that Dalí considered stolen what belonged to neither him, nor Cornell—at least not according to the definition of intellectual property. Everything in the film shown at the Julien Levy Gallery that day, with the exception of one or two shots, was taken from the adventure film *East of Borneo*, made in 1931 and lacking all artistic distinction. Reviewers of the original film noted the implausible plot, the incredible number of disasters and the wooden acting of the actress playing the lead role. She was called Rose Hobart and her high cheekbones and auburn hair was a combination potent enough to ensure her immortality.

The action-packed *East of Borneo* lasted 77 minutes. It was soon dropped and forgotten, and the reels of film could be hunted down in the shops selling antiques and second-hand goods—there were plenty of such shops around Times Square. Cornell, who collected up anything with even a passing relevance to his many *love interests*, had a particular fascination with Hollywood's cast-offs: photos of auditions, film stills no one needed, memorabilia from b movies, all nameless starlets and aging divas. When he got hold of the film reel for *East of Borneo* he simply cut out the superfluous—anything that had nothing to do with Rose, or got in the way of seeing her. In his film, named in her honor, absolutely nothing happens—but then that is perhaps why it's so captivating.

Instead of rushing about on a mission, the heroine, always dressed in a colonial white, is doomed to live out what might be called a "pure" organic existence. In the first scene the camera creeps through the jungle darkness toward a lit hut where Rose is asleep and we see her through a transparent curtain: she looks quite diminutive, as if we were looking at a scene in one of Cornell's boxes. Her white hat lies on a table. She moves in the lit interior, her face is quite expressionless, and only her outfits change in Cornell's edited frames: a dress, another dress, a soft white raincoat with rounded lapels. She speaks, pressing her hands to her breast, but we can't hear anything: the film has been silenced. Some of her movements are repeated, some two or three times as if we are being asked to follow her every gesture in its flowerlike unfolding. For the most part this is a narrative of looking: the heroine freezes and looks, staggers back, looks again.

In one scene a lovesick raja draws back the curtain and offers the white woman the rare sight of a volcano erupting. They watch it together, like moviegoers on a dark balcony. He wears a turban of fine material and she wears a floor-length evening dress—and before them the fire and the darkness. In the same shot there is a huge parrot, one of Cornell's favorite creatures.

Almost all Cornell's films are constructed in this same way. Not one lasts more than twenty minutes and as a rule they are usually much shorter. They are rarely talked about, perhaps because they are so strange. In one of his films, called *Centuries of June*, the camera is held at the eye level of a nine-year-old and its gaze wanders endlessly, over a wooden staircase and up a wall, up at the sky through the leaves, at the knees of children digging in the earth, the white socks of a little girl walking away down a street. Another film tells the story of a children's party (one of the characters is gnawing at a huge apple, which grows to the size of the moon by the end of the film). His films are a sequence of strange and wonderful images: a black hole opening in the sky; a circus acrobat in white hanging from like a fish on a line, swinging her legs in the darkness and circling like a bud opening. Branches crash and rustle, the arrow on a weathervane turns to point like a bird's beak, seagulls clap their wings; a fairy girl, her hair loose about her shoulders, rides a white horse; and a terrifying caricature of a Red Indian pulls a black mask down over his face and throws knives at his gentle squaw without ever hitting her. In another film a blonde-haired girl runs about a park holding a ripped cream-colored umbrella. Pigeons bathe in the fountain, the pigeons suddenly fly up, a sullen girl stands in the middle of a square and doesn't know where to turn. Water flows. It's a little like something filmed from a phone—as if the camera was set to record and left to capture life in all its pointless capaciousness.

Cornell saves everything that is dear to him, rescuing it from the passing of time in the same way that a child might take scissors and cut a picture of a favorite prince or princess out of the page of a book. And in the same way, in 1930s Soviet Russia, people would repeatedly go to watch a famous film about a Red Army Commander. The film, named after its eponymous hero Chapaev, was the site for the last encounter between the old world and the new. There's a scene of "psychological warfare" in which White Army soldiers advance, with cigarettes in their mouths, only to be mowed down by Chapaev's machine gun. As they fall, they are replaced by new soldiers with cigarettes in their mouths. The poet Mandelstam, exiled in Voronezh, describes this scene: the men come out, a cigarette "in the death grip of their teeth / machine-pressed officers / in the open groin of the heath." The White Army men march in parade formation to the beat of a drum and they fall silently, one by one, to the stutter of machine gun fire. "How beautiful they are," says one Red Army soldier to another. The White Army extras for this scene were dragged out of their oblivion to demonstrate once again that the victor is always right, and the beautiful are always the vanquished. The marchers included the poet Valentin Stenich, the first Russian translator of *Ulysses*. He was executed in 1938. It's said he did not conduct himself with honor at his interrogations. God forbid anyone should find out how we conduct ourselves at ours.

There's a myth connected with this film. In the end brave Chapaev, the hero of legends and jokes, dies. Injured, he swims the icy Ural river ("The water colder than a bayonet"—so the song goes), and the enemy shoots at him as he swims and we know he won't survive. In more than one memoir from the time, the author tells the story of going to see the film three or four times, because it was rumored that in a cinema somewhere on the edge of town Chapaev swims free.

Stalin's order concerning the poet Mandelstam, which led to his exile, was "isolate and preserve." This feels like a good summary of Cornell's long arduous years of hard labor. For him, to isolate (to pick out, reserve, and place in the correct context; to surround with correspondences and rhymes, bottle up, and seal; to find a space *where neither moth nor rust doth corrupt, and where thieves do not break through nor steal*) meant to preserve. In the Old Church Slavonic version of the Gospel of Matthew the treasures must be "hidden," so "to preserve" in this interpretation means "to hide," whereas in the King James Version the phrase used is "lay up," as you might "lay up" supplies for winter in an attic or a barn, or in a vast warehouse. One such warehouse was the place of a revelation that changed Cornell's life.

He told the story of this single ineffable moment of vision more than once. Circumstances had made him the breadwinner for his family, providing for his mother and invalid brother, and his job as a sales rep involved trawling round the little Manhattan fabric shops with samples. One evening at sunset, when all the windows of the big warehouse on West 54th Street were aflame with light, he saw in each window the image of Fanny Cerrito, the Italian ballerina, famous in the 1840s. She stood up on the roof of the building, and at the same time she was closing the blinds in hundreds of windows. "I heard a voice, and I saw a light," as he said about another similar incident. After this he had many more visions, and became a connoisseur of these moments of sudden transformation. Cerrito was born in Naples in 1817. Cornell's series of Neapolitan boxes (maps, views of Vesuvius, the blue of the sky) offered her a new and eternal home.

In Cornell's diaries a passionate love of the past combines with a hunger for new and related practices to his. He is absolutely a contemporary artist: he reads Breton and Borges, he is friends with Duchamp, he follows Dalí's work with interest, he is in correspondence with half the art world, he cites Magritte (he has a grief-filled collage dedicated to his brother's memory with Magritte's locomotive flying out of its fireplace like a bird let loose from its cage). He makes reference to Brancusi and Juan Gris, and his library of books on contemporary art is worn thin with constant handling. This is his context, he is in conversation with these artists. The peculiar thing is, of course, that no one ever really answers him. He knows all of them, and yet he is barely recognized—he spends his life in a vague periphery. The history of art eventually incorporated him, but he was still somehow the odd one out, like the obligatory weirdo at a fashionable gallery opening.

It's not surprising: people and animals can sense an outsider. The task of the leader of any regime, any avant-garde, is to change the world: familiar objects need to be transformed, or to be viciously mocked so they are forced to renew themselves. Cornell used the tactics of the avant-garde in order to achieve something quite different; his colleagues sensed this and treated him with justifiable distrust. Duchamp's hat rack, with its horns turned outward, conveyed its essentially alien nature (its "estrangement," as the Formalists would have described it), but for Cornell the holiness of the ready-made was inviolable. In a world in which the artist had a right to everything, he behaved with the scrupulousness of the collector, keen to preserve his property in its very best state. His found objects were not the starting point for further distortion, but much-loved creatures with their own subjectivity. In a sense he continued C. S. Lewis's theory that pets who are drawn into a loving relationship with a human grow their own soul, and in doing so are given a chance at eternal salvation. For this to happen, as I understand it, the dog or the canary doesn't even have to feel love, but just has to have love poured over it by the nearest human. Cornell's objects are redeemed in life in the same way: simply by being so very loved.

Love is an ungainly and absurd sentiment, invented to instill a certain amount of resignation and self-irony in a person; a state of lost equilibrium, created by the ridiculous situation and the inability to behave like a free and weightless being. It's too much concerned with weight, it bends the lover to the ground, to his own weakness and mortality. It's heavy to carry, even heavier to witness. I believe this partly explains Cornell's incomplete reputation, its slightly crooked nature. Unlike Hopper or O'Keefe, with their *finished* work, which has traveled a long way from its author, Cornell's boxes remain his "little secrets," the cast-offs of a barely concealed passion. The viewer becomes witness to something almost too intimate, like a domestic peep show involving plush teddy bears, but devoid of any eroticism (eroticism would be more ordinary). Cornell is simultaneously too mad and too simplehearted to be taken seriously. These qualities are usually enough to relegate an author to the nursery, the pink bookcase full of tales of gallant knights; to the children, waiting patiently for the fearful tales of the Brothers Grimm and Hans Christian Andersen.

If we consider art as a profession then Cornell was never allowed to join its trade union. He remained an awkward dilettante, the one who tries to fit in and fails: he lacked something and so the big children wouldn't play with him. Or perhaps he had too much of something: he was too fervent maybe. In his relations with life he behaved like he had a schoolgirl crush, like when a younger girl in a nineteenth-century novel followed a favored older girl around, trying to please her, keeping the precious ribbon she dropped. The chill of the experiment, which made twentieth-century art bearable, had no hold on his work, and this is important: Cornell in the world of art is rather like the huge but herbivorous elephant, surrounded by predators.

There is a famous story about the emigrant Vladimir Nabokov who once applied to join the literature department of a certain university. One of the panel was against the appointment. A clever and witty man, he noted that Nabokov was indubitably a "big" writer, but then the elephant was a big animal: you wouldn't appoint it to teach zoology. This famous put-down is almost better known in Russia than the life's work of this witty scholar. Every time I remember the story I am filled with pity for the shelterless elephant, who had neither use for nor satisfaction in his own greatness. Cornell was a similarly large beast, with no space for him in the collective landscape, and this was hardly without cause. But it didn't seem to hold him back. In one of his late notes he writes of how he has a real memory of seeing another of his idols, Houdini, at the Hippodrome—and Houdini had made an elephant disappear.

The predator senses its prey from a long way off. In the letters and memoirs of those who knew him there is often a thick cloud of embarrassment. The weight of ecstasy the artist felt at each new manifestation of the material world was not easy to tolerate: for him life seemed to consist entirely of desserts and exclamation marks, pink foam and balloons. As I read his diaries, letters, working notes, the exclamation marks, and the revelations—daily, hourly, inexhaustibly—this incontinent enthusiasm began to irritate as much as the little French words Cornell used to decorate his suburban life. His excesses went well beyond the pale of normal behavior and into areas where none of his contemporaries would have strayed: enthusiasm as a way of surviving reality had been discredited, thrown out onto the heap, it was the preserve of dilettantes and those on the margins. The constant will to ecstasy had been as natural as breathing in the age of Goethe and his Russian counterpart, Karamzin, but one hundred years later an inability to "distance" oneself was frowned upon. Marianne Moore, whose poetry Cornell loved, was in a correspondence with him, and happily accepted his gifts of boxes with their precious contents, but when he asked her to write him a reference for a very important grant, she reacted as if this might have compromised her in some way.

Fervent Joseph Cornell, with his boxes and his clippings, the teenage "fairy girls" he would go out of his way to visit daily, whom he insisted on referring to in his notes as *les fées* (apricot *fée* at the café counter, *fée aux lapins* in the toyshop), his adulation of film stars and descriptions of their hats, is in a no-man's land somewhere between the territory of professional art and the reserve of art brut, which at that point hadn't gained its later status. His means of existing put him in the same camp as those we think of as mad or "possessed," who give witness to the extreme experience, who look at our lives from a different angle, who make art without quite being aware of what they are doing. Their work needs biographical framing—it seems unreadable without this, just as you might place a stencil or colored paper over an encrypted text in order to read it.

In this sense, the artist Cornell, a Christian Scientist, a man who counted the hours till he could go and get an ice cream, was the close relative of Henry Darger, a hospital caretaker who wrote an enormous illustrated novel about young martyrs and heavenly wars in his Chicago lodgings. Both men worked and worked as if their survival depended on it, multiplying versions, accumulating essential source material in quantities that would be enough for several lifetimes, and then sorting everything into envelopes. (In Darger's case these were labeled: "Plant and child pictures," "Clouds to be drawn," and in Cornell's, "Owls," "Dürer," "Best White Boxes.") Both entered into ambiguous and undefined relationships with their own heroes. Their ardor burnt so brightly and with such an even flame of fervent revelation that even the saints would have been envious. "Transcendent feeling about swan box" or "an intolerable sadness at passing a blue house" were all part of the daily fare. "Breakfast of toast, cocoa, boiled egg, tomato, bun in kitchen—words are singularly inadequate to express the gratitude felt for these experiences."

*

"The depiction of thoughts through the depiction of associated objects" mentioned by the Russian poet Nikolai Zabolotsky is one of the very oldest mnemonic devices, a way of bringing thought back to mind. The memory is the last form of real estate, available even to those who have been denied all else. Its halls and corridors of stale air hold reality at bay. Cornell's files and drawers of preparatory work were like a cellar or an attic in a house where nothing is ever thrown away; his boxes were the drawing room and parlor where the guests sat.

In one of Cornell's diary notes he mentions a visit to the New York Museum of Natural History. He sat in the library and copied something out, all the while stealing glances at an old portrait of a Native American princess.

Had never been in this department before which is so peaceful and probably has not changed in at least seventy years [...] Wandered around downstairs and noticed (also for the first time) the breathtaking collection of birds' nests in their original condition complete and replete with eggs.

He visits the planetarium and its daytime stars and with the pleasure of familiarity he describes the glass-fronted displays of astronomical devices. It's notable that this museum, with its Indians and dinosaurs, was the model of an ever-accessible, unmoving, constant paradise for another. In J. D. Salinger's *Catcher in the Rye* the teenage Holden speaks in Cornell's words:

The best thing, though, in that museum was that everything always stayed right where it was. Nobody'd move. You could go there a hun-

dred times, and that Eskimo would still be just finished catching those two fish, the birds would still be on their way south, the deers would still be drinking out of that water hole, with their pretty antlers and their pretty, skinny legs, and that squaw with the naked bosom would still be weaving that same blanket. Nobody'd be different. The only thing that would be different would be you.

I love being in this museum, most of all in the rooms of old dioramas: the calm unassailable dignity of the stuffed animals posing against a backdrop of painted hills and forests, just as my great-grandfathers and grandmothers posed against backdrops of painted gardens and mists. The real world of sawdust and wool quietly and seamlessly extends into the illusory, into rosy vistas and nut-brown muddy tracks, a soapy soft-focus that I remember from illustrations on postage stamps in the albums I saw as a child. The blue of the sky never fails to remind me of Cornell, the okapi in their striped socks reach out to tear off an absent-minded leaf, the deer shake their antlers, and the lynx crosses the snow carefully—in the warm air every sound rings out. Then there's an image of wet autumn woodland speckled red, and I begin to cry, very quietly, under my breath, because it's the very same Moscow wood where I used to walk with my parents once, many thousands of miles ago, and we are now looking at each other again.

10. Things I Don't Know

There's a memorial in Moscow at Lyubyanka, a square surrounded by high buildings that have housed the various incarnations of secret police for the last hundred years. It's an unobtrusive
memorial, usually just called "the Stone," the Solovetsky Stone,
brought from the Solovetsky Islands where, in 1919, one of the
very first Soviet prison camps was opened. Many more followed.

Every year in Autumn there is a special day when people
gather to take part in a communal event. Everyone is given a
little square of paper with the name, surname, and profession of a
person who was executed during the years of Communist Terror.
Then they line up to approach the Stone in order to say these
names aloud. It lasts a whole day, and could go on far longer.
Even toward evening, when it's getting cold, there is no shortage
of people in line. Those who lost parents and grandparents read
their names alongside the names of strangers. Candles are lit by
the Stone. A few years ago our ten-year-old son went to stand
in line. He knew more or less why he was there, but he got cold
and miserable waiting his turn. Then suddenly, when he heard
the names and dates being read out, he seized hold of his father
and burst into tears: "They killed that person on May 6, on my
birthday, Dad ... how unfair is that, Dad?"

*

Birthdays do matter after all. My grandmother Lyolya was born
on May 9, Victory Day. I learned that important fact almost before
I learned to walk. My mother loved to remember the Spring of
1945 when they returned to Moscow from evacuation: fireworks
over the Kremlin, a long table with everyone eating together:

family, friends, all the inhabitants of the communal apartment, and all this felt like a natural ending, like a long-awaited birthday present. Grandmother was born in 1916, but the year wasn't important. The general victory celebration completed her own quieter celebration, confirmed that her birth date wasn't just chance.

The natural connection between Grandmother and May 9 was such an integral part of family mythology that it was only recently that it occurred to me that the she was in fact born on April 26, back in the old world and according to the old Julian Calendar. It occurred to me, too that her father, my great-grandfather Misha, was born under a different name and lived with it for a few years. Among the old papers there is a certificate given to Mikhel Fridman, apothecary's apprentice, and however hard I strain my eyes I can't make out the moment of transformation, when something shifts and Great-Grandfather appears in the world as the young lawyer Misha, a court solicitor in polished boots, carrying volumes of Tolstoy. All I know is that he gave his student nephew a single piece of advice: "Live an interesting life." Did he live an interesting life, I wonder? For these people, changing names was as common a matter as moving from one town to another. My other great-grandfather, the handsome Vladimir Gurevich—in his striped jacket with a jaunty group of friends at the seaside—unexpectedly turns out to be Moisey Vulf, according to his papers. How did he pull off the old skin, and how did he choose the new one? Mikhel becomes Misha almost effortlessly, Vulf becomes a Vladimir, as if he had always been a Vladimir. Sarra's brother, the wonderful Iosif, the firstborn and favorite son of Abram Ginzburg, who broke his father's heart when he converted to Christianity, was transformed into Volodya (hardly the obvious shift from Iosif), as if the age demanded of its children only blue-eyed straightforwardness.

Other surnames stayed in place and their owners wore them as they were. The Ginzburgs and the Gurevichs, who were from distant Polish and Bavarian towns, heaved toponyms around like sacks of possessions. The Stepanovs, with their bland newly built surname (with its vaguely Greek root: "stefanos" meaning crown or garland), had nothing distinctive in their names. The branches of the family tree are curiously bare of "Rosen" and "Mandal," of stars and precious jewels. But it is peopled with apparently gentle, peaceful Libermans and Fridmans.

In our own history the most interesting part is what we don't know. In other people's histories it's the animal magnetism of elective affinities that singles out *this one* from hundreds of others. Sebald's method, his way of thinking and speaking, is founded on refusing to choose. Although when you begin reading, his books can seem riddled with tunnels like an ant nest, all leading to unexpected consonances. "Across what distances in time do the elective affinities and correspondences connect? How is it that one perceives oneself in another human being, or, if not oneself, then one's own precursor?" If we are to believe him, then these connections come about of their accord, in the way that a magpie drags everything it can find into its nest. Sebald was touched above all by dates that coincided, birthdays, deathdays, and events through which you could see your own life.

When I bring to mind a date or an important event, sometimes it gives rise to a thought experiment, the point of which I hardly know myself. "If a child had been born to that day," I think to myself, "then that child would now be x years old." I express it like that—born to the day, and not to me or someone else, as if the event that changed my life had also given birth to someone new. There are by now lots of these invisible children, and they are growing up; but I remember one of them more often than the others. The child born to January 15, 1998, a frosty, radiant day in Moscow and a gray tricklingly damp day in Würzburg—the date of my mother's death—would now be an adult.

*

One evening in Moscow in E. P Peshkova's flat, Lenin, who had been listening to Beethoven's Sonatas, played by Issay Dobrowen, said, "I don't know anything better than the Appassionata. *I could listen to it every day. It's wonderful, superhuman music. It makes me think, perhaps childishly, naively, but with pride, of the wonders humans are capable of." And smiling and narrowing his eyes, he added sadly, "I can't listen to music often, it acts on my nerves, it makes me want to say sweet and stupid things, stroke people on the head, who can still create such beauty although they live in filth and horror. But right now stroking people on the head is out of the question. They'd bite your hand off, it would be better to beat them about the heads, beat them mercilessly, although ideally we are against all violence toward men. Hmmm, it's a hellish task."*

This paragraph from Maksim Gorky's *Days With Lenin*, which was censored by the Soviet authorities, is often quoted, and especially the bit about "beating them about the heads." It's also been noted that Lenin got the Sonatas confused. Dobrowen himself later confirmed (from emigration) that he had actually played the *Pathétique* to the Great Leader. The story of the evening when Lenin was Gorky's guest is fixed in the nation's official memory, so much so that the 1963 film of the meeting *Appassionata* simply lifted its visual composition from the previous painting by the artist Nabandyan, "V. I. Lenin at A. M. Gorky's home in 1920": the striped divan, the warm half shawl worn by Peshkova, and the low-hanging lamp in the painting were as much part of the mythology of the evening as the music and the discussion, and the snowstorm whirling outside the window. The film opens with a shot of snow falling over the crenelated Kremlin walls; it's an epic, hungry, terrible winter. Lenin and Gorky are feeding firewood into an iron stove in the icy apartment, a little girl runs in and begins talking about Crimea: "It's not safe! The Whites have occupied Crimea!" In fact winter was still a way off. Dobrowen was summoned to play for Lenin on October 20, an autumnal evening. They say that Lenin constantly pressed Gorky to go abroad during that evening, and as he left he famously said: "If you don't go, then we'll exile you anyway."

So everything happened—and yet it didn't happen. They played music, but it was a different piece; there was a snowstorm, but only ten days later; the famous "we'll exile you" comment was made, but was it really made then? Gorky himself was only a guest in the apartment, he hadn't lived with his former wife Ekaterina Peshkova for many years; Dobrowen was actually a strange and invented pseudonym (meaning "good wine," as he later explained). The pianist was by then a celebrity—schoolgirls treasured postcards with his portrait. I found one such portrait in my family archive: curled hair, a starched dickey, circles under his eyes: *an artist at the height of his powers!* Across the image is a sprawling signature, and on the other side there is a dedication:

To my dear friend
Isai Abramovich
With warm affection and in memory of graduating
from the Conservatoire
Your Isaichik

Moscow
20
May 1911

How did this postcard find its way into our family album? Isai Abramovich Shapiro, my great-grandfather's brother-in-law, was a doctor with a practice in Nizhny Novgorod and a specialist in skin and venereal diseases. He was well-known locally and he lived in an expensive part of town. In another picture in the album he is with his wife and three children—sheepskin caps, coats with half capes—in a snowy garden among the birch trees, sitting on one of those ubiquitous slender bentwood chairs. Isai

Abramovich could only have known the pianist from Nizhny Novgorod, where they'd both lived. Gorky was from Nizhny Novgorod, too: the hilltop house where he lived with Ekaterina Peshkova as a young man is still there. It's one of the few places in the world where everything is as it was—plates with a cheerful pattern around the edge, the long table in the dining room, a relaxed couch with bolsters, metal-framed guest beds, porcelain washbowls, and slightly macabre bouquets, gathered by the owners a hundred or more years ago from the profligate green roadsides, and now condemned to last forever. I was told that the reason for this rare degree of preservation was due to "womanly foresight": Peshkova knew she was married to a great writer and she made efforts to save everything for posterity: the blinds, the shutters, the toys of her living son and her dead daughter. When her marriage to Gorky fell apart she conceived of a time-delayed monument to their short life together. Their possessions were put away into boxes, inventoried, wrapped in fabric, and left until they could be brought back to the old house and placed in their former positions.

*

Whenever I go into a bookshop, I see there are more and more such inventories of possessions, especially in those parts of the world where they use Latin alphabets. In a New York bookshop the books lie with their covers catching the light: *Proust's Overcoat, Monsieur Proust's Library, Rembrandt's Nose, Van Gogh's Ear, Catullus's Bedspread, Vermeer's Hat, The Brontë Cabinet,* the history of a family in eight objects, one hundred photographs, ninety-nine discoveries.

I wondered if I had been too wrapped up in my thoughts to notice that the old world had breached its banks and flooded the current world; the search for lost time had become a general obsession, and everyone had thrown themselves into reading, writing, and describing our relations with the past. What I was still preparing to write turned out to be simply part of a much bigger movement. Everyone was engaged in "getting a good view" on the past, as if there was nothing else worth doing, as if this was the new form of the Grand Tour. The emptiness that fills villages burned to the ground, and the people inhabiting the rooms of others—all this has become part of the cultural program, like the Roman forum or the Paris Opéra.

I devour all these books, one after another, hardly pausing to marvel at my own unsated appetite as each new text requires me to seek out and devour the next. Pointless knowledge expands at an unstoppable rate: not like a building, which grows with the slow addition of floors, more like that terrifying wartime spring thaw when the bodies were slowly exposed by the melting snow. Perhaps I might have preferred to stand alone in the chalk circle of my obsession, but the circle is as crowded as a waiting room at the doctors where everyone is pronouncing gloomily on each other's afflictions. It matters to all of us. When I meet someone new I hardly notice the moment when we begin talking about our grandparents and ancestors, comparing names and dates as happily as animals who have finally reached their watering spot and drink, shuddering with the delicious cold of the water. It usually happens about half an hour into the conversation.

One thing saddens me. This search for the past, like the search for the Holy Grail, separates the successful from the failures, and I belong to the latter: assiduous, but unlucky. I have never lost my hope of discovering the kernel at the center of the mystery, a key of some sort that opens the door to a secret corridor in our old apartment, where a shaft of sunlight falls on a host of other unseen doors. Not since I was taken, aged seven, to the green meadow where the Battle of Kulikovo had been fought. I knew about the battle, of course: the bloody encounter between a Moscow Prince and a Tatar Khan had taken place not far from Moscow, a few hours by car. I'd read and reread the Pushkin poem, where the hero, sometimes a knight at arms, sometimes a

Russian warrior, wanders onto the site of the ancient battle, *the valley of death*. There, under the bright sun, he sees something along the lines of a vast educational installation: a heap of yellowing bones, armor and shields, arrows stuck into the ground, heads rotting in their helmets. All of it overgrown with ivy, the organic and inorganic piled up, as if that's how it had always been. The hero grieves a little, then chooses himself some armor, and knows it will serve him faithfully and true.

I knew exactly what to expect. The excitement of this dramatic and possibly terrifying sight was augmented by the promise of booty: I'd find myself a souvenir, a little thing to remember it by, sure to be such a thing among the skulls and shields, rusting under the sky. A few arrow tips to carry in my pocket would be nice, although an elegant little dagger would be best of all.

The field was quiet and empty, and the wind blew waves over the bare green grass. Our dog ran about madly but found nothing; there was a little obelisk at the side of the field, nothing else. The main quality of an ancient battlefield turned out to be how transitory it was—all the interesting stuff had been dragged home by others well before I got there.

*

I once heard that "a small bag of Marina Tsvetaeva's possessions" was kept in the drawer of a table at a certain literary museum (which is after all a place where the words and possessions of writers come, if not for immortality, then at least for a rest). The bag had been brought back from the place of her death, Yelabuga, by her sixteen-year-old son Mur after her suicide. Despite its survival, nothing had been written about it, and it hadn't been exhibited—turn Proust's overcoats, jackets, and all the other items inside out and this is what you get: objects that disappear, slipping easily through a tear in the lining into absolute oblivion, the deep pocket of nonexistence.

The bag's contents hadn't been cataloged, and so might be

considered not-quite-existing. There was no way of guessing from the museum catalog that the single *unit* of the bag in fact held many items. It contained objects that have been passed over, despite the last forty years of passionate attention to Tsvetaeva's every word; objects that were too damaged or homely to merit a museum cabinet. Tsvetaeva took them with her into evacuation, packing hastily what could be sold (anything French), things to remember others by (mustn't be lost), and other unnecessary bits and pieces that found themselves in the pile almost by chance. No one knows why Mur thought these things important enough to gather up and bring back to Moscow from his mother's dark hut in Yelabuga. Was he trying to save and preserve them—or was he in a blind haste, as his mother had been, simply seizing everything? Battered little tins, their contents unknown, beads, a pen, locks of children's hair, some other nameless bits and bobs, which might have just been stuffed in the bag. But perhaps they were the dearest things, things that reminded her of her mother, her husband, daughter: a special stone, china fragments of an unforgettable cup. There was no one to tell. Objects no one knows anything about are instantly orphaned, they seem to protrude more, like the nose of a dead man. They join the ranks of those who are no longer permitted to enter.

Among the books, papers, chairs, dickeys that I inherited, there are far too many things life forgot to label—or to leave a reminder for, even a hint of where they came from and how they are connected to me. In the family album, Dobrowen's portrait is next to a good quality reproduction of Nadezhda Krupskaya, Lenin's widow. On the back my great-grandmother has written in her big handwriting: "Who gave you this picture of Nadezhda Krupskaya? I saw quite a different picture of her in a big portrait at Moisey Abramovich's. S. Ginzburg, July 2, 1956." It seems likely that Sarra's companion took this picture. He had a photographic studio nearby in Moscow and his stamp is on this image. But I will never know the details. These huge and terrifying people who strode the century, Krupskaya, Sverdlov, Gorky, have slipped out of the family memory as if they were never there, and I will never be able to confirm their presence.

Once when I was fifteen my mother showed me something I'd never seen despite my endless rummaging in search of curiosities. It was a tiny, delicate lace purse, half the size of my palm. Inside, folded into four, the paper beginning to tear at the folds, was a piece of paper, and on it, written in a clear hand, the name Victor Pavlovich Nelidov. My grandmother Lyolya, Sarra's daughter, had kept this little purse in the pocket of her bag, which she carried pressed to her side. I began asking about it, but my mother didn't know who it was. I persisted, I wanted to know what to make of it. "Make of it what you will," said my mother, and ended the conversation.

Do I need to say that I've tried more than once to find a trail to the invisible Nelidov? Who was he? A doctor? Why a doctor? I have had no success, only the usual feeling of walking into yet another empty green field and realizing once again that the absence of an answer *was* the answer, and if that upset me, I just had to get over it. As soon as I appeared, the past immediately declined to make anything useful of itself, or to weave itself into a narrative of seeking and finding, of breakthroughs and revelations. The division between what was mine and what belonged to others was the first to break down. Everything around me belonged in one way or another to the world of my dead. I was no longer really surprised to discover paper strips with French on them in the drawers of an old writing desk I had bought: tickets to a cinema in Paris to see two prewar films. One of the films was named after a poem by Victor Hugo "Lorsque l'enfant paraît." If Great-Grandmother Sarra had been to the cinema in Paris one hundred years ago, then she might well have seen this film, even though the writing desk had nothing to do with her. Perhaps she didn't see it, perhaps she saw other films (so of course I then rushed off to immerse myself in the chronicles of cinema, as if the names of films would reveal something to me). She must have gone to the cinema, to cafes and exhibitions, and met up with Russian and French friends—she must have had some interests. I've always felt that the popular device of making your fictional hero meet Gertrude Stein or Picasso or Tsvetaeva on the Paris streets was a rather shameful example of a sort of coercive literary logic, but in my head I did this constantly, chasing after any coincidences and proximities that might have helped my independently minded great-grandmother feel less lonely.

So, for example, in May 1914, only weeks before the outbreak of war, a postcard from Paris arrives in Saratov. It is decorated with almond blossom and Spring, perhaps the personification of April, leans down over a sleeping infant. The caption reads: *sogno primaverile*. On May 30, the day my great-grandfather received this card (in which Sarra writes that she is returning from an exam "quite shattered"), the young pilot Alfred Agostinelli, former chauffeur of Marcel Proust and the model for Albertine, crashed his plane near Antibes and drowned in the Mediterranean. Agostinelli registered for his flying lessons as Marcel Swann, as if the hero and the narrator of *In Search of Lost Time* had merged into one person. Proust paid for these lessons and he'd even promised to buy Albert an airplane with Mallarmé's lines about the swan who couldn't fly etched on the fuselage. "A poem you loved, even if you thought you didn't understand it," Proust wrote in a letter that was never opened. On the day it arrived the addressee didn't come home.

*

Sometimes touch alone is enough to establish kinship. I'm thinking now of the famous 1950s experiment with baby monkeys. The babies were taken away from their hairy birth mothers and put in an enclosure with surrogate mothers: one made from wire and another from soft plush. All the babies without exception tried to squirm into the arms of the "soft mommy," to hold on and press themselves against her and hug her. As the experiment progressed the soft mommy began to cause them pain: under the soft fur she was covered in spikes. But this didn't stop the baby monkeys—they made little cries of pain but they didn't release their hold. Perhaps she even became dearer to them because of the efforts they had to make to stay close to her.

Month after month I transcribed my family's letters and documents, poring over the microscopic handwriting, the rapid accounts of long-dead conversations. I began to understand them better and love them more. I wondered whether imitation often ended in this way: the young poet who was exiled to Voronezh together with Mandelstam began to think he himself was the author of Mandelstam's poems and I, too, carefully copying out the commas and little mistakes of my ancestors, was no longer able to see the line that divided their lives from mine.

I typed up my father's thrilling and surprising letters, sent from Baikonur in 1965, where secret space installations were being constructed. There was a military presence on the steppe, and my father and his friend Kolya Sokolov were civilian instructors. I remember from my childhood the accounts of how my father had caught a wily little vixen, a *qarsaq*, on the Kazakh steppe and was attempting to train it, but the proud little beast wouldn't eat or drink and wanted its freedom, so after three days they let it go. I found his letters among the papers at Aunt Galya's, and there were lots of them: about the *qarsaq* and life on the steppe, everything down to how they made their camp and slept under an awning made from a damp sheet, and rinsed the floor with water every night. The people and circumstances of these letters became firmly fixed in my head as I typed them up, page by page. It was as if they had always been there, a natural progression of my own internal landscape. My twenty-six-year-old father hitching a ride to spend an evening drinking with a group of geologists from Moscow; arguing with the foreman over the empty shed under the workshop; losing patience with his team of fitters; stuffing a marmot; trying to send a rifle home wrapped in a fur jacket—behaving like the hero in a Soviet-era "cheerful-young-men-building-Socialism" film. This didn't much surprise me: the letters were written fifty years ago.

At some point in the process, without giving it much thought, I sent the file with the letters to my father and asked him whether I could quote from the letters in my book. I didn't doubt for a moment that he would give me permission: they were wonderfully well-written texts; lively, funny, and very distant from our world now. Yet there was something else: in my head, the letters I had typed up had become my own. I had become used to considering them part of a collective history of which I was the author. Papers found in a pile, of no use to anyone else; do what you want with them, throw them away or keep them—their fate depended on me, their publisher. Quoting from them meant saving them, leaving them in their box meant consigning them to a long darkness. Who else, if not me, should decide how to deal with them?

Without being aware of it, I had internalized the logic of ownership. Not in the sense of a tyrant, lording it over his hundreds of enslaved peasants, but perhaps like the tyrant's enlightened neighbor, with a landscaped park and a theater in which his serfs acted and sang. The subject of my love and my grief had become my property, to treat as I wished. My other heroes couldn't object or react, for obvious reasons. They were dead.

The dead have no rights: their property and the circumstances of their fate can be used by anyone and in any way. In the first few months and years after death, humanity attempts to restrain its enterprising spirit and behave with decency—its interest in the not-yet-cold corpse is kept in check, if only out of respect for the living, the family and friends. Years pass and the rules of decency, the rules of the collective, the laws of copyright, all give way like a dam breaching under the weight of water; and this seems to happen more rapidly now than in the past. The fate of the dead is the latest gold rush; the history of people we don't really know much about has become a major subject of novels and films, of sentimental speculation and sensational exposure. No one will defend them, no one asks us.

A homeless person would have the right to be angry if her photo were used on the cover of a family calendar. A man condemned to death for murder is still able to prevent the publication of his letters or diary. There is only one category denied this right. Every one of us owns his or her history, but only to a point, only while we own our body, our underwear, our glasses case. At the beginning of the new century the invisible and indescribable majority of the dead became the new minority; endlessly vulnerable, humiliated, their rights abused.

I believe this must change, and change within our lifetimes, just as it has changed over the last hundred years for other groups of the abused and humiliated. What unites all the minorities, puts them in the same boat (or on the same many-decked liner) is other people's sense that their subjectivity is incomplete: women who *need to be looked after*; children *who don't know what's best for them*; black people who are *like children*; the working classes who don't know *what's in their own interests*; the dead, for whom *nothing matters any more*. Even if you aren't in any of the former categories, you are certain to be in the last.

My father didn't answer for a day or two. Then he Skyped me and said he wanted to talk. He wouldn't give me permission to reproduce his letters in the book. He really didn't want them published. Even the one about the vixen? Even that one. He hoped I would understand. He was absolutely against the idea. Because, he added very clearly, nothing happened quite in that way.

I was horrified and offended. My *Not-A-Chapters* with their family histories were working out nicely: a chronicle, an arpeggio, a ladder running up the book from the beginning of the century to 1965, and my father's tales of jaunty builders and soldier's boots felt like a necessary rung. How could I make do without it? I argued, I questioned, I gesticulated. When we'd both calmed down a little, my father said, "I can't bear to think that someone will read those letters and think that's what I am."

I could have carried on trying to persuade him, I still had things to say: it's not about what you are, I thought petulantly. It's not about you at all: it's not you writing to your parents and sister, it's the time itself writing, it's a thousand Siberian radio programs and a hundred novels about Siberian construction projects and the vanquishing of the virgin earth, and about decent people and conscientious workers. I could have said: in our family's letters you can see how the language used to describe the everyday experience changes—how the tone changes completely between the 1910s and the 1930s, how newspapers and films form internal speech. Your letters belong in that history, they are templates of the 1960s, not "how it actually was" but written in that concentrated form that gives us a feeling for the age. It's not a book about what you *were*, it's about what we see when we look back.

I said none of this aloud, luckily—we were already saying goodbye, and my sense of self-righteousness was growing—and it grew until I realized exactly what I was really thinking. I was very close to saying "I don't care what you were," but happily I didn't get that far. Blessed are those who destroy all the letters and diaries they don't want others to see. The written text creates a false impression of its own immortality: a silly billet-doux is set in stone, an irritable exclamation puts down a claim to be the last word. This was the subtext to our conversation: to put it crassly I was prepare to betray my own living father for the dead text, because I believed in it more. It then felt to me as if the letter itself had spoken and said: "Don't touch me!"

I am afraid to think what Great-Grandmother Sarra might have said if I'd asked her whether I could publish her correspondence. But no one asks the dead.

I understood my father's objections to be that his reports on life in Kazakhstan were stylizations of a sort, written to please and entertain his family. What I saw as a picaresque novel, adventures against a colonial backdrop, was a memory of dirt, depression, and desperate drunkenness for him; of barracks and sheds at the end of the world, swearing soldiers and constant and interminable thievery. The tone of his letters was faked, but time had preserved only this stylized bravado. Another sobering realization: if these letters, so detailed in themselves, couldn't be used as witness accounts—those little fragments of bone from which the skeleton of the past can be reconstructed—then what hope was there of building anything from scratch, made of letters and handkerchiefs? It was what a psychoanalyst might dismissively term a "fantasy." In the place of respectable research, I had been occupied all this time with the Freudian family romance, the sentimentalized past.

That is how it must be. We look at the photographs of our ancestors as we might look at a human zoo, wild beasts whose lives lie out of sight, deep within the enclosure. It reminds me a little of a folder of recipes I have. The recipes are written out by my great-grandmother, my grandmother, my mother (and I spotted with a sort of shudder my own childish handwriting among them). For a long time the recipes were a call to action—wouldn't it be marvelous to make all these recipes, to unite them in their culinary succession, to pretend to be each generation of woman in turn, bringing to life their circle of relationships, some known to me, some unknown: Murochka's recipe for pie, Rosa Markovna's biscuit recipe, Auntie Raya's pike. Although in fact each possessive was a reminder to me that all these people with their pikes and pies no longer existed, and all that was left was the folder of paper. And it was unusable: when I sat down to read through the recipes, I immediately knew I would never cook these dishes. They were full of ingredients that had long since disappeared, Soviet-era cereals and grains, Soviet margarine. Mostly desserts and confectionery, each one so calorific it could replace an entire meal; rich creams and heavy sponges, endless biscuit recipes, tortes, pastries, and shortbreads, as if the lack of sweetness in life could be made up by ingestion. The diet of another, lost world. I had no desire to go back there, despite my nostalgia for its black-and-white inhabitants.

*

One of the strangest things I found in the boxes of papers belonging to the Stepanov family was not really even a "thing." It was a page from a notebook, folded vertically into four and kept by someone. On it, a single sentence, unaddressed and without date or signature and written in a hand I didn't recognize—unremarkable handwriting, perhaps Grandfather's, perhaps Aunt Galya's. But the sentence was as much of a shock as if it had been addressed to me, although perhaps the shocking part was the fact that it was intended for no one, spoken as if from inside a silent mouth. It read: "There are people who exist on this earth not as objects in themselves, but as extraneous specks or tiny spots on objects."

I didn't recognize the quote at first, although I did briefly appreciate the phrase's beauty and precision. I thought that the sentence was perhaps an attempt to say something about the self, but in a way that didn't upset or put anyone out. Someone who was known to me and yet quite unknown had secretly come to this phrase, and the fact that the words originally came from Gogol's *Dead Souls* didn't actually make much difference. The writer had altered one word. In the original this word is лица, which can mean both "faces" and "types (of person)," and they had changed it to the unequivocal люди ("people"). This small shift had surprising consequences: ripped from its context and framed by the notepaper the phrase had been transformed into a sort of poem, or a verdict.

Here is how it was:

... It was hard to say definitely who she was, a married lady or a spinster, a relative, the housekeeper, or a woman simply living in the

house—something without a cap, about 30, and wearing a multi-colored shawl. There are types of people that exist on this earth not as objects in themselves, but as extraneous specks or tiny spots on objects. They sit in the same way, they hold their heads in the same way and you are almost ready to take them for a piece of furniture.

And here's what it became:

> *There are people*
> *that exist on this earth*
> *not as objects in themselves,*
> *but as extraneous specks*
> *or tiny spots on objects.*

This, I feel, is how I see my family: their fragile, barely noticeable existence is like a speckled bird's egg, so delicate it is crushed by the least pressure. The fact that they were tested and proved resilient in life only makes them more vulnerable. Against the backdrop of history and its well-constituted heroes, these lodgers with their photo albums and New Year's greetings cards seem destined for oblivion. I hardly even remembered them myself. But although much was unknown or half-known or under a veil of darkness, I thought I knew a few firm facts about my family:

No one died in the Stalinist purges
No one perished in the Holocaust
No one was murdered
No one was a murderer

Now this seemed doubtful, or even simply untrue.

Once when I was ten or a little older, I asked my mother one of those questions you only ask at that age: "What are you most scared of?" I don't know what kind of response I expected, probably "war." In Soviet society at the time Kant's starry heavens had been replaced by peaceful skies. The country lived in the fearful expectation of a third world war; in school we had military training in how to assemble Kalashnikovs and what to do in the event of a nuclear attack (it seemed clear that a machine gun wouldn't help much). The abundance of old women arranged on the benches in the yard spoke as if in one voice: "If we can only avoid war ..."

To my confusion, my mother answered momentarily and enigmatically. It was just as if she had held this answer in her head for a long time, waiting for someone to ask the question. I was puzzled by her answer—and I have always remembered it. She said: "I'm afraid of the violence that can destroy a person."

Years passed, decades. Now I am the one who fears this same violence that can destroy a person. In me this fear has a sheen on it, as if my feelings of fear, anger, and resistance predate me and have been polished to a gleam by the many preceding generations. It is like entering an unknown room as if you had lived there all your life (and the demons I share the space with *find it swept and garnished*, as in the Gospels), in this room an undated film is being shown. When I awake I realize that the Germans have entered Paris and I need to hide the children; that the fearsome woman who sweeps the snow in the yard will interrogate me about my right to live there, that Mandelstam has been arrested and is entering a stadium through iron doors that resemble the doors to an oven. I was eight when I was told about Mandelstam and seven when I was told: *we are Jews*. But the black hole of the unspoken that lay at the center of the tale (perhaps because they themselves didn't know) was more ancient than any explanation or example.

Every example, every photograph and book among the dozens I have read only confirms what I remember too well, with my gut memory. Perhaps this ancient horror began in 1938 when my still-young grandfather Nikolai gave up his service pistol and sat waiting to be arrested. Or perhaps later, in 1953, with the Jewish

Doctors' Plot, when Great-Grandmother and Grandmother, both doctors, both Jews, came home in the evenings and sat silently under the hanging lamp at the table in their communal apartment, waiting to be taken away. Perhaps in 1919, when my overly successful great-great-grandfather Isaak, "the owner of factories, property, steamships," disappeared. We don't know how or when he died, but we can well imagine what was going on back then in postrevolutionary Ukraine. Perhaps, and probably even earlier, in 1902, 1909, or 1912 when pogroms were taking place in Odessa and all across the south of Ukraine and the bodies lay on the streets. My relatives were there (a person is always *there*, in close proximity to the death of others and one's own death), and it turns out I didn't need to hear any of this from them. The knowledge has lived within me.

Many years later I visited the Holocaust Memorial Museum in Washington in search of help and I am still thankful to the advisor who spoke to me there. We sat at a long wooden table in the library, which appeared to hold every book written on any matter that might be considered Jewish. I asked questions and got answers. Then the museum advisor, a historian, asked me what I was writing about and I began to explain. "Ah," he said. "One of those books where the author travels around the world in search of his or her roots—there are plenty of those now."

"Yes," I answered. "And now there will be one more."

PART THREE

She saw all her knickknacks fly straight to heaven, tray cloths and photo frames and tea cozies and grandma's silver cream jug, and the sentences in silver and silk, every single thing!

—Tove Jansson

At this point I must speak of my ancestry.

—Viktor Shklovsky

1. You Can't Escape Your Fate

"... And all this time," said my mother, in her séance-like story-telling voice, "all this time Misha was waiting for her in Russia, Misha, who was to be her future husband and your future great-grandfather. And when the First World War broke out, she returned to him after all her wanderings and they met at last, and after that they were always together. At their wedding he gave her a little brooch, the one I always wear for special occasions. On one side it has her initials, SGF, for Sarra Ginzburg-Fridman, and on the other, the words *you can't escape your fate*."

This *you can't escape your fate* was inscribed on a round gold disc, like a dog tag, which was fastened to the front panel of the dark-blue "best" dress, and for a long time I thought it was awful (because fate chased and chased and finally caught up with them — Misha, who was irresistible and fun, with his high boots and long, long legs, only lived another seven years after the wedding). The "best" dress was always the same, made of a brushed cotton gathered at the bust, and hugging the waist. It was a comforting uniform that only came out on special occasions. In my early childhood my mother had more dresses for going out, and one of them, a brown dress with a white pattern on it, gave me a silent thrill. By the 1980s, when my parents had reached the age I am now, it was the unchanging nature of any special occasion that gave it its appeal. The blue dress came out of the cupboard; the brooch was fastened in its place; the white box of perfume was taken out of the little wooden medicine cabinet, always the same uncomplicated scent, or perhaps the bottle simply never ran out. The perfume was called *Signatyur*, and it was from Poland; the round crystal bottle with its gold-flecked contents lived in a silken nest on a cardboard pedestal, its cold little scented beak touched my mother and me behind the ears, on the chest, and at the nape of the neck. A few minutes before guests arrived I always took a quick peek at the back of the golden brooch with its blue stone to check the inscription was still there.

"And all this time," my mother repeated, just to make sure there was no doubt at all who the heroine of the story was, "she was in France." *Your great-grandmother studied at the Sorbonne* (this, I surmised, was a sort of medical institution, the most important and famous, that much was clear without any explanation) and she returned to Russia as a qualified doctor. The milk-white certificate from the Sorbonne, with its inked calligraphic tails, its concave little letters, and its seal the size of a barn-door key, was another piece of proof of the seriousness of the deed and the righteousness of the victory. But none of this was important. The mesmeric heart of the story was that great-grandmother spent a biblical seven years in Paris, the length of time Jacob worked for his Rachel—and she returned from there, returned to the future "us," as if from under the ground, as if her wonderful life over there had meant nothing to her. Working my way through the shelves of French books from the Musketeers to Maupassant, I couldn't come to terms with how carelessly she had thrown over Paris's dizzying possibilities (or impossibilities for my mother and me).

I was five when she died, aged ninety, having outlived her beloved daughter by two years. Those two years she spent patiently searching for her daughter in her two rooms in a communal apartment, looking in the cupboard, then the sideboard: "Lyolya?" Gradually she began calling her granddaughter by her daughter's name, as if the various nesting dolls in the family matryoshka could be moved around without changing the sense of order. She would sit on the divan at the dacha in a stripy housecoat: a tiny little woman, shrunken to a husk. In the jasmine-white light she looked almost transparent, but her gaze had a spiky, insect-like tenacity, you could see that whatever was coming for her would have a tough job of swallowing her down. *Oh, she's a rock*, Lyolya had said, forty years before, and even now, in her minute and weightless state, she was a monument to her own past strength.

"Surely we won't turn into old people like them. The very thought horrifies me. I'll never allow it! It must be that in old age we think differently and want different things—otherwise life would be unbearable." In February 1914 something made her send her future husband a few postcards with pencil sketches of old women, together with this note, and a few weeks later she wrote to ask him if the old women had arrived. She still had her university exams ahead of her—and then two wars, the birth of a child, revolution, evacuation, her daughter's and granddaughter's illnesses. Then the Jewish Doctors' Plot, which didn't quite reach our family, and the milky skin of poststroke life, simply termed "senility" back then. The deft precision of her youth didn't leave her, but it seemed to stand out more sharply, like her ribs, her mandibles, her wing cases, or the heavy line of brow over the little, almost childlike face.

A little earlier, at the beginning of the 1960s, Rufa, one of my mother's distant cousins, came to Moscow from Saratov and stayed with us. She came home one evening to find Sarra sitting on her own in a rocking chair in a dark room: "Why on earth didn't you turn the light on? You could have been reading a nice story!"

"Oh I just have to shut my eyes and I see such stories, my sweet girl."

*

In her old age, or so I was told, she used to sing. There was always music in the house (on the title page of one very old romance published in 1934 there was an inscription by the author, who went to the same Moscow holiday camp as Sarra: *For you to sing*). An old Blüthner piano with yellowing keys stood neglected in the corner of the apartment. Occasionally Rufa's husband, Alik, a professional pianist, visited from Saratov to play in Moscow's concert halls, and in the mornings he would slide his hands into the Blüthner's mouth and the piano would growl and lisp obediently. But Great-Grandmother remained indifferent to hers or anyone else's musical accomplishments—she saw music as a trivial occupation, something to fill an idle hour. I remember tales of her calling the guests, who had just gathered at the piano, to the dinner table, saying, "Alik will play along as we eat."

Her return to singing, just before her death, was of a different order, as if the songs of her youth had returned and settled in her throat, releasing their long-forgotten words, shorn of meaning, dim and terrible: "You Fell, The Victim of a Fateful Battle," composed in the 1870s and sung at the graveside, the basis for the funeral march in Shostakovich's Eleventh Symphony. Or the "Song of Warsaw," the revolutionary song from the Barricades in 1905, with its "March, march ye toilers and the world shall be free." And all the repertoire of underground songs sung by the kids of 1900, which formed the living language of their battle and their slightly postponed victory. Fifteen-year-old Mayakovsky in Butyrka prison, schoolboy Mandelstam with his Erfurt Program, thirteen-year-old Tsvetaeva at revolutionary gatherings in Yalta—all of this was infused with historical necessity, and hovering overhead, the gramophone buzz of the relentless "Worker's Marseillaise": "Let Us Denounce the Old World."

The memoirs of the revolutionary movement at the turn of the century make it sound as if they were always singing, even rather demonstratively replacing speech with song. The stories of strikes and the secret meetings of conspirators were punctuated by musical interludes: "we set off up the river singing revolutionary songs," "we returned by boat singing revolutionary songs again and waving red flags," "after his speech we ended the meeting with songs." "The Marseillaise" is seamlessly replaced by "The Internationale."

Somewhere among the students and girls, the Mayday meetings and leaflets, is the indistinct shadow of seventeen-year-old Sarra Ginzburg, marching, clutching hands with another, as the letter describes. The gymnasium she studied at in Nizhny Novgorod was only a few houses away from the Sverdlovs' Engraving Workshop. It was noisy and busy in the workshop and this is where she met all of the comrades of her best friend Sarra's brother, Yakov Sverdlov. In the darkly mysterious memoirs written collectively by three Sverdlov siblings many years later, there's a story about one brother going for a boat trip with their sister and her friend (the waves were rough and threatened to overturn the boat, but the girls didn't cry because they were more afraid of the brother than the water); *Sancho Pancho* moves through the work silently like a shadow; long lines of schoolboys engage officer cadets in fisticuffs; prison visitors bring sweets to the prisoners. A strange combination of comfort and horror dyes the eggshell of their youth, as if with onion skins. "Between 1901 and 1903 she [Sarra Sverdlova] often passed on notes, carried proclamations, printed leaflets on the hectograph, and did other tasks that were illegal." Her friend must have done much the same: in 1906 Sarra Ginzburg is predictably arrested for distributing leaflets at the barracks.

When I was fourteen, in 1986, my mother decided to take me to Leningrad—she had long promised to show me her favorite city. It was summer, the time of the "White Nights," when the sun hardly sets, and we sat together, first on one damp bench, and then another. She got quickly tired, so all the walks we took were short, and ended with us resting on benches, the mass of pigeons pecking at the cracked paving stones around us.

Occasionally I would badger her for presents, as if a new place was hardly worth visiting without a little souvenir of some sort that I could carry home as a memento, to console myself when the adventure was over. I grieved over a completely useless piece of tat being sold for the outrageous price of three and a half rubles in the theater shop Maska on Nevsky Prospect. It was a theatrical prop, a "historical" ash-colored lock of hair that fastened at the temple and fell as a long curly braid down to the lady's soft neck. The braid felt completely plastic to the touch, it was impossible to think of an ordinary nontheatrical situation in which it could have been worn, but with my mop of black curls I only yearned all the more to keep it treasured in my desk drawer.

On the first evening in Leningrad we went walking toward the stretch of river and, beyond it, the dark walls and glinting golden spire. "That, Masha, is the Peter and Paul Fortress," said my mother, "where Great-Grandmother Sarra was imprisoned." And we both made a goose-like movement with our necks, stretching and leaning down at the same time, as if we were both bowing to Sarra, and attempting to escape our own skins.

We gave the Peter and Paul Fortress our minute attention, as we did the fountains of Peterhof, the side rooms and staircases of the Hermitage, and even the Chinoiserie of Oranienbaum. It beggars belief how much we managed to see on that trip. The Fortress that June was as bare as a parade ground, hollow as a Christmas decoration. It bore no resemblance to anything. Everything that had happened there was long over, my Sarra had been blinked away, like a mote in the eye.

Whenever I have visited Petersburg since, I have always gone out to the banks of the Neva to face the granite wall of the Fortress, the angel at the top of the spire and the narrow river beach below — and I've made the same goose-like bow, my neck stretched forward, bowing either to my great-grandmother or to the place that held her and then spat her out, as the whale did to Jonah.

The Trubetskoy Bastion Prison was built in the early 1870s. It had sixty or so cells and two solitary confinement cells, allowing for a constant flow of hundreds of "political prisoners." Sarra's stay in the Fortress was sure to have been in here: dirty-white ceiling, gray walls, prison issue sheets, round-toed prison shoes.

The corridors have a life of their own, twisting abruptly like elbows; the cells breathe their underground chill on you as you approach the doors, and the iron bed frames cast their cross-shaped shadow on the stone wall. The beds and the iron tables, bolted to the walls and floor, resemble the furniture in sleeping cars on a train: a white mattress, two pillows, a coarse blanket. Every possession had to kept in plain sight, books, mug, comb, tobacco. The archivists in the Fortress could not help me with my inquiries. It was too late, there was no trace of Sarra Ginzburg in the papers left in the Bastion—the place would not acknowledge her existence.

And now where to look for her? There were so many like her. It isn't easy, after everything that has happened, to picture the wholeheartedness with which those young people threw themselves into battle, yet it still rises, like steam from bread, from the memoirs, documents, the crudely typed police spy reports: "They unrolled a red scarf with 'Down With Autocracy' written on it in ink"; "Propaganda classes take place one-to-one or in small groups on boats"; "In the Passazh Inn we caught a group of new recruits singing 'The Marseillaise' among a very different crowd: 'Arise, arise, working class!'" And over all this the constant refrain: "Participants were singing revolutionary songs." In the soft-gray fortress corridor, carefully researched panels of information about past prisoners hang on the walls: "sentenced by military court and executed in 1908"; "committed suicide in her cell"; "killed in Mexico by an NKVD agent"; "died in Moscow in 1944."

Alongside the panels hang photographs of the graffiti found on the walls. The photographs were taken in the mid-1920s, when the Bastion was no longer a prison. In one photograph, there's a drawing of a woman in a light blouse with puffed sleeves. The picture has a frame drawn around it, as if to pretend that it's a proper picture, or even a window we are looking through. The woman sits at a table, on which there is a tall vase of flowers, a silver butter dish and a samovar on little iron feet. She's ugly, and it feels as if this is because she has been drawn from real life. Her simple face has an expression that combines both concentration and surprise, she has just brought a match up close to her cigarette and is now taking the first drag, smiling all the while. Her hair is drawn into a bun. Through the window the play of summer shadows and light. It is terrible to consider the degree to which we are absent from this picture.

The letter from Platon with its Pushkin quotes was sent to Sarra "in her fortress" in February 1907. Ten years later, in Autumn 1917, in the general collapse and confusion, something strange happened to the Fortress archives—they disappeared in murky circumstances and less than half of them were saved. Any trace of Sarra might have been wiped out then, which worked to her advantage. She never once, on any paper or form, mentions her revolutionary past or her prison stay. "In Russia, as a Jewish woman, I couldn't study in higher education and I was forced to study abroad," she wrote about her French sojourn. Although, in fact, as a daughter of a merchant belonging to the 1st Guild, she could have lived and studied in both Moscow and Saint Petersburg, and in any of the cities' universities. The story handed down through the family is different: efforts were made on behalf of this girl with her revolutionary past. Connections were used, levers pressed. And it worked: she was offered the choice of exile to somewhere in the remote east, or departure in the opposite direction, to Europe, to study, recover her health—to get her out of the way, in short. Her next postcards were sent from Montpellier.

In her declining years, on her way home from a walk with her old friend Sarra Sverdlova, the two of them in their weighty coats, fur hats and ancient fur muffs, Great-Grandmother spoke of herself as a "Bolshevik without a party ticket"—another cliché of a time when phrases were minted like postage stamps. But it was true, she never did join the party, not in forty years of living in Soviet Russia and knowing all the right (and wrong) people, and coming from antediluvian Nizhny Novgorod, with its exhortative speakers, assemblies, tea parties with Maxim Gorky. Sarra Ginzburg worked in managerial roles, she survived purges, and attended party gatherings—but she never signed up. There were plenty of opportunities, but she didn't take them. Her departure for Paris, like crawling up on dry land after flailing in the deep, symbolized some deep and irreversible break: for her the revolution was over. Something else had begun.

Many years later she went back to Nizhny Novgorod from Moscow for the first and last time. The Soviet town was now named Gorky. She was taken to the local museum, which stood high above the town on a promontory over the river. The museum guide gave a detailed account of the heroic lives of the Nizhny Bolsheviks, moving between one photograph and the next. On one photograph, which looked dirty because of the grainy snow whirling down, a group of young people stood by a low fence. There were four of them. One young woman's face was covered in an absurd black bandage, her bonnet was in disarray, wedged on the side of her head, and bits stuck out from it like rabbit's tails. The museum guide commented that this was on the barricades in December. "We know very little about these people," she said, "it seems most likely they are all long dead."

"Most likely," agreed Great-Grandmother Sarra, and turned away to view the next picture.

*

Pochinky's main square is empty in this old picture. A cart is being pulled by two horses, a factory worker stands in a shop doorway where some bold chickens have gathered expectantly. It looks like a quiet backwater, a place at the far corner of the earth. The horse fair, when people gathered in the town, was a huge event and the town's main source of entertainment. Pochinky was built of wood, it stood waist-deep in orchards and gardens. Everything was small in scale but designed to impress: the little local hills were respectfully referred to as "mountains"; a one-and-a-half-yard-long prehistoric tooth was once dredged out of the local river; the cathedral was tastefully built; and the town could boast a notary's office and mutual savings association, part of a growing bureaucratic presence that also regulated army recruitment, drink, and tax collection. Abram Osipovich Ginzburg brought his sizable family up here, very far from the center of things, in the hinterlands.

I found no traces of his life in this little town, which is now only a hamlet. A handful of memories of his son Solomon, Uncle Solya, who sold Singer sewing machines, the reluctant heir in the place of the cursed prodigal son, Iosif. Great-Great-Grandfather Abram, with his baobab tree of a beard, had sixteen children, garnered a good deal of wealth, saved Sarra from prison and exile, and died on June 22 in 1909. He has been forgotten by Pochinky.

The merchants of the 1st Guild were not subject to corporal punishment. Among their other privileges was the permission to deal wholesale in Russian and foreign goods within Russia and abroad; to own shipping and to send their trading ships to foreign lands; to own factories and production plants, with the exception of distilleries and vineyards; to own shops, storage and cellars; to provide insurance; to carry out transfers of money and much else. There was one special provision for Jewish merchants: after 1857 membership of the 1st Guild meant the merchant's whole family and even a servant were guaranteed permission to live in Russia outside of the Western Pale of Settlement in any town in the Russian Empire, including (with some conditions) the cities of Moscow and St. Petersburg. Membership was an expensive matter: annual fees were never less than 500 rubles (one percent of declared capital over 50,000 rubles). The Jewish community in Nizhny Novgorod was still small at the end of the nineteenth century and in the tiny town of Pochinky Jews were downright exotic. Statistics compiled in 1881, four years before Sarra's birth, show that in the whole district there were eleven people of the

Jewish faith—I have a suspicion they all shared the surname Ginzburg.

Great-Great-Grandfather didn't live to see a time of mixed marriages and integration, when the children of the Priest Orfanov from the Cathedral of the Nativity of Christ would marry descendants of the Ginzburg family. His estate was divided equally between his children and Sarra's inheritance was spent on her studies in Paris. She returned without a penny to her name, with "nothing more than a hatbox." I close my eyes and I see her standing on the platform of the Brest Station in Moscow, holding her hatbox, a little independent woman who would walk alone all her life. If I screw up my eyes and really focus I can see the black Paris hat, with its long curling ostrich feather. The hat outlived its owner. It appears now and again in photos from my childhood.

No matter how hard I concentrate, in my mind's eye I can never see the texture and the sound of everyday life back then: tea in the Gethlings' garden; her sister Vera clutching a book of Nadson's poetry; the endless hours on the coach to Nizhny Novgorod; skirts damp with the dew and catching on the burdock; the little river; smoking a secret cigarette in the attic. Pochinky was home: where she came to rest, to cry her eyes out, to be *fed up*. Her little sister Rakhil once wrote in a letter that she'd just come back from the theater, they'd staged Ostrovsky, and then about forty people had come for dinner—but where did that happen? Surely not in child-size Pochinky, which never had a theater? Then again, it was the age of the amateur performance, home theater, Hamlet strutting the boards of the dacha terrace in black hose. The fine dust of the friendships and flirtations has settled for good, nothing can be made out now. All that is left is what Balzac calls the ruins of the bourgeoisie: "An ignoble detritus of pasteboard, plaster, and coloring."

In all this pasteboard detritus there is one other photograph I've loved since I was a child, although it makes a comic impression more than anything: the Ginzburg women are standing in a line, from the oldest to the youngest, one behind another, looking sidelong at the camera. In front are the powerful matriarchs with their wide behinds, heavy busts, helmets of hair, and the calm faces of heroines. Then, in order of decreasing magnitude, a series of ladies with a more ordinary appearance, in bustles and puffed sleeves, and at the end of the tail, erect, frowning, and dressed in a simple, dark dress, the almost fragile figure of Sarra behind her more majestic sisters. Lastly the miniature Rakhil, and she and Sarra radiate a misleading warmth: it feels to me as if I understand them better than the others.

The medical report of Sarra's childbirth, written up in 1916, offers a range of exhaustive detail—the process of acquiring information is almost unnaturally easy. Only I, in the whole world, now know that this was her first pregnancy, that she went into labor in the evening, that contractions lasted nineteen hours and forty minutes, that her tiny and still nameless baby girl weighed only 2,420 grams and was healthy the whole week they stayed in hospital.

There is nothing more distancing than the documents of a dead person with their contradictions and lacunae, their dated habit of apparently meaning something. On the identity documents issued to Sarra Ginzburg in 1924, her birthplace is given as Saratov, but in later autobiographical writing it is Pochinky. There is no discrepancy in the dates—on both it is January 10, 1885 (January 22 in the new calendar). In her autobiography she calls her father a "minor" merchant, but her marriage certificate says he was in the 1st Guild. Perhaps these discrepancies are due to her fear that in a new Communist era it would be all too easy to find traces of her "inappropriate" bourgeois background in tiny Pochinky.

She graduated from school at twenty-one, in 1906, and by 1907 she was in prison. She was in France from 1908 to 1914. She returned to Russia, took the state exams, which allowed her to practice medicine with her foreign diploma, and made the "Medical Faculty Promise," with its delightful phrasing:

I accept with the deepest gratitude the rights of a doctor, given to me by science, and understand all the importance of the duties placed upon me by this calling and I give my word that throughout my whole life I will never besmirch the honor of the association I am now joining. I promise to always help those who come to me in suffering, to the extent of my abilities, to keep sacred the family secrets entrusted to me, and not to abuse the trust placed in me.

This is 1915, the year of her marriage. Her daughter Lyolya is born in 1916 in Saratov, the same year Sarra opens her medical practice.

I have the bronze name plaque with its stout prerevolutionary lettering: ДОКТОРЪ С.А. ГИНЗБУРГЪ-ФРИДМАНЪ (Doctor S. A. Ginzburg-Fridman). It didn't stay in place long: a year later there were spelling reforms and it became redundant. Then all normal life was turned upside down in the revolution. The plaque and a full box of unusable visiting cards were kept and brought to Moscow, like unfulfilled but unforgotten promises. So much back then was begun but never finished. In March 1917 Mikhael Fridman, Sarra's husband, finally became a solicitor. It is hard to grasp just how much work that would have entailed. As well as an education in law, a solicitor in state practice had to go through an apprenticeship scheme and work for at least five years as a solicitor's assistant, traveling many miles on state business, spending hours on the minutiae of regulatory law. The pages in Great-Grandfather's passport, where they put stamps for any overnight stay in a place away from your registered home, are bright with the names of Russian towns.

This passport was issued by the Saratov Police Department (no expiry date, price 15 kopecks) on May 23, 1912. The owner is named: Mikhel Davidovich Fridman, the language of the document did not indulge any attempts at assimilation or the desire to be like everyone else. He was born on December 15, 1880, of medium height, Jewish faith. In the section about military service he is listed as having military training. He has black hair and no distinguishing features. A few pages later there is the registration of a marriage with the spinster Ginzburg by the "government" Rabbi, Arii Shulman, and later it is noted that "The Fridman couple have a daughter by the name of Olga." Lower still on the same page, a note to the effect that the Board of Court Officials accepts him into their ranks. The next document referring to my great-grandfather's affairs, in a similarly minimal style, is his death certificate.

How large and intense and decorated their lives seem before *events* caught up with them. How very full they were of other events: of post-horses, telegrams, and plans opening out before them like a gift box. There's a bright, clear period of about ten years from 1907 to 1917, but if you attempt to go back further than 1907, a torpid darkness falls and nothing can be made out. Misha's father, David Yankelevich Fridman, was a doctor, or so my mother thought, but he appears nowhere in the Saratov or Nizhny archives. A David Fridman (tradesperson) appears once in a list of members of the Jewish community in Nizhny Novgorod, complied by the Rabbi Borukh Zakhoder in 1877. This Fridman is not significant enough to be counted as a full member of the community and is listed under: "Those who can't be named either because they don't give money for prayers, or because they are illiterate and not in trade, or because some of them are soldiers on leave who can be sent away from the town by the town administration, or those who are under age." The unnamed David Yakovlevich could easily be the father of Mikhel. We are told nothing else about him. I have lots of photographs of David Fridman in his golden pince-nez, slowly aging and imperceptibly thinning about the face. The last picture, taken with a dog, is a studio shot from 1906, shortly before he died.

He, too, like everyone else, had several children, scattering like berries across the roads of the new age: his sons Misha and Borya used to tell stories of their beloved nanny, who was round and quick to grumble, and they would tease by lifting her up on a high cupboard to quieten her. One of the many uncles married the young wet nurse, fascinated by her embonpoint and the blinding white of her uniform—women in this useful profession usually wore a smock robe decorated with rows of red beads. Then there were ferry trips along the Volga river, and a samovar heated with pine cones. Mikhel was not a particularly good student, but he passed the exams to become an apothecary's apprentice. He had wanted to become a lawyer and in 1903 he resigned from the Association of Tradesmen "to gain a place in an institution of higher education and continue his education." The document confirming his resignation is decorated with an official stamp: a pensive reindeer lifts its right leg as if it can't quite decide whether to take a step forward.

Mikhael Davidovich Fridman, who told his nephew to "live an interesting life," died on November 11, 1923, of severe appendicitis in Botkin's Hospital. His death certificate gives his profession as "employee." In Sarra's autobiography, which she wrote in the *far too interesting* year of 1938, she carefully avoids naming his legal work: her husband "worked as an economist in Central Mining Management." He was only forty-three. Lyolya was barely seven. Just the year before they had moved to Moscow from Saratov, but there is no way of knowing when exactly, or why. At almost the same time, as if driven by some invisible gust of wind, another family moved to Moscow: the boy Lyonya, who will one day marry Lyolya, and his still young mother.

*

The ability to skip large chunks of time might be useful in the writing of novels, but it starts to frighten me when I realize I am doing it in life, and with real living people—that is, with dead people, of course, although there isn't really any difference. Great-Grandmother Sarra's youth, before Lyolya is born, feels like the beginning. Everything is ahead of her, anything could happen. After 1916 time begins folding itself up, tightening into the felt roll of collective fate. A hundred years later I began following in her footsteps, visiting her St. Petersburg addresses, buildings with rebuilt facades, missing apartments, and whole missing wings in poor areas of the city, lit by the setting sun and inhabited by flocks of Sunday soldiers. It always seemed that if I took just another turn to the right, then that would be enough, I could transform her life, restore it, make it fit to be seen again.

In my own family history, I am interested more than anything in the period of ten to fifteen years after the revolution, when a way of life suddenly slowed, convulsed, and belly-flopped onto a new set of rails. These were the purblind years, the years when my great-grandparents died, or left the country or moved—that period of their lives is barely documented. They preferred not to keep diaries, and all the photographs that had been preserved are only partial, the tiny corners of a much larger picture, and something is going on in this unseen bigger picture that I don't understand. Here's a photograph of croquet at the log-built dacha; here are some hefty women doing exercises under banners with rhymes on; Sarra with her daughter Lyolya, who is looking sad and pinched, standing on a little hill by a stream, and by them some faces from the past, family whose names I don't know. As her daughter grows up (school class group pictures, the little girls pressing themselves against their teacher; postcards from friends; the *La Bayadère* sheet music), the mother slowly fades out. She works in numerous medical institutions, there's a tired love affair with a relative of her dead husband who owns a photo studio, postcards from her travels, pictures of holiday resorts where the gray sea rushes up to meet a gray skirt and then squirms back like a dog at a command.

Sarra never disappeared altogether, and that was her great achievement. She sank into the comfortable life of a qualified medical professional, doing the rounds of sanatoriums and women's clinics. Her daughter, too, was drawn into a constant purposeful activity. She had long decided to become a doctor like

344

her mother, and the permanent bustle radiated a sprightly sense of inclusion, everyone working together. I can't even attempt to guess what they thought about what was happening around them. There is no evidence, no basis for such guesswork. There are no preserved letters, and there never were any such letters, nor books from the home library (the usual Tolstoy, Chekhov "ex libris M. Fridman, Court Solicitor," some early twentieth-century poetry) that might allow me to put together a collage of Soviet or anti-Soviet inclinations. When eighteen-year-old Lyolya decided to get married in 1934 her mother gave permission on the single condition that she first graduate from medical school. They could get married and they could live with Sarra, but they weren't even allowed to think about having a family until Lyolya had her diploma in medicine. This white-hot near-religious belief in higher education was handed down through the generations and I remember it in my own childhood. *We are Jews*, I heard this at the age of seven. You cannot allow yourself the luxury of not having an education.

Lyolya, pink-cheeked and responsible, complied obediently: according to the agreement, Lyonya and Lyolya's child was to be born at the beginning of August 1941. But in early August they and Sarra were part of a convoy evacuated east, toward Siberia. The child sat tight in the womb, as if she understood this was not the time. After a few weeks of changing trains, dragging belongings, the fear of being left behind or being lost, they finally reached Yalutorovsk, the furthest point on the map of our family's wanderings. This tiny town with its wooden duckboard pavements and blackened little buildings had barely ever changed, and even now is probably much the same. It had always been a place of Siberian exile: the Decembrists settled there in the 1820s after their failed uprising against the Tsar. My mother was born there on the third or fourth day after their arrival, on September 12, 1941. Her very earliest memories were of the neighbors chopping the head off their cockerel, and when the head fell on the grass the bird suddenly took to its wings and flew across the astounded yard.

Yalutorovsk, in snow and in steam, with its milk production plants and nurseries, needed an experienced doctor, and it was one of Sarra's finest moments (*Oh, she's a rock!*) — she found her feet straightaway. In the general panic in Moscow in the first weeks of war no one knew what to do or where to go. Marina Tsvetaeva's sixteen-year-old son Mur kept a terrifyingly detailed diary recording the daily changing shades of hope and despair: the hope it might be possible to sit it out, the fear of being buried in the rubble, the fear of flight, the fear of staying put, the endlessly torturous discussion of all the possible outcomes. It's hard to believe now, but in the middle of July 1941 Tsvetaeva went off to a dacha with friends "to rest." The dacha was outside Moscow, on the Kazan road, and the three middle-aged women and one lonely boy stayed out there, filling the time between lunch and dinner with discussion, waiting for news from town, like a scene from a Chekhov story. This sojourn turned out to be their last chance to catch breath. When mother and son briefly returned to Moscow they were caught up in the whirlpool of fleeing crowds trying to get on the last train or the last ferry, and they were *the lucky ones*. They left Moscow by themselves with no help from the Literary Fund, no money, almost no baggage, nothing that could be exchanged for food. We know how the story ends.

Moscow wasn't prepared for war or siege. In Spring 1941 a commission was set up to research the evacuation of Moscow's population in case of war. They discussed possible ways to evacuate a million residents away from the front line. Stalin sent an angry riposte to their suggestions:

I consider your suggestions on the "partial" evacuation of the population of Moscow in "a time of war" untimely. I want the commission for evacuation liquidated and all discussion of evacuation ceased. If and when it is necessary to prepare a plan for evacuation the Cen-

tral Committee of the Communist Party and the Council of People's Commissars will inform you.

This memo is dated June 5, 1941.

The city was in a state of frenzy for several months. People fled precipitously as you might dive through a hole cut in the ice. All the government ministries and offices evacuated their staff, and those who didn't go were simply left to their own devices. Some fled on foot. On October 16, when the German army was very close to Moscow's outskirts, the literary critic Emma Gerstein missed the evacuation train she'd been promised a place on. "I walked through the streets and wept. All around scraps of shredded documents and Marxist political brochures whirled about me in the air, carried by the wind. The hairdressers were all full and 'ladies' were lining up on the streets. The Germans were coming, they needed to get their hair done."

*

They returned to Moscow in 1944. On May 9, 1945, Lyolya's birthday, the high windows of the apartment on the boulevard were thrown open. Spring was everywhere, its green streaming like tears, and all the residents in the communal apartment were gathered around a table laden with food: the family, friends, chance passersby brought in from the street, and young Viktoria Ivanova, a singer whose name reminded them of Victory, who wore a blue dress, and sang for them in her divine voice: "The Blue Scarf" and "Come Buy My Violets," and anything else they asked her to sing. Then they went out to the Ustinsky Bridge to watch the fireworks blooming over the Moscow River.

After this evening Sarra's light begins to dim, to disappear into the darkness that will last for nearly thirty years. I remember my mother linked Sarra's stroke with the "Doctors' Plot," which should by rights have consumed her, and Lyolya as well. Her little gray "record of work" book, filled out up to 1949, shows that even before the "Doctors' Plot" there was no dearth of terrifying events. The whole country was at war with "cosmopolitanism," a code word for Jewishness. The Jewish Antifascist Committee was disbanded, there were arrests, books by Jewish authors were removed from libraries, all publication in Yiddish ceased, and there was the usual wave of sackings across the city. I don't know what would have been more dangerous for Doctor Sarra Abramovna Ginzburg: her native Jewishness or her assumed Europeanness. I wonder, did she ever discuss what was going on with her close family, was she scared that it would also affect those around her, her very successful son-in-law, daughter, and grandchild? Her stroke, and the resulting "senility"—that long-awaited inability to be responsible, make decisions, take steps—removed her from the group at risk, and placed her in a cool, safe place, where she could sort through her photographs, make little notes on them, and put her hand out and touch any beckoning memory.

I remember listening to a school talk on Byzantine architecture in the darkened auditorium of the Pushkin Museum when I was ten. The powerful shoulders of the Hagia Sophia and the sky above the minarets appeared on the projector screen. You could say that this was a later invention, or a stereotype I have retrospectively revived, but I remember all too well the moment when I looked at the bright screen and thought to myself: I will probably never see this in real life. People with our lives, engineers and lowly scientists, the unexceptional Moscow intelligentsia at the beginning of the eighties, simply never went abroad.

I started traveling as soon as I had the opportunity and I have never stopped. Perhaps this is why I get an almost physical thrill from being under the glass-and-metal roofs of railway stations. It's as if the roof's ribs are mine and the circulation of people is my own body's vital circulation, filling sixteen platforms, the wide glassy wings, the lofty arcs supported by sunlight. I have the same feeling in airports, with their laundrette fumes, their inhuman cleanliness. I have to cling to every opportunity for travel like a monkey wrapped around a branch. The aerial state, the gaseous state, invisible, elusive, passing across borders and breathing in the air one chooses—yes, for this I strive! When we moved apartments and all the cups and sauce boats, photographs and the books of our home life were put into storage, I started traveling twice as much as usual, as if these possessions had weighted me down to the earth.

My travels had a solid justification: I was writing a book about *my people*. I moved about from place to place, archive to archive, street to street, places where they had walked. I tried to coincide with them, hoping this would engender a memory of them, however implausible it sounds. I diligently gathered up everything I knew, and entered dates and addresses into the computer's memory, mapping a route like anyone who embarks on a long journey.

On the corner of a Paris street, in a building where my great-grandmother had once lived, there is now a small hotel. Here I could spend one or two nights under the same roof as the young Sarra, I could quite literally get under the skin of history. I arrived from London on the train, threading itself through the undersea tunnel and appearing suddenly in the midst of green French fields. Looking out of the window, I thought how terribly tired I was of family. I couldn't look away from it, I saw nothing else. Like the wrought iron fence of the Summer Gardens, I couldn't see beyond the captivating design and into the space within. Every past and present phenomenon had been tied to my indistinct relatives, I had *rhymed it all*, emphasized the simultaneity between them and me, or the lack of it. I'd had to learn to put off my own relations with the world for later, just as truffle pigs are trained to ensure they don't eat their precious findings. My journeys had only the most oblique connection with me, I made my way from town to town like a traveling salesperson, dragging a wheelie bag. It wasn't that the wheelie bag was out of place or filled with the wrong things—not even when it clattered down the cobbled Parisian streets—no, it was just that wherever I went it insisted on its presence.

There I went with it, weaving along the verges, down the long rue Claude-Bernard in the fifth arrondissement, where only people like Sarra Ginzburg lived, and not because it was near the Sorbonne and the Val-de-Grâce hospital—this was the area of rented rooms and cheap lodgings where sparrowlike students flitted from perch to perch, never going far, huddling together for collegiate warmth. On this very street Sarra had spent a few weeks or months in a green-tinged seven-story building with metal balconies. It was a cheap, fierce neighborhood, the stairwells smelt of smoke and damp face powder. It had been rebuilt in the 1860s, but had become no more respectable for it. As the architect of these changes Baron Haussmann said "Paris belongs to France, and not to the Parisians, who inhabit it by birth or by choice, and definitely not to the flowing population of its rented rooms, who distort the meaning of 'referendum' with their unintelligent voice." A few decades later the Russian Mademoiselle Ginzburg joined this floating population.

Waking one morning in the attic room on the sixth floor, I slowly began groping mentally for what might have been back then: the number of rooms, the crooked ceiling, the old table and the chimney pots, very white against the gray sky. Without even getting up I could see at least ten possibilities. My great-grandmother might have stayed in this very room—why not, the cheapest rooms would have been up in the attics—or she could have lived in any of the other rooms. If I had expected a supernatural happening (paid for in advance and online with my credit card), a dream peopled by Sarra and her student friends, a sudden nighttime revelation, an injection of understanding, no such thing happened. Instead the usual tourist morning, the light, the smell of coffee, the quiet murmur of a vacuum cleaner.

The owner of the hotel was an older man with grief-stricken eyes. He held himself with the dignity of a caryatid. It was clear that he could carry on a conversation with me, and at the same time carry all the weight of his elegant hotel, with its staircases and the starched envelopes of its beds. He bought the building in the 1980s, reconstructed whole floors of tired rooms and sunk a lift shaft through the building, but left untouched the ancient underground passageway leading into the darkness toward the Seine. He knew little about the life of the building before that, except that the designer Kenzō Takada had lived in one of its microscopic rooms during his early days in Paris. There were no memories back to the beginning of the century, but the building had always housed the cramped, narrow, warren-like living quarters of the poor. "You're Jewish, aren't you?" he suddenly said.

Twenty or so years ago I was sitting with my future (now former) husband in the little porch of a Crimean café and waiting for it to open. It was noon, a lazy August day, the holiday season was nearing its end and no one was hurrying anywhere, especially not the ragtag band approaching us across the warm asphalt. A man in dirty trousers with a greasy blond beard was leading an elderly horse, and up high on the saddle, gripping on to the pommel with both hands, sat an unusually pretty curly-haired little boy of about six. Even at that hour of desperate longing for Crimean fortified wine, their appearance seemed unreal, like a shamelessly direct quote from a Soviet film about the White Army during the Civil War. The horse was white, too, but red with dust. The man led the beast right up to the porch and said, without any particular expression: "Excuse me but aren't you *ex nostris?*" I was so surprised I didn't immediately grasp what he was saying.

Ex nostris, jid, as he added in his next phrase, meaning the very same "we are Jews." He took the coins we offered and went on, him and his child toward Feodosiya, without offering any detail in return, and for this reason I sometimes wonder whether we didn't just invent it all, sitting there in the shade of the porch. But I couldn't have invented it, the Latin, the *jid*—in my assimilated experience the space for such an understanding was absent, along with the reflex for such an exchange of passwords. "Yes, I'm Jewish, too," said the owner of the hotel, hardly doubting either himself or me. "At the end of the streets there's a synagogue, a very old one. You can understand why your grandmother would have wanted to live here. It's very hard here for us again. I give us at best another five years in France. After that it will be worse. Far worse."

*

The oldest medical institute in France in Montpellier accepted foreign students with open arms. The diaries of the Swiss physician Thomas Platter the Younger, who studied here at the end of the sixteenth century, describe the area's reddish and very fertile soil, the local wine, so strong it had to be diluted by two thirds, and the elegant townspeople, adept at trickery and intrigue, fine dancers and sportspeople. Thomas noted the seven courts for ball games in the town: "Where do these people get so much money from, just to fritter it away?" Sarra's life abroad began here, either under the glassy dome of Gare du Nord, if she had arrived via Berlin, or Gare de l'Est, if she'd come via Vienna.

There were hundreds like her, if not thousands. The medical education in France was the cheapest in Europe. From the end of the 1860s, when universities gradually began accepting women, Russian women began filling the quotas. By 1914 they made up 70 percent and sometimes 80 percent of the women studying medicine. They were treated with disdain, their fellow students needed no encouragement to complain about them, their manners, their slovenliness, their political radicalism—and most of all their desire to be at the top of the class, pushing local students out of the family nest like cuckoos. Even Pyotr Kropotkin described how the professors at Zurich University would without fail and very insultingly hold up the women students as examples to their male counterparts.

One of the women students remembered years later how

in the 1870s "the Russian women demanded not just the usual rights, which applied to everyone, but special privileges, always occupying the best spaces and putting themselves first." They lived in a tight community, in areas where spoken Russian dominated, and they ate a diet of bread, tea, milk, and thin slices of meat. They smoked heedlessly, they walked around unchaperoned. They discussed in all seriousness whether one could eat a plate of plums or raspberries and remain a thinking woman and a comrade. The newspapers in Bern called them the hyenas of the revolution: "unhealthy, half-educated, uncontrollable creatures." But by the end of the 1880s there were already 698 women doctors in Russia. In 1900 there were only 95 in France and 258 in England.

A huge number of the Russian students were Jewish. This was their chance, their golden ticket—a doctor with a medical diploma could practice anywhere in the Russian Empire, and not just in the Pale of Settlement. By the beginning of the new century more than five thousand foreign medical students had converged on Paris, fighting for places with the locals. In 1896 students in Lyon protested on the streets, claiming that foreign students, in particular women, were crowding French students out of the clinics and lecture halls. In 1905 students in Jena signed a petition against giving student places to Russian Jews with their "pushy behavior." In 1912, when Sarra was already studying at the Sorbonne, there were student strikes all across Germany and everywhere the demand was the same, to limit the influx of foreign students. In Heidelberg, Russian students made a public appeal to the local student body to understand their position and not to judge them too harshly. Mutual annoyance hung in the air, like smoke. Women, those *corrupters of youth*, were an easy target, widely caricatured in the tabloid press.

My other great-grandmother, Betya Liberman, also dreamed of becoming a doctor, but nothing came of it, except this family legend: Betya felt she had to test herself—would she cope with seeing a dead body or would she be frightened by it? So as a fifteen-year-old she went alone at dusk to the town morgue, and for a small fee she was allowed to sit there, night after night, until she was sure that she was ready and could cope. She wasn't able to continue her studies, however—instead of medicine she got the fairy-tale prince she deserved, an early and (I want to hope) easy marriage, the wealth, peace, and sparkle of a *vie heureuse*. I look at them, like two playing cards in the hand: on one card strong-minded Sarra and her battle for a diploma; her stubbornness and drive, once set into motion an unstoppable force. And on the other tender Betya, who worked as an office accountant her entire prosaic Soviet life, while her son was growing up, and for a long time afterward. What difference is there between them? History is such a strange thing—it canceled all the choices they made before 1917 and quickly reduced both to old women, hardly distinguishable in the grandeur of their last years of life.

*

Medical students were much noisier than the other students. The memoirs and police reports are filled with accounts of merry rowdiness: in Thomas Platter's time the lecturers were given *the slow stamp*: "Students began banging with their fists and feathers, and stamping, and if they felt that the lecturer wasn't paying any attention they would make such a noise that he couldn't continue." In the nineteenth century Platter's equivalents rivaled this riotousness with snowball fights, and boxing matches in the laboratories, and plans to throw a sentry from a high balustrade. But the First World War changed a great deal, it put an end to the youthful boisterousness, which is quite normal when the young are left to their own devices. The games were over, everyone became more serious and angry. Between 1905 and 1913 there hadn't been a year when student protests in Paris hadn't disrupt the medical training for a time. The system had ceased to work.

The university in Paris was the largest in Europe at the time.

The huge lecture halls were overflowing. Late in the winter of 1914 Sarra wrote to my future great-grandfather: "best not to even try to predict when you might finish [university studies]." In 1893 three quarters of Paris's medical students were spending up to six years studying before their final exams. 38 percent of students spent more than eight years on their degree, and many spent as long as eleven years studying. Studies were full time, six or seven days a week, with daily dissections in the big anatomical theater, lab work and compulsory morning shifts in the hospital: examinations, assisting with electrotherapy. By the point when the student took the rigorous final exams, he or she would have racked up many hundreds of mornings in the hospital. The exam season lasted two months and the exams were oral and public. They required knowledge, but also a measure of artistry. In the letters written during Sarra's last Parisian year (and the last year of the *old world*) Sarra can't think of anything else: "Just back from my exam. I'm quite shattered," "I have another exam tomorrow—on birth and midwifery. If it goes well I can rest a while," "Still hard at the revision, lots of people have been left behind, they'll take their finals in autumn," and so on until her diploma, her long-awaited victory, which happened only a little while before the catastrophe.

Prince Sergei Trubetskoy, who was in Paris in 1913 (like the rest of the world, or so it seems, all enjoying a last stroll along the Seine), wrote in his memoirs: "I recall that on this trip [...] there was something that surprised me. The hotels I stayed in in Berlin, Amsterdam, Antwerp, and Paris—on the day of my arrival I came down to eat in the hotel restaurant, and in each town they were playing versions of the same popular tune of the time, 'Pupsik.'" This unprecedented "simultaneity" of life, barely noticeable back then, is frightening now when we look with clear eyes at the date and the places. Those few prewar years are a time when the entire future twentieth century, together with a large part of the nineteenth century, swept its skirts along the same boulevards, sat at neighboring café tables and side by side in theater stalls, hardly suspecting the existence of each other. Sometimes you have to die to find out who lived on the same street as you.

My brave, lonely great-grandmother lived in Paris from 1910 onward. In September 1911 Kafka briefly visited Paris. At the beginning of his travels he and Max Brod conceived of a plan to write travel guides. It was a brilliant idea, anticipating the Lonely Planet series, for readers who didn't mind going third class across Italy, or preferred streetcars to barouches. Brod wrote a business plan, including details of accompanying discounts and free concerts. Two phrases are written in Kafka's hand—one of them is "exact amounts for tipping." They also included shopping advice on where one could enjoy pineapple, oysters, and madeleines in Paris—this, less than two years before the publication of Proust's *In Search of Lost Time*.

That same September Rilke was strolling in Paris, having just returned from a trip around Germany. The newspapers were discussing the theft of the *Mona Lisa*, which the obscure poet Guillaume Apollinaire was suspected of stealing. 1911 was an ordinary sort of year, no better and no worse than any other year. The Ballets Russes premiered Stravinsky's *Petrushka*. Romain Rolland's *Jean-Christophe* was being slowly published, volume by volume, an endless novel that was much loved by the women of my family (and despised by Proust, who was planning an article "Against Romain Rolland").

In April, Lenin began a successful lecture series on political economy on the avenue des Gobelins (another place where my great-grandmother took lodgings). Gorky came to visit him at the end of the month and they discussed the current situation: "There will be a war. It's inevitable," said Lenin. In the Jardin du Luxembourg Akhmatova and Modigliani sat on a bench—they couldn't afford to pay for chairs. Each of these people hardly suspected the existence of the others, they were quite alone in the transparent sleeve of their own fate. Opera hats unfolded with a familiar click at the Opéra—the interval was just beginning.

A May morning in Paris, close to the Jardin du Luxembourg, with its stone lions and its now free chairs: there's no question in my mind that Sarra must have strolled here and suddenly—waiting for the place to tell me what I must do—I'm bewildered and lost. The night passed as nights do. The chimneys in the view from the window resembled flowerpots, Kafka said something similar about them. I had no memorable or distinctive dreams or thoughts. I'd spent half the day on a tour around the Sorbonne, gently but firmly led down the usual tourist routes. I'd smiled at the birds, stood motionless looking at shop windows, and checked the museums' opening hours. The city basked in the sun, showing its pearly innards. People stood, sat, lay in its every fold. I didn't remember these people from previous visits, they silently stretched out cupped hands from piles of rags and damp newspaper, or approached café tables, one after another with the ancient entreaty. I had nothing left for the last of these, and he shouted hoarse furious words in my face.

Not far from this place were some little specialist shops selling old cameras and camera accessories: on their shelves lenses and filters stood alongside daguerreotypes and equipment for panoramas, dioramas, and night photography. Forbidden images of the buttocks and breasts of the dead were folded in leaves of rolling paper and placed in boxes. There were large amounts of cards for stereoscopes, those wooden, bird-headed instruments, lending every image a capacious depth. The glossy stereoscope cards had two images on them: you inserted them into a special slot in the instrument and twiddled a wooden beak until the doubled imaged gathered itself into something singular, alive, and convincing. There were hundreds of these cards, showing the streets of Rome; a whole ant heap of quartiers and alleyways from San Pietro down to the Tiber that no longer exist because the wide modern Via della Consiliazione has been driven through it all.

There were colorized cards of family scenes; train crashes from a hundred years ago. And there was one card that was unlike any of the others.

This card also appeared to be made for a stereoscope, but it was a pair of illustrations, rather than photographs, and the two images, although intended for each other, had nothing in common. They were both black cut-out silhouettes (silhouette profiles enjoyed huge popularity in the past). The left-hand image showed a doorway with a curtain across it, a colonnade of some sort and a tree a little farther off. In the right-hand picture was a detailed but unmatching composition: a hussar in a shako, and a goat with horns. When inserted into the stereoscope the two pictures came together into a suddenly animated tableau: the hussar leans on a column's capital, the goat grazes under the tree, and we see the scene through the curtained door. Two unrelated images shift and come together to make a *story*.

The following days and nights I spent in my hotel room. I had flu, a high temperature, and the chimney stacks outside the window multiplied and divided stereoscopically. An endless storm raged outside and it comforted me at first, and then ceased to have any significance. I lay lifelessly on the bed, listening to it crashing overhead and thinking that this wasn't the worst ending to a pointless sentimental journey. There was nothing for me to do here and I had done nothing in this beautiful foreign city, this large empty bed, under a roof that might or might not remember Sarra Ginzburg, her Russian accent, her French books.

In the 1960s, quite by chance, a Frenchman visited the family's Moscow apartment. God only knows where he came from or who he was, but he was royally received, as all guests were, with all the salads known to man, and a homemade Torte Napoleon. All the family joined him at the table, including eighty-year-old Sarra, who had long since disappeared into herself. But when she heard French being spoken she became terribly animated and began speaking in the language of her youth. She sat up talking to the guest until long after midnight—they were both delighted with each other. In the morning she'd switched to speaking French completely and irrevocably, as a person might take vows and vanish into a monastery. When the family spoke to her in Russian she would answer in long French sentences. After a while they learned to understand her.

2. Little Lyonya from the Nursery

It was the middle of the night in November. Telephone calls at that hour were always a cause for fear, especially in the years when a single telephone rang in the deep womb-like corridor of a communal apartment, waiting for someone to run to lift the receiver. The voice at the other end was like nothing else they knew, hoarse and gulping, like a voice emerging from a gutter: "Your old man is dying. You should come." And they went. I was two years old at the time, and fast asleep in a room. I don't remember anything. Only four months before, my mother's mother Lyolya had died, at just fifty-eight.

The building they went to was near-invisible in the night, on a Moscow side street and surrounded by identical, low-eaved two-story buildings. The door swung open and a woman wearing only a slip staggered out in the thin yellow light. There was a room and a bed, and in the bed, in a tangle of bedsheets, lay my grandfather, dead. His naked body was covered in blue bruises. All the lights were switched on, as if it were an operating theater.

He was hardly an old man, only sixty-two. Only a few years before he had moved into his own cooperatively owned apartment with his wife. Grandfather Lyonya had been very active in the block's community affairs, planting out a strip of land in front of the white facade of the high-rise with lilac and, most importantly (this was his idea), a row of poplar trees. He wanted to plant the same trees in the backyard; my mother said they reminded him of the south—*Grandfather was from Odessa*. Now the poplars grew up around the tower block, but the box inside, like the chamber in a pyramid, was empty: no one lived there anymore. The little bouquets Lyolya had picked gathered dust.

The box where Grandfather kept his savings books was empty and my mother didn't know what had happened to them. There were phone calls to the authorities, and police promises to get to the bottom of the matter. Eventually my parents received a single terse call. They were advised not to pursue the matter, it would only make things worse. Although, really, what could be worse?

This year was a turning point for my family; a whole generation suddenly gone. My mother, Natasha Gurevich, had lost both parents, and she found herself the shepherd of a strange flock. Apart from me, chattering merrily away, she had under her care two ninety-year-old grandmothers, Betya and Sarra, who had always been politely indifferent to each other and suddenly had to live together. The loss of a single son and a single daughter offered their misaligned lives some insulation, a soft layer between them and the new life with its strange cold drafts. Someone once said that the death of our parents marks the loss of the final boundary between ourselves and nonexistence. The death of their children was a wedge jammed in the inner workings of my great-grandmothers. Now nonexistence washed at their boundaries on either side.

My parents were quite certain that my grandfather had been murdered, but no one knew why or what he'd done, what sinister criminality resided in the place where they had found him, or even how he, a calm, untroubled man, came to end his life there. They could only guess. After Lyolya's death, when the funeral was over and the family plot at Vostryakovsky Cemetery had opened its mouth for the first time in fifty years to allow a new resident to enter, and then sealed it again, Grandfather called his daughter for a conversation. It turned out he had another woman. He appealed to my mother to react with understanding, to discuss things like adults—the situation might be seen as advantageous for all parties. My mother could go and live in the apartment on Banny Pereulok, where there was more space for a child, and Grandfather and his girlfriend could live in the communal apartment. This was all discussed with a calm businesslike logic, along with the other details: his girlfriend didn't work and perhaps she could even babysit Masha. She loved children.

I gathered this story slowly, in its constituent parts, many years later. When I asked how Grandmother and Grandfather had died, I always received the same unwavering, darkly symmetrical response: he died of "lung inflammation," she of a "heart attack." I couldn't quite understand either, and so they disproportionately upset and fascinated me. The heart and lungs were magnified in my child's imagination, I understood that much depended on them, these human parts that could treacherously inflame and attack. Still, I remember my sense of horror as if it were yesterday, of everything being turned on its head, when my parents told me for the first time at the age of seventeen "what really happened." I heard the story again a few times, each new account fuller, and in more detail. The story was in itself frightening and unclear, offering no answers. Worst of all was the manner of telling, as if my parents, reluctantly and against their will, were attempting to push back a steel door. The door had rusted into place, it stood in front of a black hole, whistling with an otherworldly chill. They had nothing to say in answer to my questions, not even "who was his girlfriend?"—they knew nothing about her. Back then, in August 1974, my mother had angrily refused to have anything to do with her, or to accept that this unwanted woman, eclipsing Lyolya's memory, even existed. Three months later Lyonya, with his grand plans, his bristling mustache, and his joyless jokes, was gone, too.

*

Lyonya and Lyolya. They were always a pair in my head, their names matched like snap cards. Their childish correspondence, freckled with exclamation marks, beaded with ellipses, dates from 1934, when life still seemed eternal, a thing of substance, when the summer move out to the dacha was undertaken on a horse and cart, and the line of hired carts stretched through the Moscow morning, laden with goods and chattels, trunks of bedlinen, kerosene stoves and samovars—as if this was the only way to do things. Some of the previous generation's rituals and formalities were still in place despite the *new life*, the circus-ring gallop of new friends and lovers. In time Lyonya proposed, and his proposal was gladly accepted, but accompanied by a few clauses and conditions. They didn't rush to have children, just as they had promised, and life had the faintly lazy feel of a holiday in the warm south. They went to the sea and their photos show a slope of rocks, and the holidaymakers posing against it, the black beetle of a car, and the bright moth wings of dresses. Lyolya completed her medical training, Lyonya graduated from the Construction Institute with very respectable grades and began working. And then there were the things that weren't ever discussed: both these young Soviet professionals filled in the usual forms, and in the box marked "social background" they, like others, avoided mentioning certain things, or twisted the facts slightly to make them acceptable. Lyolya's father's legal title was downgraded to "clerk," and then hurriedly to the even less objectionable "employee." "Merchant of the 1st Guild" became "shopkeeper" or "tradesperson." There was a special box for relatives abroad and that was better left empty. In that box, Lyonya wrote: "My dead aunt's husband was transferred to London for work. I do not keep up contact with him."

In 1938 the forms asked whether Lyonya had served in the old Tsarist army, or in any organization connected with the White Government, and if so in what capacity? Did he serve in the Civil War and if so, when, where and in what capacity? Did he suffer persecution as a result of revolutionary activity leading up to the October Revolution? The form also asked how the subject had fared *in the last purges in the party*. There were even more questions in the 1954 form: Have you been in prison? Fought in a partisan group? Lived in occupied territory? In every box a blue-inked NO is scrawled.

His daughter Natasha never quite forgave him for his lively haste to move on to a new life after his wife's death, nor for her sudden realization that the old life had had a false bottom. When we spent our evenings together, with the old photographs and memories, this was never mentioned, but later, when I began studying the inexhaustible contents of drawers and boxes, I discovered strange objects, artifacts that fell outside of the "tone" of the household: postcards, notes, little objects that fitted a different shape or order—not ours, but not Soviet, either. A drawing in color, for example, of a very carefully drawn heart, divided in two. The dotted line down the middle was highlighted in red, and at the bottom someone had written: "IT'S HARD FOR BOTH OF US." Teardrops with light reflections were dripping down on the letters. Or a New Year's greeting card in a homemade envelope with the inscription: "Open on December 31 at 10:00 p.m." The woman who wrote the card and sealed it with wax and the impression of a Soviet kopeck had known that the addressee, at his own family celebration, would have no time for her at midnight on New Year's Eve. Inside was a poem and a letter, signed, "your little friend." The miniature nature and inexperience of the "little friend" were given rather insistent emphasis by the letter: "I am writing to you and drawing a Christmas tree, my head on one side with the childish effort, I'll put the clock hands on the picture when it reaches midnight. Happy New Year, Leonid!" And the poem carried this further: "Like your daughter, I'll find my place too / under the Christmas tree." And all of this, the picture and even the kopeck imprint, had survived for some reason.

Later, when my parents had left Russia and the flat was empty, I would still find marvelous things from time to time (a whole handful of silver spoons scattering from an overhead cupboard where we kept nails and bottles of turps), but I was beginning to lay its depths bare. I found, among the papers, the most various things: my acquaintance of old, the unknown naked woman on the divan, and another picture, which I have before me right now.

I am touched, not by the "piquant scene" as they might have said back then, but by all the objects indicative of an era. A blonde woman in dark-colored knickers and bra sits with an unlit cigarette. It reminds me of a home movie from the nineties, a genre painting adapted for home and for a single viewer. It's a stylized shot, a Russian pin-up, done with half an eye on seen or invented examples of the genre, and an attempt to adapt them to a set of completely unsuitable circumstances. It's a conservative image, most things are strategically covered up, but this doesn't stop it being reckless and even indecent.

A fresh copy of the Soviet newspaper *Pravda* makes the photograph dangerous (placing a naked lascivious ass on the *party organ* could get you a few years in prison), not to mention the packet of Belomor cigarettes (with the emblem of the White Sea Canal, built by slave labor) in her left hand. The country's main newspaper and its cheapest cigarettes, stubby and potent, are brought together like heraldic symbols, linked by the female body. The body seems indifferent to both. The room looks like a temporary lean-to, an institutional bathhouse dressing room. The high heels resemble cabaret costume, along with the underwear, which is too well cut for Soviet underwear. All this at the end of the 1940s, or the very beginning of the 1950s, the holy winter of Stalin's rule with its ponderous sensibility, the rows of party cars lined up at theater stage doors, a second wave of terror, the "Doctors' Plot." In the corner of the picture, stuck up on a limewashed wall, is a crass caricature of a "capitalist" doffing his hat.

In later, safer years Grandfather Lyonya found himself another occupation to add to his many activities: he began writing and publishing satirical sketches of various kinds. These were mostly funny little anecdotes, short jokey dialogues or paradoxical phrases, sometimes also didactic prose, and some strange little hybrids—work reports in verse, for example. His ease with rhyme—he had a natural virtuosity, he could fit any subject into its neat envelope—did not improve his writing. His anecdotes were funny, though, and were even sometimes published in the top Soviet satirical magazine of the era, *Krokodil*. He stuck the clippings proudly into special exercise books. I remember some from my childhood: "Never eat on an empty stomach!" was one. A favorite mode of his was writing little stories about "other cultures and customs." He would write about different, half-invented worlds, peopled by hopelessly bourgeois Frenchmen called Pierre and Antoine, but the satire slid into something stranger, as if the story was about a dream that could never be realized, and all that was left was to make fun of it.

Any anecdote is just a novel compressed down to a point, and it can equally well be reinflated to elephantine proportions. The opposite must also exist, when your intended meaning is too large even to want to try to fit it to a form. My grandfather's jokes (they were printed anonymously) were based on the belief in another world that bubbled up with attractive possibilities, a world in which erotic excitement hung in the air, a world of live and let live. There was something perennially old-fashioned in them, as if the characters wore bowler hats and cuff links: "At his wife's funeral Mr. Smiles comforted his wife's weeping lover: now don't you take on so, I'll be married again in a tick!"

I should add here that in contrast to his generation of compatriots who never left the Soviet Union, Lyonya was a lucky exception. He had been abroad—this family story was repeatedly told to me from my earliest childhood. Lyonya was born in 1912 with clubfoot. I couldn't see anything wrong with his feet in the old photographs, just a baby with such pale eyes they looked white, lying on his stomach. They treated the condition thoroughly, took it all very seriously, and managed to cure him. Every summer Lyonya's mother took him to the same Swiss sanatorium where there were green hills, and Lyonya learned to walk better and better on the hills until he was ready for the *new life*, in which all travel would cease. But he remembered Switzerland very well.

When he was privy to those classic Soviet intelligentsia conversations about where one would go if one were able, and Paris, Tokyo, and Rome were flung down like hands of playing cards, he would sit without saying a word. If you asked him directly he would answer without hesitation: I would go to Switzerland.

*

Lyonya, or so I was told, wrote his first academic thesis on a hospital windowsill, during a period of recuperation when he was supposed to be resting, although he couldn't bear to sit still. He was full of curiosity, he always had a new interest, and the range of these different interests brought its own financial rewards: they always lived well.

Articles, books, lecturing in three different academic institutes didn't satisfy him. It was as if he sensed that he'd been made for bigger things, or other things, and he threw himself into ever newer pursuits, ticking more and more boxes on some invisible form. I suspect that the shadowy "little friends" were all part of this hunger, if they didn't fill a hole, then they momentarily satisfied a need that was invisible to everyone else. His cup of life ran over. He designed transport interchanges, he played chess, he invented things, and applied for patents for them—including an object that always fascinated me. I boasted about it in childhood, and I am still proud of it today: a complicated mechanism for testing whether a watermelon is off. The pointlessness of its complication gave it a special thrill because you knew even as you used it that you could tell whether a watermelon was off simply by flicking a finger against it and listening for the tight echoing of its belly.

These displacement activities were joined by the constant rhyme-mongering. His talented nature found expression here too, and the verses came tumbling out whenever there was an occasion for such jokes in verse. Before the war he had enjoyed a reputation as a very witty man, adept at table talk. Nobody I spoke to remembered him from that time, though. My mother's friends remembered him as a preoccupied and glum man, who would greet them and then disappear off to his own business. Lyolya was the life and soul of the house, everyone loved her and she loved everyone. She baked cake after cake, embroidered tablecloth after tablecloth, knew everyone and remembered everything. She kept a whole huge family of second and third cousins together, held them close to her heart. The Doctors' Plot left her without work until a contact of Sarra invited her to work with them at a medical inspection point. Offering work to a Jewish doctor was a gesture of extreme nobility, almost a suicidal act at that time, and she remained there for the rest of her working life, either out of gratitude or because she had no more desire to move.

After Lyolya died my mother didn't mention her to me for a very long time, and then suddenly she asked if I remembered Grandmother. I did. "And what was she like?" "She adored me," I said with certainty. And I know this of her: she was adored by everyone, near and far, the light of collective adoration is blinding to this day and prevents me from seeing any detail. What *was* she like? Auntie Sima, my old nanny, who remembered a time when everyone was young, answered my questions brusquely: "She was a happy creature. She'd put on her perfume and her lipstick and run off to a meeting on the boulevard." What meeting? Who was she meeting—the mysterious Nelidov? My mother's friend came to see me to tell me more family history, and when I asked for details, she said simply: "She was a ... she was a proper lady," and would say no more.

What she meant by this couldn't actually be said in the language of a new age. By "proper lady" she perhaps meant a living anachronism, a person of another era with qualities and virtues that had long since disappeared. And this demanded a language that had vanished too, full of "properness" with regard to long-defunct rules and obligations. Lyolya's good-heartedness made her way of surviving bearable for those around her. The alternating softness and harshness, the uncompromising, and then the suffering, spirit—it is all so familiar, and it can't begin to be lined up against how we see the world today. I remember I was once stunned by my mother saying, "If I'd done that my mother would have slapped my lips," Even now I shudder at the thought. *Her lips?* These were the words and actions of a dead language, and even if you wanted to, there was no one left to speak it with.

Among the various traditions lubricating the family machinery, there was Lyonya's New Year's poetry. Lyonya would write a number of funny poems to members of the family: daughter, wife, grandmothers Sarra and Betya, and guests, if guests were expected. These were simple ditties, rhyming "new year" with "cheer," they radiated the coziness that comes of repetition and settles on the walls like scale in a teapot. But there was one constant motif that always surprised me and I wondered how Lyolya felt about it: the poems addressed to twelve-year-old Natasha recommended she "be like Daddy and not like Mommy."

They were by all accounts happy, and they got on, Lyolya the beauty, with her cameo brooch at her throat, her Dickens (she'd made marks around her favorite passages with her fingernail), her embroidery and her sullen, busy husband. She baked and cooked and had people round, grew jasmine and went, as before, on holiday as a couple with Lyonya. Natasha was sent with her nanny for "feeding up" in Svyatogorsk, where she waited, desperately missing her parents, growing her hair into a thick long black braid down to her waist. By the time it reached her knees she had quite grown up. Like her father she wrote poems with ease, and wanted to be a poet: she wanted to be Pushkin, as she said as a child.

At the time poets were produced in industrial quantities, in a special production plant called the Literary Institute, based in an old building on the Moscow Boulevard behind a wrought-iron fence and surrounded by trees. It was a complicated place with its own heritage and an ability to attract those who needed to be there. In earlier Soviet times both the writer Platonov and Mandelstam managed to survive there briefly and unhappily, and at the end of the 1950s it was considered to be, and perhaps even was, "the place to be." Natasha dreamed of studying there, but her father, who'd never denied her anything in her life, unexpectedly said no. He forbade her to apply to the Literary Institute with absolute and unbending resolve, reminding her of the age-old, *We are Jews. You need a profession.* So she obediently went to study in a Construction Institute, graduating with an excellent degree (everything she did was excellent) and receiving as her reward the title of "Pile Foundation Engineer." Then she actually worked under the ground, in a little basement in a research institute, spending half the day in the underworld, like Persephone. Around her, women in black lab coats stared into microscopes, swapping slides with their friable contents, and the most enormous range of weights was laid out by the old weighing scale; they gleamed and had a pleasant heft in the hand. I dreamed of stealing one.

The subject of Lyolya's icy and near-nonexistent relationship with her mother-in-law, Betya, was off-limits in the family (and this silence was just one of the expressions of Lyolya's famed obstinacy). They weren't good at hiding their mutual dislike, in both women a sense of dignity demanded the highest standards of behavior. At celebrations and gatherings, the lifeblood of a big and welcoming family, where everyone was loved and everything remembered, they watched each other closely and suspiciously. Natasha was dragged into all of this, and she made valiant attempts to love everyone, but sometimes it was just too hard. Her mother was the most important person in her life: her mother's shape and her content were the story she had learned off by heart. Even years later, in her own stories of family life, although she never judged Betya, she pushed her away, held her at a distance, at the very margins of the family's history.

Betya Gurevich, born Berta Liberman, lived quietly and independent on the fringes, cherishing and saving every line of poetry written by her son and granddaughter; all the children's pictures, little poems, telegrams. She spent fifty years working as an accountant for various state institutions with unpronounceable acronyms for names, and in her free time she led a spartan life, never permitting herself any form of excess, especially of words. She left behind no letters, no diaries; she was the odd one out in our family, everyone else was constantly occupied with noting everything down, rhyming it, putting it on a postcard. Inscrutable Betya preferred to say nothing about herself, she was cloaked in silence. I don't think anyone ever asked her any questions about herself, and that is how I know very little about her—apart from the air of disapproval that I breathed in my childhood. I remember that my mother was wounded when someone commented that I looked like my great-grandmother Betya. She didn't respond but her silence spoke volumes. I remember the ring Betya left my mother, which my mother never wore. The ring had a chunky setting and a large opaque stone and my mother thought it "too ornate." All in all, hardly any space was left for Betya, the bête noire, in the family's accounts of itself.

I have her school photographs and I can see her, curly-haired, among the lines of girls with their heads held high. There are a few photos from her girlhood and youth, though not many. Her childhood was spent on the edge of poverty; with eight children in the family, and no hope of a decent education, she was forced to give up her dreams of becoming a doctor. Both she and her sister were reputed to be real beauties, fair-haired, fine-boned, with dark eyes and a melancholy gaze. Family legend has it that she married young and well, to the son of a man who manufactured agricultural machinery in Kherson. They were wealthy (among my parents' papers I found the plans for a large house), and took their son to Switzerland for treatment. And then one day they appeared in Moscow, where everyone appears, sooner or later. This is how I imagined it, and in some details at least I was correct.

My grandfather was from the southern port city of Odessa. *He was an Odessan*—this little description stands for a million words. In a well-known Soviet wartime film a girl asks a soldier, "Are you an artiste?" "No, an *Odessan*," answers the soldier. Heroes like him became artistes by birth, not by calling—it was an inevitable outcome of being born in Odessa. The soldier in the film then sits down at a grand piano and plays a blithe little song, nothing to do with the war, all chestnut trees and boats and the love between a fisherman and a girl. I can't entirely explain the charm of the song, but it's still weaving a spell on me.

By 1925 Odessa was known as a special place, its uniqueness agreed upon by all; not wholly Soviet, but definitely not quite Russian either: a strange anomaly, cherished by the entire population of this vast land. The nineteenth-century writer Ivan Aksakov called it "foreignized," tied neither in body nor in soul to the rest of the huge imperial carcass. And it was true: rules and customs that applied across the rest of the Russian territory had no sway here, simply weren't taken seriously. A German traveler who found himself in Odessa in the mid-nineteenth century wrote: "They say whatever they want about politics, when they speak about Russia it's as if it's a foreign country." Currency exchange signs were in Greek, Odessan writers wrote in French and Italian, high society spoke in French, and the theaters produced plays in five languages. The dark figures of Moldovans, Serbs, Greeks, Bulgarians, Germans, Englishmen, Armenians, Crimean Karaites all walked its blinding-white streets like shades. As another witness at the time put it: "If Odessa had to put up a flag that represented its dominating nationalities, it would probably be a Jewish or Greco-Jewish flag."

In fact Orthodox Jews didn't have an especially comfortable time of it in Odessa. According to a local proverb, "The fires of Gehenna burned for seven miles around Odessa" ("zibn mayl arum Odess brent dos gehenem"). The profound indifference to officialdom crossed all borders of nation and faith—both churches and synagogues were less frequented here than in other places, and more than a third of couples with children were unmarried. But the opera was very good. The poet Batyuskkov thought it better than the Moscow opera. Everyone went to the opera, including religious Jews in their sidelocks and hats who were mocked in the stalls for their loud and excessive enthusiasm. The cab drivers sang opera arias as if they were gondoliers. The Odessan way of things was unusually tolerant of difference; it demanded of Odessa's citizens not so much a readiness to assimilate, as a readiness to hop from one language to another, one idea to the next.

Odessa resembled one of the ancient Mediterranean towns, in that it belonged to no single culture or nation. Laws ceased to have effect here, its mafia was immortal, its cuisine had no equals. But unlike Naples (for example), Odessa only rose from the sand and the foam two hundred years ago, and at beginning of its history it barely had time to invent a mythology of its own. The mythology was gradually invented around it, and it fitted surprisingly well. A Russian officer wrote that

everyone is younger and having more fun in Odessa. A yid walking along the street doesn't cringe as much or look over his shoulder, and a foreigner looks you more squarely in the eye. On the boulevard people stand around chatting and laughing and eating ice cream. They smoke on the streets.

This is confirmed by an anonymous Jew from Lithuania, quoted in Steven Zipperstein's *The Jews of Odessa: A Cultural History* praising the "dignity and stateliness of the community, the calm way they walked along the streets, conversed in the Café Richelieu, enjoyed music at the Italian Opera House, and conducted religious services showed how at ease they felt."
A particular way of being, and a particular language: by the beginning of the twentieth century Odessa was becoming known

as a preserve of the grotesque, and for its distinct style of humor, jokes peppered with Yiddish phrases. This is the warm south, where everything is more theatrical and histrionic, where street runs seamlessly into street, and house into house. The sea and the port were the ideal backdrop in a town where everything followed the comedic principle that the scaffold of the joke existed only to deliver *the punchline*. Lightness of touch, tethered to the ground but always pulling at those tethers (like a hot air balloon)—these were the necessary conditions of life in Odessa. Their flair for criminality stemmed from these conditions, and they cultivated it, enjoying their Wild West image—young hotheads, indulging in hotblooded violence as a natural process and therefore somehow an acceptable one. The gangsters of Isaac Babel's *Odessa Stories* gave generations of readers a warm fond feeling: this was humanity before it could be civilized by reading, and in its natural habitat: exotic beasts in a brightly colored zoo. Occasionally this happy-go-lucky sunlit life came undone, revealing its own ugly stuffing—and this began to happen more and more until it became an equal part of the bubbling pot of daily life. Violence racked the city like an involuntary convulsion. The port was full of arms and early in its history you didn't even need permission to own a gun. Street fights crackled like Roman candles; striking workers and bombers were newspaper heroes. In the period February 1905–May 1906 alone, 1273 people died as a result of "terrorist activity" in the Odessa District: policemen, civil servants, factory owners, and bankers. Politically motivated requisitions were hardly any different from gangster heists. Expropriation became a popular cross-cultural sport. Everyone was at it, from Anarchists to Communists and groups of Jewish vigilantes in black shirts. Suicides were also in vogue—the number of suicides had dramatically increased in the years before 1900, and though the number of those who took their lives in little Odessa was hardly less than in Moscow or St. Petersburg, in Odessa it was done with theatricality: the victims shot themselves on balconies with a sea view, or on the smartest street in town, Deribasovsky. Other approaches included the following: "An actress from a minor theater had her hair done at the best hairdressers, put on perfume, a specially chosen dress and white satin shoes, and holding a ready prepared bouquet of flowers she climbed into a warm bath and opened her veins."

All this happened in what you might call the public domain, spaces in this cosmopolitan metropolis that were set aside for theater; when you approached its white-hot nucleus, the town began dividing into tribes: "one's people" and "strangers." In Vladimir Jabotinsky's novel *The Five*, there is a passage in which the narrator describes this phenomenon:

in our homes, it seems, we lived apart; the Poles visited and invited other Poles, Russians invited Russians, Jews, other Jews; exceptions were encountered relatively infrequently; but we had yet to wonder why this was so, unconsciously considering it simply an indication of temporary oversight, and the Babylonian diversity of our common forum, as a symbol of a splendid tomorrow.

Jabotinsky also remembers that despite his secular upbringing he had no close childhood friends who weren't Jewish. Pogroms and rumors about pogroms, the terrified chatter about what was coming and the much quieter conversations about what had happened, were everyday matters from 1882 onward (and up to 1905, when Odessa seemed even to frighten itself with the violence, and finally put a stop to it).

News of pogroms spread like wildfire around Southern Ukraine. It traveled on trains with the railwaymen, down the Dniepr with the ferrymen, jostled at hiring fairs, and served as a model for new outbursts of pointless cruelty: "Let's do it the Kievan way!" All the towns with a connection to my well-heeled predecessors bore the traces of this violence. My grandfather Lyonya was born in Kakhovka in 1912, and could well have witnessed the pogrom there in 1915, initiated by retreating Cossack forces. Kherson, where the family owned a fine house with *figures on the facade*, saw its own pogrom in 1905. Death could come at any moment, it had not a shred of dignity, it was coupled with shame and horror. None of my relatives ever mentioned the pogroms. Were members of my family killed in Odessa in 1905? Were they among the dead, laid out in the streets, barely covered with sheets, their chins jutting out? Or among the ones who hid in attics, in basements and dog kennels, or sheltered by Samaritans? I will never know.

I do know other things now. In one of Lyodik Gimmelfarb's letters from the front he adds, "I expect you know that Grandfather stayed in Odessa. I am very worried about what will happen to him." Both Lyodik's grandfathers were in Odessa and both were Jews. Israel Gimmelfarb, Lyodik's paternal grandfather, was shot in October 1941, immediately after Romanian forces occupied the town. The other grandfather, father of Betya and Verochka, was called Leonty, or Leib. I only now realize that although I know the year and the day, and almost the hour of the deaths of my other great-grandfathers, I have never found out anything about him—he vanished, quite as if he had never existed. In youth he was incredibly beautiful with a waxen pallor; in pictures taken in the 1870s he looks as dapper an advert for a tailor. His daughters had no pictures of him in later life.

Lyodik's note is perhaps the last time this man's life floats to the surface. On the Yad Vashem database eighty-one people come up when I type in "Liberman, Odessa," and only a few of these have first names. A few are listed with initials or short forms of their first name, Busya, Basya, Besya. Some of them crop up in lists of the evacuated, but most were killed: shot or hanged during the October roundups; burned to death in the munitions depot at Lustdorf or sleeping side by side in the ghetto at Slobodya; slaughtered in Domanevka, Akmechetka, Bogdanovka. By the end of the war Odessa, with its Polish, Greek, Italian, and

Jewish streets, had no more than six hundred Jewish residents, and none of my family were among them.

*

As a child I was always very disappointed by the professions and activities of my family. Engineers and librarians, doctors and accountants, my relatives represented the full range of the ordinary and humdrum; nothing special or exciting, nothing adventurous. Although one of my great-great-grandfathers did sell ice cream in a shtetl near Nevel, and that was far more interesting to me as a child than the agricultural machinery sold by the other. The black-and-white television at the time showed endless newsreels of combine harvesters chewing through the thick corn and I could not have predicted that anything of interest would ever come of those fields.

At the beginning of the 1990s, when food was scarce, my father traveled to the south of Ukraine with a friend to see whether he couldn't sell something in return for food. He came back from Kherson with some photographs, and he and my mother spent ages looking at them before bringing a set of old architectural plans down from a top cupboard. Grandfather Lyonya's family house in Kherson was a fine-looking building with a wide balcony supported by two bearded Atlases in loincloths. It was odd and pleasant to imagine all those rooms and windows occupied by just one family, but it seemed outlandish in comparison with my day-to-day life at the time: ration books were being reintroduced, we had coupons for cigarettes. Very well-to-do people, my mother said, repeating someone else's words from long before, and for some reason their well-to-do-ness seemed even more tedious than their agricultural machinery.

There are so many stories in which a person turns out to be not what they seem at first sight. The frog prince, for example, or the superhero masquerading as a bespectacled boy. When I began my blind groping for family history over the last hundred years, what had seemed initially to be well-documented and interesting momentarily evaporated as I reached for it, crumbling like ancient fabric. My guesses were confounded, my witnesses slow to step forward, but there was one exception to this. When I entered "Gurevich, Kherson" into the search engine, the answers came tumbling out as if I'd won on a slot machine.

A side street in Kherson now bears the name of my great-great-grandfather—it had once borne the name of a Communist, but Ukraine was removing traces of its Soviet heritage. The Gurevich concern had included a number of factories (so many I couldn't immediately distinguish them all) with substantial income—a Soviet brochure described with disgust the more than four million rubles of total profit he made in 1913. By current standards this amounts to about fifty million dollars, which explains the provenance of the Atlases on the facade. On a history website I found an image of a blue-and-white bond issued in December 1911 in Basel. The Société Anonyme des Usines Mécaniques I. Hourevitch was attracting new investors, and in the oval medallions on the bonds you could see, as if through an arrow slit, two model factories, surrounded by what look like poplars, smoke issuing through the chimneys and ponies-and-traps driving through the front gates.

This predecessor of ours was a famous man. A telegraph addressed to him read simply: KHERSON, GUREVICH. He appeared in the area at the beginning of 1880s and began with a workshop repairing carts, and then an iron foundry. Over twenty-five years he achieved a great deal. There were a few big factories in the southern town of Kherson (kerosene streetlamps, parks, five chemist shops, six libraries, 227 hansom cabs)—and Great-Great-Grandfather's were the largest, employing five hundred people. I was even able to track down wages at the factories: nine and a half rubles a day for a qualified worker, forty kopecks for an apprentice.

I was vaguely bothered that I hadn't found anything "living" in all the array of documentation I had unearthed, anything that wasn't simply an illustration of the history of capitalism in Russia. The internet was happy to tell me about Isaak Gurevich's income and expenditure, but there wasn't one photograph of him online. I found a catalog of produced goods, printed in good taste, with curlicues at the corners and attractive diagrams of plows and seed drills, resembling large insects. The implements had fashionable names from the era, vaguely reminiscent of racing horses: "Universe" and "Dactyl" and "Phryne" and even the unlikely English word "Dentist."

"One may always choose a layer of earth moist enough for the successful growing of seed," the sales brochure says. But I found nothing at all about Isaak Gurevich's seed, as if neither he, nor I (by extension) existed. Even the website of the Jewish cemetery only promised to show the monuments "to the *family* of the founder and owner of the agricultural machinery factory Israel Zelmanovich Gurevich"—it seemed the man himself wasn't buried there.

There was a dissonance between the excess of information about one aspect of his life and the absence of information about the man himself, and it began to gnaw at me as if something invisible was pulling at my sleeve or twitching my collar. In my home, where nothing of sentimental value was ever thrown away, and lace collars and dickeys lay moldering in suitcases for decades, there was absolutely nothing from the wealthy Kherson household. This in itself was strange. I made a mental list of all the old furniture I had grown up with, the worn bentwood chairs and the ancient crockery, and I realized that my assumptions were right: everything came from that short period when Sarra and Misha were married, working, and setting up house. There was nothing from the Gurevichs, apart from the ring my mother refused to wear. Then, for the first time, I asked myself what I really knew about my great-grandfather, the son of Isaak / Israel.

I had two documents. The first was on thick card, pleasant to the touch, with a tiny ribbon attaching a second card to the first. It was an invitation to the circumcision of the tiny Lyonya. The second was a death certificate for my great-grandfather Vladimir Gurevich ("Moisey Vulf" in brackets) who died in Odessa of brain inflammation at the age of thirty-three on June 25, 1920. At the beginning of February that year the very last refugee boats from the Civil War left the Odessa harbor. An eyewitness remembers the crowd on the pier, a woman with a pram desperately searching for her husband and child, and another woman dragging a gold-framed mirror behind her. The Red Army entered Odessa soon after and set up their infamous secret police. News of my great-grandfather's death only reached the family two years later in 1922.

My taciturn great-grandmother Betya did have one story about the past she loved to tell. When guests once came to see her little son Lyonya they made a joke of asking him, "And who are you?" The little boy shied away at first since he didn't know them. Then he answered in a deep voice: "I'm little Lyonya from the nursery." In the same year, 1922, Betya and her son appeared in Moscow, quite alone: no one knew them and they knew no one. They had nothing from the old life with them, apart from a few photographs: white dresses, stripy pajamas, and the cheerful mustachioed Vladimir sitting on a bench with friends. On all the Soviet forms Vladimir is described as an "employee," as was customary. Betya worked at home to begin with, typing with two fingers on a heavy Mercedes typewriter. Then she eventually found work. Lyonya went to school. They began to settle in Moscow.

I found one other thing, almost by chance: Grandfather Lyonya's brown wallet lying in a drawer all these years. It had nothing in it, just a colorized photo of my mother, the dark square of a negative with the young smiling Lyolya, and a postcard cut around its edge for some reason. It was sent from Kakhovka to the city of Kharkov in 1916 and it read: *Dear Lyonya, Daddy is*

*missing you very much and wants you to come home very soon. To-
mochka hasn't been round since you left, and won't come back until
you do. Much love to you, Lyonya. From Daddy*

*

I couldn't get to sleep on the first night I spent in Kherson. The
night was streaked with early morning light, the remote pools of
yellow streetlamps dimmed, but the dogs never once stopped
their noise, the whole district rang out with the deep bass of their
barks, passing between one dog and the next. Then the cocker-
els began their crowing. From my lace-framed window I could
see lonely roofs and boarded fences stretching to the horizon.
My great-great-grandfather's factory was next to the station and
the yellow building hadn't changed in a century: it was built in
1907 right on the edge of the steppe. That year there were huge
celebrations to mark the arrival of the railway, with an orchestra
playing. The new railway meant you could get to nearby Niko-
laev in only two hours, and a third-class ticket to Odessa cost
just over seven rubles—a first-class ticket cost an impossible
eighteen rubles fifty kopecks. A strange and frustratingly vague
account describes Isaak Gurevich in the crowds on the square as
the "gentleman in a black frock coat standing by the only car of
the English 'Vauxhall' make in the whole area." The gentleman is
offering the train driver a cigarette from his golden cigarette case.

We got off the train from Odessa at midday, when the leather-
ette of the train seats was beginning to stick to the thighs, and the
white steppe was tired of loping alongside the train. The town
was deserted; it was just because of the midday heat, but it felt
terrifying, like the whole town had been left in 1919 just as it
was, and the newer concrete buildings were simply the scar tissue
that had grown over the burned flesh. In the town center, where
Suvorov Street and Potemkin Street crossed, stood the family's
former house, the "House with Atlases" as the guidebook called
it, although it mentioned neither Isaak, nor his heir, Vladimir. I

began my research at the town archives, where I was treated with great kindness, and given access to a wealth of material.

Our predecessor, Isaak Gurevich, seems to have come to Kherson from the Urals, where few Jews had ever lived—he was described as a "Chelyabinsk merchant" until at least 1905 in the town's documents. There were heaps of papers documenting his many and various occupations: steel and iron foundries; machine building works; all managed with a very steady hand. The machinery in the workshops cost around a hundred thousand rubles; production increased incrementally. He fought a legal battle with someone over a patch of land on the edge of town and then built another factory on this land. I was brought the blueprint of the buildings, white lines on a storm-cloud blue paper. The table at the archive wasn't large enough for us to unfold the plans—they hung over the edges. The archive also held lists of Gurevich correspondence, probably mostly written by his secretary; in vain I listened out for the tone of his voice in the dictated letters, "I urgently need money right now, and I have the honor of asking you to transfer the requested amount if possible." But his signature was *real*, and I followed it across the page with my fingernail when no one was watching.

I really wanted to know only one thing: when he had died and how. I'd amassed a few scraps of half-plausible information from various websites, including an article with the following anecdote: in his old age the former factory owner Gurevich, sitting in the warm sun, said laughingly that he remembered the war and the revolution, but he couldn't recall making a present of his factory to the Communist Petrovsky. I tried to imagine what was meant by this "warm sun": a park bench of pensioners and pigeons at their feet? That seemed profoundly unlikely. The article gave no clues. I wrote to the author, but never received a reply. In the period from 1917 to 1920 there were about twenty changes of power in Kherson: the Bolsheviks, then the Austrians, the Greeks, Grigoriev's army, and then the Red Army again, who immediately took hostages from among the wealthier citizens and demanded payment. No one had any money left by then and lists of the executed appeared in the newspapers. The last information I found was just before my visit to Kherson, in the minutes of a factory board meeting from February 28, 1918:

we heard a report on the transfer of the factory to the management of the workers. We decreed that the factory must be taken out of the private ownership of Gurevich immediately, along with all the assets: buildings, stock, raw materials, and manufactured products transferred to the workers. No decisions will be taken on the nationalization, socialization, or municipalization of the factory until this matter is decided by central government.

*

Before transferring the factory to the workers in February 1918 the factory board made it clear to the owner that he was to blame for the factory stopping production after the revolution, when there was neither money nor raw materials to be had.

1. It is determined that Gurevich, rather than the workers, is more to blame for the lack of working materials.
2. The materials may be obtained by the workers, if not now, then in the near future.
3. In firing workers Gurevich sought to rid the factory of elements unfavorable to him.
The united board demands:
1. That without permission from the board no worker shall be fired.
2. All the workers must receive full pay until the resumption of normal activity.

The sequence of subsequent events is hard to reconstruct. Life in the town was in constant flux, time was measured by a new calendar. The factory fell silent. The merchants, landowners, homeowners, landlords, and self-employed had until February 23 to gather 23 million rubles for the Red Army, and those who didn't pay were arrested. And yet the pianist Mogilevsky gave a series of successful piano concerts—he played Scriabin, with the intention of giving the public an understanding "of his last masterpieces." Outside the concert hall the anarchists were having a street battle with the police and the trees in the park were being chopped down for firewood.

When the Austrian army entered the town, they restored a flimsy semblance of order. Local government was conducted in Ukrainian; the weather got warmer and the townspeople played football and lawn tennis at the sports ground. They opened a conscription office for Denikin's Army for "officers, landowners and students." A head of local government, Boris Bonch-Osmolovsky, was elected, and died of typhus in 1920. They held a charity day in Kherson to raise money for those suffering from TB, and set up an Esperanto Club. This was at the same time as bands of peasants moved across the steppe, murdering landowners and attacking Jewish communities. In July a local newspaper announced that the "The Gurevich agricultural machinery factory has resumed production after a deal was struck between the owner Gurevich, the local authorities and the Austro-Hungarian army."

And that is all. News of arrests, burglaries, and deaths are woven together with football matches and charity bazaars in the newspapers, much as they are *in real life*. For a while the town resembled the sun-warmed seaside shallows: masses of brightly colored crowds from Moscow and St. Petersburg passed through, drawn along by an invisible current. There was a popular series of lectures in the town on the theme of "Theater and the Scaffold." Spanish flu replaced typhus. On December 11 the Austro-Hungarian army left Kherson. It was then occupied by volunteer armies, Petlyura's Ukrainian army, Grigoriev's army again, Greeks and

French, Red Army, White Army, Red Army ... Sometimes the bodies of the executed were returned to their families. At the beginning they were even given proper funerals.

My ancestor's name slowly fades out. The archive has a few more papers, tax notifications sent to him by the authorities in 1919. In March 1920, when the Kherson Revolutionary Committee is wondering who to tax for the land and assets of the factory, they received a declaration back from the factory's own revolutionary committee, refusing to pay since the factory already belonged to the state. By then Isaak Gurevich has disappeared: he can't be found in March or April, nor even when they begin selling factory assets, or when the factory begins working again. There are no more traces of him; no shadows, no photographs, nothing human I could grasp on to and consider my own, apart from a few ink markings and a single iron object.

This object occupies nearly an entire hall in the local museum, which is otherwise stuffed with amphorae and embroidered blouses. It's huge and lumbering, balanced on iron paws, with a long, outstretched neck and wheels hanging to the sides of its carapace: a "Bunker Plow for shallow plowing." It wore the sign of its provenance—both our provenance—like a birthmark, embossed in unambiguous Cyrillic lettering: ЗАВОДЪ ГУРЕВИЧА КАХОВКА (Gurevich factory, Kakhovka).

*

Isaak Gurevich Street had been given its new name only a few months beforehand, and had not quite inhabited it. It was in fact simply the space between the gates and fences that lined it on both sides, and seemed narrow as a result, but it was hardly used anyway. On the corner hung a plaque with the old name: Bauman Street. The place had no particular link with my great-great-grandfather but I was still grateful to Kherson for its act of remembrance. The house with the Atlases was now painted a chestnut-brown color, with a boarded-up basement

and a little shop selling souvenirs. It gave me no sense of familiarity, although I walked through to the yard and even stuck my
head in to see the creaking staircase to a veranda, where the colored glass windows looked out onto trees.

A corridor led into the depths of the building, and I followed
it as far as the bright square at its furthest point—no one ever
locks a door in the south. Washing hung on a line, a cat leaped
out of our way, I was momentarily blinded by the light as I came
out onto the veranda and saw the sky above it. All this was alien,
belonging to the woman who shouted cross words at our tres-
passing, and I had no sense of sadness or loss.

Neither my grandfather Lyonya, with a mustache just like his
father's on his babyish face, nor his severe mother Betya, ever
came back here, and I could see why. Apparently Grandfather
had gone back to Odessa in later years, and even visited someone
he knew. But Kherson and Kakhovka slowly faded, sank to the
deep seabed of memory, as out of reach as Switzerland. There
was nothing left to find here. Still, for the sake of propriety, I did
have one more place I needed to visit.

The New Jewish Cemetery, as it was once called, was founded
in the nineteenth century. We'd arranged to meet a local historian in a café on the day before, and when I'd told him we were
planning to visit the cemetery he'd politely commented that it
wasn't in the best state. Natural enough, we supposed, as there
were very few Jews left in the town to tend it. We took a taxi to
the cemetery; the afternoon heat had settled like a lid and my
skirt stuck to my legs. The town had petered out, its remains
lay scattered over the scrub, half-built houses on large plots of
land, looking for all the world as if someone had taken a bite out
of them and then left them half-eaten. Everything was sky blue
and yellow flax. We drove past a space of wild grassland behind a
wire mesh fence and the driver suddenly said that this was it, but
he wasn't sure where the entrance was. A little way ahead were
some garages or storage units and we walked for ages along the

perimeter fence until we came across a locked gate. Beyond it was what looked like an empty kennel and then the tombstones. We could have scrambled over the low fence, but the lock gave way and the door opened. I went in. My husband waited outside on the road.

I had no real idea what I was looking for. The tombs of my unknown relatives could have been anywhere, and it was instantly clear that the cemetery had given up the ghost, had allowed the land to consume it—and this had happened not recently, but many years ago. A little farther off were tombstones, obelisks, and what might have been a crypt but looked more like a ruined military dugout. These seemed to have lost all purpose, they had collapsed into the ground, and between them patches of spiky scrub sprouted like mangy fur. The place was quite overgrown, it was an effort to reach them, and I felt a rising fury—at my husband who had left me on my own, at the spikes and thorns catching on my skirt, at this senseless search, which had never once brought me closer to my goal. The fury kept me struggling forward, I walked three hundred meters without even noticing, and only then did I hitch up my skirt to examine my legs, which were striped with scratches like a cuneiform tablet, and I gasped with the realization of pain.

From here, wherever I looked I found myself surrounded by pale-colored scrub, like a mess of untidy hair. From a distance it looked like high grasses, but in fact it was a mat of thorns, burned by the sun to transparency and covered in tiny shell-like growths. I had walked farther and farther in, and I now stood waist-deep in the thorny plant and it clutched at me. The tombstones were not far off now, but there was no way to reach them. I could make out yawning holes around their bases, and I could see that some of the older stones had name plaques that couldn't have been from before the 1950s or 1960s. I could see the stumps of old railings around the tombstones, one little fence still shone with a flame-blue paint. The fallen tombstones were hidden by wild flowers, burdocks, and snail shells, and their surfaces resembled burned skin. There was no reason to go farther, nowhere to go, but it was equally beyond me to retrace my hundred or so steps across this merciless landscape. It was perfectly clear to me that even if there were some Gurevichs buried here, I wasn't going to find them, and I didn't even want to anymore. The past had bitten me, but it was only a warning nip, and it was still prepared to let me go. Slowly, very slowly, step by step and bawling gently at the effort, I made my way back to what had once been the beginning of the path through the cemetery.

3. Boys and Girls

A mother and her son and two daughters once lived in the district town of Bezhetsk. By their village standards it was practically a capital city, with houses made of stone and even a cathedral and monastery. They'd come from Zharki, their native village. The father, Grigory Stepanov, did seasonal work in a St. Petersburg factory and traveled back and forth. There is no record of what he did there. They lived as people generally do, causing no trouble to anyone; they were not poor, the children could all read and write and the oldest, Nadya, who was sharp-witted and sharp-tongued, wanted to study in a school. There was a girl's gymnasium in the town and her parents were just considering this. Nikolai was born in 1906, his sister Masha was a year younger. Nikolai later remembered them sitting together in the summer heat on the riverbank, reading the exciting *Two Little Savages* by Ernest Thompson Seton, and Walter Scott.

There was an accident at the factory: their father was *dragged into the machine* and the machine, like a living creature, bit off his right arm, his working arm. So he returned to Bezhetsk for good. The factory owners paid him a huge amount in compensation, as he was a qualified worker who was no longer able to work. No one knows how much, but it was enough to buy a house built partly of stone, and a cow called Zorka, and to send Nadya to the girl's school. In the aftermath, in the suddenly empty life of an invalid, Grigory took to drink and his drinking killed him. It happened terrifyingly fast. By the time they buried him, a few years later, they'd lost both cow and house.

There's no one left to tell the rest of the story. A family of local gentry took Nadya on and treated her as their own, paying for her school books and school aprons, but they didn't help the others; poverty swallowed them like a black hole.

I remember how my grandfather Nikolai used to sit for hours by the silent piano and recount his story to my mother. Some small fragments I can remember to this day, not because I was listening particularly carefully, but simply because it was always the same story, repeated countless times—only my mother's courteous attentiveness shielded him from the realization that everyone knew the story already. Once my grandfather began to lose his memory, nothing between his destitute childhood and the death of his wife interested him anymore: the sense of being abandoned returned as if it'd never been gone, and he was quite alone again.

He often returned to the same part of the story, the lowest ebb of their fortunes, the year when he and his mother were forced to go begging for alms. They sewed a canvas bag to put offerings in, and went hand in hand in the sunshine from one house to the next, knocking at the low windows. They stood at the cathedral's entrance at one o'clock when mass was over and the churchgoers thrust bronze coins into the outstretched palms. The utter disgrace of this changed his life for good, and at this point his story began to break apart into strings of confused phrases. He ran away from home and lived rough, slept in railway sheds, derelict houses, in foundation pits (I still don't know what he meant by this). Then he went home, because the family couldn't manage without him. He was working by the age of fourteen, minding the community herd of cattle, weaving their cumbersome way down the Bezhetsk streets in the evenings. His mother considered returning to their native village, but there was no one left to help them.

When I was twelve I was inexplicably occupied by the fate of runaway children and juvenile criminals. I drank in the books of the Soviet educationalist Anton Makarenko, who had run a juvenile detention center in the 1920s, where hard-nosed young villains were recast as exemplary young Communists (obviously I preferred these heroes in their former guise, it fitted with my own longing for a more exciting life). I kept bothering my grandfather with questions but I could see that he had nothing more to tell me. He didn't want to recall those years of sleeping rough for a reason I couldn't then comprehend. He shook off my pleading with an expression of morose revulsion. Only once, in response to my endless questioning, he agreed to sing "Lost and Forgotten," a song you could hear back then in every railway carriage and at every flyblown little country halt.

I will never forget it. Grandfather Nikolai began to sing in a quavering tenor, closing his eyes and rocking slightly, as if he was using his body to inch his way down into a dark and seemingly bottomless well. He no longer saw me, he'd forgotten my request. In his stumbled phrasing, and shorn of its upbeat, romantic qualities, the simple song was a horrifying spatter of sound. It sounded like nothing I'd ever heard, as if something very ancient had fought its way back to life and stood in the middle of our room, twitching and blinking. The original song was a sentimental thing, about a boy in a foreign country and his lonely little tomb, all of it very lovingly described, but there was nothing human in that performance, neither in the words, nor the voice of the singer—it was as if he was singing from the afterlife, already indifferent to the fate of humankind. A deadly chill touched the room.

*

Back in the mid-1970s my grandfather suddenly decided to visit the town of his birth, to see whether it was still standing. What happened then resembles a film from my youth: my father and my seventy-year-old grandfather, shaved and smartly dressed, set off after lunch on a motorbike, the older man holding tightly to the younger. The pair traveled for 300 kilometers along broken roads, staying over somewhere when it got dark, and reaching the town the next morning. They wasted no time looking around, but drove down one street and then another, my grandfather pointing the way, until they reached a featureless low house, identical to those around it. The ground floor was uninhabited, and they climbed up to the first floor. The owner answered the door. She didn't want to let them in—what did they want with the house, she'd been there since the war—but Grandfather said in the terse voice of a military officer that he hadn't come to claim the place back. The woman wasn't convinced, but it shut her up. Grandfather stood under the low ceiling for a few moments, looking about him, and then said they could go. They got on the motorbike and set off back to Moscow.

Bezhetsk was once part of the lands owned by Tsarevich Dmitry, Ivan the Terrible's son, who died aged nine in May 1591. The bell tower with its tented roof was built ten years before his death. When we visited the town it was untouched, as if time was just beginning. A four-cornered pool encased in pondweed lay behind the tower, right under its tiny square window; the window had been blocked up because drunken locals used to climb in hoping to steal things. The church the bell tower had once belonged to was gone—it had been razed to the ground.

"Those thieves who climbed in the window after the icons, they all came to a bad end," reported the old woman who looked after the box of candles in the chapel in the former bell tower. "They drove off in two cars and the cars crashed and no one survived." Only three or four of the original twenty or so churches in the town were still standing, although the half-destroyed, half-reconstructed outlines of some of the others could just about be made out in garage and warehouse buildings. The weeds had been given free rein: every gap and space was occupied by growth, proliferating and swelling with the sense of its own importance, dock leaves the size of sheets of newspaper, and cheery pink and blue lupins lighting the town. The main square, once named Nativity Square after the cathedral where my grandfather had been christened, was now named Victory Square, and a puddle, fringed by grass, ran the length of it. The cathedral itself was huge, with eight radiating chapels. Built in the eighteenth century, it boasted "a ciborium of rare beauty," supported by sixteen columns, and oval icons. It was entirely destroyed in the revolution, when the building was turned into a sewing factory. When we visited it was bare, its windows yawned, its domes had been lopped off; it belonged to the realm of the lupins and the towering cow parsley.

We walked down a street that had already had three names, the last the name of a Bolshevik: the little town had got used to each in turn. On the corner was a building that had not changed very much. In the 1920s another little boy had lived there, Lev Gumilev, the son of two poets. His father, Nikolai Gumilev, was executed in 1921, when the little boy was only seven; his mother, Anna Akhmatova, lived in Saint Petersburg. Lev was brought up by his grandmother in Bezhetsk; his mother visited the town only twice. It was a two-story house, like most of the houses there, still residential, with a vegetable plot in the garden behind a fence. My family lived only a few hundred meters away—any of the overgrown buildings nearby could have been ours. In the same year, 1921, Nikolai Stepanov, a blacksmith's apprentice, had just started work. Lev Gumilev went to a Soviet school, where, as he later said, he was beaten half to death.

The two boys barely shared a world, apart from the dust and the burdock on the walk they must both have taken toward the market square and the library, which Lev Gumilev remembered in old age: "complete collections of Mayne Reid, Fenimore Cooper, Jules Verne, H. G. Wells, and many other exciting books." The library was free and open to all; anyone could come and borrow those books beloved of boys of all ages: Dumas, Conan Doyle, Walter Scott. There, without knowing each other, two boys reached for books from the same shelves: a teenage boy whose childhood had been drawn into the whirlpool of history, and my grandfather, who might have been delighted to have been drawn into the whirlpool, but was luckily saved.

*

I have to reassemble his life from its constituent parts, from various accounts, breaking off and beginning again from the same place, from records of employment, military ID and photographs. The most detailed of these is the "record of employment," which begins in 1927 and gives Nikolai Stepanov's nationality (Russian), his employment (joiner), education (three years at a village school, elsewhere it is recorded as four years), first employment (cowherd in Bezhetsk and Zharki). At sixteen he found work at a privately owned forge, but only lasted a couple of months there. From November 1922 he was employed as a joiner's apprentice in the Bezhetsk Mechanics Works. It is there that he joins the Komsomol, the Communist youth movement created in 1918 as a first step to joining the party. At eighteen he is the secretary to the workers' committee in the same factory, and at nineteen he moves to Tver as a cadet in the local party school.

To try to imagine this journey, I had to wind the film back to its beginning, to its very source, where there is nothing, just the midday heat, and him walking behind his mother, moving from yard to yard, and when they open the gate to her and she mutters "for the sake of Christ," he can only focus mutely on the cracks in the loam. My paternal grandfather was the only person in my family for whom the revolution was like rain in July, like the emptying of a full load of grain onto the waiting earth. His life began just as all hope was over; all of a sudden everything was made good and filled with meaning. The injustices could be set straight like a broken arm, and the world made better for people like Nikolai Stepanov. Each and every person had a birthright to land and work; working class young people could finally access learning, it was there for them to reach for, like library books on freshly scrubbed shelves.

This new and more caring reality spoke in the language of newspaper headlines and party decrees, and all its promises were directed at him and his interests. It was now possible to gain an important set of masculine skills without leaving work, like handling arms properly, and learning to shoot and to command the groups of fighters the factory workers were producing munitions for. The Bezhetsk Mechanics Works was also called a Munitions and Firearms Works, and it ceaselessly strove to provide the young republic with what it needed more than bread: revolvers, rifles, mortars, and machine guns. In time, their grim production was watered down with the needs of a nation at peace—plows and coffee grinders—but it was clear that the workers in the factory were intent on defending what they had won in battle, holding onto the gains of the revolution. Nikolai was the secretary of the factory committee, an organization combining management and union, which dealt with everything from purchasing raw materials to paying workers. This committee was also responsible for forming battalions of armed workers who were familiar with the tactics of street fighting and conventional combat.

It was a time of confusion and uncertainty. The peasants in the surrounding villages—in the family's native Zharki, for example—weren't so keen on giving up their grain for the new state. It was quite as if they *hadn't realized* that it was in their own interests, and they hid the grain wherever they could, and when asked for it directly they were sullen and hostile. Rumors circulated around the villages that there would be a war soon, or certainly an uprising, and that the Bolsheviks were about to bring in new taxes: five rubles for a dog, thirty kopecks for a cat. Waves of peasant uprisings moved across the area, thousands joined in. Tiny Bezhetsk District saw at least twenty-eight riots over three years. Newly formed detachments of Red Army soldiers were sent to put the rebellions down. Both sides had meetings, passed resolutions, beat up offenders, executed them, buried them alive. After the war, the natural fear of killing another human had gone.

It was easier to pull the trigger, and there were more arms "lying around"—the piles of requisitioned rifles had multiplied. The political "agitators," who were in charge of convincing the peasants to cooperate with the Soviets, set off for the villages as if they were heading into battle: "A revolver hanging at his waist, sometimes two, grenades stuffed into his pockets."

There are moments in time that seem characterized by blindness; or rather by darkness, like the inside of a sack in which people are thrown together, hardly distinguishable from one another, and yet all agitated by a sense of their own righteousness. The great animosity between the new Bolshevik government and the rural peasantry—reviled, strange, uncooperative; twitching and turning in its unwieldy and unchanging twilit world—could have ended differently. But the villages gave in first, and this was the beginning of the end for Russia's rural communities.

Tax collection was undertaken by special detachments, whose arrival in the villages was feared like the Day of Judgment. These visitors dug up supplies that were being saved, turned over the houses, looked in underground stores, took the last of the provisions. Unused to this practice, communities at first tried to resist, everyone playing their part: sometimes firing warning shots from the rooftops, and sometimes unexpectedly killing someone. There were also attempts to steal from the collection points where precious grain was stored: the peasants went in groups with pikes and axes to demand their portion. Red Army soldiers were set loose on them like guard dogs let off the chain, and the crowds slowly dispersed.

There were not enough people who understood combat and military discipline and they needed people just like Nikolai, people who were warmed by the sun of the new regime, who saw it as the beginning of a new time of justice and were ready to die for it. Aged sixteen (not even old enough to order a drink now), he joined a special task unit. There are no documents or photographs in the family album to prove this, but they are hardly needed: the terrible scars on his stomach and back, traces of something that pierced him through, are proof enough.

The advantage of these special task units was that they were somewhat like volunteer militia groups, but together they made up a huge militarized organization (600,000 soldiers in 1922), well-armed, with weapons they kept with them at all times (hidden behind the stove, or under the bed). Three-quarters of them had no professional military training. They were flying squads, ready for action, and a living manifestation of the idea of the Soviet Union as one big military community, where every person could leap from his or her job at the lathe or the kitchen sink to fight for socialist justice. The units had their own uniform and motto, and they were sent to tackle flare-ups as if they were proper military units, but all the same they had a kind of tangential relationship with the Red Army itself, as if they were considered by the army to be so much dross and sawdust. You could join a special task unit from a young age: they recruited at sixteen, and you were handed your Mauser as soon as you enlisted.

At the margins of the country, where everything still hurt and smoke was still rising, the special task units fought in straight combat. In the central areas it was a different matter. Here the class enemy had learned to hide, to mask himself and pretend to be the old man fetching water at the well, or your mother's brother, or even you yourself. The stories of what these units did, sometimes in their own villages and communities, flit like ghosts in the communal memory. My grandfather joined up in 1922, when the work of the units was coming to an end. In April 1924 the organization was officially closed. Nikolai had not turned eighteen. What he did in those two years, he never revealed. When he went to wash in the bathhouse his scars were visible, and he always said that he had been jabbed with a pitchfork when collecting taxes from the peasantry—and immediately changed the subject. What he had in his memory, I will never know. In the box marked "social background" on the ubiquitous form, he, the son and grandson of peasants, stubbornly wrote "factory worker."

*

In childhood, when my father woke up in the morning he could see his own father in the blue and ever paler light, already awake, doing push-ups or lifting his dumbbells, or bent over the washbowl splashing water, or in front of the mirror, soaping his jaw. His boots shone like lamps, and his officer's shirt was pressed, and he was so very tall and so very dear to my father.

Among the very ordinary faces of my relatives there is this one very handsome man, handsome in the way Marina Tsvetaeva defines as: "war heroic, seafaring, savage, most real and unbearable male beauty," the sort that sends three villages wild with desire. There are no photos of Nikolai Stepanov as a child, and there probably never were; he must be about twenty in the earliest picture I've seen, and wearing a cap and tie. This is before the shaved head, his later impressive stature, the military uniform, but it's clear he already belonged to that generation of Soviet dreamers with their fury-fueled desire to carry out anything the country demanded of them: *to get on with the job of building the future's garden cities—and then to get on with the job of strolling about in them.* Their generation had disappeared by the end of the 1940s, but I still see them in photo portraits (some in caps and leather jackets, others in overcoats, but all cut from the same cloth, with the same weary expression on their faces, as if they'd seen too much). I see them, too, in later films made by the children of these men, who never tire of the subject of their fathers.

We choose to remember them as young men, *birthed by the revolution,* as if their youth, or their enthusiasm, gives us permission to think of everything that happened as a children's game. Those they killed, and the ones who murdered them, will get to their feet again; stand up from the dusty roadside or the commu-

398

nal pit; they'll push back the cement slab; run a hand through their hair and set off about their business again. Secretaries, representatives, commissars, policemen, army officers, they all walked with their heads held high, as if the renewed world had made them a promise. Every man's job was a fine job and even the long-held contempt for the police went away briefly. In my family archive there are a few pictures of librarians in Tver posing in front of the camera with their crushes: drivers from a convoy, a detachment guarding prisoners. These young girls are so very serious, they are kneeling on one knee and holding rifles, pressing them against their chests and pointing them into the white light, taking aim. One of them is my grandmother Dora, who had just arrived in this big town to study.

Dora's parents, Zalman and Sofya Akselrod, were from a village near Nevel in the North West. All I know about Zalman is that he made soap, and delicious ice cream, and his ice cream was in great demand in another town called Rzhev. They had six children who all lived happily together and were all members of the local Communist youth movement. Their father, who was a religious Jew, and was not a man to welcome in the new, used to lock all the doors at eight o'clock, so the young ones couldn't leave the house, and then he would go to bed. The children would wait for an hour or so at the attic window, then one by one, they would drop down a ladder and run to the Komsomol meeting. At one such meeting they were told that the country urgently needed librarians, so Dora set off to Tver to train as a librarian.

The story goes that a local school needed a book fund, and Dora was sent to see the newly appointed head teacher. He wasn't in the staff room so she went to the empty history classroom and stopped at the door. Dora was a little woman and at her eye level all she could see was a pair of gleaming high boots—a tall man was standing on a desk and screwing in a light bulb. This is how my grandparents met and they were never ever to be parted. He was teaching history (after his four years of education in a village school, and two years in a party school) and political knowledge, until he left to join the Red Army.

You might think he'd have found his fulfillment in the Red Army; that, deep at the heart of the embodiment of "people's power," his life would be given meaning and purpose. But even here there was no sense of connection; it was as if the proletarian Nikolai, with his tragic longing for order, was once again on the margins, not needed by his country, never quite fitting in. He read constantly, he had a wife and a young daughter, he was an officer in a Far Eastern garrison, but none of this could quite disperse the somber clouds; the Stepanovs lived among other garrison families, but were not of them. The War Commissar rarely bothered to drop in.

It bears repeating what a handsome man he was. Upright, never a word in the wrong place, with careful movements and terse, measured speech, and a dimpled chin. He had a chivalrousness, inculcated by reading Walter Scott, which had no practical application in a garrison town with ten thousand newly imported inhabitants. Time passed peacefully enough for the first while, when the only changes were in the various libraries that fell under Dora's management. Then, in the seventh year, misfortune befell them.

In our family there has always been a tendency to link the terrifying tectonic shifts of the external world to smaller human-size explanations, and so it was always said that grandfather's eldest sister Nadya was to blame for everything. By this time, Nadya had already worked for the representative of the young Soviet Republic in Berlin, and she sent back from there a brand-new bike for her brother. Now she was climbing the greasy pole of the party, in charge of a whole swathe of land in the Urals, or perhaps Siberia. From this posting she sent her brother the dangerous present of a service pistol, and for some reason my grandfather accepted it. One of the accusations leveled against him in 1938 was that he had owned an illegal weapon. His daughter, my aunt

Galya, remembered the last happy summer, walking across a huge field of rye to fetch the newspapers, and one of her father's comrades insistently asking her, a tiny girl, whether her father possessed the tenth volume of Lenin's writings.

In 1938, in what was later known as the Great Terror, the country's punitive capacity was strained to the utmost: the Gulag could no longer cope with the quantity of prisoners. Production, so to speak, *ground to a halt*. Annihilation was the solution and army officers found themselves at the front of this grim line: hundreds and thousands of foreign spies were suddenly found among their ranks. So when people suddenly stopped talking to Nikolai, and his colleagues began looking at him as if from the far bank of a wide river, and then at a party meeting someone openly called him an enemy of the people, he went home and told Dora to pack her bags and go back to her parents. Dora refused: if they were going to die, they would die together.

He was never arrested, although he did have to hand in all his weapons nearly straight away. It was as if they were waiting for an order that was never given. All the same, in the small garrison town where everyone knew everyone else, the Stepanov family was very visible; if they went to the only shop people kept their distance, as if they were infectious. My grandfather was quite certain he had nothing to be ashamed of, and he began mentally preparing for interrogation. His preparations were suddenly cut short: he was told that an investigation had shown him to be innocent, and he was doing important work. He should wait for further orders. These orders arrived at the end of October and the Stepanovs were transferred to Sverdlovsk in the Urals. It was all completely mystifying.

The "unspoken" Beria amnesty lasted for a short time, during which a few of those who had been accused of crimes were pardoned, and some who were already in the camps were released and sent home. It confounded all logic and people sought out their own reasoning, if only for their private family stories. Our family was accustomed to believe that the mysterious Nadya had saved her brother by sending judicious word from her eastern realm. This was her very last gift before all contact lapsed. This version of events is not inherently less likely than any other, but given the unexpected shifts in policy, it feels more embroidered than the probable truth: two thirds and more of those who were under investigation on January 1, 1939, were freed, cases were closed and defendants, against all odds, were found not guilty. The amnesty didn't last very long, but it gave Nikolai Stepanov his chance: this "reassessment" of political cases began with army officers.

The house in Sverdlovsk amazed them; they weren't used to such big city glamour. It had a granite-faced plinth, the entrance to the building was tucked away in a yard, and the apartment had two rooms, a large kitchen, and a bright blue bathroom. Their transfer to Sverdlovsk was long awaited and a huge relief. My father was born there in August 1939: a child born to those who had survived.

*

Once a week Nikolai would take a walk around the bookshops to check whether anything new had appeared. Soviet distribution was organized in such a way that going to a bookshop was an adventure, with all the pleasure of the hunt: every shop had a different selection, and some were notably better than others— there were books that only very rarely appeared, but the hope of a find, and the occasional successes, kept the hunt alive.

My grandfather collected a huge library over his lifetime, and there was never any doubt that he had read it all: it was clear from the pencil markings. He would make notes and even corrections, underlining in blue where he didn't agree with the author and in red where author and reader were of the same opinion. All the books on his shelves were covered with these red and blue lines. In special instances he took on the heroic task of transcribing a book, a task that seemed slightly ridiculous even then, and now that the internet has made any text accessible, it seems utterly mad. I think he was probably one of the last people in the world to copy books out by hand.

I have a few hand-sewn notebooks, in which my grandfather, in his calligraphic script, embellished by illuminated initial letters, wrote out one of the volumes of Klyuchevsky's nineteenth-century *Histories*, chapter by chapter. Why this book? It wasn't easy to get hold of, especially given Grandfather's principled refusal to buy on the black market. But then there were many books like that at the time, and the choice of this one is enigmatic. Someone lent him the rare copy and for long months he copied it out, returning Russian history to its original manuscript state. I don't know if he ever returned to his work as a reader, but this secretive and unfulfilled passion for everything to do with books and art did not begin with Klyuchevsky, nor end with him.

There's a small brown notebook, made at some point after the war, which fits nicely in the hand; a page from a calendar inserted between the leaves: December 18, 1946, sunrise at 8:56, sunset at 15:57. It was around then that my grandfather began writing in the notebook. Everything about it, from the best handwriting to the colored inks he used to write his name on the endpapers, indicated that this was no working instrument for the quick noting of thoughts and trivia. This was a book, a selection, intended to be read time and time again.

The selection of quotes is eclectic to the point of eccentricity. Alongside the classics, from Voltaire and Goethe to Chekhov and Tolstoy, are folk sayings and "Oriental" anecdotes. The Marxist classics are there of course, the ones every Communist needed to study, Marx and Engels—but no Lenin, for some reason. To make up for Lenin's absence there is a full set of Soviet writers from the time: Erenburg, Gorky, and the German writer Erich Maria Remarque with his lessons in brave solidarity. There's a speech by Kirov, who was murdered ten years before, and the obligatory Stalin ("without the ability to overcome … one's self-love and bow down to the will of the collective—without these qualities—there can be no collective").

The whole book is an exercise in autodidacticism. The man who put it together and then diligently kept adding to it saw himself as a clever but lazy dog who needed leading, training, pushing toward activity. Life for him, and for his favored authors, is simply an exercise in continual self-improvement: endless heroism, valiant deeds and sacrifices in the white-hot air, with eventual immolation as a natural requisite—*for you, my son, are Soviet man*! But none of this was ever demanded of him: in the offices of army bureaucracy and the garrison towns and the little schools and remote libraries, life was humdrum and basic, it was bare existence, waiting for payments, standing in lines. The world was immutable, as if the efforts of Communists were superfluous: the party schools and the factories, with their clear and unchanging rules just didn't seem to want to make that *leap forward*.

My grandfather was desperately and carefully preparing himself for the grand finale, and so he fell through time, as if it were a hole in a coat pocket, too big not to catch on the lining, too perceptive not to know himself lost. The brown notebook contained lots of quotes about undying service and higher callings, but it also contained words of loneliness and the unrelieved desire for warmth. Toward the end I found this note: "Never rail against fate. A person's fate is like that person himself. If the person is bad, then his fate is bad, too. Mongolian folk saying."

*

Galya was reminiscing, and I sat by the telephone making notes on little squares of paper: how her father used to sing to her as he put her to bed when they were in the Soviet Far East. He sang Neapolitan songs, one very beautiful song about a fisherman and a girl wearing a gray skirt. I also remembered Grandfather's songs, but by then his repertoire was different, more grief-stricken, often his voice was on the edge of breaking up entirely. He sang the ballad of a young suicide by the poet Nekrasov: "grievous grief, that wanders the wide world, suddenly came upon us."

Galya told me the story of my one-year-old father walking around the Christmas tree, which was covered in sweets and gingerbreads, and taking a bite out of everything he could reach. This was in Sverdlovsk, a year before the war; my father's own first memories were from the same period. He remembers a stuffed shaggy moose being dragged to the very top of a wide staircase in the Officers' Residence where they lived, and him being lifted up onto its wide woolly back. The announcement of war came during a Sunday excursion in May. The whole military unit had gone on the outing, the officers' wives were in their best dresses, the children carried baskets of food. They had traveled for an hour or two to the picnic spot, and had already begun laying out picnic cloths on the grass and paddling in the river when the messenger arrived: "All officers report to base immediately, and families to follow on." The men left straightaway, and the rest is history.

My grandfather spent the whole war in the Urals, right at the back of the rear guard. It seems probable that the suspicions toward him lingered on ("when Grandfather was an enemy of the people" as the family remembered the episode). The front-line was barred to him, and how he must have felt injured by the rejection, this man who had prepared all his life for sacrifice. He was demobilized in 1944, very early, before the war was even over, and he hardly even protested when the door was slammed in his face. Perhaps he hoped there would be a change of heart, and he would be kept on, but this never happened.

The Stepanovs moved to Moscow and saw with their own eyes the huge Victory Day firework display over the Kremlin and the enormous portrait of Stalin, lit up in the sky by salvos. In Moscow they lived in long barracks and my grandfather continued to wear his army uniform, as if the work he was assigned by the party in various offices and factories was simply a continuation of his military service. I absorbed my father's stories of childhood through my skin, like adventure books of pirates and Indians: how once with a friend, for a dare, he ran down the roof of a moving train, or how they called his enormous mountain of a gym teacher, Tarzan. How after years of boys' school he suddenly found himself in a mixed classroom—with girls. How a red-haired little boy called Alik was killed when he fell into a quarry one summer. At the end of the summer he bumped into Alik's mother, and she asked him about his holidays and all his plans, and then she suddenly said, "For Alik all that's over now."

A communal apartment was home to endless human variety: one family's rooms were filled with hoarded relics, another family ate extremely well; the pampered resident lapdog had a liaison with the heroic stray dog in the yard and disappeared. My father once found his father's gun in a drawer and ran out to the yard to play with it, shrieking in excitement. By the evening the police had been called, and there were remonstrations. My father got a hiding. There were plenty of cats, there were the parallel bars the grown-ups used for grunting exercise while curious children watched. There was the only toy they possessed, a much-loved woolen rabbit in army uniform. Grandfather worked at a car factory and left first thing in the morning. My grandmother, their mother, worked in a library, surrounded by her "girls." She took on staff others wouldn't employ: a Jewish woman; the daughter of a political prisoner. Yet at home their father reigned and everything revolved around him: his rules, his whims, his periods of unconscious sullenness. No one ever came round to see them.

One day Grandfather came home from work covered in blood, his head cut open. An underground conflict had been simmering away at the car factory, where someone had been stealing goods, and Grandfather, out of principle, had made efforts to stop the thieving. That evening, as he walked through the January snow, two men caught up with him. They attacked him from behind with a piece of metal pipe, but the blow was uneven and Grandfather managed to turn and hit one of his assailants. The man fell to the ground and his hat fell off and was left lying there. The other ran away, covering his face. Grandfather picked up the hat, an expensive, thick fur cap, and took it home. His son, ten-year-old Misha, wore it for ages since he didn't have one.

It was a simple life: every detail distinct, as when all the tiny stones can be seen through the thin trickle of a stream. Once, my grandparents went on holiday to Kislovodsk in the south and brought back some branches wrapped in newspaper: cypress and larch and a brown hard leaf shaped like a saber or a violin bow. Dora kept these branches until they crumbled away to dust.

Her mother, hooknosed Grandmother Sonya, sometimes came to stay with them; in the old photographs she sits with an ancient weariness on her, her skin the color of tree bark. The family remembers her as a beauty, so it must be so. Grandmother Sonya lived with Dora's sister in a tiny room, together with a vast gleaming grand piano, which her husband had somehow got hold of. Guests slept on the prized piano's lid. When Sonya came to stay Nikolai would get down a collection of Sholem Aleichem stories and place it on the table like a cake, so Grandmother Sonya could read it.

They sometimes visited Auntie Masha, Grandfather's sister in the country. Auntie Masha's husband had a Mauser pistol and he allowed my father Misha to take it apart and reassemble it, and even once let him fire it. Then he took Misha down to the river and he threw the gun with all his might into the middle of the river, and they silently watched the rings of ripples where it fell. My father remembers that summer well. He remembers lying next to his own father in the hay, warm and sleepy, his father's cigarette glowing in the darkness, and his father so big and solid and real, his close presence giving the boy such a sense of lasting contentment it felt like it would never leave him. And this sense of contentment lasted and lasted, until one day it was no longer there. Years later, when Dora died, seventy-year-old Auntie Masha wrote in her letter of sympathy to my grandfather: "At last you can get married to a real Russian girl." And then, shortly afterward, she and my grandfather were dead too, and there was nobody left.

*

The more I think about our family history, the more it seems like a series of unfulfilled dreams: Betya Liberman and her hope of becoming a doctor; her son Lyonya, spreading himself thin and clutching at straws all his life; Misha Fridman who didn't make it to forty, and his stubborn widow, who couldn't quite bring the family ship safe into harbor; my mother Natasha Gurevich, who wrote all her poems without any hope of publication, in faint pencil as if she intended the words to fade almost before they reached the paper. My father's family were no different: Galya would sing her endless romance songs, written up by hand and bound into a book, but only when no one was listening; Grandfather Nikolai had his drawing—he spent all his childhood painting, producing sketches, and he kept going into adulthood. "He painted even better than your father," my Aunt Galya told me (and for Galya my father was the highest being on the earth so this was extraordinary praise). The pile of drawings and paintings grew until 1938. She remembered the day when, awaiting arrest, her parents burned all the family papers. All the correspondence and the photographs went into the stove, and last of all Nikolai's stack of paintings went into the fire: everything he had ever painted, his life's work. He never picked up a paintbrush again.

There was something in each life that didn't work out. We did have one distant relative, a singer, whose voice on the radio filled the kitchens and corridors of communal apartments. It was as if she represented an intentionally mute family. She was our triumphant voice—although of course she was never aware of her role in our lives.

Viktoria Ivanova is to my mind one of the most gifted singers of the twentieth century. She was married to Yura, a descendant of one of the Ginzburg clan. Her life, which began as a celebration, filled with Schubert and "The Blue Scarf" and applause and concert halls, ended in tragedy. Her only daughter, Katya, fell ill, and after an unsuccessful operation it became rapidly apparent that Katya's development would forever be stunted, that she would remain at the mental age of a ten-year-old all her life, although her body would grow and age. Viktoria's life became much harder, the fans fell away, and the performances dwindled. Only her voice remained the voice of a young woman, strangely at odds with her expanding body. Her voice could fill any space, make it swell with sound, and the chandeliers would tremble, and a shiver would run across the skin.

All this time Viktoria was the subject of an absolute obsession. I am talking now of Aunt Galya, my father's sister and Nikolai's daughter, whose name in the family was a byword for headstrong behavior, doing exactly as one pleased: "Let people say what they want, follow your own path," she often repeated. In the fifties Galya qualified as an engineer and got a job in Kyrgyzstan. There are family legends about this period: how she bought an expensive camera with her first wages and then just abandoned it; how she ordered Muscat wine by the crate from a Southern resort; how she gave princely gifts to her friends, and maintained a princely indifference to her family. When I give some thought to her life, and everything it lacked, then these pathetic efforts to give some panache to her existence seem far more human and understandable. There were rumors about an affair she had as a young woman with a married man, but Grandfather didn't approve, and *that was that*. She dressed in expensive clothes, she went to exhibitions and discussed her friends' children with them.

At the beginning of the seventies Aunt Galya fell ill with cancer. She was operated on and the operation was successful, but the episode had a lasting and severe impact on her mental health. She was hospitalized once, then again. My father took on the role of caring for her, as her own father, who had never experienced anything remotely like this, was paralyzed by shame and horror. Hospitalization was followed by periods of remission, and then hospitalization again. Her condition had a direct link to her unfulfilled dreams, and to the singing voice. When it deteriorated she began desperately trying to attend every concert she could, and this rush of excitement always ended in hospital. Viktoria Ivanova's angelic voice (or perhaps rather her far-too-human voice) was especially important to her. She was a relative, if a very distant one, and I suspect that made Galya think of her as a more "victorious" version of her own self. I dimly remember my parents' perennial anxiety if Galya asked them to get hold of tickets for her: every time she attended one of Viktoria's concerts it ended in another attack.

They are both long dead. Viktoria died first, barely outliving her daughter, who had needed constant nursing for the last years of her life. Galka was chatting brightly to me from her bed, when she suddenly said, very clearly and distinctly: *It's time I went back to Mother.* But Viktoria Ivanova's whole singing repertoire is stored in the deep silos of the internet, all the lighthearted tunes from the fifties, as well as the Schumann and Mahler she sang in later years. There's something macabre in the very youthfulness of the recorded voice, which floats above both their tombs, above the heaps of paper and the concert programs, as if nothing had happened; all being is inviolate, immutable, immortal.

*

When my son was only a few months old I developed an unexpected talent (it opened in me like a drawer, and then later slammed shut again). It was at its height in the metro on my way to work. I only had to glance at the faces of the people standing and sitting opposite me, and something would shift, as if a shroud had fallen from them, or a curtain opened. A woman with carrier bags coming home from the dacha; an office worker in a suit with too-short trousers; an old woman; a soldier; a student carrying a folder—I could suddenly see them all as they would have been at the age of two or three, with rounded cheeks and serious expressions. This sudden skill was akin to an artist's ability to note the clear structure of the skull beneath the skin: in my case it was a forgotten defenselessness that began to shine through the worn faces. The whole carriage looked to me like a nursery. I could have loved them all.

On our way back from Bezhetsk we passed the town of Kalyazin, which was flooded by the Volga river and now lies deep beneath its waters, with only the monument of a lonely church spire to show where the town once stood. We sped on to Sergiev Posad, where there is an ancient and much-loved Toy Museum. It was opened in 1931 and the collection of rag dolls, dolls made of clay and wood, lead soldiers and ice skates has been gathered lovingly over the years. It includes Christmas tree decorations, the close relatives of the baubles and figures my grandmother and mother hung on our tree: children holding snowballs, little rabbits on parachutes, skiers, cats, stars, a jaunty troika, with a line of terrifying women, impassive as a frieze of korai, riding in the sleigh. The poorer children of Bezhetsk might have played with some of the simple toys on display: swaddling their baby dolls, or blowing on whistles that hadn't changed their design since the twelfth century. I gazed longest of all at a glass case containing a simple piece of canvas folded to resemble a baby, fabric twisted into a bonnet shape where its head should be: the most basic doll shape. It had something approaching human features, but you could see these were unnecessary, the unknown owner of the doll needed nothing more than its little babyish bulk to wrap her arms around and love.

The museum had two new spaces for an exhibition of toys belonging to a single famous family. The exhibits: dolls, Indian canoes, drums, and tiny sentry boxes with sentries in, were on display for the very first time, although they had lain in museum stores for nearly a century. They'd been brought there from the royal palaces at Tsarskoe Selo, Livadia, and Gatchina, and had belonged to the Romanov children, who were all killed in Ekaterinburg on the night of July 16, 1918. The four girls and the boy had names: Olga, Tatiana, Anastasia, Maria, Aleksei—he was the youngest child, aged fourteen—and they had probably outgrown the games of Lotto and the tiny suitcases for dolls' clothes, and the mechanical theater with its single play: *A Life for the Tsar*, but they wouldn't have been able to take these games with them into captivity anyway. It seems unlikely they would have played with the huge rocking horse with its dashing profile and foolish expression—that had come from a different palace and had belonged to another little boy, Pavel. He grew up and became the Emperor of Russia and was assassinated one March night in 1801. The horse, in its fine crimson saddlecloth, was left waiting for a new rider.

All old things are the property of the dead, and the simple wooden toys in the neighboring rooms were no exception to this. Here I knew exactly who the owners had been and what had happened to them, and even their little lead cannons seemed orphaned, let alone the mechanical parrot in its gilded cage. Most of the toys from the royal household were given to children's homes in the early thirties but these had survived, lying in storage, and now behind glass, like forgotten memories, suddenly rearing their heads and blocking out the light. I can't remember what I was thinking about when I stood and regarded them. Perhaps I thought of the little boy Yakov Sverdlov, who loved to suck on caramels and, later in life, according to popular opinion, gave the order to shoot the Romanov family. Or perhaps little Misha Stepanov with his woolly rabbit soldier who took bites out of the gingerbread on the Christmas tree. My own little boy hadn't wanted to go to the cemetery in Bezhetsk and sat cross and lonely on the baked earth while I strolled the paths between brightly colored tomb railings, reading the names of the countless former residents of the town. Then he changed his mind and announced he still didn't like cemeteries, but he'd like to photograph all the monuments in this one. "I'd put them on Instagram," he said, "and then no one would ever forget anything."

Soft, plump Grandmother Dora died in 1980. My grandfather never did learn to live without her. Right at the end of his life, in autumn 1985, he moved in with us, and he would wander from room to room, waiting for my mother to come home after work. Then he'd take her by the hand and they'd sit down and chat. He desperately wanted to talk, there was so much that needed to be said, over and over: the death of his father, his fear of adult life, his first shame, first hurt, running away, work, loneliness. My mother listened as if she were hearing it all for the first time. His forgetfulness grew and grew, I used to come home from school to find him sitting in the hall as if about to go out, in a coat and cap, shoes polished to a high shine, clean-shaven, his shirt ironed, a string bag with a few books by his feet. He wanted to go home, to Dora. He had two months to live.

I have one of the little notes he used to write while he was waiting for my parents to come home:

Thank you to the friendly people who live in this lovely house. I am off home now, as they are waiting for me there. Please don't be angry. We'll meet again, I'm sure.
Love
Nikolai.
I don't know today's date
Please ring, I'd be delighted!

4. The Daughter of a Photographer

Let's suppose for a moment that we are dealing with a love story.
Let's suppose it has a main character.

This character has been thinking of writing a book about her family since the age of ten. And not just about her mother and father, but her grandparents and great-grandparents whom she hardly knew, but knew they existed.

She promises herself she will write this book, but keeps putting it off, because in order to write such a book she needs to grow up, and to know more.

The years pass and she doesn't grow up. She knows hardly anything, and she's even forgotten what she knew to begin with.

Sometimes she even startles herself with her unrelenting desire to say something, anything, about these barely seen people who withdrew to the shadowy side of history and settled there.

She feels as if it is her duty to write about them. But why is it a duty? And to whom does she owe this duty, when those people chose to stay in the shadows?

She thinks of herself as a product of the family, the imperfect output—but actually she is the one in charge. Her family are dependent on her charity as the storyteller. How she tells it is how it will be. They are her hostages.

She feels frightened: she doesn't know what to take from the sack of stories and names, or whether she can trust herself, her desire to reveal some things and hide others.

She is deceiving herself, pretending her obsession is a duty to her family, her mother's hopes, her grandmother's letters. This is all about her and not about them.

Others might call this an infatuation, but she can't see herself through other peoples' eyes.

The character does as she wishes, but she comforts herself by thinking that she has no other choice.

If she's asked how she came to the idea of writing a book, she immediately tells one of her family's stories. If she's asked what it's all for, she tells another one.

She can't seem to be able to, or doesn't want to speak in the first person. Although when she refers to herself in the third person it horrifies her.

This character is playing a double role: trying to behave just as her people have always behaved, and disappear into the shadows. But the author can't disappear into the shadows—she can't get away from the fact that this book is about her.

There's an old joke about two Jews. One says to the other, "You *say* you're going to Kovno, and that means you want me to think you're going to Lemburg. But I happen to know that you really are going to Kovno. So—why are you trying to trick me?"

*

In Autumn 1991 my parents suddenly began to think about emigrating. I didn't think they should. They were only just in their fifties, and the Soviet regime had finally fallen—they'd waited so long for this moment. It seemed to me that now was the time to be in Russia. Magazines were openly printing the poems and prose we had known only from typewritten copies passed around. Colorful things were being sold right on the street, nothing like the boring stuff we'd had before. With my first ever wage I bought blue eyeshadow, patterned tights, and lacy knickers as red as the Soviet flag. My parents wanted me to go with them, but I held my peace and hoped they'd change their minds.

This lasted a good while, longer than anyone could have predicted. Permission to move to Germany came only four years later, and even then I couldn't believe our inseparable life together would come to an end. But they were in a rush and wanted me to decide. There was nowhere else I wanted to be. Apart from anything, this new life fascinated me, it stood half-open, constantly inviting me in. I simply couldn't see what was so clear to my parents: they had lived through enough history. They wanted to get out.

A process began, and it was somewhat like a divorce: they left, I stayed, everyone knew what was happening, no one spoke about it. The guts of the apartment had been ripped out, papers and objects were divided up, the Faulkner and Pushkin *Letters* disappeared, the boxes of books stood ready-packed and waiting to be dispatched.

My mother spent more time thinking about the family archive than anything else. Under the Soviet rules still in place, all old objects, whether they belonged to the family or not, could only be taken out of Russia if you had a certificate stating they had no value. The country had sold priceless paintings from the Hermitage, but it wanted to make sure that other people's property didn't escape its grasp. Grandmother's cups and rings were sent away to be certified, along with the old postcards and the photographs I loved so much. Their old order was disrupted; my mother, not trusting my memory, wrote down names on the backs of photographs and placed them in piles. She stuck the pictures she'd selected into an album with a once-fashionable Japanese patterned cover. On the first page a crooked line of writing read: *For Sarra. To remember me by, Mitya.*

Now *everything* was in this album: everyone she remembered by name, everyone she felt compelled to take with her on this freshly provisioned ark. Grandmother's school friends rubbed shoulders with mustachioed men and the pink-cheeked children of the London aunt, who, it's said, became close to the exiled Alexander Kerensky. Lyolya and Betya shared the same page, I was there in my school photographs, and Grandfather Nikolai sat glumly on a hill. Our dogs, Karikha and Lina, and then me again, grown up, aged twenty, stuck on one of the last pages, in grand company, squeezed between two newspaper portraits of the dissident physicist Andrei Sakharov and the priest Alexander Men. We were all listed, even Sakharov, in my father's hand: "Friends, Relatives, Family Members from 1880 to 1991."

They left on the train. It was during the hot month of April in 1995, and the weather was celebratory: the sky above Belorussky Station, formerly Brest Station, in Moscow, was a giddy blue. As the train's tail lamp zigzagged into the distance, we who were left behind turned and wandered back along the platform. It was Sunday, quiet, and I was just considering whether I should be crying when a man holding a can of beer glanced at me from out of a train door and said: "Kill the yids and save Russia." It's all too neat, but that is how it happened.

Later, I went to Germany to visit them and stayed a month, not convinced I could build a new life there or elsewhere. In the huge hostel in Nuremberg where ethnic Germans from Russia occupied ten of the twelve floors, the top two floors had been allocated to Jews, and they were half-empty. I spent two days there, all on my own like a Queen in my enormous empty room with ten bunk beds fixed in two lines like a sleeping car. No one else was put in the room with me. I was given food tokens to buy food with, a little like green postage stamps (Germans were given orange tokens). When I first arrived I made myself a cup of tea and sat down to watch the European night: in the distance, surrounded by black trees, I could see the twinkling lights of an amusement park and the shape of a stadium. I could hear the sound of someone playing the guitar from the floor beneath.

My parents came back to Moscow once, six months before my mother had her operation. The coronary artery bypass she needed was not an operation undertaken very frequently in the 1990s, but we were sure that they'd be good at that sort of thing in Germany. Anyway there wasn't much choice, the congenital heart defect first diagnosed in wartime Yalutorovsk had deteriorated and now needed urgent treatment. I was twenty-three, and I felt quite grown up. We'd lived with my mother's condition for as long as I could remember. At the age of ten I used to wake up and stand in the hall outside her bedroom to check that she was still breathing. But the sun always rose and the morning came, and all was fine. I slowly got used to it and never asked any questions as if I was afraid of upsetting the already delicate balance. We never properly spoke about the operation itself, perhaps just the insignificant details of her hospital care. So it was not to us, but to her friend that she said wearily: "What's to be done? I don't have any other option."

Although I tried very hard to ignore all the signs that this was her last visit to Moscow, I wondered at her unwillingness to enjoy old memories. It was a carefree summer, and Moscow smelt of dust and dried up ponds. I was sure she would want to visit our old home and sit on a bench outside on the boulevard, or go and have a look at the school where her mother, she and I had studied. I'd also planned a long conversation about "the olden days" just as we'd always had in my childhood, and I was going to make notes this time, so not a drop of precious information would be lost. After all I was going to write this book about our family. But my mother resisted the idea of a nostalgic stroll, at first with her usual gentleness, and then she simply refused point blank: I'm not interested. She started cleaning the apartment instead and immediately threw away some old bowls with chipped edges we'd had since the seventies. I would never have attempted such blasphemy and I looked at her with a mixture of shock and excitement. The apartment was cleaned and polished until it shone. Her school friends and relations visited, but no one spoke the truth aloud: that they were all saying goodbye. And then my parents left.

I remembered all of this many years later when I tried to read the old family correspondence to my father. He sat and listened for ten minutes with an increasingly downcast expression, and then he said that was enough, everything he needed to remember was in his head anyway. Now I understand him almost too well: over the last few months my state of mind has likened looking at photos to reading an obituary. All of us, both the living and the dead, seemed equally to belong to the past, and the only possible caption: "This too will pass." My father's old and new photographs in his Würzburg apartment were the only things I could look at without feeling shaken: the empty leaf-scattered riverbank with a black boat, a yellow field without a single human figure, or a meadow of a thousand forget-me-nots, no human touch, no selectiveness, just purity and emptiness. None of this was painful to look at, and for the first time in my life I preferred landscape to portrait photography. The Japanese album with the grandparents lay in a drawer somewhere and neither of us wanted to let it out.

*

One spring I had the pleasure of spending a few weeks in Queen's College, Oxford, where my book and I were received with open arms, as if my occupation were reasonable and respectable, rather than some embarrassing obsession, a sticky flypaper spotted with quivering, half-dead associations. My college lodgings had white walls lined with bookshelves, but I had nothing to put on them. In the dining halls and libraries memory had a different meaning, one that had so far been alien to me. It was no longer the endpoint of a wearisome hike, but the natural result of *duration*: life generated memory, secreted it, and it deepened with time, disturbing no one and causing no one anxiety.

I'd come to Oxford to work, but I found it hard to get down to writing because life there was tranquil and it made me feel stupefied, as if I'd been placed back into a cradle that had never in fact existed. Every morning I touched my bare feet to the old wooden floorboards with the same feeling of gratitude. The gardens were vessels of trembling greenery, and the nightingale rattled its empty tin above them; even the way the delicious rain dispensed itself on the perfect facades and stone follies filled me with tender delight. I sat at my desk every day with my pile of pages and stared straight ahead.

The road outside the college was called the High, and it loomed very large in my life. The right-hand side of the window was turned toward the interior of the college, and its cool shade. The left-hand side faced the High that in sun or rain drew my gaze like a television screen; it stubbornly refused to disappear into the horizon as a road should and instead tilted upward like a ship's deck, higher and higher, so the people and buses seemed to become more visible as they moved away from me and no figure, however tiny, ever quite disappeared. Against all probability they seemed to move closer and become more distinct—even the mosquito cyclist, the slant line of his wheels—and this trick of perspective preoccupied me, halted my already intermittent progress.

The endlessly fascinating life of the street moved in intricate patterns like a puppet theater, to the hourly ringing of bells. The long-distance coaches thundered down the street, eclipsing the light, and at the bus stop the drivers changed places; people appeared from a distance and moved closer, while remaining always in view, and sometimes deliberately standing out, like the long-legged lanky girl who came out into the middle of the road, performing a circus-style leap. In short, my idleness could not be justified, but like a character from a Jane Austen novel I sat for hours at the window watching passersby who did not fade into oblivion, but became larger and more recognizable with every passing day. I was continually amazed that I could look out of the window and count the buses at the top of the street where it twisted away, and I became obsessed by the way people, with their tiny jackets and even tinier sneakers, remained forever in focus. It was like watching the mechanism of a clock that had moving figures to mark the hours. A large and glossy black car turned the corner as if this was the deepest past, when even the smallest detail gained the aura of a witness. Only there was nothing to witness, it grew warmer and lilac shadows brushed the opposite pavement.

Then one day Sasha took me to the Ashmolean Museum, to see a picture by Piero di Cosimo called "The Forest Fire." The long horizontal picture resembled a multiplex wide screen showing a disaster movie. It occupied a prime position in the museum, but in the shop there wasn't a single postcard or coaster with an image from the painting. Perhaps that's understandable, as the painting is far from any notion of comfort. It was painted in the early sixteenth century and is supposed to make reference to Lucretius's poem *De Rerum Natura* and contemporary controversies over Heraclitus's doctrines. If that is the case, then Piero agreed with Heraclitus, who said fire coming on would "discern and catch up with all things." Something similar is depicted on the wood panels of the painting: Doomsday on the scale of a single island, overgrown with bushes and trees and inhabited by all flesh, both of fowl, and of cattle, and of every creeping thing that creepeth upon the earth.

The painting resembles a firework going off, as if a carnival were taking place in the forest: flashes of red, yellow, and white streak the panels to an inaudible and deafening crack. The fire is not only the center of the picture, but the *omphalos* of their universe, and from it the dozens of stunned beasts canter, crawl, and fly in dotted lines, not knowing what has happened, or who they are now. My sense of it is that this is an image of the Big Bang, although the painter wasn't yet aware of such a name.

Animals, like the newly created galaxies, scatter from a central point—you can't look away from it, it's like the open door of a stove, or the mouth of a volcano. Like lava they have not yet ceased their flowing, to the extent that some of them have human faces. There were doubtless also people in this world, at least there were *before* the fire. They have a wooden well on an outcrop. And there are a few people, just sketched lines, like frescoes in Pompeii. They are definitely humanoid, although alongside the beasts with their warm corporeality, they look like shadows, like the outlines of humans on a wall lit by an explosion. There is one survivor, a cowherd, clearly drawn, standing half-turned toward us, as bewildered as his lumbering cattle, ready to lower his head and charge with them. His face is not visible, just the stick, the implement he uses because he knows, like Heraclitus, that "beasts are driven by blows."

The beasts cross the painting in pairs, like the inhabitants of the ark, and the fact that some are partly human causes neither distress nor affront. The human faces grew on the beasts as they ran—on the domestic pig and the deer—and they are notable for their expression of gentle thoughtfulness. It's said that the artist added the faces at a late stage, when the picture was nearly finished: one theory is that they are caricatures done at the patron's request. Yet there is not a shadow of comedy about these wreathed hybrids, they look more like students of philosophy who have gathered to stroll under the oaks. Still, even this I can't quite comprehend—a transformation is taking place, but its logic is hard to grasp: is man becoming animal before our eyes, or is animal becoming man, growing a human face, just as it might grow horns or wings? Did Daphne become a laurel, or did the bear become its human hunter?

It would seem that in a postapocalyptic world the beasts *are* the remaining humans; and all hope resides in these animate creatures. There they are, the family of bears bowing fearfully before the lion's fury; the unbending golden eagle; the melancholic stork—all the carriers of distinct qualities, ready to emerge as egos, as "I"s. In contrast we, the humans, are barely distinct, we seem no more than raw material, or rough drafts for a future that might or might not come to pass. The rest were saved and they inherited the earth, and walked upon it, live and blocklike like the figures in paintings by Pirosmani or Henri Rousseau.

It's surprising that the focus of the picture falls not on the predator, the King of Beasts, but on the harmless ruminant. A bull with the powerful brow of a thinker stands dead center, aligned with the tree of knowledge, which divides the picture into two equal parts, and the furnace mouth of the fire. His expression of tortured reflection makes him look a little like the sinner in Michelangelo's "The Last Judgment," mouth opened in incomprehension, furrowed face. But here the creature is without original sin and it has a choice: the bull is free to decide whether or not it becomes a human.

In the dark days of 1937 the German-Jewish art historian Erwin Panofsky described Piero di Cosimo's pictures as the "emotional atavisms" of a "primitive who happened to live in a period of sophisticated civilization." Rather than a civilized sense of nostalgia, Piero is in the grip of a desperate longing for the disappeared past. In my view this interpretation stems from the age-old desire to see the artist as "other," as a transported creature, an Indigenous person at the Exposition Universelle in Paris, a Martian on a foreign planet. It might be worth arguing but he is right in one important way: the state of mind he describes is also a sort of metamorphosis, the result of a terrible disaster that has thrown the world out of joint.

In "The Forest Fire" we see the moment of exposure, the flash, when light burns out the image and replaces it with the blinding white of nonexistence. The point at which everything shifts into its final shape is beyond memory and impossible to convey. It's the moment we first open our eyes.

Piero di Cosimo's picture is for me a close equivalent of Courbet's "L'origine du monde"—its exact rhythm, even the way it shocks and spellbinds, is the same. This equivalence is due in part to the directness of the message, the documentary scale of the narrative of the formation of the universe, how it casts off new detail, forcing life to roll ever onward down the eternally angled slope. Is catastrophe then simply the starting point of genesis? The kiln for firing small clay figures? The crucible for transmutation? This is how creation happens in a post-Promethean world, and this is how the fall from heaven must have looked in an age of aerial warfare and chemical weapons—the flaming sword of the forest fire, and partridges swooping in the skies, triangular as jet fighters.

*

In one of the exercise books where my mother wrote down all my childish phrases and conversations, right at the top of a lined page filled with notes about summer and dandelions and cows, she has written: *My mother died today. And we didn't know.*

I remember that day well. I can see in my mind's eye the morning light in an unfamiliar building; a huge dog coming out from under the table, which was too high for me; the strange window frames; and then later that day, a vast stretch of water, as far as the edge of the world, and bobbing and flickering in it, my mother's head, for my mother had decided to swim out into this waste of water, and had near vanished. I was certain she was gone—a new and strange life had just begun and I was completely alone. I didn't even cry, I stood on the bank of the river Oka, where it meets the Volga, and there was no one to hear me. When the adults swam back, laughing, something had changed irrevocably.

I don't really think life can begin with a catastrophe, especially not one that happened a long time before us. *Misfortune*, sweeping low and fierce overhead like an Orthodox banner, crackling with burning twigs and tongues of white flame—maybe it's simply a condition of our existence, the maternal womb from which we emerge screaming with pain. Maybe it isn't even worthy of the name Misfortune. When we got home that August and went out to our dacha, grandmother's bouquets of dried flowers decorated the walls, and her bag still held her purse and season ticket; it smelt of phlox; and our life was already arranged for years to come, like a song with a repeating refrain. Grandmother Lyolya was only fifty-eight, she died of a heart attack before we could come home to her. And now my mother's life had been given its shape, its model for imitation. If up till then she had just been wandering along, following her heart, now she had an impossible standard to meet. She never spoke it aloud, but she seemed to want to become someone different, for herself, for us: she wanted to become Lyolya, with her easy hospitality, her radiating joy, her cakes and hugs. She couldn't do it, no one could.

The story of our home, as I heard it, began not a hundred years ago, but in August 1974. Grandmother reluctantly let my mother and me go off on holiday, away from summer at the dacha with its curtains, patterned with red and green apples. When we returned it was to an empty house, and we were alone. My mother blamed herself, and I sat by her. I remembered the terrifying story of the little girl who was slow to bring water to her sick mother and by the time she got to her mother, it was too late. Birds flew overhead, and one of them was her mother, and it sang: *too late too late I won't come back.* Somehow this story seemed to be about us, although no one had precisely said this. I just knew it, and I wept over the untouched water like an accomplice.

All my later knowledge was in light of this story: my mother spoke, and I fearfully tried to remember everything although I still forgot. I ran away, like the child in the story, to play, to grow up and live a little. I think that must be how she felt too, a young woman, younger than I am now, with her exercise book of recipes written out in pencil, and her dependents: a two-year-old daughter and two old people who no longer recognized themselves or each other. Later she began wearing Sarra's wedding ring; on the inside it had the name Misha, which was my father's name as well. Nothing ever comes to an end.

Squares of glinting photographic paper floated in ribbed trays in the red light of the bathroom, which served as my father's darkroom. I was allowed to watch as shapes appeared: the complete blankness was suddenly roiled with lines and angles and they slowly became a coherent whole. I loved the contact sheets best of all, covered in miniature images that could potentially be enlarged to any size, just like me at that age. The tiny portraits of my parents fitted in my pocket and made the evenings spent at nursery school more bearable. I remember my parents realizing I'd torn the picture of my father out of his passport so I could keep it with me.

My own first camera was a little plastic Soviet 35mm, a Smena-8, with dials to change the aperture and shutter speed. I was given it as a present when I was ten, and I immediately set about saving and preserving: the graying pines, the sleepers at the railway halt, someone my parents knew, water running over the stones—all industriously rescued from oblivion. The images, lifted from the fixing tray with tongs, dried on a line, but didn't regain their former vitality. I soon gave it up, but I didn't learn my lesson.

This book is coming to an end. Everything I wasn't able to save is scattering in all directions, like the dumpy birds in "The Forest Fire." I have no one to tell that Abram Ginzburg's wife was called Rosa, I'll never write about Sarra's joke, in the middle of the war, that mold was good because it produced penicillin. Or how grandfather Lyonya demanded that Solzhenitsyn's dissident masterpiece *The Gulag Archipelago* (despite strenuous efforts to get hold of it) be removed from the apartment after only one night as it would "kill us all." Not even how all the women in the Moscow communal apartment would gather in the kitchen with tubs and towels to chatter through the weekly ritual of a pedicure. Or even that a squirrel lived on the balcony of a Moscow apartment seventy years ago. The squirrel had a wheel and it would run round and round, watched by a little girl.

In the 1890s the family in Pochinky sat down at the table for dinner every evening and waited silently for their meal. The soup was brought it. Amid the silence Father took the lid off the tureen and a cloud of fragrant steam rose. He would sniff the soup and then make a pronouncement: "I doubt it's any good"—only after this the soup could be served. The terrifying *paterfamilias* always drank down all of his soup and asked for more.

Before Mikhailovna became Lyolya's nanny, she was married to a soldier. In the drawers of the archive where everything has settled like sediment, there are three photographs and an icon. The icon shows the Virgin Mary appearing to Russian troops somewhere in the Galician marshes. The three photographs told the story of Mikhailovna's life: here she is as a young woman standing head-to-head with a dour and innately weary man in a worker's smock. And here she is holding a pitifully skinny little baby. The last picture shows the man in the cap and thick great-coat of a soldier. Her husband was killed, the baby died; her entire earthly estate consisted of the paper icon, depicting a Pre-Raphaelitish Madonna, and once framed by a heavy silver surround that my great-grandfather gave her. When life got hard again after the revolution, she secretly took the silver surround off the icon, sold it, and brought the money back to the household she stayed with for the rest of her life. In all later photographs Mikhailovna is in her own icon-surround of pale gray, her cone-shaped black headscarf covering everything except her face. All that is left of her are a few cheap religious images and a Psalter that she read every evening.

Aunt Galya made me a present of a colorful Indian dress not long before her death, saying that she'd only worn it once, "for half an hour, when I had a dog come in here." I knew of her secret and unrequited love for her neighbor who walked his dog in the yard and who died without ever guessing why she used to come out every evening to see him.

Sometimes it seems like it is only possible to love the past if you know it is definitely never going to return. If I had expected a small box of secrets to be hidden at my journey's end, something like one of Joseph Cornell's boxes, then I would have been disappointed. Those places where the people of my family walked, sat, kissed, went down to the river's edge, or jumped onto streetcars, the towns where they were known by face and name—none of them revealed themselves to me. The green and indifferent battlefield was overgrown with grass. Like a computer game I hadn't mastered, all the prompts lead to the wrong gates, the secret doors were just blank walls, and nobody remembered anything. And this is for the best: the poet Alexander Blok tells us that no one comes back. The poet Mikhail Gronas replies that "living comes of oblivion."

The parcel had been packed with all possible care, the box was lined with cigarette paper and each of the items was wrapped in the same thin, opaque stuff. I freed each one from its swaddling, and they lay on the dining table in a line so you could see all their dents, all their cracks, the earth ingrained in the china, the absences where feet, legs, hands should have been. Most of them still had heads, and some even had their little socks, the only item of toilet they were permitted. But on the whole they were naked and white, as if they had just been born, with all their dents and flaws. Frozen Charlottes, representatives of the population of survivors; they seem like family to me—and the less I can say about them, the closer they come.

Author's note

The author would like to thank the publishers who believed in this book even before it slowly began to take shape: Suhrkampf and Novoe Izdatel'stvo. It seems likely that the book would not exist if it wasn't for a conversation with Katarina Raabe, who convinced me to finally get on with writing the book.

Some of the book's parts were conceived of and written with the help and support of a number of institutions. They gave me time and library resources, but also space for intellectual debate and discussion. They include the Institut für die Wissenschaften vom Menschen (Vienna), Tatiana Zhurzhenko and Klaus Nellen, the Kennan Institute/Wilson Center (Washington), Isabella Tabarovskaya and Matthew Rozhansky; Marion Dönnhoff Stiftung (Berlin) and Maria Birger, New York University and Josh Tucker, the Queen's College, Oxford and Charlie Louth.

I am deeply grateful to Anna Glazova, Linor Goralik, Sasha Dugdale, Helga Olshvang-Landauer, Olga Radetzkaja, Mikhail Yampolsky, Vadim Alskan, Anna Golubeva, Anton Karetnikov, Erich Klein, Sergei Lebedev, Anna and Maria Lipkovich, Maria Mushinskaya, Olga Naumova, Elena Nusinova, Katya Petrovskaya and David Riff.

My thanks also go to Irina Shevelenko and Andrei Kurilkin, my friends and the first readers of this book.

And of course to my beloved Gleb and Grisha.

Translator's note

Maria Stepanova's *In Memory of Memory* is a living text and the English translation has been changed and modified from the original Russian in collaboration with the author.

The Russian text embeds unattributed quotes from other texts in a flowing narrative, and the English translation follows this convention. The translators whose work has been quoted in this English version are listed here in the order they appear:

Harold N. Fowler (Plato's dialogue *Phaedrus*); Thomas Scott-Railton (Arlette Farge's *The Allure of the Archives*); John Felstiner (Paul Celan's "Conversation in the Mountains"); Don Reneauith, (Thomas Mann's letter to Heinrich Mann of February 27, 1904); C. K. Scott Moncrieff (Proust quotes); Richard and Clara Winston (*Thomas Mann's Diaries*); Anthea Bell (W. G. Sebald's *On the Natural History of Destruction* and *Austerlitz*); Michael Hulse (W. G. Sebald's *The Emigrants* and *The Rings of Saturn*); Maureen Freely (Orhan Pamuk's *Istanbul: Memories of a City*); Alan Myers (Lydia Ginzburg's *Notes from the Blockade*, revised by Emily van Buskirk); Alistair McEwen (Robert Calasso's *Tiepolo Pink*); Robert A. Maguire (Nikolai Gogol's *Dead Souls*); Seán Jennet (*Journal of a Younger Brother: The Life of Thomas Platter*); Michael R. Katz (Vladimir Jabotinsky's *The Five*); Charles H. Kahn (Heraclitus fragments). Translations of Charlotte Salomon's *Life? Or Theater?* are taken from the digitalized version online at the Jewish Cultural Quarter in Amsterdam.

Thanks are due to Aviva Dautch, Henry Hardy, Ruth Martin, and Robina Pelham Burn. I'd also like to thank J. O. Morgan, for his invaluable and patient help, and my family, especially Max and Paul, who have contributed words, sense and encouragement.

I've benefited from Maria Stepanova's highly literary understanding of English and English-language culture, and the generosity and freedom she gave me to recreate her brilliant work in a new poetic language.